Return to Aramon
A New Moon

EZRA FERGUSON

Songmyth
MEDIA

Edited by Anika Saphiloff
anikasaph@outlook.com

Book cover by Jeff Brown
www.jeffbrowngraphics.com

Chapter illustrations by Isaac Ferguson
isaac.ferguson.art@gmail.com

First edition 2025

Songmyth Media, LLC
www.songmythmedia.com
www.returntoaramon.com

ISBN: 979-8-9927862-0-0 (hardcover)
ISBN: 979-8-9927862-1-7 (paperback)
ISBN: 979-8-9927862-2-4 (ebook)
ISBN: 979-8-9927862-3-1 (audiobook)

10 9 8 7 6 5 4 3 2 1

For Jesus Christ

In whom we have redemption through his blood, even the forgiveness of sins:
Who is the image of the invisible God, the firstborn of every creature:
For by him were all things created, that are in heaven, and that are in earth,
visible and invisible, whether they be thrones, or dominions, or principalities,
or powers: all things were created by him, and for him:
And he is before all things, and by him all things consist.

ARA
ARREGALT
The Shrine
Voldigar's Farm
Pirvale
A R A
Maghaltani
The Adionel
WESTFORT
THE GREAT SPAN
THE CHASM
The Haroel
THE WENDING SEA
N
W
E
S
0 1 2 3 4 5
Miles

MON

THE FAR MARSHES

MON

The old well

Dizghizádè

DANEK

EASTFORT

FORT DROMVEDYA

The Vedkorya

TO KURATH >

TITURIA

PROLOGUE

ON THE DAY LUSÁNT Sispérus lost his mind, the faintest whisper of a beard was finally crawling on his chin. Briefly, he brushed his hand across his neck while he pondered what it meant to trespass in his own house. One more glance at his trembling fingertips before he held his breath and plunged ahead into the gloom. No more dithering.

Lusánt descended the spiraling stones by leaps, steadying with his hand against a mossy wall. The air was still, but his black cloak billowed like a proud banner, the Gray Sun of House Sispérus emblazoned upon it. This deep in the Vaults, he could more clearly hear the waterfalls of Arregalt, echoing and tumbling through the city and into the sea far below. They drowned out the clatter of a huge ring of stolen keys against his belt. Into the darkness he raced and carelessly thrust a bronze-handled torch before him. The sparks streamed past his eyes in a tiny finger of flame.

With luck, just as above, no guard would stand post at the iron portal below. Though Lusánt would burn precious minutes guessing at the keys, it was better to go unseen. For weeks, all semblance of order in the palace had turned to disarray. Meticulous routines, carefully obeyed, were upturned as small and great awaited the fate of Lusánt's mother, the Queen—and now Empress—Eleanora.

Every learned man throughout Aramon had gathered round her apartments in The Golden Spire, offering prayers and incantations, herbs and alchemy.

Fools, the lot of them.

Lusánt's lip curled, and he fought back tears even as he ran. He had seen her drawn face, the skeletal fingers clawing like talons through layers of thick quilts. No, as with Father, she was beyond the aid of doctors and magi. Only true power could save her now, and he would provide it.

He slowed as he neared the landing. It was cold here, and the steps were older masonry—broad and slick. A shimmer of moisture reflected his torch and the flicker of some other source of light round the last curve of stairwell. Lusánt cursed under his breath as he splashed through a small puddle, tensing under the surprising echo of both sounds.

The low opening of the stairs gave way to a soaring ceiling, uneven and vanishing into shadow. Viscous dripping from somewhere above spattered the floor and oozed off into the murk. Before him a huge iron door recessed into the stonework, its rounded face red with rust and pitted—daring him to take another step.

A single guard in unkempt, gray livery rose to his feet, rubbing his eyes with one hand and holding a lantern in the other. "Hello?"

"Open the door," Lusánt replied. He quietly slid the key ring to the back of his belt and stepped from the shadows. Perhaps this guard could be of use. He seemed to be alone.

"Begging your pardon, young man?" the guardsman asked. Even from this distance, the smell of alcohol drifted with every word. He looked like he could barely stand and had probably slept his entire shift.

"I said open the door. Are you deaf?" Lusánt flashed his golden signet ring, holding the light of his torch near the broad octagonal ruby, intricately carved with the eight-pointed sigil of Sispérus.

The guardsman brushed a damp lock of curly hair from his forehead. His eyes widened as he stammered. "Your Highness! I-I-I can't."

Lusánt stepped closer. "Open it. Or shall I have you flogged for drunkenness? Give me your name!"

"M-Manric," he sputtered, "and I don't have a key, m'lord! How did you get down here?"

Lusánt lunged forward and brought the back of his hand hard against Manric's face. The guardsman cried out and staggered into a three-legged stool behind him. Lusánt was tall for his age but slender, and though the man outweighed him five stone, still Manric toppled over and smashed into the ground. His breath shot out in a spray of spittle through his ragged beard.

"The sergeant let me in, Manric!" he lied through clenched teeth. His hand hurt, especially under the signet. The man was a pitiful heap on the floor. Lusánt blinked and looked away, moving swiftly toward the iron portal. Unclasping the ring from his belt, he cycled through the keys. Manric gasped.

Lusánt had been in the Inner Vault once as a small child with his father, King Olwis. He remembered how the King's Marshall flicked through the keys in an instant, neatly fitting and twisting the door open. Now in the half-light, the forest of keys all looked the same. He fumbled with a few. This was taking too long. He turned back to the guardsman who now sat against the wall. He looked like a frightened animal, waiting for his chance to bolt into the brush.

"I wouldn't go anywhere if I were you," Lusánt said. He sighed and softened his tone. "Look, help me with these keys and we'll forget anything happened. I was just frustrated, and you can't leave anyway. I locked the upper portal from the inside."

This much was true. The Vaults were the innermost structure under The Golden Spire, a last redoubt, and whether for security or paranoia, they could be sealed from either side.

The guard glanced up the stairs as if to somehow discern the truth of Lusánt's words, then to the keys in his right hand. "I . . . I can't allow anyone inside the Vault alone, m'lord, not even you. I'm not sure I know which key it is."

Lusánt sighed again, crossed over to the man, and crouched down—his olive face a few inches from Manric's pinkish nose and rancid breath. He spoke in a paternal tone. "Listen to me closely, Manric. If my mother perishes, who then will be Emperor? You, or me?"

Manric subconsciously moved his stinging jaw from side to side. "You, m'lord. Gods save the Queen."

"Empress, Manric. Empress." He paused. "Good answer. Now, if you value your Empress, and you serve her, you should know I am here on her business." His face twitched with irritation. "I'm sorry I can't follow protocol. Truly, I am. Now will you help me with this door?"

Lusánt splayed several of the keys in a fan before the cowering and rapid-ly sobering guardsman. Manric shook his head meekly and frowned. A second display, and the man lifted a wavering index finger to a plain-looking key, heavy and angular at its base.

"Probably that one, Your Highness."

"Good."

Lusánt slid the key into the lock. It gave an easy turn and click, but pressing against the rusted mass gave no response. Lusánt set his feet and lowered his shoulder into the edge, straining and twisting against it. Red powder streaked his cloak, but the portal held fast. He stared at it a moment and then erupted like a caged animal, ramming the door heedlessly with his shoulder, kicking and cursing—but it did not move. Stopping for a breath, he looked as if he might bore a hole in it with his bloodshot eyes. His chest heaved, and his mouth hung open in distorted rage.

"That door's not been opened in years, m'lord," Manric said quietly.

"You don't say!" Lusánt spat. "Give me that!"

He waved his hand at the guardsman's flanged mace, propped against the wall. Manric, still not risen to his feet, walked his fingers to the weapon. Never taking his eyes off Lusánt, he swiped at it twice before catching hold and tossing it to him with a grunt. In a single motion, Lusánt dropped his flickering torch, grasped the mace from the air, and brought it down hard against the outer rim. All his fury renewed in an onslaught of two-handed blows. The deafening clang of iron on iron shook the stones of the hall. Red flakes peeled from the door until the head of the weapon cracked off its haft and shot through the now steaming air, narrowly missing Manric's face. Lusánt tossed the useless handle clattering into the dark. He leaned against the door and wheezed.

"Come. Help me, Manric."

Manric scurried to his feet and shoulder to shoulder, the much bigger man laid his added weight to the effort. With one final heave there was a pop, and the door scraped open, sliding less than a foot before it caught fast on uneven stones within. The opening was far too narrow for most men, but the young prince slithered effortlessly through, sweeping his torch off the wet floor. He stopped and peered back through the crack.

"Don't follow me, Manric."

"I don't think I could, Your Highness."

The Inner Vault was like stepping out of the rain, quiet and sacred. It smelled of old metal and musty underworld unseen by human eyes in a decade. Just past the opening, the uneven stones gave way to thick red carpets and matted furs. Spiders skittered away in every direction, fleeing the light of his torch waved side to side. Lusánt shuddered to think that their only food in this endless night was each other. The entrance to the Inner Vault was a long gallery with sconces evenly spaced between columns on either side. With effort, Lusánt caught the damp fuel of a few and revealed the lofty roof and many treasures within.

Just as he remembered, rows of ancient weapons and gilded armor stood rank upon rank to greet the viewer—pieces from Tymicha's Uprising, exquisitely maintained through centuries. As a boy of five, these prized possessions dazzled his wide eyes and filled his heart with fantasies of battlefields and glory. He paid them no heed. His prize lay deeper within.

Past the ancient armaments, the Vaults split in three directions round an eight-pointed altar of swirling gray marble. He had not been allowed to see all on his prior visit to these chambers but knew that each hall contained artifacts of interest far beyond Tymicha's Arsenal. '*Some things are hidden because they must be,*' Father had said. When he tearfully protested, the old man shook his gray head and said no more. Since then, he learned the halls were loosely organized around ritual objects from the three major cults of Aramon and its neighbors—those of Sun, Star, and Moon.

The red carpeting gave way to flat gray stone in this intersection, but then to brilliant tiling and mosaics of hallowed scenes in white and blue and green, receding into the long halls beyond. The thrill of what discoveries awaited mingled with the secrecy of his crime and sent a shiver through his body.

These halls are mine. It is I who says who comes and who goes.

Even as he reveled in his mischief, his thoughts sounded shrill and thin. The image of his grave father lingered in his mind. Lusánt hurried into the greenest of the three rows to his left.

Green . . . green for the moon, and green for the sea! There was no better place to start his search. Aramon had ever lain on the shores of the Wending

Sea, plied by the Miridas and their great galleons, coming and going with the surging tide far below the cliffs of this great City of Arregalt.

Shortly before his birth, the Cult of Mirvánè, of the moon, had been dramatically purged from Aramon in the Great Dispute. It was said even the Miridas spoke no more of the power behind that great green flame circling the interior of the sky. Lusánt had never understood the purpose of it all. So much lost, and for what? Fear? What had the adherents of Star and Sun done for his mother, far above, muttering their wisdom in cold chambers at the pinnacle of the Spire? What had they done for his father? Of course he'd read his textbooks, listened to the lectures of his learned masters and their warnings—but for all their distinction, Olwis was now dead six years, and Eleanora would soon join him. What were they hiding? If they were powerless, what good were they? *'It is in such times that the brave must have courage to face peril, to master those things others fear.'*

"I'm going to save you, Mother," Lusánt whispered.

Not many paces into this Gallery of the Moon, for that is what it was, the mosaics were punctuated by low doors under shouldered arches spaced evenly between. So alike and so numerous, a bewildering forest of openings—he did not know which to choose. Along the left-hand wall several yards ahead, one door drew his gaze. Unremarkable in contrast to the others, but to his eye, a faint glow emerged from the crack below. As he approached, the emanating gleam could not be mistaken, and he perceived a low hum at the edge of hearing.

He grasped the handle. Locked. He tried the angular key from the round portal without, but it did not fit. Nor did the next, or the next. His hands shook, and his breath poured out in wavering cries. He stabbed key after key.

It was then he realized the glimmer of green light was radiating not only from the door but also from above. A narrow strip of nearly opaque glass lined the wall about eight feet up, the dim glow just barely passing. It looked the sort of material his mother hoarded in other parts of the palace to provide her light while keeping prying eyes at bay.

Lusánt rushed back to the red hall and wrenched a poleaxe from its stand, sending a suit of mail crashing to the floor. Dashing back to the green gallery, he thrust the weapon up at the thick glass in two sections. It chipped, cracked, and then shattered in a crystal shower. Lusánt smirked in satisfaction and dragged a nearby chest against the tiled wall.

Bounding atop, he could see the jagged gap he'd created was even more narrow than the crack he'd squeezed through at the outer door. No matter. Once he pulled himself up and slid his head through sideways, it was only a few clammy moments of scraping boots and torn skin until his torso squirmed through to the other side. Lusánt grasped a small support where one gap ended and the next began, then swung his legs through and lowered himself to the floor of a small room. The deed was done.

The room was unadorned save for a low granite stand in the very center on which sat a golden box, delicately etched with scenes of the sea. Greenish light gleamed from every joint. Lusánt stood motionless, gathering his courage while drops of blood dripped to the floor from gashes in his arms.

A thrill of wonder and fear raced down Lusánt's neck as he willed himself to stride slowly toward the stand. He raised the lid gently, and the sight within stole his breath away.

There it was, perfectly round and shimmering in prism with even the slightest movement of his eyes. Like a great pearl, its surface looked delicate, glass the width of silk. Strange radiance flowed and flickered just below its face. It was small, yet barely too large to hold comfortably in one palm. A dark depth, like the onyx of a night sky, gathered round a pulsing core of green lightning woven into a beating heart of electric strobes. Each vibration echoed a deep and resonant tone.

Lusánt placed his two trembling hands on either side of the orb and lifted. The light shone through all his fingers, creating a green glow within his skin. He could see every vein and artery. Even the movement of his blood came into sharp relief, beating and flowing in time with the pulsing object. The relic was beyond beauty and beyond grace, and Lusánt loved it with all his heart.

PART ONE

Chapter One

The Old Fountain

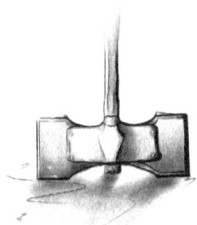

A CLOUD OF DUST sprang up under Voldigar's boots as he shifted round the old horse-head fountain and parried each of his student's swings in rhythm. The boy he taught was strong for his age and possessed a quickness most of his peers would not gain for another year or two. Grass did not dare grow here in the old stableground of Arregalt, trod over by countless steps, hard against the inner wall of the great city.

"Good! Good," Voldigar said as he lowered his blunted blade and wiped a sleeve across his charcoal black beard, flecked with gray. Though a light breeze mercifully blew across his broad back, it was uncomfortably warm for spring. Today he was the only sparring partner for his only pupil.

Voldigar stood a head above most men, creating an amusing difference in reach, but Tepic's gaze was steady, his eyes set in concentration. The boy never missed a lesson, even today when no one else had showed. No doubt the others were all in The Golden Spire, or so they would have their instructors believe. All the houses of nobility waited with bated breath for the fate of the Empress, but not Tepic.

Dantic, Tepic's ever-present father, leaned over the railing of a pine fence that surrounded the training yard and its lichened fountain. Both his hands were gloved, but he seemed unbothered by the heat. He probably should have been in the Spire too, but he was a practical man. What could he do for Lady Eleanora? His short-cropped, rusty hair mirrored his son's in the military style, and a smile adorned the corner of his mouth.

"Your feet are decent, Tep, but you're leaving yourself open too long!" Dantic said from across the yard.

Tepic did not turn back but looked up at Voldigar, squinting into the sun of late afternoon. "It's heavy, Sword-Lector."

Voldigar smiled and held his blade out. "I know, lad—answers though, not excuses." He rested the blade on his shoulder. "Your father's right. You can't hack me in two with every swing. You face men, not firewood. Understood?"

"I think so." Tepic sighed. "Why is this so hard?"

"Fear. Nothing more, nothing less. It drives men to foolish action. Conquer it, and you'll progress."

"I'm not afraid."

Voldigar raised an eyebrow and crouched down. "So says you, but fear takes many forms. Do you know what you fear?"

Tepic stared at the ground in quiet contemplation.

Voldigar continued. "Fear will drive you to wisdom too, if you master it. Courage and faith, Tepic. Learn what those mean."

Tepic sniffed and nodded, setting his feet for another go. Voldigar shook his head. "Find something to eat. That's enough for now."

Class would normally run another hour or two, but he doubted the young man would find any more benefit on his own today. Voldigar knew he himself would be unlooked-for in the Spire, and Gwenyth would no doubt be pleased to see him home early. A quick run to the apothecary, then back to the farm. He subconsciously patted her empty medicine pouch in his waist pocket and noticed a strange look on Dantic's face. The commander stiffened from his casual pose on the fence, glanced nervously at Voldigar, then gestured through the open gates with his chin.

A tall youth with olive skin and a dark shock of hair hanging over his half-lidded eyes walked toward the opening with a bored expression and something resembling a glare. Behind and beside, an entourage of five other young men flanked the youth. Save one wary-looking warrior with the dusky face of the Xerimadi, all had the look of haughty ignorance and unearned pride.

The five retainers spread out around the opposite side of the fence while their disinterested leader wandered into the training grounds, pulling a pair of close-fitting gloves onto his long fingers.

"Hello, Sword-Lector," Lusánt muttered softly without raising his eyes.

"Your Highness," Voldigar replied. "I did not expect to see you here today."

"Yes. Well, I come and go as I please." Lusánt sighed and met Voldigar's pale blue eyes. "The air in the Spire is so close I could suffocate. My mother's *doctors* thought perhaps some fresh air and a little bit of sword-play could clear my mind. Where are the other students?"

Voldigar studied the prince's face for a beat. He'd been weeping, and something else lingered in his eyes. Was it anger? "God save the Empress. Seems we're short today, Lusánt."

"Mhmm. Well, let's not be informal, Sword-Lector. What about him?" Lusánt pointed across the training ground where Tepic sat in one of the unrenovated stalls, working the heel off a dry loaf of bread a servant had left unguarded in the morning.

"You're looking to spar? Tepic is a good student, but you're not properly matched," Voldigar said. "I'd be honored to train with you myself, of course."

Perhaps this wouldn't be an early day after all.

Dantic swung his legs over the fence and strode to the fountain, resting his hand awkwardly on a worn knob that used to be a hoof. "Tepic would be delighted to train with his majesty! Isn't that right, Tep?"

The boy looked up from his bread and took a moment to catch up. "Y-Yes. Of course." He grasped his blade off its perch against the wall and walked back into the ring with a wary eye toward Lusánt, loaf forgotten. As far as Voldigar's height rose above Lusánt, the prince's height rose above Tepic. Tepic was advanced, but at this age, even two or three years separation would make for a world of difference.

"I appreciate the enthusiasm, but I'll handle the sparring personally today. Tepic, you're dismissed," Voldigar said with a duck of his chin.

Lusánt stood motionless, an expectant palm held out to Voldigar. He gazed at the matching blunted sword leaning against the basin of the dusty fountain.

Dantic snatched up the sword. "It's alright, Voldigar, really. I don't mind. Just light sparring, right?" He handed it to Lusánt who turned his back and wandered a few paces away, slashing the air left and right. These were heavier instruments, able to be gripped in one or two hands—two always for the younger students. The prince tried a few strokes with a single grip before settling on a double. His retainers shuffled into the grounds to help him with his padded coat.

"His reach advantage is less than yours, Voldigar. Don't worry about it," Dantic said in a hushed tone, slipping Tepic's helmet back over the young man's ears.

"Don't be daft. It's not the reach. How old is Tepic? Fourteen?"

"Thirteen yesterday!" Tepic interjected.

"Come on, Dantic! Lusánt's half to a man and he's . . ." Voldigar glanced again at Lusánt. "I won't allow it."

Tepic stopped straightening his thick padded coat and looked between Voldigar and Dantic.

"It's on me then. Consider it . . . extracurricular," Dantic said.

Before Voldigar could protest further, Dantic stooped to Tepic and gave him some whispered advice. The boy nodded nervously at each instruction and then began swinging his practice sword in wide arcs.

Voldigar briefly considered kicking the lot of them out of the training ground but thought better of it. He took a few paces over to the fence on the far end of their makeshift arena. *Fine*. If they wanted a foolish duel, they could have it—within reason. Still, Tepic was a good student. Breaking his confidence with a mismatched contest could take weeks, even years to undo. Voldigar leaned against a fence beam and tightened his hand around the pine wood while he ground his teeth.

"Put your helmet on, Lusánt!" Voldigar barked across the yard. "No blows to the head. Half force. No thrusts! Just practice, boys."

Lusánt gave no visible reaction to the commands, his eyes fixed on the single withered strand of ivy dangling from the fountain. Tepic made a final adjustment to his helmet and moved hesitantly to a patch of chalky earth several feet from Lusánt. True to his threat, Dantic stepped forward to officiate in the place of Voldigar—one hand in the air, waiting to signal the start of their bout.

Without warning, helmet still lying in the dirt, Lusánt sprang forward with a crashing overhand blow from right to left. Tepic leapt backward just in time, raising his heavy blade with a cry. Lusánt swung himself nearly in a circle and followed with a heaving backhand swipe. His eyes lit with fury and his mouth gaped wide, uttering a wild howl. Tepic caught this attack with his own blade and rocked to his left, barely keeping balance.

Voldigar startled forward, raising a hand. "Hold!" His warning caught in his mouth as Dantic jerked a hand up and skirted to the side, eyes fixed on the mock battle. "No, no! Let them continue. It's alright. Go on, Tep!" This was madness.

Lusánt seemed to hear neither of them and charged forward to send a third swing at the younger boy's legs. This one Tepic caught in balance and deflected Lusánt's blade in a clanging recoil. Now was his chance.

Tepic launched forward to close the difference in reach and took two rapid slices at Lusánt's chest. Lusánt lurched back grimacing and dodged both blows with an exaggerated bend at his waist. The fury in his eyes deepened, and he returned the attack with a series of withering downward strikes, heedless of his aim or any semblance of control. Tepic raised his guard high, no longer able to hide the look of boyish fear on his face. He blocked one blow after another, shifting round the fountain while Lusánt drove him backward toward where Voldigar stood. Voldigar clenched his jaw and squeezed the railing of the pine fence with his broad hand.

Tepic was visibly tiring. The firmness of his guard drooped with every strike. Lusánt breathed heavily, letting out something between a whimper and a shout with each swing. Tears left lines in the grime at the corners of his eyes. A huge cloud of dust swirled around their feet, and the wind of afternoon picked up in reply. The onslaught neared Voldigar as a blow caught Tepic's sword against his own body and rocked him onto his heels. Lusánt continued to advance as Tepic tripped over his own feet and rolled to the ground near Voldigar's boots. The boy lay dazed from his fall, blinking dust from his eyes and limply resting his blade on the earth. This had gone on too long. "Enough!" Voldigar shouted.

Lusánt's eyes widened, and he jumped forward with his blade raised high, shrieking as he swung it from behind his head in a huge arc. Voldigar saw red.

The old man's hand crushed the husk of the railing like dry mud. The beam, wide as a handsbreadth, came loose from the fence with a crack as he wheeled it through the dust cloud in a flash of slivers. It connected with Lusánt's blunted sword in a tremendous crash, splitting the weapon in two. Lusánt stumbled rearward onto his back and something like the chime of a bell echoed through the old pens. Broken shards of the sword flickered through the air.

"I said *enough*!"

Voldigar's chest heaved, and his roar lingered in the now silent arena. He held the beam in his hand. His eyes were fixed on Lusánt.

The prince slowly pushed himself from the ground. Confusion mingled on his face with disgust and fear. "How . . . how dare you."

A gust of wind scattered the dust cloud as Voldigar stepped forward. "Lusánt!" he said firmly, dropping the improvised cudgel from his hand. "This is not a game. Your fellow pupil is not a block on which to vent your frustration." Lusánt's companions had filtered into the yard. The Xerimadi's hand gripped the sword at his belt.

Lusánt regained his feet and stared at Voldigar under a tilted brow, the corner of his mouth raised in disbelief. "Sword-Lector, know your place!"

Dantic had come round and knelt by Tepic, who sat against the fence and fought back tears as best he could behind a brave, stern face.

Voldigar continued. "You should not have come here, Lusánt. I know you suffer. We all suffer for our queen, but that does not excuse your lack of discipline. You cannot let hysteria overtake you on the battlefield, nor here."

Lusánt smirked in naked disdain. "If I wanted to talk about my feelings, old man, I would have visited a nursemaid."

Voldigar began to reply but Lusánt thrust his head forward and continued, "I will contend in my training however I *wish* to contend!"

"You will contend as instructed, Lusánt! And if you think yourself a man, you contend with me. You will not abuse your comrades. Go back to the Spire."

Lusánt's men moved forward in alarm, but the youth raised two fingers without looking back. He searched Voldigar's gaze for several seconds before his mouth settled in a hard line.

"I've learned a lot today. Thank you, Sword-Lector." With that, he spun on his heel and stalked out of the stables, only stopping long enough to sweep his unused helmet from the ground and fling it against the city wall.

Tepic had fought off most of his tears and stood some distance across the training grounds, his back turned and fists clenched. He was doing his best to make it clear he had *not* been crying. It was a tough age. Dantic wandered over and stood awkwardly by Voldigar. The two stared in silence as Lusánt and his entourage made their way back to the heart of the city, rounded a corner, and disappeared from view.

Dantic exhaled and trilled his lips like a horse. "Are you out of your mind, Voldigar?"

Voldigar ignored the complaint. "Is Tepic injured?"

"No. No, he's fine, I think. I suppose. It was just . . . the anger of it all. He's never seen another student like that. I didn't realize—"

"That was incredibly foolish, Dantic."

The Commander swallowed whatever else he had meant to say. "He's never seen you like that either. Are *you* alright?"

Sighing, Voldigar stole a glance at Tepic and flexed his hand a few times. "I'm fine."

Dantic shook his head and looked down the road again. "Not one to cross, that boy." He waved his hand dismissively. "Bah, you know. The young just aren't the same anymore."

Voldigar made no reply but picked the beam up off the ground instead and stared absently at the broken fence.

Dantic continued. "It's fathers, friend. No one takes responsibility, no one—and his Lordship doesn't have a chance." He paused long enough to give Voldigar an appraising nod. "You would have been a good dad, you know?"

Voldigar glanced up at Dantic and gave a halfhearted laugh. The sun was beginning to fall behind the highest buildings. "Still trying."

"Well, you're not getting any younger, Voldigar."

"Ship hasn't sailed," Voldigar said with a hint of irritation.

"Sure, sure. You know, I wish I'd had more than just my two. They're a blessing. Which reminds me." Dantic fished a small pouch from his belt and tossed it to Voldigar. "This is from Lyrusia."

Voldigar caught it and looked inside. His eyes widened. "Falam Root?"

"Yes, of course. Saved you a trip. Lyrusia's a good girl—and also happens to live in my house. Still the only thing that works?"

Voldigar nodded.

"Well give Gwenyth our regards. Lyrusia just says, *'be careful'*—that she doesn't use too much at once."

"Right. Grind it up. Only a pinch. . . . Dantic, friend, I can't afford this. It's incredibly rare."

"Well, I'll save you the money too. It's on me, Voldigar. I'm a wealthy man." Dantic grinned. "Consider it my appreciation you didn't skip work when God knows everyone else did."

"Thank you, I—"

Dantic shifted his weight and interrupted before Voldigar could offer anything more profuse. "Really, it's fine. Just take care of your family."

Voldigar fell silent, pointlessly trying to fit the fence beam back into its broken ends. Dantic stared at him a few moments before letting out a long exhale. "Just be sure you don't live on hope too long, Voldigar. You can be some kind of a father to these students in the meantime, maybe even his Lordship Thunder Pot."

Voldigar scoffed and snorted a laugh. "I'm here to teach them swordplay, Dantic, and war. I train young men to be soldiers, I don't coddle them. If they learn a good lesson or two along the way, fine."

Dantic raised an eyebrow. "Doesn't sound like the Voldigar I know. God forbid it, but that 'young man' may soon be an orphan." Pulling his gloves off, he crossed back over to Tepic and called out over his shoulder. "And there's a lot more to fatherhood than coddling, old man." With that he strode away, placing a weather-beaten hand on the back of Tepic's head and leading him out of the training yard. "Why'd you let that scrawny vine pole shove you around?"

Voldigar was left in his thoughts as the two and their conversation slipped away into the deepening shadows.

———— ◆◇◆ ————

Voldigar's shadow stretched out before him, nearly touching the red aspen trees waving at the edge of his small farm. Though tied off, his black hair whipped behind him in the unrelenting wind. Ominous clouds had swept in from the sea and caught on the mountains, but though the earthy smell of rain hung in the air, a bright sky still lingered behind.

At this hour, when the sun sank below the sea cliffs behind him, the much larger shadow of the Spire—impossibly high—pointed directly at his farm, extending half a mile from the walls of the capital. It was as if his home was a mark on some enormous clock, measuring not hours but days of the year. Each spring this meant the same thing: Planting Day.

He would be late of course, as every spring before, but barely—and this time he had the whole week ahead. No students, not even Tepic, were scheduled. What's more, Old Man Hobyn's nephew had already loaned and delivered a small plow, a harrow, and a sturdy draft horse that Hobyn befriended and took to calling "Mack." Hobyn kept Mack on the far side of the field, grazing freely on spring grass next to his humble hut, well away from the only other four-legged resident of the homestead: "Rory," Voldigar's eight-year-old Titurian hound.

On cue, Rory sprinted from the aspens and hopped around Voldigar in his daily ritual of unexplained joy and slobber. He was a lean breed with a long snout, square head, and floppy ears. Rory loved nothing more than dirt but somehow kept his short brown coat glistening around a dark line that ran along his prominent backbone.

Voldigar squatted and placed Lusánt's dented helmet on the ground, quickly pulling a small bundle out of its opening and holding it behind his back.

"What have you done today, Rory? Anything useful?"

Rory sat and cocked his head to one side. If he didn't understand the expectation, sitting was usually a good bet.

"Well, if you promise not to bark at Mack tomorrow, I've got something for you." He held his empty palm out and gave Rory a serious look. Rory stared a moment and then dropped a heavy paw into Voldigar's hand. "Good, then we shook on it."

Voldigar produced a sizable beef bone from behind his back and swept the cloth off in a flourish. "Your dinner, master." All decorum lost, Rory snatched it from Voldigar's hand. He lay on the path, gnawing and jealously guarding the bone between his paws, only to scramble to his feet again and follow Voldigar through the aspens. Beef in mouth, he looked warily from side to side for phantom bone thieves.

The field between his low stone house and Hobyn's wooden shack was striped with long shadows from hundreds of near-identical trees, but as of yet, no furrows. This year he'd prepared its border almost to the door. He wouldn't waste his chance at a plow.

Gwenyth was stooped there with a wrinkled brow, levering a large stone with all her might and a rusty spade. Voldigar set the helmet on a bench by the front door, making a mental note to work the dent out later. Rory was left to stand watch over his bone.

Gwenyth's auburn hair was swept back in a sweat-soaked scarf, her breathing labored. Old Man Hobyn, with his skin like dry crumpled parchment, worried his hands together and pleaded with her. "Now m'lady, you've been at this long enough, wouldn't you say? It's well nigh to evening and the young lord is home."

Voldigar frowned and watched her work at the stone. "Gwen."

She didn't seem to notice, but Hobyn pursed his lips and hobbled off to his hut, shaking his head.

"Gwen," Voldigar repeated.

"The stones have to come out, Vol. It's Planting Day," she said as she drew the spade back and skipped another strike off the surface. She didn't look up.

He watched her for a few more attempts until she finally rolled the stone out of the grasp of its earthy clutch. He noticed four more rocks like it strewn out in a trail behind her. She walked a little further, pounding the edge of the field until another clang rang out. Once again, digging and prying, her face twisted in frustration. The shadows had now dissipated into the blue gloom of dusk, and somewhere overhead, the first gray cloud began to drip.

"Gwen, it's a great big field. You've done enough. Hobyn and I will finish tomorrow."

Gwenyth continued to focus on the ground and struck the new stone again and again. Voldigar stepped forward and caught the handle of the spade mid swing.

"Gwenyth . . ."

Gwenyth let go. Her head drooped and her eyes welled with tears. "I'm . . . I'm just so useless. I can't do anything."

"Nonsense. Look at your garden, look at your—" Voldigar stopped short as he caught sight of her red eyes. He sighed and wrapped a long arm around her, drawing her to his chest. Gwenyth made only muffled sobs into his shirt.

Rory could bear it no longer and padded between their knees to lick Gwenyth's hands that hung limply at her sides. Voldigar rested his chin on her head and stroked the damp locks away from her cheeks. "It's alright, Gwen. It's alright." He never knew the right words to say. "Come on inside."

The rain mercifully waited long enough for them to pass through the front door and then burst open upon the bare field. Rory slipped in with his bone and lay down in front of the hearth. Voldigar continued to hold Gwenyth close, gently rocking her side to side as the wave of emotion worked its way through her. "Just sit down a minute, love. Sometimes that's the work."

He led her to the old rocking chair with Rory at its feet and dropped a blanket over her shoulders. He could see her hands were red and blistered. She let out a few rasping coughs and closed her eyes—but thankfully no fit of coughing this time. Voldigar stared into the glowing coals in the hearth and spent the next several minutes in silence, stirring a fire back to life.

"How's my cousin?" Gwenyth asked, her eyes still closed.

Voldigar looked over his shoulder to make sure she was smiling. "Which one?" Gwenyth bore some passing relation to House Sispérus—real royalty if ninth cousins were to be counted, and the self-conscious nobility of Aramon were always counting.

"You know which one," she continued.

"He's fine, I suppose."

"Don't lie to me, Vol."

"Alright, he's a pest—and yes, he showed up for his lessons today. How did you know?"

"A squirrel pranced along a bough and chirped rumors in my ear, old man." She walked her fingers along the arm of her chair.

Voldigar laughed softly and carefully rolled a log into the center of the fire. He turned back to Gwenyth. "Lucky guess, eh?"

"Mhmm."

Voldigar wiped the soot off his hands and sighed. "I'm unfair really. The boy isn't well. His mother's illness is wearing on him. I pray God she survives. He isn't ready for the throne, not with a host of councilors would he be ready."

"Lanathor is helping her, yes?"

"Yes, he's been there for several days."

"Then she's in good hands."

Voldigar nodded and thought of his stolid old friend cooped up in the tomb of the upper floors of the Spire, bending every fiber of his learned mind to find some answer for their Queen Eleanora, for the legacy of Olwis the Shield. "Oh! That reminds me. Look what I have." Voldigar pulled a small pouch from his pocket and another pouch from within. "Falam Root."

Gwenyth sat up with a smile that quickly evaporated. She blinked. "You know we can't—"

"Don't worry. It was a gift," Voldigar said. "Dantic," he added before she could protest further. He hurried across the room and pulled a clay mortar and pestle from the cupboard, eagerly crushing the dry root into a fine powder.

"Is it really safe?"

"Just a pinch of powder, Lyrusia says."

"But for how long?"

Voldigar walked back to Gwenyth, ducking under the beam. Nothing worked and they both wondered why Falam Root *did*. No pain, and most importantly, no coughing. He squatted down with a wooden cup of water. "I don't know. But it works, and that's enough for me. There's plenty here for a few weeks." He sprinkled a dusting over the water and stirred it with his finger. Perhaps a little too much was in the cup. "Drink."

Holding his gaze, she sipped at the mixture, quickly hiding a grimace with a grateful smile. "What'd you do to get in his good graces?"

"I don't know," Voldigar said. "Something about doing my job. I don't understand the man."

Gwenyth finished the drink and stared into her lap. "I'm sorry, Vol. I really am."

Voldigar shook his head and lifted her chin with a finger. "Don't be."

She closed her eyes, interlocked her small pale fingers behind his neck, and leaned her forehead against his. Voldigar could smell the aromatic root, a hint of clove and cinnamon on her warm breath. He started to speak, but she placed an index finger on his lips.

They stayed in this pose for several minutes until she finally leaned back in her chair, rocked a few times, and let out a long exhale. Voldigar sat back on his haunches and studied her face. She was no longer young, but she was lovely. He knew she would be beautiful until the day she joined the Song. He'd do anything for her. "It's going to be a real crop this year, Gwen. We'll buy all the Falam Root you want. We'll get you well."

She made no response but rocked in her chair a few more times. Several minutes passed while the only sound was Rory cracking away to get the marrow from his prized beef bone. Thinking she was asleep, Voldigar quietly rose from his seat and walked across the room to dim the lamp.

"Voldigar," she said. Her voice sounded further away than the hearth by which she sat.

"Yes?"

"Before I die, give me a child."

Voldigar's hands trembled with the lamp, and he felt a tightness move from his face to his chest and shoulders. "Get some rest, Gwen."

Chapter Two

The Long Vigil

S OARING FIVE HUNDRED FEET above the streets of Arregalt, in the uppermost chambers of The Golden Spire of Tymicha, vigil for the Empress had continued since the last full moon. Lanathor balanced a leather-bound tome upon his knees and shifted awkwardly on a low carved chair near Empress Eleanora's headboard. Though he knew every phrase by heart, still he squinted at the text in dim half-light. Whenever he was called upon to perform the office of Reader, he found himself following familiar words along the page. There was value in the tradition itself.

Thick layers of furs and red velvet blankets were pulled up to the frail woman's chin. Her breathing remained shallow but had grown even. Perhaps she had fallen asleep this time. Lanathor trailed off his last sentence, a Chant of Wisdom near the middle of *The Words of Ralm*. He waited for the Empress to raise a hand or mutter for him to continue, but she remained silent. The heavy bedding rose and fell almost imperceptibly. There was very little color left in her face. The olive skin she shared with her son had long since faded to an icy pallor.

Lanathor inhaled and blinked. It was well past midnight. Sweeping one dark hand to close the cover, with the other he rubbed the bridge of his nose. These could be her final hours, and every learned man in the Spire knew it.

"I don't think your quaint superstitions will have quite the same effect on her," Doctor Challeric said from across the room. He was illuminated by a row of candles on the windowsill near which he perched. With his foggy glasses and mouth perpetually drawn to a point, he looked like an owl waiting to sweep down on an unsuspecting rodent.

"She asked me to read these," Lanathor replied quietly, hoping Challeric would match his tone and not wake her again.

"Hmph." The doctor released a clinical-sounding chuckle and brushed a wisp of gray hair from his brow. "Where did you find that book anyway? I know for a fact that none of your scriptures remain here in the Spire."

"A member of my order lives near the city, Doctor. He was kind enough to lend me a few tomes."

"Well, unless you have some further purpose, Lector, the Empress needs her rest. You should depart and wait until called again." Challeric turned his head to the dark window through which he most certainly could not see.

Lanathor could guess the result, but he might not have another chance to ask.

"Doctor, as you know, none of us may be called again. While Her Highness sleeps, it would be the ideal time for me to provide you with further insight—"

"Absolutely not." Doctor Challeric snapped his head back from the window. "If you believe your *abilities* to be useful, I expect you to discuss it with Diocesan Ragat and Master Hyrodan. They will inform me."

"I've been here for a week, Doctor. Time is short. There is unique information I can provide."

Challeric wrinkled his brow and looked away again. "I have made my decision."

Lanathor watched him for a long moment. Stubborn and arrogant, as always. Neither Challeric nor the two magi would have the sense to listen, but duty demanded he at least suggest it. Lanathor gave a small nod and with *The Words of Ralm* tucked under one arm, crossed the chamber and pressed the ivory doors open into an empty parlor beyond.

Only seven short years prior, he stood in this same spot, delivering a stack of books to the Reader King Olwis had requested. They were read to the King on what became his deathbed also. Eleanora's request to hear the same readings came as a surprise. But while Olwis had been eager, Eleanora regarded every reading the same—a flat expression, eyes closed, no questions. Lanathor wondered if the gentle voice of Olwis's Reader would have pleased the Empress more, but she would have to make do with his own rough bass.

Lanathor collected several more books from the polished floor. He balanced them in a heavy stack to his chin and rapped his foot against the next set of double doors, leading to a bustling antechamber beyond. Day or night, four Stonepike guards held these doors and four more held a final pair, leading out from the Empress's apartments.

"Haslor," a muffled voice came urgently through the doors. "Haslor!" After a short pause, the heavy brass panels groaned open. The porter guard rubbed sleep out of his eyes below a low-brimmed helm. *Haslor, apparently.* Another guard finished an angry glare and shook his head.

Lanathor held Haslor's eyes for a moment and did his best to forgive the breach in protocol. Duty had been lax indeed in the Spire of late, but sleeping on your feet in the Empress's chambers was a step too far. "Guard Haslor. You would do well to maintain your attention, and also . . . please call for the prince. I fear Her Ladyship may be in her final hours."

Any residue of sleep fled from Haslor's face. A hush interrupted the din of the room, and several eyes turned to Lanathor. When he did not continue, the crowd returned to its murmurings with only a few more nervous glances. Haslor spoke hurriedly to a young page who scurried off a moment later.

Despite the bare furnishings and marble floors, the warmth of the crowded antechamber was stifling at this late hour. No less than three dozen priests and prophets, magi, generals, and servants of every sort came and went, or dozed on their feet like Haslor, waiting to be called upon by the Mistress of The Golden Spire.

Lanathor found an empty patch of wall near a narrow servant's door and a small table on which he heavily dropped his stack of books. He leaned his head back against the marble and closed his eyes. He could still picture every detail of the antechamber. Long years of wariness and necessity had sharpened this talent of his mind's eye.

Directly across the chamber, General Gamad snored. His huge form and wide white beard spilled over the Empress's delicate alabaster chair. His good eye was closed, and a patch for the other hung to the side, revealing a pit of scars and liver spots. To Gamad's right, Diocesan Ragat argued animatedly with an apothecary. The ill-fitting blue robes and tall matching hat made a comical frame around his small red face.

At arm's length from Lanathor, Master Hyrodan had an equally ridiculous hat, but all in white and gold to match his flowing robes and those of the three female votaries who waited on him with veiled eyes. Lanathor subconsciously dropped his palm on his own bald, black head and smirked. *No hat. Maybe that's why Doctor Challeric doesn't care for me.*

The most intriguing figure leaned against the same wall as the heavily armed Stonepike guards. Lord Commander Caliras had two flattened wings of jet-black hair to match an oily, pointed beard. He was much older than he looked and the source of unending and unbearable gossip—a favorite of Eleanora who'd bought his way to title and position. Ruthless, and if rumors were believed, too intimate with the widowed Empress. The Stonepikes were his own and with them the security of the Spire.

It was an odd collection of men who might otherwise never voluntarily share the same room.

Lanathor opened his eyes to find Master Hyrodan staring down at him from under his obnoxious white hat. He was slender, and his long robes hung like the corners of his mouth behind a cascade of square gray beard that would shame the Empress's beautician. Hyrodan made no attempt to hide a contemptuous glare from his darkling eyes, set so deeply in his brow that only the pupils could be seen. He had not yet succeeded in driving Lanathor from the vigil with withering disapproval. Lanathor returned his stare silently.

"Still hoping for another high-profile convert are we, Lector Lanathor?" Hyrodan finally asked.

Lanathor's expression remained unchanged. "I would be delighted if *The Words of Ralm* rang true to her, Master Hyrodan. The Empress asked me to read."

"Of course. Well, good luck. I understand from the doctor you have a matter of medicine and lore you'd like to discuss with me?"

For a moment Lanathor thought to reply and then noticed the sarcastic smirk on Hyrodan's face. "Perhaps later."

It was time for a break from the suffocation. Lanathor gathered up his heavy stack of books and slipped through the final set of huge, thick doors. He passed another four Stonepikes into the red-carpeted balconies beyond where a vast array of staircases flowed out below him to the great hall a hundred feet below, illuminated by a thousand lamps and sconces. One long delicate causeway extended over open space to a brass-doored lift that traveled from the crown of the tower to far below in the Delvings. The sight of the hall was breathtaking no matter how many times he saw it.

Lanathor did not ring for the lift nor descend into the hall, for at one end of the balcony, a small door led to a walkway on the exterior of the Spire. Nearby, the plump, hairless scribe Bolran sat on a stool behind a podium and eyed Lanathor, glancing occasionally at his logbook to jot something while he hummed softly to himself. Lanathor liked Bolran the night scribe best. Of all the appropriately fastidious eunuchs who sat in that stool, he at least was no fool and possessed a modicum of humor.

"Good evening, Bolran," Lanathor said as he set the books down with a thump. "Would you mind keeping an eye on these?"

Bolran looked up from his podium and blinked tiny eyes underneath two sparse eyebrows. "Not at all, friend."

"How's your wife?"

"Very funny. What can I do for you, Lector?"

"Just need some air. It's a full moon tonight and the rain has cleared. I would like to record the next observations."

"Again?" Bolran snorted a chuckle. "You keep this up, you'll put the Imperial Astrologer out of work. Sign in here."

"Perhaps if he drank less and observed more, he'd have nothing to fear."

Bolran coughed uncomfortably and spun the podium around to Lanathor. Leaning back, he locked his hands behind his head. Where other scribes relished in painfully and slowly handling all notation personally, Bolran seemed to prefer sharing the load. Lanathor glanced at the ornate water clock behind him and wrote quickly. *Third Watch. Second Hour. Second Quarter. Observatory. Observations.* He finished with his name and handed the quill back to Bolran who exchanged it for a set of keys.

Outside, though the rain had let up, a strong wind enhanced the effect of the dizzying heights. Lanathor grasped the stone railing of the winding staircase with one of his hands, covered in a network of scars like spider webs. He caught a glimpse of Arregalt far below. While the sky was clear and unveiled stars stared down round the great green moon, a fast-moving rush of fog brushed along the tiny rooftops in little islands of light where the new gas lamps of the city would burn until morning. He was glad to round into the observatory turret at the very tip of the Spire and forget the subtle sense of swaying.

The observatory was a marvel of engineering. Of the many famous accomplishments in Aramon, Lanathor esteemed it most. Here at the pinnacle of the Spire, a thirty-foot telescope rested on a pneumatic disc that he could rotate along with the domed roof using nothing more than a single hand. Lutz, the principal engineer, should have been a national treasure, and Lanathor often noted with some pride: he was a fellow member of his order. That this was accomplished without the magic of a Teller only added to its wonder.

Lanathor cranked a handle to open the port of the domed roof and smiled when he took up his seat at the enormous eyeglass. He possessed a similar device at home in lesser scale. What a delight to sit at the greatest example. Tonight would be a simple pleasure, to measure the arc and motion of the full moon, Mirváné, in relation to the pole star, Patradavi. He could have precisely recorded her slide along the great roof of the world with calculation alone, but there was no joy in it, and he would not miss a chance to observe the wandering stars and dim constellations along Mirváné's path.

He slipped his notebook from a fold in his robes, adjusted the instruments at the base of the telescope, and began to jot down familiar figures as he saw them. A mechanical clock on the wall to his left clicked out each minute as it arrived.

The figures were wrong.

Lanathor frowned and slid down from his seat to examine the pneumatic disc at his feet. He had performed the calibration and leveling himself. To his knowledge, and that of the logbook, no one else had been here all week. The telescope itself bore no signs of tampering. After a few minutes of frustrated disbelief, Lanathor put his eye to the lens again and adjusted the overlay to ensure it was in place. Nothing. He hurried to the exterior stairs and craned his neck as if to somehow correct his lying eyes. Mirváně looked down, the same placid green orb as always.

Had the Spire itself shifted? Some structural problem? No—it would be obvious. Perhaps someone else had been in the observatory. Lanathor could recall entire pages with only a glance, and in his mind's eye, he saw no other entries besides his own for weeks. Perhaps through weariness, he had somehow missed a detail. He rushed back into the inner balconies.

"Bolran!" he shouted down the hall with more intensity than intended.

Bolran started and nearly fell from his stool. "What! What?"

"Has anyone else checked in for the observatory—in the last week?" Lanathor didn't wait for an answer and spun the podium around, flipping open to a random section. The guard logs, as it happened. He flipped back furiously in search of the observatory logs until Bolran slapped his pink forearm over the book.

"Pardon, Lector. My logs are not for public consumption. Give me a moment and I'll find what you're looking for." Bolran spun the podium back to himself and thumbed through a few pages, shaking his head like a bemused grandmother.

Lanathor mumbled an apology and reviewed the pages that lingered in his mind. Unfortunately, only logs for each set of four guards posted at the doors of the inner chambers. Bolran began to answer, but Lanathor's mind continued to drift over the pages he'd just seen. Something else was missing.

"Wait, turn back to the guard logs."

"What? Why?" Poor Bolran began to sweat profusely but did his best to keep up, turning again to the guard logs.

"There's a name in those logs? Haslor?"

"No, there isn't!" Bolran protested. He caught himself with a gasp and shut the book. "Lector, I'm sorry. These records are private. Lord Commander Caliras's eyes only. What's this have to do with the observatory?"

"It's . . ." Lanathor stared blankly a moment. "It's nothing, Bolran." He turned quickly and walked down the hallway toward the Empress's chambers.

"Wait, that's it? Lanathor!" Bolran shouted after him.

Lanathor ignored the man's confusion and mulled over the guard logs again. He knew they were private, of course, and he knew how paranoid Eleanora had grown and how firmly Commander Caliras reinforced that paranoia. Every set of doors locked from either side. Each set of chamber guards were selected daily by the Lord Commander. They did not know who they would serve with, and the Lord Commander himself reported their names to the scribe no more than a day in advance. There were no exceptions. A thousand such rules and protocols existed to prevent any attempt at conspiracy or failure in security. There was a name missing from those logs: Haslor—the sleepy guard he'd gently reproved a few minutes before.

Maybe it was just another dropped protocol in the Spire's recent disorder, but it bothered him. No one unrecorded should be within a hundred yards of the Empress's chambers. *No one.* Neither Bolran nor Caliras were men to make such a mistake.

Lanathor's thoughts were interrupted by the sight of Prince Lusánt rounding the opposite end of the balcony, marching in firm strides with his head low toward the Empress's antechamber. The small page Guard Haslor had dispatched hurried along in front of him, and half a dozen young men followed with serious expressions.

Realization sprang like fire into Lanathor's mind.

"Your Highness, wait!" He hurried forward.

The party stopped as one, and Lusánt looked up with red-rimmed eyes, noticing Lanathor for the first time. In his arms, he clutched a small chest, and a look of weary determination further soured his sallow face. "Another lector, come to say what's best for me and Mother," he said quietly. "I think not, Master Teller. Be gone!" Like a school of fish, his entourage moved again toward the entrance of Eleanora's chambers.

"Please! Your Highness, wait. There's a discrepancy with your guard logs. It's highly unusual!"

Lusánt stopped again as his shoulders tightened and raised. "Discrepancies? With the log books?" One hand rose from the chest he carried to spasm and flex. Without looking at Lanathor he responded more firmly. "I do not wish to discuss minutia with you! Leave!"

Lanathor stepped forward to implore the prince again, but two of his entourage broke off and menacingly barred his way. Before Lanathor could further protest, Lusánt shouldered the confused outer guards apart and flung the doors of the antechamber open with surprising strength. "Everyone out!"

Lanathor followed as closely as he dared. The crowd within ceased all motion and conversation for a few bewildered moments.

"Out I said! Out!" Lusánt bodily thrust the first courtier stumbling into the hallway and took hold of another. Within moments, the milling group were funneling through the door with useless protests. Even General Gamad heaved his great bulk from the groaning alabaster chair to lumber through the exit—all save Commander Caliras who no longer leaned against the wall but stood at attention with the inner guards of Eleanora's bedchamber, facing Lusánt and his young men.

"Which part of *everyone* do you not understand, Lord Commander?" Lusánt said.

Caliras held the youth's gaze as Lanathor watched through the open doors. "I am the shield of Eleanora, Lusánt. Respectfully, I must maintain my post."

Lusánt bared his teeth and spoke in a sharp, seething tone. "Shield? The Empress is unable to speak, Commander. I am the voice of this house! Address either of us without title again and you will lose your tongue. Take your men, and get out!"

Caliras's face flushed red, and the corner of his mouth lifted in a near imperceptible sneer. He held Lusánt's gaze a moment longer, then looked from one of his helmeted Stonepikes to the next. With a nod of his head, the group exited. Lusánt watched each step until they cleared the room and then waived his own men out with a flick of his wrist. Slipping through two more sets of doors into his mother's chamber, he emerged a moment later, dragging a complaining Doctor Challeric by the back of his collar to the hall. The Empress and her son were all that remained in the apartments. Lusánt closed the outer doors with a thud and the click of a key.

Forty of Aramon's inner circle now stood awkwardly in a crowded hall outside the dying Empress's chambers in silence. The warning in Lanathor's heart grew, and the itching heat of emotion rose in his chest. Thoughtlessly, he reached into the folds of his robes and discretely opened a small wooden capsule to retrieve a tiny piece of aromatic root within. When he was certain no one was looking, he turned briefly to the side and placed it under his tongue. Within seconds, he felt the reassuring calm and clarity wash over him like starlight through scattering clouds. The hall renewed its murmurings.

"Commander Caliras," he said. "I need to speak with you urgently."

Caliras stood on the far edge of the crowd with eight of his Stonepike guards. He looked up from a whispered conversation. "Excuse me?"

"Privately, Lord Commander."

Caliras crossed to Lanathor with a frown. "What do you want?"

"There's a discrepancy in your logs. They're missing a name."

"My logbooks are private."

"I know they are—and they're missing a name."

Caliras sighed. "A name? Really, Lector? Well, that's very interesting, but maybe now is not the time?"

"Do you know those eight men? Each of them?"

Caliras looked over and laughed. "Yes. Of course."

Lanathor was about to detail what he'd seen but caught himself short. "The logs should not be in error, Commander. Why are they wrong?"

A flicker of annoyance crossed Caliras's face. "Perhaps you should bring this up with the scribe." He raised his brow and pointed down the hall, then turned to walk away.

"I've spoken to him already," Lanathor said.

Caliras turned back. A silent duel took place between their eyes until the commander blinked and looked at the floor. "Are you . . . getting to a point, Lanathor?"

"Should I be?"

Caliras smiled briefly. "As much fun as this is, Lector, I do have work to do." Caliras returned to his guards and whispered to them again. The outer guards looked at Lanathor while the other four followed Caliras round the curve of the balcony. Where were they going?

Lanathor hurried forward, but the remaining Stonepikes converged in front of him.

"Where to, Lector?"

"Let me pass."

"Sorry. Need to understand where you're headed first."

Lanathor bit his lip and watched Caliras disappear beyond the corner. *The servants' entrance.*

"I don't have time for this. Let me through!"

The guard shook his head. Lanathor tensed and considered a rash act, but turned to the front doors instead. He gave them a fruitless tug. "General Gamad, there's something wrong with this guard detail. I need your key," he said with urgency.

Gamad had found himself another chair and growled as he stirred from his dozing. "The guard detail?"

"Yes, I need to get in."

"You heard the prince, Reverend. No entry."

"You have the only other key, General."

"So what?"

"I'm telling you, there's something *wrong.* Give me the key," Lanathor demanded. Even through the mask of the root numbing his mouth and his thoughts, he felt his body stiffen once again.

"Or what?" Gamad said, rising and towering above Lanathor.

Lanathor groaned and hastened back to the opposite balcony, just beyond sight of either crowd or night scribe. There he leaned against the wall and closed his eyes. Precious seconds were passing. His mind had to be clear. Breathing deeply, he bit into the root and let all sense of his surroundings pass away. He needed quiet, just quiet in his mind, and then a single focus. This was never easy.

The sounds of the milling, canting crowd faded to a muffled blackness, and then a point emerged in his mind. It was a single memory, vivid and painful, like a tiny marble on a sightless horizon. He steadied his breath and fixed himself on that point. He was a child again and the room was cold, bitter cold, and black as the ebony expanse of night. It was alright to be alone, he liked alone, but he could hear the steps of a visitor. It was the only thing darker than his lightless room, a terror a hundred feet high. He should be afraid, he should cower, he should hide, but he felt . . . nothing. *Good*. That was it.

In that instant, Lanathor heard the crackling structure of the Song all about him, its adamant pillars and a great web of resonating, vibrating threads. The harmony was so beautiful and overwhelming, he longed to hold it forever, yet if he did, he would be lost in rapturous tears and never wake again.

The moment passed. He flashed open his eyes and grasped the threads about him. With a pull, the red carpets of the Spire, the thousand lights of the great hall below, and the very air itself stretched, turned, and vanished like smoke. In a blink, he was in the corner of the Empress's antechamber.

——◦——

Sound took longer to catch up in the moment of a Shift. It always did. Lanathor suppressed a gag as bile rose in his throat and he adjusted his eyes to the dim light of the antechamber. Across the marble floors, not only did the servants' door hang open, but the heavy brass doors of the parlor before the Empress's bedchamber stood ajar as well. Through them, five men crouched low and crept toward the final set of fastened ivory doors. In the hands of the central figure, Caliras, were a key in one and a glint of steel in the other.

Lanathor fought off the lingering nausea and refocused his memories, swallowing the remainder of the root whole. A sensation of flame erupted from within as the spidery scars on his arms and hands fissured and glowed with pulsing violet. The pain was exquisite, but the fading threads about him snapped into sharp relief.

"Halt!" Lanathor bellowed from across the room. He was not ready, but there was no time. His voice, still delayed, crackled with an electric rattle in his ears as the nausea swelled once more. Five heads turned as one, eyes wide and weapons brandished.

Caliras froze at the sight before him but regained his wits just in time to leap aside, pulling the nearest guard with him. A shimmering distortion burst forth from Lanathor's mouth and hurtled through the open doors with a boom.

The force of the projectile caught another guard squarely in the chest. The hooked hand weapon he wielded snapped and clattered against the floor as the man himself was lifted from the ground and smashed into the ivory doors of the bedroom behind with a grunt. Lanathor grimaced. Only one. Just off the mark.

"Go!" Caliras yelled as he dashed for the outer doors. The remaining three guards charged Lanathor with a cry, their cruel hacking instruments held high. Haslor was among them.

Grasping the threads on both sides, Lanathor pulled them together, and a rounded void of pitch black bent the floor and ceiling before him for a split second. All three charging men were knocked to the floor in a tangled heap, but the force of the impact swept Lanathor backward in the opposite direction. He slid several feet on his red cloak, striking his head hard against the carved molding of the antechamber. He tasted blood.

Rather than escape, Caliras only confirmed the handle of the door was secure and then whirled on the prone Lanathor. "How did you get in?" he roared as he leapt on him with a stab of his dagger.

His head throbbed and his body burned, but through the haze of vision, Lanathor caught only the tip of the blade briefly against his forearm and then grasped Caliras's wrist. The two struggled and rolled on the cold floors, flailing and striking with their free hands.

Occupied as he was, Lanathor could not take hold of the threads about him. They flickered in and out of perception as the room spun around him and the Lord Commander. No man could seem to gain advantage, but two of the guards were scrambling to their feet and drawing daggers of their own. In seconds they would be upon him.

Under the calm of the root upon his mind, time seemed to slow. Lanathor knew that fear should strike him, some last cry of desperation—but nothing came. He wondered if a man at this moment should rather feel resolve or resignation. Twenty years he had been free, he had done his duty, and he now faced this treachery alone. Perhaps it was a good way to die.

With a last shred of focus, Lanathor somehow held Caliras in place, brushed against a thread, and tightened his hold around the would-be assassin's wrist. He had a sudden surge of strength. Twisting from the tiles and pushing his grip, he felt Caliras's arm give way before his own. The Lord Commander cried out in agony as the dagger clattered away and his hand curled backward at an impossible angle.

Just as the two guards arrived, Lanathor rolled to Caliras's back and hooked his other arm tightly around his neck. He scrambled backward against the floor, pulling the gasping Lord Commander with him. The two wide-eyed attackers hesitated and weaved side to side, looking for an opening. Blood seeped from the corners of Lanathor's mouth and from the scars on his arms. It gushed from the fresh dagger wound. His strength was fading and the threads were all but gone.

The doors of the Empress's chamber flung open behind the guards, but rather than a wrathful and petulant Lusánt emerging, Lanathor beheld a wondrous and terrible thing. The boy indeed stood beyond the doors, leaning at an odd angle, but he was almost entirely obscured by the form of a being, not fully opaque.

It shimmered and roiled in the half-light, and though liquid in its form, its borders were distinct and green, like clouded glass in ancient bronze. No face could be discerned, but the creature held the form of a huge man some nine feet high while presenting the distorted limbs of an injured beast. It seemed to stand with difficulty, and its body continuously took on new shapes, alternately collapsing and regaining its footing.

It lurched forward before the two guards could turn to face it. Caliras shrieked and flailed in Lanathor's grip as a hundred tendrils of green fire shot forth from the creature. The guards were pierced through and rent. Blood sprayed in every direction, their forms obliterated in an instant. Lanathor winced as the gore spattered across his face and arms and the ceiling of the room.

He released his grip on Caliras who howled again, squirmed to his feet, and bolted for the outer door where he produced and then fumbled his key to the floor. Rather than make another assault, the beast stood still and pulsated. Caliras gave up trying to retrieve the key from the slick, bloody marble and frantically jerked at the handles, screaming for help against the massive, muffling doors.

Lanathor fixated now on the green behemoth. In wonder, he slowly rose to his feet, hands at the ready for some final desperate defense. All about him the blood on every surface vibrated in unison and gathered first in droplets, then in rivulets of red, flowing to the creature.

"Orun!" Lanathor shouted. "You cannot enter this place." His hands shook, but he did not look away. Slowly, the threads of magic gathered about him once more. The movement of blood on the floor ceased, and something like a newly formed head turned toward Lanathor. The creature was now a patchwork of flesh, like soiled rags, riddled through with holes to reveal the walls behind—and glimpses of Lusánt, who stood as if entranced.

Sounds, akin to speech, but low and guttural, unintelligible, shook the room as they emerged from the thing he called *Orun*. The sounds ceased and the creature tottered, beginning to break apart and looking as if it might suddenly collapse. But at once, the flaking, stumbling mass reassembled and lurched toward Lanathor with blinding speed. This time he was ready.

Thrusting both hands up and forward, a prismatic arc burst forth from his palms and caught the creature just as it crashed into him. The fiery green tendrils again sprouted from every inch of its body. A terrible crack rattled the room and dust fell from the ceiling. Caliras collapsed to the floor and covered his ears while the creature let loose a horrific cry in its strangled, gurgling voice.

Eyes wide and teeth gritted in concentration, Lanathor pushed against it as the tendrils lashed and whipped, flailing around the edges of the prismatic shield. The ends of some cut home and slashed his face and arms, but he held firm and continued to press toward the Orun, step by agonizing step—beholding its grotesque bulk in horror.

As the battle of wills went on for those precious seconds, Lanathor could now clearly see the Empress's chamber. Lusánt still stood with distant gaze, seemingly unseeing. Beside him the Empress lay upon her bed, eyes wide in the long stare of death. She was no more.

Lusánt took one slow step toward the struggle in the outer room and then another.

"Emperor, no! Do not!" Lanathor bellowed.

The boy paid no heed and took another step, and then one more. Beads of sweat poured from Lanathor's brow and he could feel the ache of the scars upon his face that oozed blood and shimmered a burning, violet light into his eyes. One more step.

"Lusánt! No!"

In a desperate surge, Lanathor pressed into the creature with all his might, but its mass was too great, and it was growing with every passing moment. It thundered again and matched his pressure with its own. Lusánt was nearly just behind. Lanathor glanced at the prince one final time and then rotated his arms and forced them through the shield, just as they erupted in a flash of violet. Grabbing hold of the Orun, he thrust into its horrid flesh and twisted to the ground. There was a terrible radiance, then a burst of fire, and Lanathor saw no more.

Chapter Three

CHASING PHANTOMS

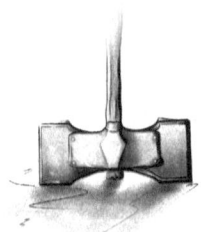

V OLDIGAR LAY AWAKE, ABSENTLY rubbing the small brass key that hung from his neck. He stared into an inky sea of silence where an old lacquered beam would be and tried to remember his dream. He was in his field again, but now the clotbur could move. Each time he stooped to pull one up, the weed slithered from the ground and skittered across a row. He gave chase, but it was too swift. Before he could lay hold, the little devil planted a tiny version of itself.

A ridiculous dream but not unusual. Though he rarely had even two days in ten to work the land, it was his farm he dreamed of most of all. Now he'd missed Planting Day. One day late. What did it matter? The chase of herbaceous phantoms left his head to swim. He wouldn't fall asleep again.

He tried to chant softly to himself, but his mind wandered while he lay in darkness. Every year it seemed he awoke more and more, before even the hint of dawn. Had he slept at all? The smell of a recent fire lingered. Gwenyth must have lit the hearth again some hours before. It was never warm enough for her, even in this unusual spring.

She had been in his arms hours ago, and instinctively he let go of the key to reach across the bed. She wasn't there. These days, she slept no better than he. He pictured Gwenyth in the only other room of the house, propped on a pillow, back in the rocking chair old Hobyn made, head lolled to the side, and a faded, woven shawl draped on her narrow shoulders.

A banging jolted Voldigar from his thoughts and the bulrush mat he called his bed. He swept his curved Daneki blade from under the edge and jerked the curtain open. Someone was pounding on the front door. Gwenyth was stirring in her chair and staring at the thick oaken entry, embers in the hearth nearly spent behind her. The two struck quite a contrast as she raised herself with slender arms. Her auburn tresses tumbled around a graceful, ever-young face, belied at the corners of her mouth and eyes by lines of care and suffering. Voldigar stood taut, blade in one hand, the other drawn into a fist—a mass of hard-won bulk and scars. His black hair was a mess down his back, jaw set in apprehension.

"What do you want?" he asked the door sharply as he gently moved Gwenyth to stand behind him. Rory crouched tensely by the hearth, emitting a low growl.

A muffled voice replied. "It's Dantic!"

Voldigar exhaled and unlatched the door. A cool blast of night air swept in, and sure enough, Commander Dantic stood wild-eyed in the frame with his fist raised for another knock. Rory clawed at the ground and let out several sharp barks. Dantic's rust-haired son Tepic trembled, face pale and lantern in hand while Dantic gripped his shoulder.

"Dantic?" Voldigar demanded, putting a hand out to soothe Rory. "What hour is it?"

"Not quite dawn. I'm sorry, Lector—this couldn't wait. There's been an incident in the Spire. Blood everywhere, the Empress is dead, the prince is in a stupor, Lanathor's hurt, it's awful!"

"It's alright! Slow down, Dantic. Come out of the cold." *What happened to Lanathor?*

Gwenyth crept out from behind Voldigar and pulled the shawl tighter about her shoulders. She shooed Rory toward the bedroom while Dantic and Tepic hurried into the room and Voldigar shut out the cold behind them.

"I'm sorry, Voldigar," Dantic continued as he gesticulated frantically. "I still can't believe it's happening. The Empress passed on tonight. The Council of War has been preparing all month—just like with Olwis. We knew the throne would go to Lusánt, but it's always a dangerous thing, you know?"

Voldigar nodded. He knew better than most but did not yet follow the Commander's rambling. He set the blade on his mantle and handed the only other chairs in the house to his guests. He motioned for Dantic to go on while he leaned against the wall. He glanced at Tepic who was staring at him and gave the boy a reassuring nod, though he suspected his face did not look particularly comforting at this moment.

"During the transition, I was to secure the city—from rioting and looting, that sort of thing. Lord Commander Caliras was to secure the Spire, as usual, and Gamad had everything else," Dantic went on.

"The preparations were cared for and in the hands of our subordinates. I received a messenger sometime after midnight that the Empress's time was near, God rest her. I brought Tepic with me in haste, but it takes a bloody long time to reach the summit, you know? Well, I'm glad we didn't come a second earlier, because the moment we got off the lift, there was a terrific blast and the Empress's outer doors came clean off. A lot of people were hurt."

Voldigar swallowed hard and crossed his arms. "You said Lanathor?"

"Aye, the Reader. He's torn up bad, Vol."

Voldigar choked back emotion and focused again on Dantic's story. "But that's not why you're here, am I right, Commander? You have the security of Arregalt as your concern, and you're two miles down the road in the house of a poor farmer. Why?"

"You're not just a farmer."

Voldigar blinked away a flicker of pain while lamplight shadows danced over their faces. "That life is over."

Dantic waived the comment off but paused to swallow. He took a long look at Tepic.

"Do you want to speak privately?" Voldigar asked.

"No! No, he needs to be here too. I'll tell you why I've come." Dantic took a deep breath. "Behind those doors was a lot of blood and bodies.

And the prince—the Emperor I mean—comes staggering out looking like a ghost. '*Caliras tried to kill me,*' is all he says, and . . . everyone just stands there dumbfounded, but wouldn't you believe it, a whole company of Gamad's men come down both hallways from who knows where. The old whale looks as confused as me, but it didn't take long for the Stonepikes and the regulars to set upon each other. There was a lot of bloodshed and nobles caught up in the confusion, but Gamad's superior numbers made quick work of Caliras's."

Voldigar narrowed his eyes. *Not again.* "And you and Tepic?" he asked.

"I'm getting to it. 'Treachery!' Gamad yells, and tells me to secure the city—and the Stonepike barracks especially. But now there's five hundred feet of Spire crawling with Stonepikes below me and I'm alone. We have a fastness for my officers a floor below the royal apartments, and I sent Tepic off to hole up there while I figured out what to do."

Tepic began to shake again as his part in the tale was told. Gwenyth placed her shawl around the youth and whispered comforting words.

"What happened next?" Voldigar said.

"Well, I made it out of the Spire with less trouble than I thought. That old fox Gamad, or rather I suspect one of his more competent men, had apparently deployed an entire brigade of regulars in the Spire, right under Caliras's nose. The Stonepikes made a full retreat and fortified themselves in their barracks. No one knows where Caliras went, maybe with them. My own men hold that perimeter now, but the distraction and rumors have let loose a bloody storm of rioting and looting in the city. I'm stretched thin."

Voldigar's face had fallen steadily as Dantic recounted his tale. Unconsciously, he squeezed the back of Gwenyth's empty rocking chair. He'd heard enough. "I'll have nothing to do with palace intrigue, Dantic. Never again."

Dantic lifted an eyebrow at the comment but quickly shook the expression off his face. "There's more than that, Voldigar."

"Go on then."

"It's Tepic . . . well . . . Tepic *saw something.*" Dantic paused. "I would hardly believe it, but you know this boy doesn't lie." He looked to Tepic who was fighting off tears welling in his eyes. "He found me a couple of hours ago in my headquarters, he was . . . he was very afraid." Dantic cut off, and caught his own emotion, reaching a hand to pat Tepic gently on the head. "Go on, Tep."

Voldigar nodded and let go of the chair. He squatted down in front of Tepic. "Tepic, what did you see?"

Tepic took a couple of wavering breaths and answered. "I was in the officers' room, where Dad sent me, and there were two of his soldiers there too. I . . . I . . ."

"Tepic. It's alright, look at me, lad."

The boy bit his lip and met his eyes. "They knew who I was and let me in, but they were scared. I think they knew what was going on in the palace. I don't know what they were talking about, but I was back in the bunks, not very long. All of a sudden, there was a great big crash, and most of the lamps went out. I-I went over to the door as quiet as I could, and then I saw . . . th-there was . . ."

"What did you see?"

"The same thing we saw at the lift, only different."

Voldigar looked to Dantic.

Dantic nodded. "There was something there when the doors came off, Vol. Not human. It was like a cloud, or smoke, only somehow darker—like the light was running away from it. I only saw it for a second, I thought the blast had shaken my wits, but whatever it was, it darted down the hall in a hurry."

"Darted?" Voldigar looked at Tepic again. "It was the same thing, Tepic?"

"Yes, sir—only it was in the officer room now."

"And you are certain this was not a man?"

Tepic nodded. "The soldiers didn't seem to notice it and were trying to light the lamps, and then . . . then it . . . it killed them both." Tepic buried his head in his hands and sobbed. Gwenyth did her best to comfort him.

"Tepic," Voldigar said, "I know this is hard, but I need you to collect yourself, son, and tell me everything."

Tepic looked up with weary eyes and spoke through his tears. "It was all in darkness, Lector, and then it had a glow, greenish, and all these terrible spikes, and the men just bled everywhere, all over, but then . . . it started to take the blood . . . to gather it up." Tepic cupped his hands in demonstration. "I just hid. I tried to be real quiet. I didn't know how to fight it, Teacher. I didn't know."

Voldigar felt a shiver run through his body and inhaled as he tried to hide his own fear. He placed a hand on Tepic's shoulder and let the boy gather himself.

"Did the creature speak?"

Tepic nodded his head quickly several times.

"What did it say?"

"I couldn't understand it, sir, but it was real deep, like a bear. It wasn't a man. It wasn't! It was something else."

Voldigar frowned as he stood and stared into the back of his house. "Orun."

Voldigar set his jaw in concentration, chewing through a thousand thoughts and memories.

"Orun?" Dantic asked blankly. "What's Orun?"

Voldigar did not hear but continued to stare wide-eyed at the back wall.

"Voldigar?"

"I have to get the Spire—now." He turned and searched frantically around the room.

Dantic jumped to his feet. "There's a carriage outside."

"Good," Voldigar said. "We'll need it. Tepic, help me gather every weapon or piece of armor in this house. Quickly now."

In a few hurried seconds, they gathered two swords, a breastplate, a brigandine, three helmets, and various other armaments in a heap by the door. Voldigar pulled another brigandine onto his broad torso, strapped the curved Daneki blade to his waist, and slung a huge maul across his back.

"All of this, into the carriage," Voldigar said, pointing. "Don't miss anything." Tepic leapt into action while Rory danced at his heels. They hurried the first items to a waiting carriage where a startled coachman watched them load piles of weaponry onto the vehicle's floor. Hobyn roused himself from the bench by the home's front door as quickly as his

old bones allowed. He must have come over from his hut in the commotion and dozed off. With a lamp in one hand, he silently helped load the
carriage.

Dantic protested. "You can't wear two coats of mail, Voldigar. Where
are we going to sit? What's all this for?"

"I'll explain on the way." Voldigar slammed the coach door and hurried
to the coachman. "Maghaltani, do you know it?"

"Yes, yes, the mountain village. About three leagues down the road,
Reverend."

"Right. Make all haste for the village. The road grows more wild, but do
not stop for anything. When you get there, you will be challenged—show
them this." Voldigar handed the man a large white coin engraved with
a flaming arrow piercing a stone. "Tell them Voldigar sent you and that
the items in this carriage must be given to 'Lutz,' all of them. Do you
understand?"

The coachman flinched as Voldigar punctuated each sentence, but
continued to listen.

"Then, you must find Medellai—and pray he's there this morning.
Tell him, 'Treachery. The Orun has escaped. Meet me in the Spire.'"
Voldigar paused. "And tell him that Gwenyth is alone." The confused
man nodded nervously, and Voldigar made him repeat the unfamiliar
names back several times. When he was satisfied, he looked the coachman
in the eye. "Can you do this, friend?"

The coachman straightened, grabbed his reins, and sniffed. "Reverend,
you're a holy man, and you preach. I'm a coachman. I drive." Voldigar
nodded and the coachman snapped his reins. The carriage sped off into
the night with its lantern swaying wildly.

Voldigar took a deep breath before he turned and grasped Gwenyth's
hand in his own. She was scared. Her face was hard as stone, but her fingers
trembled with memory. "Gwen, I have to go. I don't want to, but it's safer
if I'm not here. Medellai will send someone. I know it's Planting, but—"

Gwenyth cut him off and reached a gentle hand to his cheek. "Vol, I
know. Do your duty."

Hobyn hobbled next to Gwenyth. He held a stout staff in hand. "I'll
take care of the mistress, sir."

Voldigar let his gaze linger on Gwenyth a moment longer. "I know you will, Hobyn. Don't leave her side." Then he turned to cross his field. "Dantic, Tepic, let's go."

After the trio disappeared into the darkness, Hobyn gently took Gwenyth by the arm and adjusted the shawl about her shoulders. Before they entered the house, he stopped to sweep up the single dented helmet Voldigar had left on the bench the day before. Rory gave the air a final sniff and followed them inside.

The three moved as quickly as they dared through the underbrush in rough lands beyond Voldigar's farm. A bare sliver of light glowed on the edge of the high mountains behind them. The moon had long since set behind the waves beyond the city, and Dantic's lantern did little to pierce the darkness. It would still be some time until morning.

"Why did you send the carriage away? And with all those weapons? It'll take us forever to reach the palace," Dantic said.

"No. Not this way it won't. We'll cut a long loop out of the road. Stay close," Voldigar replied without looking back.

"What about the weapons? I'm Commander of the City Guard, Voldigar. I need to know what's going on."

Voldigar paused and turned back. "The Orun, the creature you saw, it will be attracted to those weapons. We have to keep moving."

"It wants weapons?" Tepic asked as he and Dantic caught up to Voldigar and walked beside him.

"No. Those are Vessels, Tepic. Imbued with Virtue from a Chanter. The Orun can sense it. The only thing it might seek more is the Chanter himself."

"Which Chanter?" Dantic asked.

"Me."

Dantic stopped and flung his hands into the air. "Then it's hunting you? Why didn't you say so?"

"I said 'might,' Dantic. You came to bring me to the Spire, and we need to keep moving. You can depart with your son and take the road, but it may also have his scent. There's a lot to explain, but I believe you are safest right now with me until we reach the city, and when we're there, don't be alone."

Dantic glanced at Tepic and fought down whatever it was he wanted to say next. They began to walk again and Voldigar continued.

"The creature can move swiftly, but right now, only in short bursts. That carriage should draw its attention."

Dantic cursed. "You set that thing after a coachman?"

"If it comes from the Spire, that coachman will have miles of lead, and the men of my order are well protected in their village. I do not think it will follow all that distance though. It would put itself in great peril were it to approach Maghaltani. I just need to buy time until I can gather more of my brethren."

Dantic shook his head in disbelief. "That's a lot to take in, friend."

"I know."

They continued their walk in silence while the light grew ever so slightly behind them.

Dantic broke the quiet again. "Why do you live out here anyway? Why not up in the mountains with your order?"

Voldigar left the question unanswered while they descended a shallow gully and worked their way through a wide grove of close-growing beech and maple. In the quiet of the small wood, he finally replied. "I'm retired, Dantic. I suppose nothing might please the nobles better than to be rid of me—but no, I have to stay where I am."

"But you're nobility yourself, no? House Anteres?"

Voldigar stifled a short laugh. "That was another life too." He sighed and went on. "I have my farm to tend, and Gwenyth has her duties to House Sispérus as well. And medicine," he added, "we have to stay close to your daughter's apothecary."

"You're the only one who lives away from Maghaltani then?"

"Retired, Dantic . . ." Voldigar's words trailed off before he continued more quietly. "I don't think that's particularly strange. . . . And no, there is one other. She's a long way away though."

Dantic waited for more, but Voldigar fell silent until they exited the grove.

"There's a shallow ford ahead. It's only ankle deep, but do *not* lose your footing. The current is swift, and we're not far from the sea cliffs."

The land gently dipped, and underbrush gave way to shaggy grass and lichen and finally to smooth pebbles and the uneven face of a huge, flat slab of stone. A bloated spring river splashed and skipped to the left and right of the natural bridge, but spread widely and swiftly over the rock.

"Don't lift your feet, and stay to my left. Take your time."

Gingerly, they slid their feet through the broad ford, only looking up occasionally where they could now see the dim face of Arregalt's towering outer wall, marking the edge of the great promontory on which she was built. It ran on for miles and the even higher wall of the Citadel showed behind it. The Golden Spire itself stood deep in the far end of that mass of stone. High above, the pinnacle was outlined against a dark gray sky, its windows tiny and remote with shadows flitting in those that were lit. All along its lip, the ominous flicker of fire could be seen glimmering above the wall. Smoke rose in plumes. Other tall structures peeked over the top of the battlements. A million souls lived in that wondrous city, a staggering number, and the vast majority of the citizens of Aramon. A distant chiming could just be made out over the gurgling of the river.

"The bells won't stop until coronation," Dantic said as they emerged on the far side of the ford.

Voldigar nodded. "It was the same with Olwis."

"And more treason." Dantic frowned as he squinted and surveyed the walls. "Rioting has gotten worse. Fires, and many of them. I need to get back to my men." He put a protective arm over Tepic's shoulder and looked down at him. "And I need to get this one home—with a full guard for you and your sister," he added. He produced a rolled parchment from his coat and handed it to Voldigar. "You'll have to go on to the Spire without me."

Voldigar took the paper with another nod.

"What will you do when your order gets here?" Dantic asked.

The old man wrapped his fingers around the hilt of his knife and swept his eyes over the city. "We go hunting."

Rioting had reached the outer streets, and here and there, groups of Dantic's guardsmen in blue livery chased smaller bands of opportunists or massed themselves against surging mobs of rioters. It took far longer than he wished, but with the letter bearing Dantic's seal, Voldigar was able to clear several checkpoints and slowly make his way into the city, the Citadel, and finally to the ground floor of the Spire.

The massive iron doors of the Winter Throne and its colonnade were fastly secured, so Voldigar followed a long circuit on the great tower's edge until he could cut to its core behind the throne room. A cloud of steam billowed from a many-arched landing as he arrived and cautiously made his way in.

A huge set of hatches set in the floor at the far end of the room stood open, and great puffs and streams of steam belched out. The sounds of whirring engines and ratcheting gears grew louder as Voldigar carefully drew near and peered over the edge. He was noticed at once.

"Voldigar? Voldigar! How long has it been?" A high, gravelly voice called out from the basement.

Below, a squat figure with a long white beard draped over his shirtless shoulder emerged from the coiling vapor. He beamed a toothy smile under completely opaque, foggy spectacles and balanced a huge wrench across his ample belly. Several similar workmen scurried about.

"Too long, Bajk. Everything alright?" Voldigar yelled over the racket.

"Fine! Fine. We haven't used the lift this much in years. Had to open the hatches." Bajk spat. "Too hot! How's my ugly brother?"

"Haven't seen him, unfortunately, though I sent him some presents this morning. I can take the servants' stairs."

Bajk wrinkled his nose. "No. She's fine! Get in. You'd never make it anyway."

Voldigar shrugged and walked back to the brass-doored lift in the center of the room. Its rear wall was entirely covered in intricate silver-threaded ropes. Voldigar grasped the rightmost and pulled. A single high tone rang out.

"If he does show up, I'll punch that rat in the no—!" Bajk yelled. The final word was cut off as Voldigar shut the doors behind him.

The lift shuddered to life and lurched upward with several loud clangs. It was far too large for a single man, and Voldigar, big as he was, felt child-sized in the huge moving room with its lush, red interior. Small, thick-glassed windows on each of the walls gave glimpses of the other stories of the Spire as they raced by faster and faster. Thousands of souls went about their business on every level, each a city unto itself.

The floors tapered and the lift slowed as it finally ground to a hissing stop at the peak of its course.

"Stand back!" a voice cried out as Voldigar opened the door.

A thirty-foot causeway extended from the lift to an ornate balcony beyond. A group of soldiers in deep maroon uniforms bristled with weapons and held the far end. It seemed an odd gesture, for only a few feet in front of Voldigar a whole section of the causeway had been dropped like a trap door where it hung loosely over an expanse of dizzying darkness below.

A few uncomfortable questions and Voldigar was escorted across the hastily reassembled causeway. The men dropped the trapdoor behind him again the moment he passed.

The balcony was covered in soot, shredded tapestry, and soiled rags. The two heavy doors of the royal apartments hung from their hinges at twisted angles, cracked and splintered. An army of servants swarmed the gallery, and more maroon soldiers bodily filled the gap where the doors had once stood. There was blood on the walls and banisters, and the dead and dying were tended to, carried away, or covered in blankets.

General Gamad hoisted his bulk from a nearby chair and lumbered over. "Why are you here, Lector?"

Voldigar produced his papers.

"I know you have papers," Gamad snapped, jowls shaking. "You wouldn't be here if you didn't. What do you want?"

"A member of my order, a Reader, is here. He was hurt. I understand also there was a more sensitive incident having to do with our area of expertise."

"I don't know what your 'expertise' is, Reverend, but there was an incident all right. Treachery. Leave all your weapons and don't try to speak to the Emperor. Your friend's inside."

Voldigar disarmed and made his way past the soldiers into the dark antechamber. Servants were busily cleaning blood from every surface, but it was otherwise quiet. Voldigar swallowed hard and braced for the worst.

He recognized a few of the men in the room. Master Hyrodan of the Sun Cult was being tended to by three similarly clothed votaries. His wounds seemed minor. His counterpart in the Cult of the Star, Diocesan Ragat, was dirty and disheveled. He looked unhurt though and was himself tending to wounded.

In the corner of the room, a young woman was kneeling over a man on the floor, her waist crowded with satchels and vials, hair pulled into a short rust-colored tail.

"Lyrusia," Voldigar said. "I thought your father would have you under lock and key."

She looked back briefly and returned to her work. "I'm not a child. I'm needed here."

Voldigar nodded and quietly considered his friend, lying still on the marble floor with his red cloak rolled under his head. His robes were pulled open and the deep black skin of his torso was covered in fresh wounds, scrapes, and sutures. His breathing was labored and rapid, and his face, though freshly cleaned, was covered in fissures that Voldigar did not remember.

"How is he?"

"He's alive and very fortunate."

"Has he spoken?"

"Not yet, it might be some time."

Voldigar approached and knelt next to Lyrusia. He placed a hand on Lanathor's forehead and whispered a silent prayer. His head was cool. Good.

"Can we wake him?"

Lyrusia blinked and quirked her eyes. "That would not be wise."

"You might be surprised at your ward, and I'm afraid we have no time."

Lyrusia looked questioningly at Voldigar for another moment and sighed. "Fine, but don't say I didn't warn you. Hold this under his nose a few moments." She uncorked a small vial, handed it to Voldigar, and stood with arms crossed.

Without moving his leathery hand from Lanathor's forehead, he waived the aromatic under his nose and waited.

Lanathor coughed, sputtered, and groaned. "I was having the most wonderful dream. What's that awful stench?"

"Good morning, Elder," Voldigar said cheerfully.

"Oh . . . you." Lanathor tried to roll to his side and groaned again.

"Try to hold still."

Lanathor let out a labored gasp, "Let me sleep, Voldigar. I'm no Chanter."

"Chanters need sleep too, Lan. But I'm afraid neither of us can right now." Voldigar drew his hand in a loose fist, touching his thumb to his own forehead and then crossing his palm over his heart. "Head and Heart, Brother."

Lanathor weakly mimicked the gesture. "Head and Heart." He inhaled and exhaled hard a few times and finally opened his eyes.

"Why are you here?"

"I live close."

Lanathor squinted. "The prince, is he alive?"

"Yes, he's alive."

"And Caliras?"

Voldigar shook his head. "Unknown."

Lanathor looked away and swallowed. "Voldigar, there's something you should know."

Voldigar glanced a silent gesture at Lyrusia who dipped her head briefly and left them to continue speaking.

Voldigar lowered his voice. "I know, Brother. Orun."

Lanathor ignored the prior advice and painfully raised himself to prop against the chamber wall. "How did you know?"

"One of our students was attacked on the floor below. He's fine, but the guards he was with were not so lucky. You did well to fight it off on your own."

"God have mercy." Lanathor stared at the wall. "I failed then. It's *Blooded*, Voldigar. It was very weak when I fought it. But now . . . I may already be too late."

"I know that too," Voldigar said quietly.

Lanathor rubbed his forehead and let out a long sigh. "I wish Liadov were here."

"Me too, Brother, but you get me for now." He smiled.

Lanathor looked at him in puzzlement a moment. "You're . . . coming back?"

"I'm here tonight, and I don't think I have much choice. Let's keep it at that. I've dispatched a message to Medellai and sent all the Vessels in my home to the village. He should be here soon."

Lanathor nodded. "Ten years, Vol. How could it escape?"

"I don't know, but you'd better do what you can to recover. Every second we wait only hastens disaster."

Their conversation was cut off by the approaching footsteps of a long stride. Lusánt stood above them with streaks of dry tears marring his face and disappearing into the collar of his shirt. "My mother is dead," he whispered. "I couldn't save her. She's gone to join Father . . ."

Some instinct in Voldigar compelled him to stand up and embrace the boy, to offer a word of comfort, but he found all he could do was hold his gaze. "I'm sorry, Lusánt."

"My city burns. My protector has betrayed me," he continued quietly. Gamad shouldered his soldiers aside and crossed over to listen. Lusánt went on. "Tomorrow, I will take the crown of Aramon while a fugitive assassin runs free." Gamad stepped forward to interject, but Lusánt held up his hand. His eyes came to rest on Lanathor. "You risked your life for me, Reader."

Lanathor winced as he struggled to his feet and plucked his rolled red cloak from the floor. Voldigar steadied him while Lyrusia looked on in amazement. "My life for Aramon, Emperor," Lanathor said and bowed his head.

"Loyalty and strength are in low supply, Teacher, and it would seem our traditions have been unable to stay this moment." The two lectors watched him warily, waiting for Lusánt to reveal his meaning. The boy turned his gaze to the window at the rear of his mother's chamber and stared a long while before he continued. "I want Lord Commander Caliras caught, and I want him to be made an example."

Lusánt spun the ruby signet ring he wore on his left hand and stepped closer to Voldigar and Lanathor. "Which of you is the head of your order?"

"There is equality in our order," Voldigar said, "but as there is need, Elders Lanathor and Medellai have led the Brethren for many years."

"That is correct, but Voldigar is still our titular head," Lanathor added, "our 'Eldest.'"

Voldigar tried to hide his grimace.

"Interesting!" Lusánt said and raised his eyebrows high. "Things I did not know. But why do you live so far from your subjects, Eldest?"

Voldigar considered his words, but Lusánt continued. "Then I see you are a sort of king as well, my old sword-lector." Voldigar flinched at the description but Lusánt continued in an amused tone. "Just one in exile I suppose . . ."

Voldigar opened his mouth to reply, but Lusánt cut him off again. "Here, take this." He slipped the signet from his finger and placed it in Voldigar's hand, closing it around the ring. "Let's forget yesterday. I want Caliras found and brought to me. I want your order to do this for me, and you have my full authority to see it done. You speak as me." Lusánt smiled weakly.

"My prince, we would see your will done, but you know my order has a sacred trust. Our first business is with the creature that attacked you. Commander Dantic will find Caliras, I am certain of this," Voldigar said.

Lusánt forced a laugh. "Always instructing me, Teacher. Always knowing what's best." He smiled and shook his head in mock bemusement. "The only *creature* that attacked me is Caliras."

Lanathor stole a glance at Voldigar and interjected. "Your Highness, Caliras is a dog, but Voldigar speaks of the specter that killed Caliras's men. It is *highly* dangerous and requires the urgent attention of our order."

Lusánt took on a contemplative face and nodded. "Yes, right. I know you hunt ghosts outside of your regular duties. We've all heard the tales. It's very good of you, I'm sure. But as I said, you are to find that traitor Caliras. I appreciate your . . . former roles as my professors, but I am no longer discussing. This is my will, and my command."

"Emperor," Lanathor said, with as much strength as he could muster. He lowered his head in deference.

Voldigar could only stand dumbfounded as Lusánt strode into the innermost chamber and shut the doors behind him.

Chapter Four

A New Guard

Tepic glanced occasionally at his father as they sped along the spine of one of Arregalt's many inner walls, making for the huge citadel at its core. He felt much better walking in open air, and the terror of the predawn hours seemed more and more distant while the sun rose and warmed his back.

There were only city guards along the broad walkway. They stood post at a handful of turreted entries, safe from violence in the streets below. Tepic wondered if they might rather be on the ground, rushing into fires and battling miscreants.

For all their conversation on the way in, his father had now fallen quiet. No doubt thinking about his work. He was a powerful man. Tepic felt strong walking by his side, but he could make it the rest of the way on his own.

"It's just guards up here, Dad. I can go the rest of the way myself, and you can get back to your men."

Dantic glanced at Tepic blankly for a moment, exiting his thoughts and catching up to what he'd said.

"No . . . no, I'm taking you the rest of the way, and some of my men will guard the house. I've been careless with you."

"I'm fine, Dad." The argument didn't seem to work.

The path atop the wall turned sharply as it joined its rounded counterpart on the east of the Citadel and passed through a small gatehouse.

"Sword-Lector said the monster was looking for weapons," Tepic said as they climbed a series of stone steps and landings.

"Vessels, yes. Enchanted things from their order."

"Order? Isn't he just a teacher?" Tepic replied.

Dantic looked down at his son and raised a brow, looking amused for the first time in hours. "Just a teacher?"

"Yes."

Dantic laughed. "That man's a legend, Tep. A real, in-the-flesh Brother of Aramon. Elder of the Red Cloak, and a Chanter. Most of your lectors are—at least the real ones that are still Readers."

"Really?" Tepic wrinkled his nose. "I heard the Brothers hunt ghosts."

Tepic expected his father to laugh again, but instead, he adopted a more serious tone. "Sorcery, Son, illegal magic. That's what they hunt, and it's a lot more real than ghosts. The Brotherhood eradicated it before you were old enough to remember." He looked at Tepic a moment and seemed to rethink his next words. "A lot of people don't care for their old ways anymore, and it's a shame. You should pay close attention in your classes."

"I do, Dad!"

"I know you do, and you should keep on doing so." Tepic was about to reply but Dantic went on. "You're fortunate our house is still taught by Readers, Tepic. All the nobles used to be."

Tepic thought of his classes and wondered now which of his other teachers were 'Brothers.' Vasherk who taught Alchemy? Lanathor from Rhetoric? He could not imagine either of them wielding a sword.

Dantic stopped at a guard post where a heavyset man in the same blue livery quickly placed a smoldering pipe on the wall and snapped a salute. Dantic returned it briskly. "I want a squad dispatched to my home and supplied until I relieve them."

"Already done, sir," the man replied.

"Then send a second. They'll bunk on the lower floor."

"Yes, sir." The guardsman saluted again as Tepic and his father continued along the curving wall. The sun was once more at their backs.

"What about Grandfather's sword?" Tepic asked.

"What?"

"Grandfather's sword. Mom always says it's 'enchanted.' Does that mean the monster will come for it?"

"Your grandfather wasn't a Chanter, Tep."

"But if the sword's enchanted, shouldn't it go to the mountain village, like Voldigar's?"

The question lingered on the air as they reached their home and Dantic strode over to address the guards. Their dwelling was a massive four-story turret that jutted both into the center and over the edge of the Citadel's gigantic wall. Tepic's room was at the very peak, beneath a pointed roof and atop a smaller adjoining turret. A narrow garden had been worked into the surface of the wall and grew along a row of arches, some leading up and others down beneath the turret.

"Keep this place secure at all hours, Sergeant," Dantic said to a tall young soldier with a thin mustache and a tuft of dark hair he continually pushed out of his eyes. "There's another squad on the way to reinforce."

"That's quite a guard!" The sergeant's eyebrows shot up.

"I know, and it's with reason."

"Rioters?"

"That, and worse," Dantic replied. "Be ready for anything."

The sergeant looked puzzled but Dantic did not continue. Instead, he pulled Tepic aside.

"I could be away for a couple of days, Son. You take care of your sister and your mother. And do *not* for any reason leave this house until I send for you."

"I know, Dad! What about Grandfather's sword though?"

Dantic grimaced. "It's a good thought, but it's not the sort of thing Voldigar was talking about. You've got two squads of guards here and you're atop the the strongest citadel in the world. There's nothing to be afraid of."

"I'm not scared."

"I know you're not, I understand. I'll look into the sword next time I'm home. Maybe even tonight."

Tepic began to speak again, but Dantic turned and addressed the guard once more. "My family is to stay here until I return. No one comes or goes. Is that clear?"

"Crystal, sir. But I'm afraid your daughter, the apothecary? She's already left. Said she had duties to attend."

Dantic cursed under his breath. "Fine. I'll send her back shortly, and she's not to leave again." He ruffled Tepic's short hair and looked him in the eyes. "Give my love to Mom and Lyrusia when she's back."

Tepic tried in vain to get his father's attention once more, but he and the sergeant could only watch Dantic hurry off the way he'd come while a few other guardsmen milled about. The tall sergeant looked down at him.

"I'm Galomar. Looks like you and me are going to be friends for a while."

<hr />

Tepic lay on his back, wearing his sword training gloves and throwing a small brass pitcher up and down. Light streamed through a pair of small windows, illuminating a slow-floating haze of dust that puffed away from each toss of the pitcher.

Tepic liked his room, probably the highest point in Arregalt outside the Spire, but not for more than a few minutes. He missed a catch of the pitcher, and it clattered loudly to the floor. Tepic tried to wipe away a fresh dent, thumped it backward onto a small table by his bed, and took a seat where he busily worked to see if he could fit both hands into one glove. Thwarted, he flung them into the corner and began an important ritual of thumbnail biting and toe-tapping.

Thus far, he'd been mostly successful in trying to forget about events in the officer's quarters, but he couldn't stop thinking about his grandfather's sword. What if Dad was wrong? What if Grandpa *was* a Chanter and nobody knew it—just like his teachers? What if the creature came for it? What about Mom? What about the guards?

Tepic frowned, descended two spiral staircases, and walked quietly into a windowless central den with a huge fireplace that showed through to another room beyond. Other than him and a sputtering brazier, the room looked empty and dim. Grandfather's sword was mounted above the high mantle in an intricately embossed dark leather scabbard. The hilt shimmered in glistening gold, capped by a glassy crystal pommel. It was polished to perfection by the staff of servants that maintained the household day and night.

Tepic raised himself on his toes and gently worked the weapon free from its mounts.

"I'd be careful with that. It's probably still sharp. Nice looking sword."

Tepic flinched but did his best to hide his alarm. Galomar sat in a dark corner of the room polishing a blade of his own.

"I'm trained," Tepic said.

"Oh?" Galomar said as he rose from the chair. He looked down his sword as if to ensure it was still straight. "How old are you?"

"Thirteen," Tepic replied.

"Are you any good?"

Tepic turned his eyes to the sword balanced in his palms and shrugged. "I don't know. Sword-Lector says I'm fast, but I lost a sparring match yesterday."

"Bah. That's just sparring. How old was the other kid?"

"It was Prince Lusánt."

Galomar looked impressed and held his own sword out in a mock pose of battle. "That's quite a sparring partner. A lot older than you, no?"

"I guess."

"Maybe I could teach you a thing or two? Next time, you can be the kid who beat the Emperor."

"Mom says this isn't to be struck against anything, or drawn. I shouldn't even be holding it."

Galomar laughed mischievously. "We're not gonna cross blades, boy. But why not have a look? What does Dad say?"

"Dad doesn't really talk about it. It's just art to him."

"Well," Galomar replied, drawing out the word. "There you go then. The Commander hasn't forbidden it, and you're the man of the house. Let's take a peek."

Tepic took a deep breath and chewed on his lower lip. It probably wouldn't hurt just to look at it.

One clasp and the blade slid out easily. There were gems embedded in the *cassolke* of the steel, just beyond the guard, and they caught the low light of the brazier with a sparkle.

Galomar whistled. "Better than imagined! Show me your guard, how does the sword-lector do it?"

It was a large weapon, far lighter than the training blades he used in the old stables, but still heavy and best suited to both his hands. He held it out.

"High, and away from the body," Tepic said as he demonstrated and set his feet.

Another guard walked up a wide flight of stairs into the den, adjusting his eyes. This one was bald and moved with a limp. "Your turn at the door, Sergeant. Other boys are getting mess." He admired the sword a moment. "Nice sword, kid. Lesson time?" His voice was gruff.

Tepic nodded.

"Sorry to cut it short," the bald guard continued, then walked past the den.

"Looks like fun time is over. Here, one thing before I go. What made it hard to beat His Highness?"

"These," Tepic said as he demonstrated several quick overhand strikes.

Galomar lifted his chin in appraisal. "Alright. Here. I'll be Lusánt, and you be you. When I come at you overhand, instead of holding your guard flat, turn it at an angle, like this. Don't worry, I won't actually hit your sword."

Tepic nodded again and the two squared off. Galomar shuffled forward and made a slow overhand swing. As instructed, Tepic held his sword high and at an angle, but without warning, he felt the weapon flash forward. His feet slid along the ground, and through a tremendous shower of sparks their blades met with a crack.

Galomar was thrown from his feet and skipped along the floor of the den, rolling into a cabinet that shuddered and bounced against the wall.

Tepic stood wide-eyed as the other guard ran back into the room, slack-jawed and holding a bowl of porridge.

It *was* enchanted! He knew it!

In that moment, Tepic made a decision that would change the course of his life. He scooped the scabbard up from the ground, slung the sword over his back, and ran.

CHAPTER FIVE

PULLING THE FOG AWAY

V OLDIGAR HELPED LANATHOR HOBBLE from Lusánt's chambers as quickly as he could while General Gamad eyed them warily. The Teller winced with every step, sagging against Voldigar like rain-soaked barley while they waited for soldiers to restore the causeway. Voldigar pulled the leftmost cord of the lift, and the distant tone of a deep bell chimed in the expanse below. The old man folded his arms and glared through a small window.

Lanathor propped himself against the wall. "You didn't answer my question." He shut his eyes.

"What?"

"Why you're here."

"I told you. I live close, and heard you were hurt."

Lanathor managed half a smile. "Well, you can see I'm fine now."

"You won't be rid of me that easily."

Lanathor's smile dropped. "It's not to be rid of you, Vol. It's just . . . you've done enough. Medellai and I will handle this."

"I've had a lot of years to think, Brother—don't fret on my account."

The two men fell silent while the lift remained still. Lanathor worked the smile back onto his face. "Shame we have to meet like this. You could visit, you know."

"I do know. I've been busy, and I'm sorry."

Lanathor nodded weakly and tugged the cord again. "The Emperor has given us strange instruction."

"The boy has lost his mind. That's what he's done."

Lanathor wrinkled his brow with disapproval.

Voldigar exhaled and abandoned his window to pace back and forth. "He won't be coronated until tomorrow. He's just Lusánt, and he's afraid." He paused and stared at Lanathor. "You look terrible."

Lanathor coughed a painful laugh. "I should be dead, Elder. It was weak but still Orun. Your Chants were effective, and for that I thank you."

"Not effective enough." Voldigar renewed his pacing.

"Honor God," Lanathor said quickly.

"God's honor," Voldigar returned.

"What do we do then? The Emperor forbids our duty," Lanathor said.

"What do we do? We find the Orun, that's what we do." The lift churned to life under their feet.

"You would defy the Emperor?" Lanathor asked, slowly opening his eyes and adjusting his weight against the wall.

"I would defy a foolish boy meddling with things he doesn't understand."

Lanathor coughed again and straightened himself. "Voldigar, the Code demands your obedience to the crown."

"The Code demands I find the Orun and send it back to Hell!" Voldigar snapped back. The lift shuddered as it picked up speed.

Lanathor was not cowed and held Voldigar's gaze, waiting for him to continue.

"I'm sorry, Lan."

"No," Lanathor replied and closed his eyes again. "Don't be sorry. Go on if you like. If we don't find it, we're all dead men anyway."

The lift descended until at length it came to rest on the ground with a hiss of steam. The hatch doors in the floor remained open, billowing white clouds, but Bajk and the others were nowhere to be seen. Only their distant yelling and clanging echoed in the corridors below.

Lanathor eyed Voldigar a moment before he spoke again. "No one would fault you if you went home when the others arrive."

Voldigar felt the barest hint of spring air pressing into the vestibule and pulling the fog away. "We put this thing back in its cage, Lanathor. Then I go home. Come on."

Voldigar slipped his arm under Lanathor's and walked him slowly along the endless circuit of the Citadel, returning to the somber space before the huge sealed doors of the Winter Throne. There, four hooded figures in deep red cloaks stood together in silence watching their approach. One stepped forward. "Head and Heart, Brother."

In unison, the others repeated the salute, touching thumb to forehead and crossing their hands over their chests.

Voldigar embraced the man and stepped back, still holding his shoulders. "Medellai. It's good you're here, Brother. How fare you?"

"I'm well, Eldest."

"And Gwenyth?"

Medellai removed his hood. Long auburn hair and beard to match were streaked with white, and he regarded Voldigar with the same striking green eyes of his sister.

"Gwen is fine. Your coachman told me she was alone, so I sent Wulf," Medellai said.

Voldigar sighed in relief. "Good, very good." Though a mighty man, Wulf was no Chanter. The Orun would have no reason to seek him.

"I'm surprised you left her alone at all," Medellai continued.

"Not alone. Hobyn's with her—and you know I had to."

Medellai nodded and peered around Voldigar. "Lanathor, you look terrible."

"Thank you," Lanathor offered. "Voldigar let me know."

The other three men laughed and dropped their hoods to their shoulders. Lutz was *mokja*, short and heavy like all his people. His belly bulged in a black leather jerkin against his broad belt while strange mechanical lenses protruded and retracted from his eyes. Urias laughed least, and his angular face returned to a severe expression, framed by a great cascade of thick black hair to his waist. Last of all was Soris, whose huge pale eyes were a pool of unending sorrow, like glaciers melting under a sun-swept highland. They matched the glistening rings of beryl stones that lined his sleeveless arms.

"*Good,*" Voldigar thought. A more potent collection of the Brethren could not have been assembled.

Medellai watched Voldigar as he assessed the party. "Taro and Vasherk are in the Sanctum," he said. "I'd have brought them here if I knew Lanathor's condition. Your message was very short."

"I was in haste, Elder. What of the Orun?" Voldigar asked.

"You're joining us then?"

Voldigar narrowed his eyes. "I am."

Medellai hesitated but buried it with a curt nod. "It's definitely here, in the city. I haven't been able to get a sense of its direction though."

Voldigar stroked his chin. "Odd."

"No sign of it in Maghaltani," Lutz added. "And your Vessels are secure, Eldest."

Voldigar nodded in appreciation. "We can speak more on our way to the Sanctum. There are ears in the walls here, friends."

Medellai and the others flanked Lanathor and prepared to move. Voldigar continued to Lutz. "Your brother inquired after you."

"Well Bajk can rot," Lutz said and stepped forward holding a red cloak. "Here. You'll need this."

———◦———

Voldigar did not relish the attention their red cloaks would bring and thought the theatrics overwrought. All the same, he was glad to have them—and especially the warm hoods as they escorted Lanathor through the streets of Arregalt in as much haste as they dared. A biting rain had picked up around noon, but Lanathor seemed to be regaining a little strength. It would have been quite a Planting Day and he wondered how Gwenyth fared under the watchful eyes of Wulf and Hobyn.

Few of the folk of Aramon understood the red cloaks anymore, but whether they did or no, all kept distance from the strange party that knifed through the city and steadily made its way south toward the Sanctum. They walked close and spoke in low voices.

"Caliras made an attempt on the prince's life," Voldigar said.

Soris shook his head and frowned. "The crown of Aramon does not pass without conspiracy . . ."

"We heard, on the way in," Medellai said. "And at the very moment of his mother's passing. Shrewd, and cruel. I wonder how long Caliras plotted."

News traveled fast. "Yes. We're fortunate Lanathor was there." Their backs were turned, but Voldigar felt as though all the brethren's eyes were upon him.

"Caliras seemed as surprised at the Orun as any of us," Lanathor added. "I don't think that complication was his doing."

"I would not be so sure," Voldigar said.

Medellai glanced over his shoulder. "It is as before, Brothers. You recall these manifestations occur in heightened states of emotion and consequence."

"Yes, but Orun don't run free," Voldigar replied. "Something or someone let it out."

"And that is no mean task," Medellai continued.

Voldigar helped Lanathor over a murky hole in the road. "You said before you couldn't sense it."

Medellai stopped and closed his eyes. "No, not that I couldn't sense it." He inhaled deeply. The brethren fell silent and waited. "I can smell it. I can hear it. It's like it's everywhere in the city." He opened his eyes. "I can even see it, Vol. But I cannot find its direction."

Medellai strode ahead and they resumed their march. It had been many years since even three or four, let alone half a dozen Brothers of Aramon walked openly in the capital. Whether it was this show of force or the turn in weather, they remained unmolested into early afternoon despite the lingering disorder that raged on in the streets.

Soon they arrived in a lonely ward of Arregalt under the shadow of her wall. Here it turned along the sea cliffs to overlook the bay far below. A blind alley behind crumbling tenements hid a gate blocking a square passage beneath the street. Medellai whined its rusted hinges and led them from the cobblestones to crouch and plod through ankle-deep runoff.

"Emperor Lusánt forbade our search for the Orun. This you should know," Lanathor said, his voice echoing in the tunnel.

Voldigar groaned. "Yes, he demanded the full efforts of our order in finding Lord Commander Caliras instead. He gave me this." Voldigar flashed the signet ring from his pocket.

"That's . . . odd. Was he not appraised of the danger?" Medellai asked.

"Oh, he was and more. He spoke as if the whole thing were imagined," Voldigar said.

"Troubling," was Medellai's only reply.

They emerged in a curious dead-end row. Tall brick structures stood behind, and a series of two-storied stone facades with boarded windows sat opposite. The street was a time capsule of old Aramoni architecture, invisible to any eyes save from the curtain wall high above.

After a brief survey, Medellai unlatched a moldering door and ushered the brethren through, all stooping low, save Lutz who squeezed his wide shoulders last and shut the door behind. They crowded in the dark to the sound of each other's breathing until Medellai lit a small lantern. The light revealed a tiny dirt-floored chamber and the wooden front of what was once a tavern, now walled off from the street. He knocked a quick pattern on the door, and a tiny slide flashed open a moment later, followed by the clunk and creak of thick wood.

A smartly dressed man with wispy white hair and a rapier hanging from his waist stood in the entry. "Welcome back to the Sanctum. Head and Heart, brethren."

"Head and Heart, Vasherk. We have much to discuss, and quickly." Voldigar stepped inside.

———◆———

Musty smells of mold and long years of disuse greeted Voldigar's nose, but there was pleasant familiarity too—memories of pipe tobacco and strong ale, of laughter and ancient wood. This had been their headquarters, a gift from Olwis the Shield long years ago when the Brethren gathered daily and needed secrecy. Here they'd plotted against an endless flood of sorcerers and their vile conspirators. The Brethren seldom gathered at all anymore outside their village, the wicked plots of madmen only a whisper of their former fear.

Taro stomped up the cellar stairs, sputtering and meticulously plucking a mass of cobwebs from his mop of black curls. *Skullcrusher*, the thick, knobby staff he never parted with, was in his plucking hand, and with the other, he brushed flour from his plain brown tunic. He caught sight of the newcomers and beamed. "Brothers!"

After customary salutations, he took notice of Lanathor and hurried to his side, eyebrows folded in concern. "Elder. What happened to you?" He didn't wait for an answer but tucked *Skullcrusher* under his arm and scooped Lanathor up like he was a child.

"I'm fine, mother," Lanathor managed while the others snickered. Taro set him gently on the only comfortable-looking chair, stuffed in a quiet corner of the room.

"I'll be right back," Taro said and dashed into a back room from which wafted a savory smell of herbs and meat. It made Voldigar's stomach growl.

Vasherk swung his rapier to his back and stooped over Lanathor. "These sutures are fine work," Vasherk said as he examined his wounds.

Voldigar found a mealy apple and bit into it, speaking around the bite. "Commander Dantic's daughter."

Vasherk nodded distractedly, then closed his eyes and began to Chant a quiet, peaceful song. His hands hovered over Lanathor. Taro emerged a moment later and handed a bowl of stew to their patient. Voldigar smirked. It was too much. He and the others all made for the kitchen to discover what glorious concoction Taro had created.

In short order, they were gathered round a long oval table with countless dents and dagger wounds, burning their mouths on hot soup. Urias seated last after circling the chamber holding his bowl and seemingly glaring each sconce into flame. His scowl was unchanged when he finally settled on a stool.

Within earshot of Lanathor and his new doctors, Voldigar spoke first, quickly recounting Lanathor's battle, Caliras's treachery, the cause of his rapid message, and Lusánt's troubling behavior. At each juncture of his council, he expected the others to interrupt, to question his presence, but on he went like an old wagon, rumbling again through the muddy ruts he'd made with his own wheels.

"Thus to me," he concluded, "our purpose is single. Every passing hour is another in which the Orun gains strength. All else is distraction."

"And Voldigar doubtless trusted I would be able to locate it," Medellai added. "Thus far, I cannot—except to tell you it is within the city walls, cautious, seeking poor souls to devour."

Soris's eyebrows were pinched together, the corners of his mouth drawn in pained expression. He rubbed at the near-translucent skin of his chin and spoke in his soft tone. "If we cannot go to it, then let us believe it will come to us. You, and Voldigar, and Vasherk and Taro. Chanters will be like giant beacons, as sure as the river flows to the sea."

"This occurred to me as well, Soris," Voldigar replied. "But it seems to be operating with a strange intelligence, calculating, as if it is afraid to face us all at once—at least until it's stronger. It should have come by now."

"Then we split up," Urias interjected. "Travel in twos and draw it out. Maybe it gets overbold."

"That would be dangerous, no?" Taro asked from across the room.

"No more dangerous than letting it grow," Urias said. "If we don't find it soon, it won't matter if the whole order is here."

Medellai nodded his head and carried on the thought. "In this way, perhaps we could accomplish the Emperor's will as well. Some of us could search for Caliras."

Lutz drummed his fingers on the edge of the table while he turned his eyepieces from face to face. "By two or by ten—what does it matter? How do we even stop this thing?"

"Subdue it and bind it, by every craft you possess," Voldigar replied. "But you speak true. Such a victory would be short-lived. I must retrieve its prison, and pray we can discern its use."

Lutz opened his mouth to object again, but Lanathor spoke first. "What about Liadov?" The table grew quiet. The rattle of spoons and bowls evaporated into a hush while Lanathor tried to straighten in his chair.

"What *about* Liadov?" Voldigar said.

"Medellai says he cannot pinpoint the Orun. You doubt we can even use its prison. I say there's an answer to both riddles, and neither of you has offered it."

The accusation hung in the air a moment too long. Lanathor concluded, "Liadov could tell us."

"Lanathor, there is no earthly chance that Liadov will return to Aramon. Not had the Orun devoured the Spire and the Empire with it."

"You're wrong, Vol. I could bring her back."

"You can hardly walk."

Vasherk interjected. "Begging your pardon, Eldest, but two more hours and he'll walk better than you."

"How would you do this, Lanathor?" Medellai asked.

"Brother, I perceive in your question that you do not trust me at my claim. Let me do this."

Lutz coughed and wiped a phantom crumb from the table.

Voldigar searched their eyes for an answer that never came. "Fine," he said at last. "I still believe the greatest likelihood is that our foe has already sensed Maghaltani and the draw will be too great. It will hide itself and gather strength and allies until it has the confidence to attack the village. Let us pray we find it before then."

He went on. "We stay here until evening. If the Orun has not come to us, then we go by twos at night, as Urias says—one Chanter in each pair. Lanathor and Vasherk will travel inland to seek Liadov. They have three days. Lutz and I will retrieve the prison and search for Caliras. Medellai and Soris will search the Spire and Citadel for the Orun. Urias and Taro have the rest of the city. We meet here in the Sanctum at dawn, each day. Do any object?"

"I don't like Taro," Urias said.

Taro chuckled while the brethren looked from face to face. "It's like you never left, Voldigar."

"Don't grow accustomed to it."

"We're settled then," Taro continued as he pushed himself up with his staff. "The Eldest has spoken." He grinned and fetched more soup.

The sconces were mostly put out, and in the dim light, the four Chanters sat against the wall, opposite the door. Voldigar, Taro, Vasherk, and Medellai. As they thought upon their Scriptures, they quietly sang their Chants in low throaty tones, occasionally harmonizing and ending each phrase with a glottal stop. Weapons lay across their laps. As the hours passed, they tried to get some rest, preparing for the night ahead.

In the back room, where lingered the smell of venison and herbs, the three Tellers—Lanathor, Urias, and Soris—whispered stories to one another and passed a flask of some aromatic liquor from hand to hand. While Lanathor's face remained stoic through each tale, the other two flared with emotion through every turn of phrase. Soris often turned his sorrowful eyes toward the entryway in the room beyond while they carried on their ritual.

Lutz sat alone in a dark balcony above, carefully inventorying a row of strange devices and tools while his goggles clicked and whirred. He called out each hour with a single word, just loud enough for the men below to hear. Night would come soon.

Voldigar's mind wandered to Gwenyth and his farm. A drizzle could still be heard outside, and he imagined the raindrops tinkling on the borrowed plow while the stout draft horse ate unearned hay. A team of oxen would have made the job easier, but his field was so pitifully small. He and Hobyn and Gwenyth could still have plowed, sown, and harrowed in a single day, maybe two. They'd missed the winter crop entirely, but a fine spring was predicted, and they might have more than enough for themselves and even a little to sell. Unasked for, he imagined a row of fat-faced sons and daughters, smiling round a fine oak table under a new roof. Rory went from hand to hand, filling his belly with scraps. He meant to smile but was surprised to feel his eyes wet instead. He looked into his lap.

Lutz had just fished his watch from his pocket and cleared his throat when a knock came at the door. The Tellers streamed out of the kitchen while Voldigar and the other Chanters leapt to their feet, weapons in hand. All were crouched and ready to spring.

"Orun don't knock," Voldigar said and strode to the heavy door, flinging it open and pulling the smaller door of the facade open beyond.

In the rain, a shivering messenger dressed in the full black and gray livery of House Sispérus flinched. A second to regain his composure and he recited: "His Highness Lusánt Sispérus, Lord Sovereign of Aramon, Emperor of the Baerdermyrch, Admiral of the Wending Sea, and Protector of Arregalt requires the presence of all present Brethren of Aramon at his coronation tomorrow, to commence at sunset. You are further to meet with him at the Tower of the Sea immediately thereafter."

"We're quite busy," Voldigar scowled.

"I am not to return any answer," the page responded and scurried away.

Voldigar groaned and turned back to the Sanctum.

"I see we're not so secret after all," Lanathor said.

Voldigar fastened his red cloak over his shoulder. "Prepare for a long night, Brothers, and little rest to follow. We have much to do."

CHAPTER SIX

FLOATING IN THE MIST

T EPIC'S PALMS AND FINGERS ached and his heart leapt into his throat
every time he spotted one of his father's guards in blue livery. He
shivered uncontrollably in the biting rain and kept to narrow alleys and
backways, making east as best he could.

Were he not so fixated on his present danger and discomfort, the thrill of
escape might have given him a moment to be rather proud of himself. The
limping officer had no chance of catching him. Sergeant Galomar and the
others were faster, but not as fast as he. The turreted stairs along the citadel
wall, guarded as they were, were out of the question, but Tepic found a
long rope ladder and shoved it over the wall's interior. When the guards
caught up, they had tried to pull Tepic, ladder and all, back to the top, but
it was too late. He dug his fingers into the rough stone of the Citadel and
scraped his way down the final dozen feet to a tall roof. With a plop, he was
racing across rooftops while the guardsmen sputtered and cursed, falling
further and further behind.

Getting out of the Citadel had seemed perilous indeed, and it took him
several minutes to brave one of the smaller gatehouses. The riots and fires
must have drawn them away, for only a single guardsman stood post and
paid him no heed. Perhaps on any other day, a boy walking alone with a
huge ornate sword on his back might have drawn a question or two, but

today he had been just another mouse in the wall. All the same, the weapon felt like a beacon on his back, a lighthouse calling out to sinister ships. He was glad to pass from the Citadel into the ragged wards beyond, but it was then the rain had picked up and set his teeth to chattering ever since.

"East" in the winding streets of Arregalt's less savory parts was difficult to discern. Fruitlessly, he searched for the sun through thick gray skies but had to settle for glimpses of the Citadel and curtain wall instead. These he spied only occasionally in the gaps between crowded buildings that nearly touched where their high roofs leaned over windless lanes. It was a mercy of heaven that rain had kept it all from burning to the ground.

"You look cold, sweetheart," a pink-cheeked woman called out from her stoop where she lounged with two others under a sodden awning. Tepic looked at the ground and quickened his pace. "Why not let mommy warm you up?" He felt his face redden as he turned the corner and their laughter faded into the rain behind—dead end.

The alley was filled with refuse, and shoddy brickwork blocked his way. A pair of soleless boots lay sideways on a rotted crate, dripping into a basin streaked with mold. He heard a low sound behind him and froze.

Tepic clenched his fists, but his head refused to move. He imagined the great shimmering shadow of the Orun filling the alley's entrance. He could picture its green tentacles slowly emerging and lashing into his body. He shuddered, and with painful effort finally willed himself to turn. He found nothing more than a sopping dog slinking away with a bone.

Tepic exhaled and rubbed his arms together for warmth. The enchanted sword had to go to Maghaltani. He was the only one to do it. It would be safe there and so would he.

But where *was* Maghaltani?

'Three leagues down the road,' Voldigar had told the coachman before his horses sped off into the dark. The old man's farm and that single road were somewhere east of the city—the whole world was east of the city. If he could only get outside the walls . . .

Peeking his head from the alley, a grumbling roll of thunder caught the women's attention. Tepic took that chance to continue down the street from which he'd turned. In the distance, a clock tower looked as if it floated above the misty rains. Its taupe stones were unmistakable, the same as the stable where Lector Voldigar taught—and more importantly the city gate near both. He sighed with relief and hurried forward.

He'd traveled only a few more streets when every hair on his neck stood straight. He tensed again, but this time immediately spun about. Three young men were there, accosting a blustering shopkeeper, but otherwise, the soaked lane was unremarkable. They took no notice of him, and a mundane collection of sullen townsfolk went about their business, scurrying from the rain.

Tepic wiped the wet from his brow and turned to walk again, but as he did, he caught from the corner of his eye a flit of shadow between two tilting structures. A split second and it vanished. Tepic whirled to bring it back into view, but there was nothing.

"Get hold of yourself, Tep," he whispered.

He quickened his steps again, nearly to a jog. He could see a wide avenue ahead that surely led to the clock tower and the exit. He'd first find Voldigar's house back the way they'd come, then the road, then the mountain village of Maghaltani—somehow. Two men stepped into the street, barring his way.

They were tall, faces and bodies obscured entirely by rough gray cloaks. A voice emerged from the hood of one. "That's a nice sword, boy. Where are you going?"

Tepic thrust his hands into his pockets and turned aside. Averting his gaze, he walked quickly toward a row of low houses near an outlet from a dirty canal.

"You, boy. I'm talking to you."

Tepic could hear their feet quicken behind him, and he lengthened his stride to match. A vain hope, for a moment later he was at a full sprint, stealing one quick glance to see the men give chase. Their hoods somehow remained firmly over their eyes. He looked about in desperate search for something, anything—only dark windows and shutters. The afternoon was wearing on, and the deepening shadows of the houses showed no escape, only the bare city wall ahead. There was no other choice. Tepic leapt as far and long as he could into the frigid waters of the murky canal.

The rush of water in his ears was only rivaled by the shocking cold that sucked every bit of breath from his lungs. He thought the heavy sword and the shoes on his feet would surely drown him in the depths, but he struggled with all his might, and after an eternity, broke the surface of the water, gasping for air.

On either side of the canal the two men now paced, eyeing him intently, looking for a place to wade into the water and take hold of him. Ahead, there was a culvert under the wall, barred tightly with iron. He dipped his head and kicked his feet, making for the culvert as fast as he could.

Near the wall, the men stepped tepidly into the water, seeking for their footing as they made for the center. Tepic gave one last push and thudded against the iron bars. A current picked up here where the water drained beyond the wall. The men were waist-deep and gaining.

Tepic tried his head between the bars. Too narrow! He tried again and squeezed. His ears flattened and scraped and he cried out, but he was through, first head and then shoulder. His sword clanged on the bars, stopping any further progress. The cloaked figures were upon him. He wrenched the strap of the sword and scabbard over his head and yanked it through behind him just as one of the men lurched forward into the water with a swipe. He grasped at air.

Tepic could only choke and flail as the men cursed behind him and the current carried him away.

———————— ◆○◆ ————————

Tepic was weakening and his limbs grew numb in the bitter cold water. It had been warm under the sun in Voldigar's training yard the day before, but there were few breaks in the rain since. It seemed so much had happened after his last lesson, and he wondered what the old man would tell him now.

The canal soon joined with the river, and Voldigar's warning about the current and the sea cliffs jolted into his mind. Frantically he looked for the ford they'd crossed in the morning as he fought to keep his head above the water. Off to his right, upriver, he saw it: the wide flat stone they'd so gingerly crossed to avoid being dumped into the very river in which he was now rapidly gaining speed.

Fear clutched at his heart as he fought the current and searched for shore through a blinding spray of rapid water. Panic had nearly taken hold when he *did* remember what the old man would say. *Fear drives men to foolish action, or to wisdom*—and something about courage and faith. The old ways were seldom mentioned in his home, and he wasn't sure he even understood what his teacher meant. Tepic would not remember what he prayed, but pray he did—eyes gripped tightly as the water pulled him closer and closer to the sea cliffs. When he opened them, there above his head a lonely, leafless tree leaned over the water, extending a branch like a gnarled finger in the mist.

With what little strength remained, Tepic heaved himself from the river and caught the limb in both hands, his legs sweeping up from the water and swinging wildly in open air where the current plunged over a perilous drop—twice again the height of the Spire. His head spun watching droplets of water speed from his feet and disappear into the hazy nothingness below. His grasp was failing, yet one aching hand to the next, he worked his way to a soggy bank where he lay breathless upon his back.

Tears welled in his eyes and mingled with the rain spattering against his face, but he caught them with wavering gasps. *I'm not afraid,* he told himself. *I'm not afraid.* The cold was forgotten, and all the world faded about him.

The first thing Tepic noticed was the rain had stopped. The sound of the great waterfall rushed in his ears, but the constant spatter of precipitation was gone. He then remembered the cold and felt for a cloak he did not have to wrap about him. There he shivered on his back for some time with eyes closed. Perhaps if he did not look, it would all go away. The wicked men, the bitter chill, the terror that stalked his dreams.

The sword. Grandfather's sword. *It must go to the mountain village.* He opened his eyes.

It was dark, and Tepic wondered how long he must have lain on the soggy bank. Had he been seen by his pursuers? He felt for the sword—still strapped to his back. *Good.* It seemed too that somehow rain was falling on his face again and nowhere else, tiny movements like raindrops running on his forehead and under his eyes.

He leapt to his feet and brushed the first from his brow. A spider, and then another, and another! He swiped furiously across his whole body. Dozens, hundreds of the fiends fell to the ground and skittered away in a growing stampede under the green moonlight that peeked through gaps in the seething clouds above. Tepic shuddered and spun round and round looking for more.

Through the fog of his breath, he then saw a most curious thing. The spiders were streaming in a line straight to the river, plopping in one after another to drown in dark depths where the water pooled in the weeds. On they disappeared in their macabre parade while he felt his face for bites.

A subtle glow began in the shallow shore. A trick of the moonlight it seemed at first, but then more distinct. There was a shimmer as the water bulged and flowed over some invisible, rounded surface. It rose higher and something like a translucent head emerged from the water. The mangled bodies of spiders curled in death were stuck about its face, some linked together in a ghastly weave. In an instant, the rest of the form burst from the river with a brilliant flash of green light. It loomed over him for a frozen moment of breathless terror, and then it lunged.

Tepic tried to cry out, but no sound arose. He swept his grandfather's sword from its scabbard and stumbled backward, holding it out in both hands. To his surprise, the creature recoiled and seemed to diminish in size.

There it paused again, with a tiny flicker in its heart, like a tongue of pale flame smoldering through its mannish form. Though it cowered, it stood some nine feet high, water flowing over a gossamer body. It lurched again, rising up as a blast of heat flowed forth. Its guttural voice boomed and reverberated, making some kind of demand in unintelligible speech—but it seemed unable, or unwilling, to close the final gap.

Tepic found his voice and shouted in return. "Stay back. Go away, Orun!" He swung the sword in quick jerks as he regained his feet and backed away.

The creature inched forward, its body vibrating and creating a pulse of tiny ripples in the water that clung to its frame. Arms more clearly forming, it held them wide as small coils of green tendrils began to broil from its core. Tepic could see the grass of the bank curl and blacken under its advance. He ground his teeth and held the sword high, ready to make a desperate strike. His hands felt strangely warm, the sword like an extension of his arms.

The Orun hesitated, then turned its face to the side. It shuddered and suddenly collapsed with a tremendous splash. Another burst of green light followed a scalding surge of air, and the pool of its body jolted back into the river. It vanished in the water's depths.

"Over here!" a voice cried out from the darkness.

Tepic peered along the riverbank, eyes still wide and sword held high. No less than a dozen figures emerged in the moonlight, some carrying torches aloft. Their heavy boots sloshed in the muck. Each man wore a gray cloak and all were armed. From their midst, one stepped forward with a row of daggers tucked into his belt. Two wings of jet-black hair were matted to his head, and a sharp, black beard pointed from his chin. His right hand was wrapped tightly in a makeshift splint, and his wrinkled face was marred with bruises. Lord Commander Caliras.

"What have we here? Dantic's other whelp, no?"

Tepic shook and the blade wobbled. "Stay back!" he cried and glanced to the water's edge. He retreated slowly as the men drew closer. Some of them laughed while they tightened a ring about him.

"Stay back I said! It will kill you all!"

"I wouldn't go too far, lad. That's a long drop behind you, and I'd hate to lose that sword."

Tepic glanced behind him as quickly as he dared. The ground grew more solid here as it rose to the lip of the cliff. It was only ten steps to an endless drop toward the sea and the rocks below. He continued on.

Caliras furrowed his brow and raised his good hand. "Easy, lad, easy now."

Tepic stepped to the last inch, the heel of his shoe hanging over the edge. "You don't understand!" he cried. "You can't take this! You'll die! You'll all die!"

"Just hold still now, boy. Easy."

Tepic closed his eyes and imagined the great drop behind him, imagined the Orun following him into the sea. His shoulders drooped, and the point of the sword fell to the ground.

In a flash, the men were upon him, the sword jerked from his hands, his wrists bound, and a rough-woven sack dropped over his head.

Chapter Seven

Watchmen in the Night

L ANATHOR WAS FIRST TO leave the Sanctum, hastening to prepare despite his recent wounds. The miles between him and Liadov were many, and the hours few. While the others groused and cautioned him to ease, Vasherk merely grinned and leaned against the door. Mercifully, the rain had ceased shortly after the Emperor's messenger visited. The mobs too had been put down in anticipation of Lusánt's coronation, and after a quick exit from the city, the two men were riding swiftly along Aramon's high road.

A bright green moon rose and slipped between clouds as it sailed along the dome of the world. They would make one brief stop in Maghaltani and then be on their way again. Rather than double back to the road, ten miles more by foot on a rough mountain trail remained from there to the great bridge at old Aramon's border—and then the first of two high forts at the near end of the pass that went on to the Baerdermyrch.

Lanathor realized as they rode that he and Vasherk would miss the coronation and the Emperor's summons. Lusánt would be most displeased. He dismissed the thought and tried to picture Liadov instead. Had she aged like him? Would she upbraid him as always for the flat expression he wore? Was her skin still as pale as he was dark? He placed a small piece of Falam Root in his cheek and rode on.

Soon they were enclosed by deep pine wood, and the land rose steeply. Vasherk produced a lantern and held it high with one wrinkly hand. The paving ceased, and the darkness and silence of the forest set in about them.

"We cannot stay long," Lanathor said. "I must retrieve some instruments from the tower, and we can gather whatever supplies we need."

Vasherk nodded and came alongside Lanathor. His rapier clacked against the stirrups as their mounts stepped in time. "If we hurry, we can make the Westfort a good deal before morning. Perhaps we keep going from there."

Lanathor shook his head. "Not in the dark. The pass is treacherous and still too cold to travel by night. We should bring something warm, by the way."

Vasherk nodded again. "It's good to ride with you, Elder. Been a long quiet dream. I was beginning to think I'd not live long enough to see another adventure."

"Better to die in peace, Chanter."

Vasherk smiled faintly. "If you say so. Feeling better?"

Lanathor flexed his hands on the reins. He was feeling better, much. He could still sense his wounds, but it was more akin to the aching of an early morning than a wrestling match with an Orun. "Your magic is a wonder, Vasherk. I know it's costly. I thank you—and wish we had more than one of you."

Vasherk chuckled. "The world's not ready for that much charm. I am but a humble Chanter." He dipped his head in an exaggerated bow, and a long wisp of his white hair hung toward his saddle.

"Truly. The husbands of this world would lament it," Lanathor said.

Vasherk snorted a laugh in reply and Lanathor continued. "Why are you the only one anyway? I suppose I've never asked."

"The only healer?" Vasherk said. "I don't really know. Chanting isn't strictly 'magic,' as you say. I was just good with my hands. The Chanting of the Scriptures brought out more of what God willed."

It was Lanathor's turn to laugh. "That simple? It's a wonder the world isn't full of Chanters. You have a way with words."

"I think I described it near enough," the old man replied. "I just left out the essential ingredient—time. Like anyone else, it took many years to find my First and Second Virtue, and then twice as long again to find my Third. I really am that old."

"A lifetime of Chanting for its highest prize."

"Not the highest. There's a Fourth Virtue too, but I'll be dead long before I find it."

"How long would it take?"

"Depends on the person. Taro found his already, but he's a prodigy. Voldigar too, in his own way—though he's nearly as old as I am." Vasherk shrugged and stared into the pines. "Liadov could heal too you know."

"I do know," Lanathor said. "But she was something else."

"'*Is*,' you mean," Vasherk corrected. "I'll be quite curious to see how she's getting on. A lovely woman!"

"You truly have no shame, do you, Brother?"

"No, I do not. And I shan't live long enough to change that either."

Lanathor reclined in his saddle and stretched his back with a grin. "All this carrying on about your advanced age, why still rank and file? Never a push for the Eldership?"

Vasherk returned a smirk and shook his head. "And end up like Voldigar? No thank you. Of cares, Elder Lanathor, I'd rather be free."

The mirth melted from Lanathor's face. "I don't think that's something to make light of."

"Nor I. But—"

"He saw things no man should," Lanathor interjected more firmly. "Gave more than was just. Lost his closest friend, his dearest pupil, the girl he thought of as a daughter—"

"And very nearly his sanity," Vasherk finished. "I know, Brother. I helped him fish Gwenyth's body from that pond when he found her. We all thought she was dead."

Vasherk turned his eyes to the saddle as a deeper quiet fell over their path. "I'm sorry. My tongue gets ahead of me. If we can't laugh in the dark though, we'll all be madmen soon enough."

A scowl still lingered on Lanathor's face, but he offered a conciliatory nod. "Look, the village is ahead."

The two left their words in the wood and dared a bit more speed as the first lights of Maghaltani showed through the trees. Trotting where the trunks thinned, the outer palisade of their home could be seen, interspersed with stone reinforcements and intricately carved in the forms of beasts and birds. The fortifications were layered one after another up the face of a steep hill on both sides of a sparkling river—far more formidable than a first glance would suggest. Arching bridges crossed the tumbling water all along its length and a peculiar collection of tiered structures with angled roofs and protruding log beams were built as the natural landscape allowed. Many of them were dug into the slope. Flickering watch fires of various sizes receded into the darkness where they could just make out the shape of a tall stone tower at the peak of the hill. Had there been more light, numerous tidy gardens would have revealed a colorful array of spring flowers and early crops.

The village had been well-secured that night, and though most were probably asleep, a large group of brethren escorted them through the gates, flashing a series of salutes and greetings. Their horses were collected and cared for as a slender man in rough hides descended the hill toward them with a pair of bone-blade hatchets and a thin, hollow staff across his back. His ears and nose were covered in piercings and his brown hair and beard were pulled away from his hawkish, sun-kissed face in dozens of small braids.

"Left in charge I assume, Gardoric?" Lanathor asked.

"Aye," Gardoric responded with a dip of his chin and the thick accent of the Far Marshes. "Wulf's out. Medellai left the village to me."

"Yes, he sent Wulf to his sister's house. Any sign of the Orun?"

Gardoric spat on the ground. "Nothing. I say let it come."

"Sooner would be better than later," Vasherk added.

"We're not here long," Lanathor continued. "We need to collect supplies, and then we continue by foot to the Span."

"Why so hurried? You could rest easy here for the night."

Lanathor realized how tired he was for the first time. He looked at Vasherk, but no sign of weariness was on the old man's face. He shook his head. "No, we have need of haste."

"What are you doing at the Span?" Gardoric asked.

"Better to keep our errand secret," Lanathor responded quickly and walked uphill toward the tower. Vasherk ducked under a thatched roof into a nearby house that burrowed into the earth.

Gardoric narrowed his eyes and came alongside Lanathor, speaking in a low voice. "You're going to see Liadov, aren't you?"

"Perceptive," Lanathor replied and continued walking.

Gardoric shrugged. "I miss details, and people die. It's hard to hide things from me, Elder. I hope you know what you're doing."

"Yes, you and everyone else. Don't try to dissuade me."

"No such intent." With a quick dip of his chin, Gardoric turned to other business, disappearing in the torchlight of Maghaltani.

Lanathor ascended a curve of stone steps and unlocked the tower's banded, oak-hewn door. If the ancient scents of the Sanctum were full of memory, the smells of old leather and mossy stone in the Tower of Maghaltani were its forebears. Lighting lamps within, the darkness fled into the corners to reveal a crowded floor of trunks and laden bookshelves, of desks and curious contraptions. Few came here besides Lanathor anymore, and the ordered chaos was his doing. It was the only place in the world he felt truly safe. He loved it, but he could not linger.

Passing the small chamber he called his bedroom, he snatched a rigid case from the wall and clambered to a high terrace under the rapidly clearing sky. There he withdrew his long telescope with its stand and delicately fixed it toward the moon. He held his breath before he put his eye to the device and silently mouthed the familiar calculations.

Wrong, wrong, and wrong again. There was no longer any doubt. He collapsed the device as quickly as he'd fastened it and stood as a dark sentinel on the windy roof while his robes billowed about his legs. He gazed a long while at Mirvánè with doubt in his eyes while she stared down quietly at him. On he watched and contemplated until the wind stopped and his robes settled on his feet. There seemed to be a haze about the moon's gentle curve, a shift in the light that he did not recall. *It* was happening. It had to be.

—◦—

True to their word, Lanathor and Vasherk left Maghaltani as swiftly as they'd come. Save for Gardoric and the night watch, the others might never know of their passing. They now hurried along a rugged trail, clad in thick furs that Vasherk had retrieved while Lanathor peered into the sky. The lamp stowed, they traveled by moonlight only, for the clouds had blown away sometime in the last hour.

They spoke little and watched the ground intently in the pale light, silent save for their soft footfalls and rapid breath. The land grew more wild, the forest older, and though the Brethren maintained it well, the trail was riddled with roots and stones. There was sacred memory here, as if the spirits of this quiet road to The Great Span brooded and coiled about their feet. Neither man was willing to disturb it as they went steadily on to the border of Aramon.

Hours passed, and they traveled into the deep watches of the night, the trail gently rising and falling. Lanathor's thoughts drifted, but he considered most what he would say to Liadov. The Brethren would understand in time, but she must understand now. Surely, she would have the wisdom to see, yet her mind was a deep pool, the strings of a great instrument. What could he say that would change her counsel, long determined? How could he sound those depths or find her melody? It was a strange realization that the fate of a people might rest on his words—nothing more than words.

At long length, the path declined steeply, and the distant sound of flowing water could be perceived at the edge of hearing. A short distance off a curve in the trail, Lanathor spied the glimmer of a small white flower in tiny cups growing from the side of a felled tree. He stepped into the underbrush and produced a knife that he worked carefully into the wood at the flower's base.

Vasherk approached quietly and squatted beside him. "This is Falam Root, no?"

"It is," Lanathor replied. "And very rare."

Vasherk tilted his head and carefully watched his handiwork. "I've distilled it with my students, but never seen it in the wild."

Lanathor continued delicately. "I must remove the bulb with care. The potency is lost if it is damaged even a little." He gingerly lifted the small root between thumb and forefinger and quickly placed it in a wooden capsule where it disappeared into a fold of his robes.

"I meant to ask you about your 'magic' too," Vasherk said as they rose and continued down the trail, "about your particular form of *Telling* I mean. You too are unique, are you not?" Lanathor considered the question a moment but Vasherk went on. "Soris is a Qalimist, Urias a Skeltemist, but you are . . .?"

"Unique." Lanathor finished the sentence and flashed a smile, but it quickly flattened. "And I would be careful how you refer to Soris and Urias. They indeed manipulate the elements, but the words you used describe sorcerous demoniacs."

"Oh," Vasherk replied quickly, "I suppose I owe another apology."

"It's not your fault, Vasherk. You served in Polic's time. There are many errors he did not correct."

"I'm old, Lanathor, and I've been a brother a long time. There are things I should know better." He frowned and shook his head. "But it's never too late to learn, I suppose. What of the root?"

"What of it?"

"You Tellers seem to use a number of, of . . ."

"Aromatics? Yes." Lanathor said.

"But Falam Root is dangerous, no? And you use so much of it."

Lanathor stopped and stared at Vasherk. "You are quite inquisitive."

"I meant no offense," Vasherk added.

"None taken." Lanathor held his gaze a moment and then turned back down the trail. The two fell quiet once more.

As their path flattened, the sound of water echoing off canyon walls could more clearly be heard ahead. The forest thinned and a dim outline of The Great Span's high towers could barely be made out in the darkness before them.

Vasherk placed a hand on Lanathor. "Wait. What's that smell?"

"Smell?"

Vasherk circled where the trail met the main road, lifting his nose and sniffing. "Here!"

He dashed into a copse of trees and bracken with Lanathor close in tow. There on the ground before them lay a soldier in deep maroon livery, hastily covered in vines and branches. Blood streamed from the corner of his mouth, and his eyes gazed lifeless into the night sky.

"One of Gamad's men!" Lanathor said.

"And not dead long, " Vasherk added.

Both men drew steel and ducked behind nearby trees, listening and watching intently into the darkness about them. They caught one another's wide eyes in the fading moonlight but heard nothing more than the rustling of wind.

They stayed still for several long minutes while the moon sank behind the hills to the west. It would still be some time before the sun rose over the high mountains to the east, but in their wariness, both men peered intently into the gloom for the slightest movement. Just as it seemed the danger had passed, over the bubbling of the river deep below, Lanathor heard a rhythmic sound. In a moment it was obvious—marching feet.

Lanathor sheathed his knife and stepped to the edge of the trees with Vasherk close behind. The Great Span could now be seen, clear and massive in growing firelight a short distance down the paved road. A wondrous bridge, many-arched and jeweled with tall white turrets, it soared over a vast, deep chasm at the foot of high alpine mountains. Its length was so great and the chasm so wide, it seemed like an endless pier jutting out over an enormous black sea. Unlike the observatory atop The Golden Spire, The Great Span was wrapped in thick magic. Tellers, Chanters, and even Singers from generations past had woven their spells for long years to create the impossible structure. Lanathor could almost smell the power emanating from its ancient stone.

The Span stood at a slight angle from the brethren, and to its near edge marched some two or three hundred armed men in Gamad's livery, bearing torches. The pillars of its mighty stone disappeared into the depths below. It was the only way in or out of Aramon.

"Hail, Legionnaires!" Lanathor cried and stepped onto the road as the soldiers neared the bridge's end. The column ground to a halt and four men on horseback from the head of the procession rode swiftly to the crossroads where the brethren stood.

The man at their lead approached and spoke hurriedly without dismounting. "Reverend, I have need of haste—but I recognize the symbol of your order. Why do you call for us?"

"I am Reader Lanathor and this is Vasherk, of my order. We too travel in haste, to the Baerdermyrch, and mean to refresh ourselves in Westfort before we continue on to the east when the night's cold is past."

"You have my blessing then. I am Captain Arbed of the Westfort Garrison, but you will have to seek the hospitality of the Stonepikes. I, and those with me, were recalled this morning. We've spent the day in preparation and just recently departed."

An icy gust blew down from the mountains, and Lanathor caught Vasherk's worried glance in the corner of his eye.

"Have you not heard, Captain?"

Arbed turned his horse to the side and took on a stern face. "Heard what?"

"Surely, your messengers would have told you by now. Empress Eleanora is dead. Lord Commander Caliras and the Stonepikes made an attempt on the prince's life, and that wicked man is now a fugitive."

All the blood ran from Arbed's proud face. His horse stamped as he turned every which way and his officers cursed and shook their heads.

"My messenger from this morning did not return," Arbed said through gritted teeth. "And my second is late."

Lanathor suppressed a wince. "I fear they are dead, Arbed. My companion and I found a body not far from here in the uniform of your garrison."

Arbed shook his head and slumped in his saddle. "If I had known but a moment sooner, this could have been averted. There is no way my garrison can reclaim Westfort now."

The officers murmured and jerked at their reins as Arbed barked orders, but they did not hesitate to do his will. One was to confirm the truth of the matter and sped off with other mounted men toward Westfort. Another prepared the column to march in double-time. Arbed and the last followed Vasherk and Lanathor into the woods to examine the corpse.

"I would take you for a brigand and a liar, Reader," Arbed said as he looked down on the bloody body, "but I am not a fool. I believe you. Even so, you must come with us to Arregalt."

Vasherk opened his mouth in dismay but Lanathor responded coolly. "I would ask that you bring Brother Vasherk on ahead with whatever mounted men you have left—and with all speed. He's a strong rider and will confirm the truth of all once you reach the capital. Another messenger alone would be most unwise."

"And what then will you do, Reader?"

"I must continue my purpose beyond the pass."

Arbed raised his eyebrows. "You'll be killed by the Stonepikes. No one passes Westfort unseen."

Vasherk smiled. "The Elder may surprise you, Captain."

Arbed scoffed and turned his mount out of the trees. "We'll bring up a horse, Vasherk. Godspeed, 'Elder.'"

When the soldiers had moved out of earshot, Vasherk spoke quickly in a hushed voice. "What of the Orun, Lanathor? The plan was to stick together!"

"I don't think we have a choice, Brother. You know I can work my way through that fortress alone, but I can't bring you. There is no Third Virtue for Tellers."

Vasherk bit his lower lip and struck one fist into the other. "I'll tell the others. We'll ride fast. Do be careful, Elder."

"I think the time for care is over. Head and Heart." Lanathor saluted and sped off alone into the darkness.

CHAPTER EIGHT

CONSPIRACIES AND KEYS

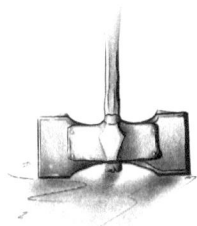

VOLDIGAR AND LUTZ MADE by torchlight for the Spire at Arregalt's heart while the other brethren fanned out in search of the Orun. Lutz jogged with an awkward gait to keep pace with Voldigar's long strides. Here and there, the city's new gas lamps were being lit in no particular order. Serious-looking lampmen scurried about, straining on step ladders with their long *hirigaels* flickering against the cobblestone.

Voldigar glanced from side to side, half expecting the Orun to leap out of every shadow. He wished it would, that Urias's gamble would pay off, that the creature would smell him out and give him the chance to end this ordeal with the head of his maul.

"We're not actually looking for Caliras, are we, Elder?" Lutz asked in his gravely tone.

"No, we are not," Voldigar answered. "Though some questions along that path may help us find the Orun."

"I thought as much. What's our first move?"

"We find General Gamad."

Find he hoped would be simple. Caliras's Stonepikes were long departed from the Spire, surrounded in their barracks by a host of Dantic's guards.

General Gamad's soldiers had taken over security of the imperial seat, and it was crawling with his men. A brief interrogation of a few at the Spire's entry revealed that Gamad now kept his command in the great hall beneath the royal apartments. For the second time that day, Voldigar found himself making for the vestibule where the brass-doored lift sped up and down the vast height of the Spire.

As they entered through one of many arches, Voldigar noticed first that the steam had subsided. Second, that the great hatch doors in the floor had just closed with a resounding bang. Within the lift, Lutz folded his arms and shifted his weight from foot to foot. Voldigar pulled the next cord from the last and watched him curiously.

"You shouldn't have brought me," Lutz muttered. The mokja jerked the cord twice more and turned away glaring. Nothing happened.

It was not unusual to wait for the lift, but it was night and the vestibule was quiet. Voldigar tapped his thumb on his knife a few times before he swung the lift door open and walked to the hatches. He stooped down and knocked loudly. "Bajk?"

"Lift's closed. Go away," a muffled voice called out from below.

Lutz walked up behind Voldigar, arms still crossed. "It's no use, Elder. Bajk hates me. I'll show you the stairs."

Voldigar was incredulous. "Can't you reason with him? We don't have all night to climb the Spire. There must be a thousand steps between here and the great hall."

"Eight-hundred-thirty-two. And no, I could sooner grow my beard back on the spot than reason with Bajk." The gears on Lutz's eyes clicked and whirred as if to emphasize his point.

Voldigar considered pounding on the hatch again but let the thought vanish with a sigh. "Lead on then."

The Spire's "stairs" were in truth a network of flights and passages of various sizes. Most of the halls were dim and little-used, smelling of the mold and moss of rainy Aramon. Sometimes they traced the outer wall or tightly spiraled in tall columns. At other times they ascended evenly, leading through a single low story. Still more paths led off in a dizzying array, but Lutz knew every curve and corner.

Halfway up they stopped to catch their breath.

"I'm completely and utterly lost," Voldigar said as he leaned over and huffed.

Lutz grinned. "As you should be. Can't have just anyone wandering floor to floor."

Voldigar looked around and shook his head. They stood in a dripping intersection of six passages. They'd hardly seen a single soul along the way. Lutz leaned casually against the wall and at length pulled a small object from one of his many pouches. He held it out.

"Here, I have a present for you. Carefully now."

Voldigar took the disc from Lutz's hand. It was astonishingly heavy for its size. "What's this?"

"Pull that knob on the edge. Like that, yes. Now hold it to your eye." Lutz was grinning ear to ear.

Voldigar did as instructed and looked into a little cylinder that protruded from the object. It took a moment to adjust his vision, but inside was a miniature map in relief, all in faint blue light.

"This is amazing," Voldigar said.

"It's the Spire," Lutz replied. "Press the lever—that bit on the right side."

As Voldigar did so, the view inside the lens went briefly black then shifted to some other section of the Spire. A few more instructions and he was able to slide and spin the map in all directions, like looking in every window of a minuscule doll house. Not merely flat, there was a clever representation of space and distance, a tiny model of the Spire.

"This must be priceless," Voldigar said.

"It's a *tharmskolp*, and it is," Lutz said, "but I have several. They're a bit out of date, but the Spire's the Spire. You can have that one."

Voldigar pulled the tharmskolp from his eye and blinked.

Lutz was still smiling. "Skill of the Mokja, Brother. I figure if you're the new Chief Investigator of Arregalt, that map will be more useful to you than Lusánt's gaudy little ring." He paused. "Caught your breath?"

Voldigar nodded. "Your people are a wonder."

Lutz raised an eyebrow. "Some of us."

"Who's the elder of you two?" Voldigar asked.

"Me and Bajk? I am," Lutz replied. "Of thirteen in fact. You'd know me better if you spent any time in the village. Why don't you and Gwenyth come back?"

Voldigar ignored the prodding. It was rote complaint at this point. "Why does Bajk hate you so much?"

"Never forgave me," Lutz muttered. He started walking again.

Voldigar took his hands off his knees and followed. "For what?"

"For joining your crazy order. What else? '*The Artificers should be in the Spire.*' That's what Bajk said. I'm an embarrassment."

Voldigar considered Lutz's words as they continued down a low passage. "And what did you say to him?"

"Nothin'," Lutz concluded. "I shaved my beard and been an embarrassment ever since. Some things are more important, Brother. I took the oath."

Voldigar let it lie at that, and they continued up the Spire in silence.

———◆———

The great hall was vast, with ceilings a hundred feet high. Several staircases led up to the balconies before the royal chambers, but the landings and lower steps of these were all enclosed, the doors secured and sealed. The floors and walls were a sea of red, in the old style of early Aramon. A starry host of twinkling sconces adorned the walls, and huge, graceful chandeliers hung at differing heights in the space above. Voldigar and Lutz entered through a small door at the far end.

Gamad and his officers had commandeered a quarter of the hall beyond the wide, round void where the lift traveled and set up desks and chairs, long cabinets of records, and rows of trunks. At this hour, they looked to be closing shop—staff collapsing furniture and sweeping papers into cases. Gamad shifted his weight to rise just as the brethren arrived, wiping a greasy hand on his coat and straightening the patch over his eye. He scowled and settled back into his chair.

"Prince's pet, back again?"

"Gamad, I need to speak with you—privately."

Gamad spat. "Sorry, Reader. Business is over and I'm hungry. Come back tomorrow—or never." A nearby officer chuckled.

"My purpose is urgent. I must compel you," Voldigar said.

"Compel me?" Gamad asked. His chair creaked, and a hush fell over his makeshift office.

"Yes," Voldigar said. This wasn't going to be easy. "I speak for the Emperor."

Gamad laughed and rose heavily to his feet. A naked sneer spread across the corner of his white beard. "Alright, little viceroy. We can talk over there." He pointed into a dim side room.

They crossed the hall together where Gamad stopped and gestured for Voldigar to enter first. His men made to follow, but the General raised a huge hand to stay them. Ducking low under the door, he turned to Voldigar, his face twisted in displeasure. Voldigar could see little of the hall behind Gamad's huge form.

"You'd better hope this is worth my time," Gamad said and crossed his arms.

"This morning outside the Empress's chamber," Voldigar said, "Reader Lanathor alerted you of the assassination attempt before it began. He asked for your key, and you refused. Why?"

"Protocol. What business is this of yours?"

"You know what my business is, Gamad. Prior to that moment, you moved a brigade of men into the Spire. Also protocol?"

Gamad unfolded his arms as fire kindled in his eyes. "Are you investigating me?"

"Answer my questions."

Gamad lurched forward catching the edge of Voldigar's collar in his massive fist. "Who do you think you are, whelp? Not enough to ruin your Brotherhood? Come to poison me too?"

Voldigar shot his hand out in answer and seized the giant's wrist like an iron vise. With a squeeze, he turned his hand. Gamad's fingers splayed and released Voldigar's collar. "Don't test me, Gamad. I am not here to suffer your foolish intimidations."

Gamad's eyes widened, and he grit his teeth in a flicker of fear. He struggled in vain as he was held in place. When the message was clear,

Voldigar allowed him to jerk his hand away. Gamad retreated and rubbed his wrist. "Cheap Chanter's tricks!"

"I said to answer my questions."

"I told you. Protocol. The men were an extra precaution. Maybe I saw something the rest of you didn't. Maybe someone should ask *you* questions."

"Maybe you should have acted," Voldigar said. "Maybe Lusánt has the same questions I do." He paused and allowed Gamad to calculate behind his sunken brow. "Your key. I will need it."

Gamad balked. "No! Why? I am the security of the tower now. Ask someone else."

"Your key is one of a kind, Gamad, as you know. There are no others like it. I will need it, and it will be returned to you at coronation—tomorrow."

"I have a host of soldiers at my call in the room behind me, Brother Voldigar," Gamad growled. "Don't dictate to me."

Voldigar gave no visible reaction but held Gamad in his gaze. "How hard do you want this to be?"

The general hesitated and flexed his jaw. It looked like two snakes were trying to worm their way from his neck. He glanced again behind him, but then slowly, he produced a large ring of keys from his belt. It looked like a toy in his huge fingers. He worked one heavy, angular key from the ring and held it up. Voldigar recognized it at once.

"Tomorrow, at the coronation," Gamad said, "or by the gods, I'll find you and take it back myself. I don't care what tricks you try or whose signet ring you wear—I'll break every finger. And let this be the end of your 'investigation' of me. I'm loyal to Aramon, loyal to its crown, and loyal to its gods."

"You are loyal to Gamad, and you should hope we find Caliras soon."

Voldigar took the key and exited the room as Gamad stood aside. Lutz fell in beside Voldigar as they walked out of the hall under the silent gaze of the officers.

When they had disappeared down a long passage, Lutz spoke in a hushed voice. "Do you suspect Gamad of treason then?"

"He's an opportunist," Voldigar replied. "But no, not anymore. That man could no more conspire than the chairs he's been torturing all day.

I doubt he even knew about the brigade, and he likely found sleep more important than responding to Lanathor." Voldigar stopped and turned to Lutz. "He's not without cunning, but I take him for a fool."

"Why antagonize him then?"

"I had to be sure, and we need his key."

Lutz let his eyepieces spin for a moment "What do you intend to do with it?"

"We retrieve the Orun's prison."

The Vaults of Arregalt were only legend to the few who had any sense of their existence at all. Rumors traveled in those circles of wondrous treasures and relics from Aramon's antiquity, when the stonecutters overthrew their masters and cast them into the Wending Sea.

They were real enough, and Voldigar had been there precisely one time, along with Liadov, the long-dead Marshall Hugan, and King Olwis when his face was fair and his smile broad. It was serious business then, and it was serious business now. Lutz, for his part, had never been inside. Like all the Mokja people, he tended to be taciturn and cross, but he could not contain his excitement as the two of them made their way slowly into the Delvings beneath the Spire.

"The Artificers built the Vaults you know," Lutz continued. "Every last vestibule and embrasure! It's warded too, the very stone. Magnificent engineering, superlative craft!"

Voldigar stopped at a wet intersection and pondered his direction. It had been a long time. "Do you happen to know the way?" He fished the tharmskolp out of his pocket and extended it to Lutz.

Lutz blinked out of his reverie and scowled in consideration. "Don't need that." He tapped the side of his head. "It's all up here. I haven't been inside, but I can guess where the door is." He stared at the dripping ceiling. "Artificers aren't allowed down here anymore. Unjust if you ask me." Lutz turned his head from side to side several times and finally pointed off to his right. "We're not deep enough yet, and the stonework dips this way."

Voldigar looked behind, then closed his eyes to listen. Only sounds of water. They turned into the hall Lutz chose and descended at a gentle slope. Lutz struck up where he'd left off. "The designers wondered if the residents of Undercity might dig their way into the Vaults." He laughed. "Can you imagine? It was foresighted if you ask me. The things which must be stored—"

Voldigar cut him off. "Here." They stood at a small wooden door cut into the masonry, mildewed but sound.

The lenses on Lutz's eyes protruded and hummed. "This?"

"Yes."

Lutz grumbled. "Wouldn't be my guess."

Voldigar grabbed the handle and pushed. Inside was a small room with a low roof and the trappings of a guard post. It was otherwise empty, save for an imposing iron door, riveted and banded. "Yes, this is it."

"Unbelievable," Lutz exclaimed. "Not even a guard."

"No," Voldigar said as he glanced around the room. "Gamad's men have done nothing to remedy the recent laxity. The guards can't open the doors anyway, and it's better we not be seen." Voldigar pulled the key from his pocket and rolled it between his fingers.

"Well? What are we waiting for? Open up!" Lutz rubbed his hands together.

"This key doesn't open the outer door," Voldigar said. "It's powerful. It can access the outer chambers of the crown, the offices of the Stonepikes, and the inner door of this vault." He shook his head. "But the outer door requires another key."

Lutz jerked his head back. "That's not Artificer work!"

"It was the work of Olwis after we placed . . . more dangerous things in here. Most of the brethren don't even know what's inside, Lutz, though I'm sure you've deduced it by now."

Lutz nodded.

"There are similar keys. After Olwis passed, Eleanora used the innovation to play her generals off one another, to make them fear. No one key can open all doors and no one person holds them all. They often don't even know who can access what. Gamad's key is unique."

Voldigar went on. "Not only is it a maze to find this place, the key to the outer door is in the possession of the crown while the highest officer keeps the inner, now in our possession." Voldigar took a deep breath. "It's my hope that in Gamad's wicked mind, we need this key for Caliras's offices or something in the royal apartments. He could certainly guess at our purpose, but if his thoughts are on the Vaults, that too would be interesting."

"Then you have the other key already?" Lutz asked.

"No, Eleanora does, or rather did, and Olwis before her. The sovereign often had to see personally to the changing of the guard below. This is where you come in, Lutz. In one thing you're wrong. This lock itself is Artificer work. Your brother Bajk, in fact."

The lenses on Lutz's face spun wide enough for his magnified eyes to show surprise. "That devil! Why didn't Olwis ask me?"

Voldigar had no more need to explain. He raised both hands, stepped away, and nodded at the lock.

Lutz turned to the door and glared. In a flash, a round container appeared in his hand, alike in shape and size to the tharmskolp. This he flicked back and forth, and a dazzling array of picks, files, and wires sprang from its edges. His lenses narrowed toward the lock. His hands went busily to work.

Some time passed, and Voldigar found his eyes wilting while Lutz muttered and his tools clicked and scraped. He must have nodded off, startled when Lutz finally spoke.

"There!" Lutz said proudly and gave his small device a tap. "Amateur!"

There was a pop and an echo behind the door. A nudge and it swung slowly with a groan. Faint smells of the sea wafted through, and for a moment, blew flat the light of their torch. Voldigar rubbed his eyes and bid Lutz follow as he stole into the darkness.

The sounds of Arregalt's waterfalls and the crashing of the Wending Sea far below grew louder, piercing stone as the Brothers descended a long spiral into the Vaults' heart. The air became cool, and soon a loud dripping echoed all around. At the base of these stairs, old masonry gave way to a great cavern covered in ankle-deep water. Voldigar held the torch high to reveal a tiny patch of the soaring roof and walls, but most of its long expanse was lost in shadow.

Ahead, stonework rose from the flooding, as though it floated on a hidden sea. There, to his surprise, the great rusted door of the Inner Vault stood narrowly ajar. Just in front, the body of a man in gray livery lay in the shallow water next to an overturned stool and a shattered lantern.

Lutz crossed to the body and gasped. "Dead a long time, this one."

Voldigar knelt beside and covered his mouth with the back of his hand. "No, only a few days. He's *Blooded,* Lutz. Every drop drained."

The face of the man was drawn and skeletal, as though it had been prepared for burial and the embalming cut short. Lutz shook his head in dismay.

Voldigar continued quietly. "No one's even come for this poor soul. Left here forgotten by his fellows." Voldigar looked around the body and found the broken haft and head of a mace in the shallow water. "Looks like he tried to fight at least."

Lutz had crossed to examine the open door. He ran his hands along its edge where several gashes showed near the lock. "Or tried to beat this door to death . . ."

Voldigar joined him in the examination and laughed ruefully as he put the angular key back in his pocket. "All the trouble we went through, and the door stands open."

"Though too narrow, and stuck fast," Lutz said as he squeezed unsuccessfully at the gap.

"Yes, it's ground into the stone."

Voldigar gripped the door and closed his eyes. With a grunt, he drove it forward a few more feet, splintering stonework and spraying sparks from its edge. He would be sure to close and lock it on their departure. His torch revealed a shimmering arsenal within, obscured in a haze of shifting dust. One suit of mail lay tipped on its side. They walked slowly, looking about in quiet reverence.

"Tymicha's Arsenal," Lutz whispered.

Voldigar found and lit a few sconces on the walls, packing nearby fuel into them. "Whoever was last here let these burn out."

Lutz was admiring a huge, ornate axe on a stand and seemed not to hear. Voldigar stood beside him and pointed at the base. "One has been removed. Let's move on."

They soon came to a gray stone crossway with a platform of marble, raised in the eight-pointed shape of Aramon's three cults, one overlaying the other.

"The altar of House Sispérus," Voldigar said. "Our quarry is not far."

Off to the right, there was a long gallery, covered in mosaics of white and gold. Bright pillars, and tiling, and many doors adorned the high walls. Their meager torch did it little justice. Voldigar led on, quietly counting doors as they rounded a corner that opened into an even longer gallery beyond. Up a flight of carven stairs and along a railed balcony. "Five, six, and . . . here."

They stood in front of a small ivory door, unremarkable and identical in every way to the others they'd passed.

"This is it?" Lutz asked. "The Orun's prison?"

"It's inside," Voldigar replied, gesturing a small shape with his hands. "A *Kishket* Liadov called it, fashioned by her own hand. And I do have one key, to this door only. I locked it ten years ago." He looked down at Lutz. "You were only a rank novice then, Lutz."

Lutz flexed his hands nervously and watched the door. "Probably should have stayed one."

Voldigar let a brief smile cross his face as he produced a small brass key from under his shirt and handed the torch to Lutz. "I don't know what we'll find beyond this door. Be ready, and don't touch *anything*."

Voldigar drew the Daneki blade with his free hand while Lutz unwrapped a curious chain with a barbed end. A click, and the door swung open.

There, in the center of the room, was a short stone pillar with a flat top and something like a birdcage resting on it. Inside the cage, a small jar of alabaster sat quietly, reflecting the light of their torch. The Kishket. Beyond this, the room was empty and still.

Voldigar felt the blood drain from his face. "I should have known. The prison is undisturbed . . ."

"What?"

"We're not hunting the same creature, Lutz." He quickly shut and locked the door and turned to the mokja. "There are rumors—rumors of other Kishket unique to the demons they bind."

Lutz raised his eyebrows in alarm and hurried after Voldigar who was rapidly descending the stairs. "How many hellspawn are we keeping down here?"

"I don't know!"

"Why don't we put this whole thing to the torch and be done with it!"

"No! The Kishket, they *want* to be destroyed. If only it were so easy. That's just it, Lutz. The demoniacs you've chased down all these years—spirits in people's minds. Mad creatures with no will but to kill, and destroy, and consume! But the Orun, they are different. They reason, after their own fashion. They plot and prepare, and desire nothing more than to manifest themselves bodily in this world. They create nothing, but in their envy, steal everything."

Voldigar stopped and stared at him wide-eyed. "They cannot be let out. The thing that Lanathor fought was nothing. What it seeks to become though . . ." Voldigar blinked and lowered his voice to a hoarse whisper. "I've seen them, Lutz."

Lutz's mouth hung open, a question on his lips, but Voldigar hurried on.

They passed the altar of Sispérus again and dashed from one gallery to the next. Soon they were racing into the Gallery of the Moon. It did not take them long to find the object of Voldigar's fear. Deep in the long hall of green mosaics, one low door lay broken in the middle of the corridor, splintered and charred. Shattered glass was scattered on the floor near a large, upturned chest, and the missing pole axe was carelessly dropped upon the tiles.

Voldigar rushed to the opening with Lutz close behind and peered in. In the center, there stood a short pillar, akin to the one they'd seen before, but empty. A golden box lay on its side on the floor.

"I've never seen this room, nor known of its existence," Voldigar said. "The broken glass is from the wall, the wood from the door." He hurried to the golden box and ran his hand within through an empty round impression of black velvet.

"Another Kishket?" Lutz asked.

"No. The box is empty, and mundane . . ." Voldigar knelt by the door and grasped the mangled wood. "But this is the work of an Orun, as sure as the earth." He spun his torch about frantically in every direction. "There's nothing else."

Lutz's eyepieces clicked and whirred as he scanned every corner of the room. "What does it mean?"

"It means the Orun was let out here, in this very room, Lutz. Its Kishket should be in a million pieces on the floor—but there's nothing. No prison. I don't understand."

Lutz moved his mouth silently, trying to offer some explanation. His voice finally emerged, thin with fear. "But . . . how do we catch it then?"

Voldigar shook his head. "I don't know." He caught Lutz's eyes and the cuff of his sleeve for a moment before he rose and bolted across the tiles. "We have to tell Medellai!"

CHAPTER NINE

THE SHADOW OF A STORM

N O SOONER HAD VOLDIGAR and Lutz fled from the winding passages of the Vaults and Delvings, than they saw Commander Dantic gesticulating wildly to his officers in the landing of the Spire's broad gatehouse. As he punctuated each word sharply with a hand, he caught sight of Voldigar and rushed across the echoing tiles between them.

"Voldigar!" he shouted angrily. "Where have you been? We've searched for you for an hour!" Dantic breathed heavily. His face was drawn, a storm in his eyes. A pair of nervous guards followed at a distance.

Voldigar tensed. "What's wrong?"

"Tepic! He's gone. Gone! They took hours to inform me. Is he with you?"

"No," Voldigar replied. "What happened?"

Dantic cursed. "Those wretches, I'll have them court-martialed. What were they thinking!"

Voldigar felt his own voice rising. "Easy, Dantic. Tell me what happened."

"The Vessels, Vol. Tepic listened too close to your story. We've an old sword in my house—his grandfather's—and there are tales about it. Tep thought it was enchanted too, and now he's gone with it!"

Voldigar's eyes opened wide. "Is it?"

"What?"

"The sword, Dantic! Is it enchanted?"

"No! There were no Brethren in our family," Dantic complained.

"But the sword, do you *know* it's not enchanted? What were the stories?"

"I . . ." Dantic looked at the floor and ground his teeth. "I should have locked that sword away, and the boy with it!"

"You should have listened to him!" Voldigar shouted.

Dantic lifted his eyes, now welling with tears. His mouth was set in a hard line. "Lyrusia's missing too, Vol. No one's seen her since yesterday morning. I thought maybe she was looking for him, but . . ." Dantic's shoulders drooped, and he shook his head.

Voldigar caught the rest of his rebuke in his throat. "Lyrusia's a willful girl, Dantic. I'm sure she's fine. We'll find her, and we'll find Tepic too." He spoke firmly and placed a hand on Dantic. "We'll find them."

Dantic blinked the weariness from his eyes. "We've scoured the city, Voldigar."

"Keep scouring," Voldigar said, "and send some of your men toward Maghaltani. More to my farm. As fast as you can. My order is even now searching for the creature that attacked Tepic. We'll be searching for your children too."

Dantic nodded, though doubt was plain upon his face. His gaze lingered on Voldigar a moment longer. "Is it hunting him, Voldigar?"

Voldigar's hands clenched and his eyes narrowed. "Cast it from your mind, friend."

The commander wiped his hand across his face and turned his eyes to the ancient walls. With another nod, he set his jaw and sped across the landing to point and bark orders among his men again.

It was still hours before sunrise. "Come on," Voldigar said to Lutz, "We have to gather everyone—now."

Voldigar wrestled with his own doubts as he and Lutz hurried from the Spire and through one of the Citadel's many courtyards under a clear night sky. The Brethren were to gather in the Sanctum at dawn, but he could not delay so long. Arregalt was a huge city, and he had little hope of how he might find the other four among a million. No, he and Lutz must search for Tepic now, alone, and send a messenger to the Sanctum.

To his surprise, the four brethren rounded a corner and interrupted his musing.

All were mounted on huge warhorses with tufted hooves and riding fast. Medellai led, with Soris and Urias at his flanks. Taro was close behind guiding a pair of riderless horses—one considerably smaller than the other. No finer creatures could be found in Aramon, these bred and raised by the wisdom of Brother Gardoric and Sister Hyfariel in green valleys below Maghaltani. They thundered to a halt just before Voldigar and Lutz while confused guards streamed with torches from their posts and looked on in wonder.

"Come!" Medellai shouted. "The Orun has left the city!"

Voldigar and Lutz rushed to their mounts and saw then that the others were fully armed for war.

"What? How?" Voldigar asked.

"No time, Elder. We ride!"

They vaulted to their steeds, and the six of them spurred from the Citadel in a clamor of dust and squealing horses.

"When did it leave?" Voldigar shouted.

"Less than an hour," Medellai said over the pounding of hooves. "We looked for you and Lutz as soon as I realized. It was sudden, Voldigar. One moment it was all about, as before, and the next it was clear and bright as a wandering star, moving east."

"Dantic's children are missing. His son, Tepic—one of my students—I fear it may be following the boy!"

Medellai's brow shot up.

"He has a Vessel," Voldigar added.

"Ride on!" Medellai cried.

Voldigar noticed Medellai's face in the passing lamplight. It was haggard and pale. Dark circles rimmed his eyes.

"You've taken no rest!" Voldigar said in alarm. "You've expended Virtue since we left the Sanctum! Have you watched it the entire time?"

"These are extraordinary times, Elder," Medellai shouted. "I'm just tired."

"Don't be careless, Medellai. You know better!"

"I'll be fine," Medellai said as they reined before a wide gate. Guards scrambled to open it under his brusque gestures. They bolted through and then on through the city as swiftly as they could. There were few on the streets to impede their path at this early hour, but all the same, Urias waved a great bright spear above his head and roared "Make way! Make way!" whenever a wandering townsperson looked ready to brave a crossing.

"Due east!" Medellai called out to the brothers.

Voldigar glanced at the city wall as it whipped by on his left. He could see there the postern door that he often used along the shortcut from his farm. *Due east.* Neither the land nor that small gate would be suitable for their horses and the main gate still lay some distance to the south. He grit his teeth and dug his heels to a full gallop. The rest kept pace and joined Urias, shouting "Make way! Make way!"

In minutes they were riding hard beside Aramon's great paved road as it bent slowly north, crossed the *Trakast Bridge*, and returned them to the course of Medellai's unseen beacon. With red cloaks streaming behind, soon they would crest a rise where Voldigar's farm would become visible under the moonlight. With each passing moment, he set his hope against a creeping shadow, willing Medellai to turn them from this path—silently pleading that somehow their chase would break away. They continued on, arrow-straight.

Had Tepic gone to the farm? Were they too late? He squinted into the dim light as they came over the hill. In the distance, the grove of aspens gently swayed, untroubled by the Brethren's frantic ride. A cool wind flowed over the long grass of the downs and brushed along his legs, but then he saw it. The borrowed plow, upturned and with one handle broken off, thrust like a skeletal hand into the darkness. The door of his low stone house dangled on a single hinge. The world went gray.

"No!" Voldigar bellowed and snapped the reins of the great black warhorse again and again. It grunted, and wheezed, stamped and pounded, faster and faster—white flecks of foam streaming across its proud face. He gained distance quickly on the others and burst upon his field, slowing only a little as he flung himself from the horse and rolled to his feet with his huge maul in hand.

He breathed heavily as he scanned all about in white-eyed fury. Save for the heaving of his own chest, it was quiet. He sprinted for the door.

A huge figure ducked and staggered through the frame, clutching his side just as the others arrived, dismounted, and fanned out around the farmhouse with weapons at the ready. It was Wulf.

He was a huge man. Even General Gamad would seem ordinary next to his great bulk. A shaggy mane of red-brown hair framed a wild face and an even shaggier beard. His arms were slick with blood and one eye was swollen shut. He held a hand up.

"Elder," he groaned as he staggered and sat heavily against the wall. "Head and Heart." He weakly flashed the salute.

Voldigar stopped short and knelt to his side, reaching one hand to pull the man's sweat-soaked hair from his eyes. "Is it inside?"

"No," Wulf managed through labored breaths.

"Gwenyth?"

"She's fine."

Voldigar exhaled a shaking breath and let his shoulders drop. Taro was at Wulf's side now, surveying his wounds with darting eyes.

Voldigar rose and stepped through the ruined door. Medellai stopped in the frame behind while the others searched cautiously around the outside.

Within was a chaotic scene, furniture upturned and seemingly nothing unbroken. Hobyn stood protectively in front of Gwenyth, his cudgel in hand, one arm rapidly growing purple with bruises. He wore a distant stare.

Gwenyth gasped and rushed to Voldigar, a cascade of sobs pouring out. He let his weapon fall to the ground and held her close. "I'm sorry," he said again and again into her tangled hair. "I'm sorry."

Long moments passed and Voldigar opened his eyes again. "Is Tepic here?"

"The commander's son?" Hobyn said. "No."

"Was he?"

"No, no—not since you left this morning."

Voldigar looked about in dismay, and then he saw it, a stout helm, crumpled like foil and tossed carelessly to the corner of the room. *How could I be such a fool?*

He crossed and grasped the helm in both his weathered hands. "I made these to protect the students. . . . How did I miss this?" he said quietly. The others did not answer, but Wulf was on his feet again and limped into the room.

"It was here, Brother. Big, nasty, just like before," Wulf said. "I hit it with the plow outside. Broke the bloody thing over its back but it kept coming. Got inside here when I was wrestling with it and these great big green arms came off it, like snakes. Got me good." Wulf held up his arms and then pointed at a mangled ornate cabinet on the ground.

"Would have been worse but I picked that cabinet up there and used it like a shield. I'm sorry, Brother. Looked expensive."

"It's alright, Wulf," Voldigar said softly.

"After I threw the cabinet at it, it ran off. Everybody fought real good, Elder." Wulf went on. "Even Hobyn and Gwen here." Wulf stopped short, swallowed hard, and dropped his red-rimmed eyes to the floor.

Voldigar narrowed his gaze. "What? What is it?"

Wulf made a quick shake of his head and sniffed. "There's something you need to see."

Medellai embraced his sister briefly, then closed his eyes and walked into the yard beyond. It was clear he was searching for the Orun again, reaching out with his senses. Wulf led Voldigar to the rear of the farmhouse while he stared at the ground.

"Rory fought real good too," Wulf managed to sputter before he looked away. "I got him comfortable."

A tuft of tall grass worked its way up the old stonework of the house. Voldigar slowly approached the patch and knelt. A whimper came through the weeds and then two brown paws. Rory whined and emerged from the grass, dragging two dangling legs behind him. He worked his way into Voldigar's lap, licking his hand and whimpering quietly between labored breaths.

Voldigar's hands shook and his chest tightened. Rory was struggling hard. All he could do was hold him and stroke his soft head. "It's alright, Rory—just hold still here."

Medellai came near behind him and said something, but Voldigar did not hear, for a moment forgetting the world about him. What did this poor beast do wrong? What did he know of gods and demons, of betrayal and empires? He was just a loyal friend. "Vasherk!" Voldigar cried out through blinding tears. "Vasherk!"

"You sent him with Lanathor, Brother," Medellai said quietly.

Rory whimpered again and squirmed further into Voldigar's lap. After a long sigh, he closed his eyes and then lay still.

"Rory no . . . no, no, no . . . Rory." Voldigar's shoulders sagged and then he sobbed in choking gasps, pulling Rory to his face. Hot tears dripped into his fur. Gwenyth had come beside him now and cried at his side, her head buried in his gray-streaked beard.

Medellai laid a gentle hand on Voldigar's shoulder. "We have to go, Brother. It's moving again, south and east. I'm sorry."

"I'm not leaving you again," Voldigar said to Gwenyth. "I'm staying."

"You have to, Voldigar," Gwenyth whispered back while he shook his head. "You have to keep going." She embraced him once more, then rose to her feet.

Voldigar met her eyes a moment, not knowing what to say. "Do your duty," Gwenyth said, adopting that same brave face she had so many times before.

Voldigar laid Rory in the grass and looked to the dark horizon. He felt the tears drying on his face. His eyes narrowed and he stood, sweeping his great hammer from the ground. He met Gwenyth's eyes again in a long gaze and then rushed to his horse, leaping and bolting away to fly over the plains.

The horses of Maghaltani were extraordinary, and the great black steed on whose back Voldigar leaned low was no exception. Like the shadow of a storm, they flew swiftly south and east over the hinterlands of Aramon. His enemy was ahead, and he saw only the horizon and the mountains rising above.

A lesser animal would have long since collapsed or thrown its rider, but their wills were united, and the horse's deep eyes glowed red with fire. The rumbling sound of a predator rolled from its mighty head. It would have run until it perished, but a lighter and swifter rider was soon at their side. Medellai, on an equally magnificent beast of red and brown, raced to Voldigar's flank, reaching his hand toward his brother's reins.

"Voldigar!" he cried over the pounding of their galloping hooves. "Voldigar!"

Voldigar bared his teeth, deaf to the world.

"Voldigar, you'll kill your horse! You must slow down!"

Like a man waking from a dream, Voldigar heard the cry of Elder Medellai from far away. He was right of course, and the wisdom of his words rang in his ears. Voldigar went on heedless for a moment more but then slowed to a rapid trot. He released a long and painful sigh, and the others soon overtook them.

"There are greater than ten miles yet from here to the mountains," Medellai said. "It cannot go further. We'll catch it, Voldigar. We'll catch it," he finished more quietly. His hand was on Voldigar's wrist as they rode in close formation. He emphasized each word with a shake and a hard look from his dark-rimmed eyes.

Voldigar rode in silence for another mile, collecting his thoughts and allowing Medellai to lead. It was only he after all who had any sense of where the Orun was. The rising sun was sending its glow over the mountains ahead and to their left, shining on the hills that hid the village of Pirvale behind the morning mists. Their horses breathed impetuously and heavily, but they could maintain this speed for a great while.

"It's growing," Medellai said. "Its footfalls heavier. Its reek more foul."

Lutz groaned and muttered. "Wonderful."

"What do we do when we catch it? Did you retrieve the prison?" Urias asked from the rear of the party.

"We did not," Voldigar said.

Soris sighed. "Then all is lost. We ride to our doom."

"No. What flesh it has can be destroyed, like any creature," Voldigar replied.

"But it will rise and strike again—until we are utterly spent," Urias said. "Without Liadov, what hope have we?"

Urias and Soris were no fools. Voldigar had relied on their mighty hands and keener minds to capture the Orun that once ravaged Olwis's kingdom. He could not afford despair.

"We have a little strength, Tellers—even beyond flesh. The Orun has reason to fear us," Voldigar said. He glanced at Lutz. "And our Artificer has some power of binding as well."

Voldigar took a deep breath. "You all should know, this is not the same creature we faced before." A murmur arose among the brothers until Voldigar held up his hand. "We found the Kishket. Lutz and I were in the Vaults of the Spire tonight and examined it. Yes, the Vaults are where we kept it all these long years, that no mischief would touch it. I'm sure many of you suspected."

The brethren nodded.

"The prison was secure. The chamber where we placed it, unopened since the moment I locked it. The demon we now chase is another, some foul kin."

Taro shifted uncomfortably in his saddle. "There could be more . . ."

"There could," Voldigar said, "but keep your mind to the task at hand. We found where this foe escaped. We don't know how, but we must face it all the same."

They soon came upon a long bridge of stone and wood that crossed the westward arm of the river Adionel, Aramon's central watercourse. Its rustic architecture was strong and impressive, but despite its great length, it was a small thing compared to The Great Span over the chasm before the feet of the eastern mountains. They crossed warily while Medellai went on a little ahead, still fixing his senses on their prey.

"There!" Medellai cried out and pointed. The brothers hastened to his side to peer to where his arm extended. There was a cloud of dust rising over the lowlands beyond the bridge. "There are riders, five of them, and one wears our cloak!"

They dashed forward across the fields to intercept the riders before they passed the crossroads and carried on to Arregalt. "It's Vasherk!" Medellai shouted as the distance closed. Sure enough, the wispy white hair of the Chanter was soon in view, his hood swept back and four other men riding swiftly behind him in the maroon livery of Gamad's legionnaires. Voldigar's heart gripped in fear for a moment, until he could plainly see they were not in pursuit but rode together. Vasherk and the other riders spotted the brethren and turned course toward them.

They soon came together, their horses stamping. The sky was alight with the morning sun, but not yet risen above the high peaks.

"Vasherk! What happened, where's Lanathor?" Voldigar asked.

"Well into the pass by now," Vasherk replied. "But by stealth. Westfort is taken!"

"Taken! How?"

Captain Arbed removed his helm. "By treachery, Reader. I am Captain Arbed. These are my officers."

"Voldigar, of the Brotherhood. These, my brethren," Voldigar said, as the others saluted. "And the Eastfort? Do Dantic's men still hold it?"

"Unknown. Stonepikes killed my messengers," Arbed went on, "and we knew naught of the capital, not even of the Empress. By ruse, they relieved my garrison who are marching some miles behind us. Westfort is bloodlessly in the hands of Stonepikes."

Voldigar's mind raced. Thus far their chase had in fact led them directly toward Westfort. If the Orun was pursuing Tepic, why would the boy have gone there, and to the Stonepikes? Was he for some reason seeking his father's men in Eastfort beyond? This far into the hinterlands, how could the Orun have not already caught him? It was too terrible to imagine, but perhaps it already had, had taken the sword and its strength, and now the demon was making for some further mischief in the Westfort or through the pass.

"Lanathor and I found one of Arbed's messengers, Elder, and found Arbed by chance. We are making haste to Arregalt to warn Lusánt and Gamad," Vasherk said.

"I found your men with the corpse of my soldier in the woods. You will forgive my insistence that one come with me to Arregalt," Arbed said.

"Yes, I do. Though I hope you are now satisfied at his honesty," Voldigar replied. "Vasherk, the Orun is headed toward Westfort. We can't linger."

Vasherk's eyes raised high.

Voldigar went on. "Dantic's son and daughter are missing, and we believe the Orun is pursuing the boy."

Vasherk looked about the broad plains. "All this way from the capital? Surely it would have caught him by now."

"Yes, but—"

"Voldigar," Medellai interrupted. They met eyes a moment as realization struck them both. Medellai moved toward Arbed and continued. "Captain Arbed, was the Stonepikes' leader, Lord Caliras, with them when they relieved your command?"

"No."

Of course. "He's not on foot. Caliras has Tepic!" Voldigar exclaimed.

Medellai nodded and looked off to the mountains again. "He means to escape Aramon, and the boy is his leverage . . ."

Voldigar urged his horse forward. "Captain Arbed, Godspeed to you and your legionnaires. I trust we will see you soon at Westfort. I have need of Vasherk." He locked eyes with the old man and spoke quickly. "Brother, you must make for Maghaltani with all speed. Find Gardoric, tell him everything. He must send as many as he can spare through the old mines, get between the forts, send more to the gates of Westfort."

"The old mines? They'll be hopelessly lost!" Vasherk protested.

"No, Gardoric knows the way—in part. He has to move fast and pray that Caliras isn't through the pass already."

Soris was aghast. "We cannot empty Maghaltani, Elder! The fort is work for an army, not the Brethren."

"We've no time, Soris. We risk it! Vasherk?"

The old man smiled. "I was just beginning to dream of food and a bath, Elder, but who needs it?"

Vasherk turned his horse about, Arbed bid him farewell, and the old man sped off with his cloak billowing behind.

"Onward, Brethren," Voldigar said, "and let us hope we catch Caliras before the Orun does." The Brotherhood surged forward, turning to the east.

As miles slipped behind them and the sun crept over the mountains, Voldigar grew more and more uneasy. He knew well the Orun had no love of day, but Medellai did not turn them from their course. They drove their steeds as hard as they could bear. The Orun was still moving, and they saved only enough strength for a frantic burst were battle to be joined. The air was chill, yet warming rapidly under a clear and sunny sky. Even the distant isles of the Ekhebiri could be seen, small and remote, drifting along their skyward course.

The Brethren continued on a path east and south, well above the main road. Medellai would sometimes slow and lean his head so low it dipped behind the shoulder of his huge warhorse. Satisfied with a scent or sound, he picked up speed again. They would adjust here and there, but their path led always toward the Span and the Westfort beyond.

Today, of all days, the blossoms of cherry trees chose to bloom. The tight buds of their delicate white flowers silently watched the passing of the Order. In the hinterlands north of the road, the forest was long since cleared, but these cherries remained, sacred and untouched. As the Brothers swiftly passed a tight row of them, Medellai reared and thrust his finger forward. "There, it's a body!"

The six riders charged forward and saw not one grizzly scene, but two. At their feet were the husk of a horse and a man in a gray cloak. Flies buzzed around the gore. They were drained of blood and their skin looked like rotted cloth. Not forty yards ahead, the same scene was repeated.

Taro dismounted quickly and examined the bodies. "*Blooded.* Even their animals." He prodded at one with the end of his staff. "It was thorough, took its time."

Voldigar jumped down and stood beside him, still holding the reins of his horse. "That's a lot of blood . . ."

"And it's catching horsemen at this point," Medellai added. "It's growing stronger. Much stronger. And look here." He gestured left and right. "There were at least a dozen riders that passed through. They gave battle."

"And fled quickly," Taro concluded.

The horses whinnied nervously and stamped side to side. Voldigar gave one last grimacing look at the horror and wound the reins in his fist. "Gather your strength, Brothers of Aramon. We are about to be tested."

They mounted again and hurried forward over the rolling hills of the sparsely populated land that neared the Great Chasm and its mighty span. It seemed with every cresting hill, they found again the handiwork of the Orun. Stonepikes and mounts, mangled and emptied.

"They were in a flight of madness here. Full gallop," Medellai said to the others.

It occurred to Voldigar as they went on that each of these Stonepikes had served alone as some twisted form of a hopeless rearguard, whether they chose it or no. The Orun, stopping to *feed* would give the others a vain hope for breathless minutes until it caught them again. Wicked men, though they seemed, they were soldiers, and they did the will of their lord. He pitied them. Would they ever properly be buried? It was a relief that among the horrific displays, they had still not seen the red hair of a foolish boy.

As they neared the edge of the hinterlands, the land rose more sharply, and a loose wood lined the crest of a final hillock. There, two pine trees were splintered, their mighty trunks cracked and tossed aside. Through that gap they rode and looked on below. They could hear the distant rumble of the river Haroel, echoing in the chasm ahead. The Great Span soared over it and narrowed into the distance through a billowing cloud of morning mist and river spray. Near its center, three horsemen charged on in panic.

Voldigar blinked in the shimmering reflection of the cloud upon the river canyon. At first, it seemed nothing more than refraction, a streak of sunlight in the air. But as his eyes took hold of what lay ahead, a crashing terror burst from the fog to shake the very stone of the Span.

The creature was twice the height of Voldigar's huge warhorse and ran heavily balanced on its massive forelimbs. Like a great ape from Olwis's menagerie, but thrice its size. Cobblestone cracked and scattered through the air under its bulk. Eyeless, its head could be made out only by a wide maw of hideous teeth. A wild plume of green fire streamed behind it, flickering from the towers that lined The Great Span. No longer dim and ghostly, its body was opaque and rippled with sinew. The lead rider was upon a great horse, most similar to Voldigar's. Between his arms, a small figure jostled from side to side, a sack over his head.

"Now!" cried Voldigar.

The Brethren plunged down the slope holding fast to their mounts. They knew the will of their riders and bounded in great leaps, eager for the danger ahead. Whispers of the Scriptures flowed from the mouths of the Chanters while the eyes of the Tellers grew distant and they searched their memories. Lutz brought up the rear, pulling an array of devices from hidden packs, fixing them upon his arms and wrists, and gripping a stout chain that he swung in wide circles.

They had not gone far when the horse of the rearmost Stonepike screamed and buckled in exhaustion. Its front legs gave way and the rider was tossed, soaring and flailing through the air. His gray cloak was torn from his body, and he skidded violently along the bridge's edge. Miraculously, he was on his feet a moment later, fleeing in his terror.

The Orun paused only long enough to grasp the horse by its frothing head and toss it from the bridge. It had fed enough, and its prize lay ahead on the lead horse. Moments later, it reached the fleeing Stonepike and caught him up in its arms. Running awkwardly on its hind legs for a few steps, it rent the man apart, gore spattering across its own hideous flesh. On it went in flaming fury, bellowing in gruesome speech.

The feet of the mountains came nearly to the Span, and the two remaining horsemen made for a sharp fold beyond which the gates of Westfort lay. There the road began to climb again, and the progress of the two slowed under the flagging strength of their exhausted horses. The Orun was gaining fast upon them as it passed the lip of the bridge. The brethren were now not far behind and gaining even faster still.

Soon all were rounding the shoulder of the mountain. The horse of the trailing Stonepike began to stumble, but rather than be thrown headlong, this rider slowed and slid from the animal's back. He grasped a long spear from the saddle just as the horse collapsed and rolled onto its side. He whirled to face the Orun. A flowing banner of the Stonepikes, a great golden spear driven into a quarried block of marble upon a gray field, unfurled from the long weapon as he set his feet.

The Orun rushed on heedless and raised one of its great forelimbs to strike. The arm was pierced through, but then it jerked the weapon from the man's hand and burst it into shards upon the hard earth. The Stonepike drew a shining cavalry sword and tried to step around the creature's vicious onslaught, but its movements were too swift, its violence too great. In an instant, the man was broken upon the earth, and only his master went on with Tepic, the warhorse scrambling and lurching up the hill.

Men were now upon the walls of the fortress that loomed ahead, and their distant cries echoed down the gorge. They were raising the gate slowly as Caliras sped on. Opening the gate before the charging Orun was a rash act of great foolishness, but it was also the only hope that Tepic and his abductor would have to avoid being dashed upon the walls of Westfort.

The brethren dug their heels into their steeds and leaned low over their steaming backs. The cool mountain air rushed in their ears, but not so loud that they could not hear the roaring call of the Orun, seeking the power of Tepic's sword. Caliras's horse bolted through the gate, and with a clatter and a crash, the portcullis fell heavily to the ground, its iron teeth locked in place. Unslowed, the demon smashed into it. The walls shuddered, a cloud of dust sprayed into the air, and the groan of metal rang against the face of the mountains—but the gate held.

The brethren sped on and fanned out in a wide half-circle as they advanced. The creature reared up in terrible height and brought its two arms down together against the iron bars. Some bent and popped, sparks flying into the air.

"Orun!" Voldigar cried as he neared at a full gallop. So close to the walls, there would be no charge of cavalry. He coiled, gripped his mighty maul in both hands, and sprang from his horse. "Be gone from our world!"

<hr />

Voldigar felt a great blast of heat wash over him, like the door of a furnace flung open in his face. His hammer flashed in an arc of steel over his head as he crashed into the Orun. The weapon sank into the creature's back with the willow crack of new-formed bone and a thud of putrid flesh.

No longer held in great breaths of wary tension, its green tendrils shot forth in an instant, wrapping around the haft of the maul and both of Voldigar's arms like a squid. He wrenched in alarm, leaning away from the creature and driving hard with both legs. Its muscles tore with a snap and writhing tendrils tumbled to the earth in a wet heap upon Voldigar as he struck the ground with his back.

The Orun bellowed and whirled to crush this new threat, but the brethren—now dismounted—were upon it from every side. Urias's shining spear burst alight in a billow of orange flame and black smoke. A huge curling tongue of fire shot forth from it and engulfed the torso of the beast, battling with its own pallid green light. No sooner was it struck than the long shaft of one arrow and then another sank into its body—fired from the great longbow Medellai drew again and again.

Taro came near with *Skullcrusher* in hand, and it was toward him the creature leapt aside with a trail of flashing flame scorching the very air about it. After its gorging horror upon the hinterlands, it suddenly knew fear again and lashed wildly with its huge limbs. Taro caught its force and held fast to one of the creature's gigantic arms. It tried to lift him from the ground with a great heave, but Taro let go and it staggered. In that opening, he struck again and again with his stout staff. Gore and detritus sprayed with every blow.

It regained balance and brought its two hands together in a thunderous clap. Taro ducked at the last second, but the creature came on in a roar, its mouth wide and teeth slavering. It brought the head-like appendage down upon him as if to swallow him whole, but Taro thrust the staff upright into its maw. The weapon, his own Chanter's Vessel, held fast and the Orun could not crush it. The fiend jerked wildly from side to side, smashing its jaw against Taro's face, tearing the cloak from off his back, and leaving a streak of blood from the crown of his head to the hem of his brown tunic.

Voldigar had come to his feet now and worked a mighty sidelong hammer-blow into the back of the creature's knee. Its leg buckled and it thrashed away from Taro, whirling another massive arm that caught Voldigar full in the chest, flinging him like a toy into the wall of Westfort. He felt the air shoot from his lungs and the bones of his body compress and rebound, but yet he lived, and the Chants of his Scriptures echoed in his mind and on his lips.

The others leapt away of their own accord, for now the men of the fort leaned over the walls and let fly a barrage of arrows, heedless of whom they might strike. The Orun wrapped its arms about itself as few of the shafts struck home and more deflected harmlessly like so much kindling. It roared again and shot forth a thin tentacle like a snake uncoiling over the lip of the wall. Grabbing one of the archers, it tore him from his perch and smashed the hapless man against the gates as if to batter them open. The others cowered behind their battlements and shot no more.

Voldigar felt the air rush into his lungs again. Ignoring the pain, he charged forward in the same instant as Urias and Taro. Soris stood a short distance away in deep concentration, a strange coil of shimmering blue light swirling between his hands and crackling along the beryl rings upon his arms. Lutz spun the heavy chain he held and inched closer while Medellai loosed one arrow after another.

The Orun, rocked by each dart as it disappeared into its body, squared itself against the attackers and fixed its aim upon Medellai. Forward it burst in fury, looking as though it would crush Urias and blaze past Voldigar and Taro in a streak of green fire. The two mighty Chanters dropped their weapons as one and grasped the Orun's arms from either side, pulling downward in desperate struggle. It was strong, so very strong, and Voldigar and Taro could not wrestle long against this titan.

Upward Urias thrust his flaming spear into the belly of the twisted giant. His skin fissured and cracked in glowing red embers as the Orun's vile energies washed over him and he turned all his will to send forth the Teller's fire through his weapon. Flame licked upon its monstrosity, searing too the brothers that held it fast, but the Orun continued to struggle forward, slowly wrenching free its arms.

"Now!" Voldigar shouted. "Now!"

A blast of frigid air and ice poured out from Soris's outstretched hands in a brilliant glow of otherworldly blue, crystallizing the air between him and the Orun. Urias yanked his spear free, dropped to his belly, and rolled aside just as the hexagonal structure engulfed the Orun. It slowed and writhed with a piercing howl, yet still it came on. Voldigar and Taro leapt aside, and

Lutz let fly the chain he had carried all this way. It wrapped full around the wreckage of the beast's chest, pulsed in a violet glow, and with a sound like the swarming of bees constricted.

Lutz hurled a stave, joined to the other end of the chain, into the ground, and a tremendous burst of brimstone and spraying sparks knocked him to his back several feet away. The chain disappeared into the earth below and yanked taut against the Orun. The brute fell to its knees, the chain loosened for a second, but then grew taut again.

For a feeble moment, the Orun reared back and grasped at the restraint. It only constricted further, and the shambling atrocity tumbled wholly to the earth.

It was then a sound emerged like the scraping of a great steel plate against the bones of the world. Shrill and ghastly, all else was engulfed in the roaring whine of its terror. The brethren clutched their ears, and a furious wind blew past them, tearing at their hands and faces with debris—sweeping dust into a swirling miasma. The Orun crumpled and grew smaller, the whirlwind larger.

There was a great crash, a clap of thunder, the sky went dark, and the sun vanished in a burst of deep shadow. For an instant, as though night, they could see even the green moon high above upon the roof of the world, and then a towering pillar of dust and flame swept into the sky. The dread of it grew until it might overwhelm their minds, and then, like a ripple on the water, it ceased. The frightful clamor echoed away along the jagged peaks of the mountains. The sky lit again with the light of the sun. The cyclone of dust drifted off. What remained of the Orun's body gathered in a heap like quicksilver, collapsed into a hissing pool, and vanished.

The brethren slowly rose to their feet and unstopped their ears. As they gathered their weapons, a whisper and a breath of mocking laughter lingered on the air. Medellai staggered forward looking back and forth and reaching with his hands.

Voldigar sped to his side. "Where is it, Brother? Where has it gone?"

Medellai continued to walk forward. "I can't sense it, Brother. . . . I can't see it anywhere."

"You're sure?" Voldigar asked urgently.

Medellai peered at the ground and then into the sky for a long while. "I . . . I don't see anything, Voldigar."

"Anything?" Voldigar asked. He stepped in front of Medellai, placing two hands upon his shoulders.

The Elder lifted his face to Voldigar. Where once there were green eyes and the deep pupils of a learned man, there were now only two yellow pools and the narrow slits of feral eyes. "I cannot see, Brother."

Chapter Ten

A Sun in Winter

THE SUN ROSE SOONER beyond the eastern side of the high pass of Aramon, and it was nearing mid-morning. Here, the narrow way opened wide onto the thirteen provinces of the Baerdermyrch beyond. Lanathor surveyed the lands ahead. Snow gave way and Spring continued unabated in the wide fields of Kurath and gentle hills of Tituria below. But it was to the north that Lanathor must go, and the highlands of Danek still held their frost. He pulled his furs about him and trudged forward while the wind blew a haze of snow across his brow.

The passage he had made through Westfort in the hours before dawn had little incident. The Stonepikes were indeed warily watching the road, and from along the parapets they had surely seen his approach. Pouring into the muddy path before its gates and waving their torches from side to side, it mattered little. Lanathor had already pulled upon the threads of the Song and passed through both of the stout walls that barred the road. The effort left him heaving in a grove of pines, but he was unharmed and beyond their grasp.

There would be no rest in Westfort as he had hoped. Instead, he was forced to ascend into the steep four-mile climb between forts in frigid darkness. Snow blanketed the ground, and despite Vasherk's aid, the wounds of his battle with the Orun ached in the cold. Those were the last gloomy hours before sunrise, and he remembered little. His mind drifted to dark thoughts and darker memories while he took comfort in a piece of the fresh root he'd found along the trail from Maghaltani. It was near the last of his supply.

Eastfort, he'd found to his relief, was still in the possession of Dantic's guard. Apart from the city, his men had watched the eastern approach of the pass for many years. It was a much larger fortification than Westfort and held three times the garrison—always wary of the Border Princes that only grudgingly made Aramon an "Empire." The soldiers were brusque and skeptical, but they allowed his passage. He could only hope that they had taken heed of his warnings too.

The trek into Danek would take him into early afternoon. He would first have to climb one more steep shoulder of the mountains and then descend a little into the high valley of the province. It was a shame Vasherk was made to turn back, for this was his home as a boy. His kin would have no doubt been more amenable to aid him than one tall Azkushan wandering alone in the winter sun.

Lanathor was jolted from his thoughts by the sudden peal of something like thunder many miles behind. He spun about and peered into the sky, but it was clear. The sound continued to echo and reverberate over the mountains, and to his astonishment, the sky went dark above him. For an instant, he could see even the great green moon almost directly overhead. There was another burst of thunder, then a great pillar of lightning shot over the crowns of the western mountains. As quickly as it came, it passed, and the sky was lit with daylight once again. A moment later, a great gust of wind bent the trees and blew his hood from off his head—and then it was over. All was still.

Lanathor stared into the distance for a long while, wondering what madness would come next, but nothing did. It was surely another sign—another harbinger of what Liadov foretold. What had happened in Aramon? How fared the Brotherhood? Two thoughts wrestled in his mind. The one nearly compelled his feet to sprint all the way back through the pass, but the other urged him on. Liadov would know. She had to be found. She had to return.

The long valley of Danek lay hidden among the mountains. It was riven through by many tumbling rivers in steep ravines, and its farmlands wound about them where Danek snaked along the eastern edge of the peaks. All was blanketed by snow, and Lanathor had passed imperceptibly over its borders some hours before.

He was so very tired, and glad that few of the locals seemed to notice him at all. For the most part, they stayed huddled in their low stone dwellings where wood and peat smoke rose in hundreds of twirling plumes. More than once, as he passed a settlement, men wordlessly followed him at a distance and then broke away, satisfied that he was beyond whichever humble village they called home.

As afternoon set in, he found the head of the trail which he sought. A winding path climbed into the mountains at his left, over the face of many treacherous cliffs and switchbacks. At the end of it, he knew, lay *Dizghizádè*. The Oracle of the Sun.

He found for himself a sturdy length of rowan wood at the foot of this trail and made his way slowly toward the top, tapping the staff at each switchback. He clung closely to the stony wall wherever the track narrowed and opened to the sky, and he moved swiftly whenever it closed again in a canopy of thick growing fir and juniper that thrust from the steep flanks of the mountain.

As he neared the end of his path, the air grew strangely warm, and he heard the sounds of waterfalls and gentle, splashing streams. Lanathor pulled back his fur-lined hood and looked about in wonder.

Here, high in the mountains, was a many-tiered garden with wide lawns of green and broad-leafed trees. It was as warm as the lowlands of Aramon, and steam rose from bubbling pools that flowed in many rivulets to small underground passages or into tumbling waterfalls over the edge of the mountain. All about were white and gold blossoms, or even leaves of the same hues. Among this natural beauty were many golden-domed shrines, some enclosed, but most on delicate pillars of white in a receding landscape of marble.

The whole edifice opened wide to the east, but the afternoon sun, now passing beyond the mountains, caught only the tops of trees in hazy golden beams while the lower part of the garden was painted in long shadows.

There were guards in white robes with curved Daneki blades upon their waists, but they paid no heed to Lanathor. A group of votaries, also in white and with their eyes covered, were descending the steps of marble daises from further back in the garden, making their way to him.

"We've been expecting you, Elder Lanathor," one of the women said. "And you are fortunate, for the Lady is not sleeping today."

A petal from one of the blossoms blew past Lanathor's face and smelled of plums. He did not know what the trees were and lamented that he'd come too early for their fruit. Winter clung to Danek over the mountain's lip behind, and a tender hush pulled his heart ahead. In years past, the enigmatic Liadov had endured many of her "sleeps," sometimes for weeks on end. She never unraveled this riddle for the Brethren, and they soon abandoned their asking. Here within the idyllic haven of Dizghizádè, Lanathor wondered if he too might like to sleep for a week.

They led him on a wandering path of small bridges, steadily ascending the garden toward the largest dome, covering a dais of many steps. It was deep in the shadow of the mountain but lit by soft lamps that hung on shimmering strands. The votaries stopped and let him walk the rest of the way on his own.

As he approached, a tall woman in a long white garment gathered about her waist turned from the shadows. Her sandaled feet glided silently over the stone, and from a circlet upon her brow, close-set strings of crystal hung over her eyes. Pulling back her hood, a cascade of white-gold hair fell about her shoulders. It was worked through with gilded threads and shining gems. A light seemed to glow about her.

Lanathor quietly laid his rowan staff on the earth and bowed low upon his knees, bringing his face to the ground while the woman descended the steps.

"See you do it not, Lanathor. A Brother of Aramon does not kneel, save to God only. His honor," she said.

He brought his face up from the ground. "Honor God, Sister Liadov."

She turned back and ascended gracefully over the steps. Lanathor could now see that a small spring bubbled up from the center of the dais and flowed down the stairs in tiny channels. It danced playfully away from her footfalls. "Walk with me," she said softly and exited the far end of the shrine.

Lanathor hurried to her side, and they walked silently into a dim and narrow path that wound its way through mossy cliffs. The air was cooler here, and the twisting stalks of tiny trees pushed from every crack, thickly bearing small, round, deep-green leaves. All about them, glowing insects in pale blue and gold floated lazily from branch to branch.

"Even here in the dark, these little ones bear the light of Tetrimázè," Liadov said as a golden insect alighted upon her finger and folded its wings.

Lanathor had forgotten his weariness and his quest. He stared at the glowing creature a long while and circled through his memories of the sun's strange name. It was not custom anymore, and odd to hear it on her lips. He did not know what to say.

"You still find it strange that I have made my dwelling here," she said.

Lanathor blinked and considered her words. Many steps further, he finally spoke. "I do," he admitted. "The votaries, the priests—long have they forgotten God. They worship the creature and not the creator."

"I care nothing for their worship, Brother, nor their idols, whether sun or moon, wood or stone. Can I not bring the worship of God here? Did he not create all things?"

"God's honor," Lanathor replied quickly, searching for her eyes behind the veil. "Yet you are all alone, Sister."

"Am I?" She smiled and continued walking. "How long have I been here, Lanathor?"

He blinked again in surprise as she awaited his answer. "Six . . . maybe seven years."

She made a soft noise in the back of her mouth. "Have I? And how is our father?"

"Father?" Lanathor squinted and tilted his head. "What do you mean?"

Liadov laughed brightly. It seemed in harmony with the small stream that trickled between them while they walked. "Our names, Lanathor. Voldigar gave you yours as well as mine, did he not?"

Lanathor hazarded a laugh as well. It had been twenty years, a lifetime ago. "Oh, the Eldest you mean. He's well—well enough, and very fond of the letter 'L.' I suppose I never realized."

Liadov laughed again. "Earthly fathers have we few, and too little of their love. I am glad this one is well."

Lanathor nodded as he thought of his friend and how he fared in Aramon. Liadov's riddle seemed to carry some deeper meaning, but the moment of levity and an image of a younger Voldigar in his mind brought his musing back to the earth.

"Things have been different, since you . . . you . . ."

"Since I left?"

"Yes. I'm sure you heard rumors. It wasn't well for him, Liadov. Not at all. Gwenyth was the final blow. He was . . . lost, and penniless. The Brethren pooled together what we could, bought him a little plot of land." Lanathor smiled. "Even a dog."

"I had heard no rumors, save for whispers on the wind."

Lanathor caught her eyes briefly behind the veil. "Gwenyth nearly died, Sister—while he was away. She's never recovered, and right or wrong, he blames himself every day."

A flicker of emotion crossed Liadov's shrouded face as she turned her gaze back to the stream.

"We urged him into retirement, as gently as we could. After everything else, it was time. And it *was* better, Liadov, for a while . . ."

Lanathor suddenly remembered his purpose, but his thoughts tangled one over the other as he considered how he might communicate to Liadov. All that he had rehearsed along the way now seemed profane in her presence. All was trite and banal. To speak the name 'Orun' seemed worst of all.

"I know why you have come," Liadov said, stealing back his attention. "The enemy is freed again and you are afraid."

Lanathor's eyes darted about the pathway. "Yes . . . yes it is. But the Order is strong. It's not that we fear it. It hides itself, and even Medellai cannot find it. We have tried to draw it out, but it will not show itself."

"I know the Order is strong. What I said is that I know why *you* have come, Lanathor. You are afraid that I will not return."

A weight fell upon Lanathor's chest, like a stone dropped into the waves. He subconsciously reached for the last piece of root in the folds of his robes, but Liadov gently grasped his hand before he could. Her eyes still obscured, she turned her face to his. "Lanathor."

He responded hurriedly. "Sister, it grows stronger with every passing hour. It must be brought back to its prison. If Medellai cannot find it, our hope will soon vanish. You can find it. I know you can."

"Lanathor," she repeated. "You will find a way—but my part in these matters is long past."

"But what of your prophecies, Liadov?" he asked. "The portents, they have begun!"

"What of them?" Liadov asked. "Can I hurt you anymore? What have my words brought but death?"

"You gave us hope, Sister!"

Liadov gently shook her head. "I gave you light when you had need. That is all. Shall I give you darkness as well?"

Lanathor felt his heart give way as she gripped his hand tighter. "Give us the words of God, Liadov. Light or darkness. We would have truth. You cannot defy the one who sits upon the throne of the whole earth."

"No," Liadov said. "No, I cannot. But shall I be the one to hurt *you* again? Shall this doom pass through *my* hands?"

Lanathor's body shook, and he dared one trembling hand slowly toward the crystal strings upon her face. Gently, he brushed them aside, swallowed hard, and looked into her deep blue eyes. "Do this for me, Sister."

"I stay, for all of you, Lanathor."

Lanathor released a deep sigh and looked into the stream dividing their feet. "At the setting of the sun then, join me in the gardens. Let me speak to you one last time before I go."

———◆———

As evening hastened on, Lanathor made his way to the terrace atop a broad temple that graced the garden's center. Its marble columns were bathed in waning crimson from a sun that would soon dip below the sea somewhere beyond the mountains behind him. He busily went about assembling his small telescope, pointing it to the east. Once satisfied, he sat upon the roof and produced a marvel of Lutz's craft—a small clock, no bigger than his hand.

He lamented the clumsiness of his earlier speech. Liadov had unraveled his mind and purpose before he'd barely spoken a word. He felt his hope and the confidence of his quest slipping away. Everything he'd thought to say came tumbling out in the worst possible way. He laughed ruefully. An instructor of rhetoric, bumbling like a child. He would not be so careless this time.

Liadov was a learned woman. In countless years past, they had often gazed at the night sky, sometimes joined by Soris, and sometimes all alone. While neither she nor Soris held all the numbers in their minds as he, she was no novice and would surely understand what he would show her.

As the shadows deepened, Liadov softly made her way beside him and sat. They did not speak for a long while, but together stared into the darkness as it spread from a distant horizon and enveloped the sky.

When the last glow of sunlight had disappeared, Liadov removed the circlet from her head and gently placed it beside her.

"I've never known your true name," Lanathor said.

Liadov smiled in the dim light of a few lamps lit below. "Nor have I, Lanathor. And I'm glad of it." Before he could question her further she went on. "I have never known yours either."

Lanathor laughed softly. "My true name is Lanathor," he said. "And I too am glad of it. I know the other, but just because it's older, that doesn't make it true."

"At some point it does," Liadov replied, "but 'L's we shall remain."

Lanathor smiled and turned to her. There was not a hint upon her face that years had passed. "It would be good to have you back in Aramon, troubles or no," he said.

"Trouble is all I would bring, Brother."

"But these things will be, whether you are there or not, Sister."

"Will they? I sense we are repeating ourselves," Liadov said. "I much prefer to watch the stars with you."

Lanathor bit his tongue, and they stayed in silence for a while longer until the first stars shimmered through the veil of night.

"I believe God, Lanathor," Liadov said at length. "Do not mistake my choice for faithlessness."

"But do you believe in his *goodness,* Liadov?"

"Does the sun rise in the east?" She asked.

Lanathor pressed on. "Do you believe he will redeem those things he brings about?"

"I—" Liadov caught herself short. The question lingered on the air.

Lanathor was surprised to see tears running down her cheeks, but she did not reply. Instead, she fixed her gaze upon some distant point of the horizon and returned to silence. Long minutes passed before she closed her eyes and placed the circlet on her brow again. She looked as though she would rise to her feet.

"Liadov, I—"

A brilliant flash of green shot across the eastern horizon, once and again, illuminating the dark forest at the valley floor. For a breath, the night was pitch, and then the streaks of green light returned, faster and faster until they were a pulsing flicker on the distant peaks. The two stared on in hushed wonder, but then, like a dragon of old bursting from its lair, a huge moon rose, swift and full—engorged to twice its size, menacing the feeble earth below. Lanathor's mouth dropped open and he scrambled to his feet, snatching the small clock into his hand.

"It cannot be!" he cried. He placed his eye to the telescope. His hands were a flurry of corrections and adjustments. "It's far too early. The discrepancies, they were minor, I had only seen—"

Liadov cut him off with a hand upon his shoulder. She moved the telescope away from his eye and the circlet from her brow—her face drawn in terror as she watched the horizon. "This was no Orun, Lanathor." She pointed into the distance where the lights had returned and gathered until they outshone even the gleaming moon above them. A crackling wave of green fire coiled and surged forward, swiftly cascading over the highlands beyond the valley, tearing trees a thousand feet into the sky and gathering into a great column. It gained speed as it rose and turned directly toward them.

"Flee!" Liadov cried, but Lanathor stood transfixed. The portents had come, and now he was helpless. A reed before the fury of a crashing sea.

Chapter Eleven

Bound for the Darkness

Someone shoved Tepic to the floor. His hands were bound and a burlap sack still over his head. He turned his face so as not to strike his nose on the stones and scraped his chin against the sack instead. There he lay a while in darkness. It smelled like a dank cellar, complete with incessant dripping.

When, by the riverbank, the sack had first been placed over his head, he thought he might suffocate. With time, breathing became easier, though his throat was hoarse from the fibers of the bag. It was his legs that really hurt. A jostling ride with hands tied, over who knows how many miles, left him aching. He shifted his legs back and forth, trying to get comfortable and trying to forget the screams of dying men he'd heard during their mad flight. It didn't help that a great clamor and crash continued to echo dully through the walls. It seemed like it would go on forever, but then abruptly ceased.

In the quiet, he awkwardly struggled to a seated position and tried to hold back his trembling tears. He felt foolish and ashamed, but what did it matter here, alone in the dark?

"Who's there?" a woman's voice called out in a sharp whisper.

Tepic flinched and held still.

"I can hear you breathing," she went on.

"Lyrusia?" Tepic asked.

"Tepic?"

"Yes! It's me!"

"Tepic! How did you—"

"I was trying to get Grandpa's sword out of the house, and I swam out of a drain, and Stonepikes found me, and—"

"Me too!" Lyrusia said. "Well not the part about the sword and the drain, but they got me outside the Spire! What about Grandpa's sword?"

"It's magic! Where are we anyway?"

"Westfort."

A door groaned and dim light glowed through the sack. Shadows flickered across his vision.

"Keep your mouths shut!" a voice snarled. The door slammed.

They fell silent for some time, but Tepic's heart soared to know his sister sat there in the dark with him. Why was *she* here? They stumbled around in the blackness as quietly as they could until they bumped into each other and sat.

"My hands are tied," Tepic whispered.

"Mine too," Lyrusia whispered back. She squeezed in closer and rested her chin on his head. "What do you suppose all that noise was?"

"It's the Brotherhood," Tepic replied. "They're fighting."

"Like a siege?" Lyrusia asked.

"No. They're fighting the Orun."

Lyrusia was silent at the wicked name. When she spoke again, Tepic noticed how small and tired she sounded. "That's the thing that attacked the Emperor, isn't it?"

"You saw it too?" Tepic whispered back. His voice was louder than he intended, and they both fell quiet.

At length, she finally responded. "No, I didn't see it. But it wrecked everything in the royal apartments, and all the nobles acted like nothing happened. I'm glad you're alright, Tep."

"You believe I saw it though, right?"

"Of course I do."

The door groaned, again and heavy feet thumped across the floor. "I thought I said to be quiet!"

Tepic heard one sharp thump and then felt a smack on the back of his head. It didn't really hurt, but he still felt stinging tears well up in his eyes.

"Why do we need them both?" another voice asked.

The first voice cursed. "How should I know?"

One more groan and the door slammed again. The room went dark.

"Why are we here, Ru?" Tepic whispered as softly as he could. He felt for his sister with his shoulder and squirmed closer again.

"I don't know, Tep." His name echoed briefly off the stone walls and faded into the quiet of their dreary cell. In time, the dripping filled his ears again until Lyrusia spoke once more. "We're going to be alright. We just have to be brave." She leaned her head back into his.

"I love you, sis," he whispered.

"Love you too."

For a while, they did sit obediently, soundless in the black. Tepic's mind wandered, and once again he thought of his grandfather's sword. He wondered what terrible purpose drove the creature to chase them all the way through the hinterlands. He had no answers. *Who were you, Grandfather? How did you get this thing . . . and how do I get it back?*

Tepic had not realized where they were until Lyrusia told him. He shuddered to imagine all the burnt-out farms and villages the Orun must have left along the miles between Arregalt and Westfort.

Perhaps an hour had passed when the door swung open again. "Get up," a man demanded roughly. Tepic shuffled out the door on stiff legs and could hear Lyrusia close behind. He stumbled blindly through winding halls and up cold stairways, pushed and pulled. Lyrusia breathed heavily beside, her feet tripping along. Soon he could feel a breeze, and then the cold touch of steel against his neck. When the bag was finally removed, he blinked and squinted in the sunlight.

"Call off your dogs, Commander Dantic!" Caliras yelled from right behind him. Tepic winced. They were high above the gate. He gave a jerk on Tepic's forehead and pressed the knife against his throat.

As his eyes adjusted, Tepic could see sidelong a crowd of brethren below in their red cloaks, standing by a long row of magnificent horses. His sword-lector was among them. Besides these, there were his father and two dozen other riders. All in blue, they were still mounted and stamped nervously side to side. Their horses nickered and wheezed.

"Tepic!" Dantic cried out. "So help me, Caliras. We'll tear down every stone of the Westfort!"

"You're not dictating terms, Dantic!"

To his right, Tepic saw another man in gray shuffle forward with his sister, similarly held at the edge of a knife. A cry went up from below.

"Let them go!" Dantic roared.

"Back up! All of you," Caliras yelled, "or we loose arrows!"

Lines of soldiers with bows gathered along the walls to either side. The men below retreated several steps.

"What do you want, Caliras?" Voldigar shouted.

"Nothing from you, Voldigar!" Caliras replied. "Dantic Banari! Give me passage through the Eastfort, me and all my men. I want out of this hellhole of a kingdom!"

Dantic leapt down from his horse. "You are a fugitive from the crown. You cannot leave!"

Caliras gave another jerk to Tepic's head and pressed the knife closer. "Can't I? Do you care for the lives of your little rats!"

"Stay your hand!" Dantic cried. It was quiet for several moments. Tepic could only hear the wavering breaths of his sister. They caught each other's eyes, and she nodded a little, as reassuringly as she could.

"I don't need them both," Caliras said. "Shall I demonstrate?"

"No!" Dantic bellowed, his voice hoarse. "Stop! I'll do as you say. I'll take you through." He heaved a sigh. "We'll pass through the walls of Eastfort, but then—you must give me my children."

"You're seeing reason."

"I will have guarantees, Caliras."

"Oh? How so?"

"I bring ten men with me. The moment we pass the eastern gates, you turn my children over."

"Ten? To stab me in the back?" Caliras called down. "I think not! If you're so lonely, bring two—unarmed. A nursemaid for each of your rats when they get tired. Your soldiers in the Eastfort will lay down their weapons too, until we're miles past. Then, and only then, do I send your whelps back."

There was a murmur among the men below, but Dantic unstrapped his sword with a grimace. He tossed it to a rider along with his gloves and gestured to one of his men who similarly disarmed. This soldier's jaw was crooked and his eyes hollow, a twisted face set in the permanent snarl of a man who'd seen too much of war. Blue livery bulged over his torso, and even weaponless, he looked like he might breach the gate with his bare hands.

Dantic scanned his riders for a second volunteer, but it was Lector Voldigar who stepped forward, laying his weapons on the ground. "Take me."

"Not you, Anteres!" Caliras yelled. "Go home."

Voldigar paused and looked as though he would reply, but a tall, heavyset man with curly black hair and a brown tunic hastened to his side. The man looked wounded, with blood upon his face and shirt, and had a mild manner about him. For a moment, it seemed to Tepic that silent words passed between his lector and the bloodied man. Voldigar scowled, but then with a nod the other man gave him his huge staff and walked forward with hands raised. Dantic narrowed his eyes, but he and his sergeant mimicked the man's pose and walked with him toward the gate.

Caliras appraised the wounded man briefly but this time did not object. Instead, he fixed his gaze on the grizzled soldier by Dantic's side. He eyed him for several seconds with a frown before he called out again. "Sorry, Dantic. Not this brute. Anteres—send me your pet mokja there instead."

Dantic looked about in alarm. There was indeed a mokja there, standing among the brethren, all in black with a strange device over his eyes. Pointed ears swept back behind the straps of the contraption, and thick black tufts of hair ran down the sides of his broad face. He too seemed to pass silent words with Voldigar, then dropped a broad-bladed dagger from his belt and waddled forward. There was an argument Tepic couldn't hear, but in a moment the mokja had replaced his father's man.

"Wonderful," Caliras spat. "These chaperons are more to my liking. I'll have spears in your backs the whole way. If you so much as flinch, I gore you like pigs, bleed Dantic's rats, and find my own way out of Aramon."

"Enough, Caliras! On my honor," Dantic said. "I'll bring you through Eastfort unharmed. Once you're beyond, you let us go. Then, you never return to Aramon."

"That would be my great pleasure, Commander. You're all as good as dead anyway."

Tepic caught one final glimpse of his father's men with Voldigar and his order as he and Lyrusia were dragged from the high perch atop Westfort's stout gatehouse. His sword-lector looked him directly in the eye with a shallow nod of the head before he lost sight of him. It was a subtle gesture, but he felt as though the old man was silently speaking to him too. *Be brave.* He heard the portcullis slam back into place.

In a courtyard below, men in gray were gathered all about, perhaps a hundred in total. Most held spears, and some had heavy packs hung upon their shoulders. Others were busily checking Dantic and the two brethren for weapons. Many more packs were lined against a wall.

"Don't touch," the mokja said sharply as a Stonepike reached toward the goggles on his eyes. "I'm blind without them."

The soldier looked questioningly at Caliras who had just come into the courtyard. "Leave him alone. We need the mokja to see," Caliras said.

Dantic caught sight of Caliras and his prisoners. "Tepic, Lyrusia! Everything's alright. This will all be over soon. Do as you're told and keep moving."

"That's right." Caliras released his grip on Tepic for a moment and adjusted the dirty brace he wore on his hand. Tepic looked suspiciously about, wondering if this was his chance to bolt, but the thought passed as quickly as it came. The ropes on his wrists were removed, and soldiers replaced them with iron manacles connected to a short chain, his arms behind his back. They did the same to Lyrusia. At least they didn't have hoods anymore.

"Leashes," Caliras said. "For my little rats. This one can scurry." He tugged at Tepic's chain.

The big wounded man with curly hair looked down at Tepic. His nose looked broken, but he had a gentle smile and seemed younger than most of the others. "I'm Taro," he said, "and my friend here is Lutz. We're going to keep you company—and bring you home."

"You'll speak when spoken to," Caliras interrupted. "Do what I say and you *all* get to go home. Don't upset me."

Taro gave a wink and one last smile to Tepic. More manacles were brought out, and matching restraints were placed on Taro and Lutz. A third set was brought to Dantic.

"I won't be chained," Dantic said. "That wasn't part of the agreement."

"Trying to negotiate again, Dantic?" Caliras said.

"You bring me in shackles to Eastfort and the garrison will kill you to a man. I have over a thousand guards posted there, Caliras."

Caliras considered a moment and then waved off the soldier with the manacles. "Fine. Try something I don't like though, and this one gets a dagger before you move a step. You keep your back to me. Understood?"

Tepic flinched and tried to control his trembling.

"For God's sake, Caliras. They're children. You've scared them enough."

"Oh? Done playing soldier with your boy, Dantic? Isn't ready to be a man yet? Hmm? The other looks grown to me."

Dantic bared his teeth in a snarl, but before he could speak, Caliras raised his finger with a side-eyed look. "I hope you're not about to say something I don't like."

Dantic shook, and a twitch flashed across his face, but he choked down his words and turned away.

Caliras spoke some hurried instructions to his men, and about twenty, all wearing packs, gathered near. The rest stood a little way off, and he addressed their officer. "Stay quiet in the fortress until we send for you. By the time they investigate, we'll all be long gone."

Dantic squinted. "What's your meaning, Caliras?"

"Unlike you and your backward friends, Dantic, I plan ahead." He smiled wickedly. "Oh yes, I know about your little ambush in the pass. And you're lucky I do. You were about to get your family killed. I considered sticking with the plan all the same, but alas—plans have changed."

Taro's face was neutral, but he stole a quick glance at Lutz.

"You, mokja," Caliras went on. "I know the mountains here are riddled with tunnels. One of them even leads us beyond Eastfort. I also have it on good authority that *you* know the way through."

Lutz scowled and his nostrils flared. "Maybe they are. Maybe you've got the wrong mokja. Why would I show you?"

"I could just kill you now, but I'm in a hurry. Show me the way, we slip past Eastfort, and then you get to go home."

Lutz looked to Taro a moment, but their faces were unreadable. He wrinkled his lips as though he chewed on the request. "Fine, come along then."

Tepic could not guess at all they meant, but he soon found himself on the move again, chained hands behind his back. Lutz led them all down several flights of stairs. The soldier holding his leash also hoisted a torch above his head. Dantic walked near and occasionally placed a hand on his or his sister's shoulder. The crowded breathing of the soldiers behind him sent puffs of gray mist into the narrowing passages as the mountain air set in. A wretched, uncanny feeling arose in Tepic's heart.

It was an entirely unremarkable patch of wall, but here Lutz stopped, turned his back and bound wrists to the stone, and silently passed his hands over the surface. With a click, a section of the wall rolled away, and an even colder flow of air crossed their faces.

"How did you do that?" Caliras asked as he stepped forward.

Lutz raised his eyebrows over his goggles. "You wouldn't understand."

"Try me."

"No, I mean you really can't," the mokja said. His face was flat.

Caliras grabbed a fistful of Lutz's collar. "Don't toy with me, little fellow."

"Shall we begin with the Artificer's Cant? Then transmute you into a mokja?"

Caliras's glare slowly turned into a sarcastic smile. Taro watched the exchange impassively, his eyes flitting between Caliras and Lutz. "A funny one, I see," Caliras said. "Leave it open then, and lead on." He clutched Lutz's collar a moment longer before he shoved him through the opening.

Tepic stole a glance in the torchlight and noticed with disappointment that Caliras still carried his grandfather's sword. Lingering too long, the

Lord Commander caught him spying, and Tepic quickly turned his eyes away. With a chuckle, Caliras took up his leash again. Tepic could feel his breath on the back of his neck. What did this wicked man want with the sword?

"Mark every turn," Caliras said to someone further behind as they marched after Lutz.

They were now in a close-walled passage of packed earth and thick beams. In some places, it turned to level stone, and in others, huge roots hung down to bar them. They would pause as a soldier pushed through to the front and hacked the obstacle away. They turned this way and that in dizzying confusion, a hundred passages leading off into the darkness.

The tunnel soon narrowed so terribly that they had to squeeze single file, and all save the mokja stooped their heads. The air was so close and thin, Tepic felt as though he'd been swallowed whole, and panic threatened to overtake him. He wondered if a burlap sack in a cold cell might be better.

They went on like this in growing dread for quite some time, alternating between passages so tight it was akin to burrowing, and others more like the long shafts of a mine wherein they could at least stand and have a bit of air to call their own. But even then, shadows danced like curious ghosts, biting at their hands.

In the flickering glow, Tepic sometimes looked back and caught sight of Taro's face, eyes closed and his mouth moving in silent words. Taro most of all was so tightly wedged in the passages that at times he appeared to crawl. Still, the man seemed entirely calm. It was the only token of encouragement for Tepic as the strange apprehension grew with every step, like vines upon his back.

Caliras broke the silence. "I saw you staring at my sword, Tepic."

"It's not yours."

Caliras laughed. "Is it not? Hmm. How came you by it?"

"Leave him alone, Caliras," Dantic said.

"Satisfy my curiosity, boy. It's a dull walk."

"It was my grandfather's," Tepic blurted out.

"Don't answer him, Tep," Lyrusia called out from somewhere behind.

"Really? That's remarkable. Did you know that I'm familiar with this sword already?"

"That's enough, Tepic. Just keep walking," Dantic said.

"Oh, come on," Caliras went on, grunting as they ducked under another low ceiling. "It's harmless conversation. What do you know about the sword, little rat?"

Tepic didn't answer. Caliras laughed again.

"What about you—'Taro' was it? What do you know?"

"Nothing," Taro said quickly.

Caliras shook his head and sighed. "I believe you. Typical ignorance."

Tepic hated the venomous tone Caliras used. He hated that he stole his sword and wished he'd just be quiet. It wasn't his.

"Your precious Voldigar thinks himself so wise, so learned. None of you provincials have any idea what's coming, do you?"

There were several more uncomfortable steps in awkward silence.

"Speak plainly," Lutz barked from the front of the column.

"Aha! Piqued some curiosity, have I? It's like all of you think Aramon didn't exist before Voldigar, before Polic! There are older things, little mokja, truer things. You wouldn't believe what this sword can do." Caliras's voice grew distant. "In many ways . . . I'm helping you . . ."

Tepic's stomach turned, and he could feel a strange new layer of fear twisting inside him, darker than the tunnel they wormed in. What did he mean? What could *he* possibly do with the sword? Caliras said no more for a time, and Tepic was glad of it.

They emerged from a low tunnel to a high craggy ceiling and the sound of running water far below. They stood upon a narrow shelf, where they could walk maybe three abreast. A great plummet into the darkness lay to their left. Four passages split off ahead. Here Lutz finally stopped.

"Well?" Caliras asked. "Which way?"

"One of the center two. It's been a long time, human." Lutz replied.

"Are we close?" Caliras asked. "Your delay is vexing me."

"Yes. It's an arrow shot down one of these," Lutz said with irritation. "Just let me think."

Tepic felt a weariness creeping into his legs and arms. Lutz continued to look back and forth while Caliras stared on frowning. Tepic sat upon a stone and expected his captor to yank him once again to his feet, but Caliras didn't seem to notice.

Taro's eyes were closed again, his lips still moving with silent words. Tepic closed his eyes too and began to nod off but was startled by Taro's voice.

"You're a twisted man, Caliras," Taro said as he passed by. His guard was walking him up beside Lutz, near the cliff's edge where his back now faced Tepic.

Tepic swallowed and watched for an angry reprisal, but Caliras only laughed.

"I'm a practical man, and you—you're a fool. Do you think you've actually killed that demon?"

"You're meddling with things you don't understand, Caliras. What is it you intend to do with the sword?" Taro's voice had subtly changed. The kindness was drained away. It was low and menacing.

Caliras dropped Tepic's chain and flashed a dagger into his hand. "It's you who don't understand." He crossed over to Taro who turned to face him, hands still chained behind his back. Taro did not look at Caliras, but instead, stared over his shoulder at Tepic.

"I intend to make a new friend. What's that to you?" He waived the dagger in front of Taro's face.

All eyes were now fixed on the two as they spoke, and Taro continued to stare directly into Tepic's eyes with a look of concentration. Tepic glanced from side to side. What did Taro want?

"Tell me more about that sword," Taro continued quietly in his strange voice.

Caliras's hand shook. "It's . . . what are you looking at?" He glanced back at Tepic and then moved an inch from Taro's face. Doubt crept into his voice. "What are you doing, Chanter?"

Taro now met Caliras's gaze. "I'm conversing with you, while we wait for Lutz."

Quietly, Tepic worked his arms and manacles tightly under his legs and then past his feet. In a breathless moment, his hands were in front of him. Though his wrists were still bound, the leash of chain lay loosely on the ground.

"Now that I think of it, Brother Taro, I don't believe I need hostages anymore," Caliras said. "I'm sure we can find the way between these two passages without you."

Tepic held his breath.

Caliras raised his dagger directly between Taro's eyes. "What is it you brothers say all the time? Head . . ." He tapped the dagger point between Taro's eyes and then lowered it to his chest. ". . . and heart?"

It happened so quickly, Tepic surprised even himself. Something awoke inside him, and he willed his legs forward in a mad dash. With a sudden lunge, he slipped the chain over Caliras's head and neck from behind. Soldiers cried out and rushed forward, but it was too late. Tepic tightened his arms, twisted, and pulled. The dagger clattered to the ground and they lurched backward. In the blink of an eye, he slipped from the edge and they were in open air.

"No!" he heard his father cry. "Tepic!" his sister screamed. He closed his eyes tightly as the wind rushed in his ears, and the sound of fast-flowing water hurried to meet them. Time slowed as he fell. The sword would now be far away, buried with him here beneath the mountains. No more wicked Caliras. No more wicked schemes. *Goodbye, Father. Goodbye, Mother. Goodbye, Ru.*

Chapter Twelve

The Sons of Aramon

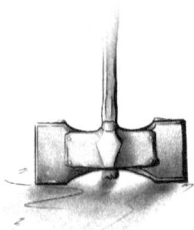

V OLDIGAR CLOSED THE POSTERN door inch by inch until the last sliver of light vanished noiselessly behind him. In a few moments, his eyes adjusted to a murky chamber within the thick wall of Westfort. Vasherk stared back, as did thirty other sets of blinking eyes, their owners all breathing as quietly as they could. No Stonepikes were here to guard this door at least. *Good*.

Vasherk had made good time. He found Commander Dantic in Maghaltani searching for his son, and together they raced on to Westfort with his men and a small detachment of brethren that Gardoric had spared them. They arrived to meet Voldigar only an hour or two after the deadly battle with the Orun and just in time for commander Dantic, Taro, and Lutz to offer themselves up as hostages.

A half an hour after Caliras and his men had disappeared from the walls, it was still quiet. There was no sign of any Stonepike, nor of the Orun. Fruitlessly, they had hovered around Medellai, only able to confirm that the man indeed could not see. Of what would become of him, there was no time to learn. With every passing moment, Caliras would bring his captives further away.

Voldigar had considered breaching the gate directly, but what of the Stonepikes? The wall was strangely silent, but surely there was a rearguard. The noise would have brought them running. Dantic had wisely left a key with one of his officers, and with that discovered, their plan was certain. By stealth, they passed through a postern door and now crouched within the fortification.

Voldigar squinted in the dim light and strained his ears. Medellai's senses would have served them well, but they would have to make do without. There could be anything beyond this chamber. Westfort's normal garrison reached three hundred men. He prayed the Stonepikes did not have so many, that they had all traveled up the pass by now, and that Gardoric and the rest were on time and unseen, lying in wait between the forts.

They made their way deeper into Westfort, keeping to the shadows and padding softly upon the cold stone. As they neared the central courtyard, Voldigar waved Vasherk forward. The old man darted cat-like from shadow to shadow. Hidden near a pillar ahead, he signaled with his hands '*Four score,*' then looked back across the courtyard. Bad luck—but it could be much worse.

Voldigar nodded to Soris, and a faint glow of blue came to life between the Teller's hands, reflecting off the rings that encircled his arms. Voldigar motioned for the other men to gather close.

"There are eighty Stonepikes in that courtyard ahead," he whispered. "Soris and I will demand their surrender."

Dantic's men looked incredulous. Voldigar held up his hand. "We can be very convincing. But no, they may not listen. If it goes ill, wait for them to break ranks, and then flood the courtyard from every side. My brethren will hold the center." There was no more to say. He rose, pulling his maul from off his back, and walked past Vasherk to the courtyard. Soris followed a few paces behind.

Voldigar stepped into the sunlight. As surprised as they were, and so out of place was he, it took a few awkward seconds for the Stonepikes to comprehend that he was there.

"Stonepikes. This fortress is taken. I am Voldigar Anteres, Brother of Aramon. Lay down your arms."

The Stonepikes were loosely scattered about the courtyard, some eating a meal in groups, others asleep on whatever dusty patch of grass they could find. Packs lay against the walls, and rows of spears were propped between them. A man with a scar through his eye acted first, drawing a sword and brandishing it in Voldigar's direction. Others by him plucked up spears and set their feet.

"How did you enter?" he demanded.

"You left your wall unguarded, Captain. Save yourself and your men. Disarm. You are surrounded."

The scarred man looked around wildly as more of the Stonepikes rose to their feet. He hesitated but then plucked a javelin from a nearby pack. "You lie!" He hurled the missile at Voldigar with practiced aim, and several men about him soon did the same in a bristling volley.

From the first, Voldigar moved aside, caught, and then snapped it like a dry stalk with a flick of his wrist. The volley behind simply stopped in midair, surrounded by a shimmering glow of ice in the midday sun. The javelins fell to the ground with a clatter, and Soris stepped from the shadows. Urias, Vasherk, and half a dozen others bearing red shields and the cloaks of their order followed swiftly behind. They rushed to set a line before Voldigar.

Again, the Stonepikes faltered but then surged forward in a mass of swords and spears. Men streamed down from the walls in fury as their first line crashed into the Order's shields. Others fanned out to surround them, but the brethren did not wait. Voldigar leapt forth and laid about with his great maul in terrible arcs while Stonepikes shrank back in dread of the glistening spear in Urias's hand.

From the sides of the courtyard, Dantic's men burst upon the flanks of the Stonepikes with a shout. The force and surprise of the impact collapsed their lines into a flailing melee, but with the Stonepikes' greater numbers, a pitched battle and much bloodshed were sure to follow. They were disciplined men, and they would not break as quickly or as easily as Voldigar had hoped. The sons of Aramon would slaughter one another in her mountains under a rapidly climbing sun.

It was then, upon the high east wall of the fort, that Voldigar saw a man swing his legs over the battlements. His braided hair hung against his tattooed face as he pressed his lips to the hollow staff he bore and blew one deadly dart after another. Brother Gardoric had come.

At first, only he stood upon the parapet, but then wave upon wave of red cloaks appeared. Arrows flew into the rear of the massed Stonepikes and panic set in. They threw down their weapons, bellowing surrenders in the chaos. It was over in an instant.

Swords were kicked away, spears taken, and packs rifled. With their hands in the air, what survived of the Stonepikes were soon stripped of their arms and bound. The scarred captain cursed and moaned of treachery, but was placed on his belly and gagged by Dantic's officer.

Voldigar ran breathlessly to Gardoric. "Head and Heart, Gardoric. Where are Dantic and his children?"

Gardoric saluted as he stowed his peculiar weapons but met Voldigar's eyes with confusion and a shake of the head. "I've seen no one, Elder."

"Nor in the mines?"

Gardoric shook his head again.

Voldigar blinked and sighed and turned his eyes to the packed earth of the courtyard beneath their feet. "It's as I feared then. Caliras took Lutz with him. They've gone underground and slipped past our net."

Chapter Thirteen

In His Hand

Tepic's eyes were fast shut. He could sense the ground rushing to meet him while Caliras flailed his arms and let out a tortured howl. In a moment, it would be over.

Suddenly, he slowed, and a searing heat raked along his sides. He flashed open his eyes, and there high above, Taro stood on the brink in torchlight, one hand flared open in blazing white fire, a broken manacle dangling from his wrist. His eyes and mouth were wide in agonizing effort, and his other hand splayed and thrust behind him. Tepic and Caliras were suspended there, a foot above the rocky shore of a roaring subterranean river.

Caliras cried out and twisted, clutching Tepic about the neck with his one good hand. Tepic tried to shout but no sound came. He grasped at his grandfather's sword on Caliras's back and tried to pull it free, but he could not fully draw its length. Reaching into Caliras's belt with his other hand he yanked free one of the man's many daggers and with his eyes shut, he stabbed again and again. Caliras's hand released.

Tepic opened his eyes again just as he fell heavily to the ground by the rushing river he could barely see. Caliras lurched to his feet and staggered, holding a hand to his bloody chest. With an open mouth, he stared at Tepic for a moment longer. His eyes rolled back, and then he toppled into the river with a splash, swept away into the darkness.

Tepic pulled his grandfather's sword against his chest and closed his eyes again. The scabbard was gone, but he hadn't lost his grip. The blade was in his hand.

Chapter Fourteen

The Chanter's Gift

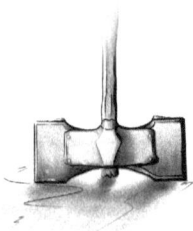

THERE WERE AN ABSURD number of cellars and basements beneath the old fortification they called Wesfort, but at length, Voldigar found the gaping black opening that Lutz had left behind. Vasherk and Urias were close in tow. Long hours spent in Westfort in years past, he should have known where it was, but mokja mazes hid in plain sight all over Aramon. No matter how many times he passed through, getting lost was a matter of ritual. He was relieved to finally see the door, still open, with cold mountain air flowing from the darkness.

"I can't believe we're going in without Lutz," Vasherk said. He returned a frowning stare into the glowering hole and pulled his gloves more tightly over his hands. "Never wanted to see this place again."

"Nor I, but I trust he left tokens for us to follow," Voldigar replied. A freezing gust brushed against his face.

"Even with his hands bound?" Urias asked.

"Count on it, and he's likely done all he can to delay them."

Urias snapped a torch into life and turned his glare ahead. "This could be many hours, Eldest. Like blind worms in the earth. We should leave tokens of our own."

"We'll miss the coronation too," Vasherk remarked with a chuckle, "and what if the Stonepikes were lying? Why not bring Gardoric?"

Voldigar had considered it, but Soris's interrogation was quick and convincing. The Stonepikes were rank and file men, overawed at the presence of the Tellers.

"They only confirmed my suspicions, Vasherk. They weren't lying. Gardoric would have seen them in the pass—and he only knows the first level of these mines. Lutz has led them deeper down. I'm certain of it."

He imagined explaining himself to a petulant Lusánt. "Lusánt will understand our absence, especially when we bring him Caliras."

Vasherk wrinkled his forehead "You don't sound convinced." He stepped in with his head low and let out a long exhale. "It's been nice knowing you, Elder. Please don't eat me first."

"The ghosts will see to that, Brother," Urias said. Voldigar followed them in.

The mines were more akin to a tomb, and even twenty years past his last step within, the dread of the place closed about Voldigar in an instant. Urias's torch sputtered against the black, and the earthen walls were full of imagined whispers and dark memory.

They had not gone thirty steps in wary silence when the sound of many feet echoed in the caverns ahead. Voldigar froze and then whirled about wide-eyed. A moment later, they were hurrying back to the basement passage. There they crouched behind whatever cover they could and drew steel.

The first Stonepike emerged. Voldigar coiled to lunge, but then he saw the man was barefoot and unarmed. A twist of chain enclosed his wrists, and it carried on to another and another as they each came forth from the tunnels, similarly bound and linked. Last of all came Lutz, Taro, Dantic, Lyrusia, and Tepic. Voldigar exhaled and rose from behind a rotted crate. Caliras alone was missing.

"Elder!" Taro called out in surprise. His nose was most certainly broken, and he looked the part of a man who hadn't slept, but Taro was Taro. "You found us!"

"What is this?" Voldigar asked.

"These clever fellows made the mistake of binding us with chain," Lutz replied. He rattled the end of the links he held in one hand. The Stonepikes stared sullenly at the floor. "A stroke of luck, if you ask me." He gave a rare grin and his lenses protruded in emphasis.

"I take it you hold the fort then?" Dantic asked. Tepic stood in front of him with shoulders slumped. Lyrusia was comforting the boy and whispering to him.

"We do," Voldigar said. He surveyed the line of prisoners. "Gardoric didn't wait long in the pass. He scaled the walls from the east while we broke in from the west. Are any of you hurt?"

"No more than before," Taro said.

"I broke the Code, Elder," Lutz interjected with a scowl.

"What?"

"I lied. Twice."

Voldigar raised his brow. "We'll talk upstairs. Let's get these men with the other prisoners."

In the courtyard, what remained of Caliras's men were bound in small groups, guarded mostly by brethren with about half as many of Dantic's soldiers. It was well over fifty red cloaks—a sight unseen in many years. They left the new prisoners among them. Gardoric was perched on a wood round smoking a pipe and cooing gentle words to a group of horses he'd brought inside the west gate of the fort. They gathered near him and the pleasant smell of his tobacco.

"Lutz told them only Artificers could open the door to the tunnels," Taro said as he smiled, wiping blood and dirt from his hands. "We left it open for you."

"I also told them we were almost past Eastfort when we'd only reached the river falls," Lutz added.

"That's not far in," Voldigar said.

Lutz grinned. "Less than a mile. Men lose all sense of time when they're underground."

"Where is Commander Caliras?"

Taro looked behind him at Tepic. The boy was leaning against his sister with his eyes closed. She stroked his head and occasionally pressed her face against his hair. His grandfather's sword he held between his knees with its point in the ground.

"The boy killed him," Taro said.

"What?" Voldigar said, lifting his brow again. He stared at his student in quiet consideration. He could see now that Tepic's chest was shaking. He tried to remember himself at thirteen.

"Yes," Taro went on. "I could hardly believe it."

"How?"

"With Caliras's own dagger."

Voldigar ran his hand across his beard. "I suspect you were in Caliras's thoughts then?"

"I was," Taro said. "The man's mind was wary, guarded even—but he was full of arrogance, Voldigar, and envy. In these, I had my wedge. He found me out as we struggled but came on in his pride. The boy was a help to me."

"A help?"

"Tepic's unusual. Very unusual. He may even have the Chanter's blessing. His will was in harmony with my own, whether he knew it or not. He was fixed on the sword, as was I, as was Caliras."

Voldigar narrowed his eyes at Tepic and Lyrusia. "What do we know of the sword?"

"Very little," Taro admitted, "but Caliras certainly thought much of it, and I believed him. He had some wicked design, Elder—cut short, thank God"

"How did the boy overpower him?"

"It was fast, surprised us all. Wrapped his bonds around Caliras's neck and pulled them both over the cliffs. That snake was going to knife me there." Taro glanced at Tepic again.

A lump formed in Voldigar's throat. "Tepic tried to save your life?"

Taro nodded.

"That wasn't your doing?" Lutz asked in surprise.

"No," Taro responded. "Of course not. It was a remarkable deed, and I was lucky to catch him! I would have stopped that knife blow, but the boy moved before I could act." He shook his head in wonder. "They were a foot from the rocks when I caught them, Elder. A foot! Caliras was half-mad, but Tepic got him with his own blade, and then the river took him. Simple as that. Mark well, there's a lot more to that sword, and the boy was willing to sacrifice himself to make sure Caliras didn't get it."

Voldigar stole a long look at the crystal-hilted blade, and the brethren followed his gaze. He sighed. "There's still time to get to Arregalt by sundown. I'll learn what I can along the way."

—◦—

Gamad's legionnaires and more of Dantic's men soon arrived in Westfort, gaining custody of nearly eighty surviving Stonepikes and the fortress itself. Captain Arbed was among them and took great pleasure in raising his banner once again over both gatehouses. After some hurried instructions, Voldigar sent Gardoric on to Eastfort to await Lanathor's return and debrief him on all that had occurred. All the rest departed west. If they traveled quickly, there would still be time to return to the capital by sunset.

Voldigar found himself riding half-awake in the saddle, leading Medellai's horse at a steady clip with one hand behind. Gardoric had been wise enough to send fresh mounts to the western gate, and upon these many brethren rode. Dantic and his children trotted along in silence some distance behind. They were to part ways with the greater portion of brethren at the crossroads to Maghaltani, and Dantic's footmen would bring the prisoners along in the evening.

Voldigar assumed Medellai was sleeping, but he felt the reins slacken, and the man urged his horse forward to come alongside. Every Brother of Aramon could sleep in the saddle. It had served them well on countless long journeys before, but apparently, his fellow Elder could not bring himself to rest yet either. The wariness of their ordeal lingered like a fog on their shoulders.

"What time is it?" Medellai asked.

Voldigar glanced at the sun. "Midafternoon. Time enough to make the coronation. Still can't see?"

"I cannot," Medellai said darkly.

"You'll be alright, Medellai. We'll get some rest and then figure out what to do."

"Don't lie to me, Brother," Medellai replied. "It's the *Wilding* and you know it. I pushed too far."

Voldigar sighed. "Maybe Liadov really will come home. She'll know what to do . . . or we'll bring you to her."

"Maybe," Medellai said and fell quiet. His shoulders drooped, and his face was downcast to his saddle. He looked like he wished to say more but then let his pace lag again.

Voldigar flexed his hands and rubbed under his eyes. His fingers felt weak, his skin parched and hot. He had not expended so much Virtue so quickly in many years, maybe never. How close had he come to the edge himself? How close had they all come? He looked around at the others. Like Medellai, they too sagged—dozing as they rode. They were bruised, but not broken. Their test would soon be over. They had only to honor the new King, and blessed rest awaited.

He recounted the battle with the Orun in his mind and wondered at its sudden disappearance. Was it truly dead? They had ground their foe to powder and witnessed a tremendous release of its power, but without Medellai's senses—how could they be sure? Taro relayed more of Caliras's dark words before they left. The man was a liar, but under Taro's influence, whatever twisted thoughts were in his mind had come pouring out. What did he know that they did not? His soldiers had been useless in further interrogation. What of the sword?

Too many unanswered questions.

Voldigar handed Medellai's reins to Soris and slowed until he came alongside Dantic.

"How are you, Dantic? How are your children?"

"Lyrusia is fine," he said softly. "I don't think that girl can feel fear. Tepic is . . . quiet." Dantic looked back at his son who was just out of earshot. "He's been through a lot."

Voldigar noted with curiosity that the sword was still on Tepic's back. Wrapped now in cloth and hung with a makeshift scabbard. "He still has the sword."

"Yes. He won't be parted from it. Rest assured, when we return to Arregalt that thing will be locked away."

"You should send it with my order," Voldigar said. "Taro told me everything Caliras said."

"Caliras was a liar, Voldigar—and a bizarre eccentric. I knew him better than you realize, a story I should share with you someday." He shook his head and stared off to the north. "That sword is an heirloom of my wife's house. There are no more heirs. Her father's long dead and she has . . . an odd attachment to it. She wouldn't forgive me. It must stay with my house"

"We would return it to you, Dantic. We just need time to examine it. There was undoubtedly truth mixed with Caliras's lies, and the creature followed it. That's not by chance. What do you know of the sword?"

Dantic shook his head again. "I know her father was not a Chanter, and he was an eccentric himself." He waved his hand and frowned. "Come, visit us soon, tomorrow. Bring whoever you like. My wife will tell you all the tales, but as long as that creature is no more, the sword stays with us. You are returning home, are you not?"

"I am," Voldigar replied. "But—"

"Then if you feel safe to do so, so do I. That thing could have followed us into the mines were it still alive. It didn't."

Voldigar thought to press further, but he'd said his piece. He swallowed his argument. "Don't relieve the guard at your home, friend. Destroying an Orun is not so simple as you might think."

Dantic nodded. The Brethren would come to Dantic's house and see the sword—tomorrow then. Voldigar just needed to rest a little and to let the others do the same. He was about to spur his horse forward again when Dantic put a hand on his shoulder.

"Thank you, Voldigar."

"For what?"

"For my children."

Voldigar frowned. "What else would I do, Dantic? Would you not do the same for me? You have a beautiful family."

Dantic released a long breath and looked down at his saddle.

———◆———

The larger host of brethren bid farewell and headed south toward Maghaltani. Soon after, Dantic and his family turned west to Arregalt. Medellai and the others went with him, though Soris now led. Voldigar planned to stop briefly at his farm and then join them in the city.

Two hours remained until sunset, and though he entertained the thought of sleeping through coronation, and perhaps the rest of the week, he was certain enduring a few more hours awake would be less painful than ignoring the prince's summons. He'd have a precious half hour to wash his face, close his eyes, and then set out once more.

A final rise in the hills and the aspen grove was below, waving its red leaves in a gentle breeze. Seldom were they ever green, and not even Lanathor could answer why. Its lengthening shadows were cast again toward his farm, but to his surprise, he could see a small figure there, walking behind the plow.

Hobyn was working a hammer busily at the front door and waved with a smile as Voldigar came to a stop and dismounted. "Just in time, m'lord. Good as new!" Hobyn took a few more swings at a nail and stepped back to assess his handiwork. Satisfied, he beamed at Voldigar and then nodded mischievously to the field.

Gwenyth looked comically small behind the plow but was finishing a fine, straight row from end to end. Perhaps a quarter of the field was already complete. Wulf sat nearby on a stump and watched, sipping a flask of who-knows-what.

"I wouldn't interfere, Brother. She's a goddess of the plow, and that horse hates everyone but her," Wulf said.

"You're drinking while my wife turns the field, Wulf?"

"You'll recall I nearly died this morning. Then, I fixed your borrowed plow, Elder. You're welcome." He took a long swig. "She'd have finished me off if I tried to stop her anyway. How went the hunt?"

"Successful. I'll tell you later."

Gwenyth completed the row and pulled a scarf from off her head, trudging back to the house. Voldigar leaned against the wall and smiled while Hobyn hurried over to attend to Mack the plow horse with an apple that seemed to materialize in his hand.

"Done so soon, Lady Anteres? Mind you don't strike your chin with that plow," Voldigar said.

Gwenyth slapped a pair of gloves against Voldigar's chest and looked up into his eyes with a smirk. "We have a coronation to attend, m'lord."

Voldigar blinked in surprise, and Wulf snorted a chuckle. Gwenyth had good days, but he did not expect this to be one of them.

"I am House Sispérus after all. Let's not offend my cousin." She wrinkled her nose. "You smell like a horse. Time to clean you up."

"So do you!"

She laughed and shoved him inside, shutting the door behind.

Gwenyth wrapped her arms about his neck and leaned her head against his chest. "I'm glad you're home." She exhaled slowly.

Voldigar pulled her in more tightly. "As am I, Gwen. Are you well?"

"I am." She leaned back and looked into his eyes again. "It was a remarkably mundane day—after this morning."

Voldigar chuckled. "Was it?"

Gwenyth frowned and furrowed her brow as she studied Voldigar's face. "Did you find the boy?"

"We did."

"And slay your dragons?"

"Aye, that too. You actually want to go to Arregalt?"

"I do." She turned his head to the side with a gentle hand upon his cheek. "You're hurt."

"Just tired, Gwen. I haven't slept."

"Sit here." She pointed to a footstool. Voldigar lowered himself heavily to it, letting his eyes close and his head sag. It felt good.

The house had been set in order again with what little furniture they possessed, though the fine cabinet was piled in pieces in a corner near the hearth.

"I hope you don't intend to burn that cabinet," Voldigar said.

Gwenyth laughed. "No, my love. I wouldn't dare. Hobyn says he can fix it. See? My rocking chair is fine. Let me help you with this."

Slowly she helped Voldigar work the tunic and brigandine from off his back. He realized with some amusement that it had been stuck to his skin for two days straight. Gwenyth sucked her teeth when it came off.

"That bad, eh?" Voldigar said as he dropped his head into his hands and rested his elbows on his knees. He might have fallen asleep in that very moment but blinked at a sting as she drew a cool washcloth across his back.

He started to drift again as he swayed gently side to side with the working of her hands. Gwenyth muttered and clicked her tongue at what she saw, but it was just soft music to Voldigar.

At length, she stopped dabbing at his bruised back and slipped her slender arms around his chest. Interlocking her fingers just under his downturned eyes, she released a long, contented sigh. It was time to doze in the silence, even for a moment.

"Voldigar," she said quietly. He felt himself drifting to sleep. "I am with child."

Voldigar's eyes shot open and he inhaled sharply. Had he nodded off again? For a long moment, he was quiet and completely still, afraid to speak, afraid to even breathe. His eyes welled with tears. "What?"

"I said, Lord Anteres, that I am pregnant."

Voldigar began to rock back and forth on his toes. A tear escaped each eye that he quickly wiped away. Still he could not turn to face her. He reached down to take her two small hands in his own and pulled in a wavering breath. It was four small words he'd waited all his life to hear, and there they hung in the air like drops of rain. If he turned, they would crash to the floor and flow away.

"When?" he finally managed in a tiny whisper. He could feel her heart beating against his back.

"Two months," she whispered in return. "I couldn't be sure at first. I was afraid to believe it, afraid to tell you."

Voldigar gathered himself and turned about to look into her eyes. They smiled silently, studying each other's faces, writing the moment in their memories forever. He slowly dropped his ear to her belly and closed his eyes again. "I love you, Gwen," he whispered. She wrapped her arms about his head and dared to laugh once more. "I am having a good day, Voldigar."

They stayed in that pose of wordless joy for some time until Voldigar suddenly leapt to his feet and swept Gwenyth into his arms. Her eyes went wide with mirth and surprise. Kicking the newly repaired door open, he charged through like a madman. Wulf fell clean from his stump onto his back, sputtering and cursing. Freshly freed from the harness, Mack bolted, and Hobyn cried out in alarm, chasing after the horse. Voldigar sped through the half-plowed field screaming at the top of his lungs. "I'm having a baby! I'm having a baby!"

Chapter Fifteen

LIGHTBRINGER

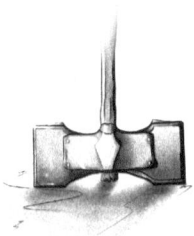

V OLDIGAR WALKED BESIDE HIS horse, half dreaming with a broad smile on his face. Occasionally, he would look up at Gwenyth who sat gracefully on the mount. She wore a dress all of black and silver with a lace covering upon her head and a woven mantle on her shoulders. "Not right for spring," she had said, but Voldigar thought her radiant.

For his part, he was able to clean the most obvious dirt and blood from his cloak and hastily squeeze into a red and gray military jacket, twenty years old and missing a button. It was not as if they had a choice. It was the only finery either of them owned, and at least the colors aligned with the noble houses of their births.

"You'll run us off the road if you keep looking up here, old man," Gwenyth said.

Voldigar laughed and kept his eyes on hers. They had just passed through the shadow of the Spire, and the waning sun of evening warmed their faces. They would soon cross the last bridge over the Adionel and come to the gates of Arregalt.

"Just keeping an eye on you—and our son," Voldigar said.

"How do you know it's a boy? Are you a wizard?"

"Never trust a wizard," Voldigar protested with a chuckle. "No, Wulf said so. We'll start with sons, and the younger can be daughters."

Voldigar stumbled on a rock, and Gwenyth hurled at him the core of an apple she'd been munching. "You don't get to decide, old man!" He failed to dodge, and a wet, fruity smear was left on his face and jacket. Gwenyth laughed. "They won't let you in now! I suppose I—and our daughter—will have to attend alone."

"Alas!" cried Voldigar. "I'll just have to go home and sleep."

"Request denied, Brother of Aramon. Don't upset my house."

Voldigar smirked and tried to wipe the apple from his coat.

The great outer walls of Arregalt towered above, hung with countless massive banners, billowing in the wind. Half in the black and gray of House Sispérus with its eight-pointed sigil, and half in the red and gold of Aramon's oldest emblem—the flaming arrow of Tymicha. The sound of bells still echoed against the stone and would finally cease at sunset when the nobles gathered at the Spring Throne.

In the press of the streets, they would not reach the far end of Arregalt's promontory until well after nightfall, but Voldigar still had Lusánt's ring with him, and this he reluctantly used to gain passage and hurry along the tops of the inner walls with Gwenyth close at hand. The news of his child had renewed his strength, but weariness crept into his limbs again as the long curve of the wall led them steadily into the Citadel.

At long last, they passed to the far side of the Spire. The Wending Sea opened wide before them where many ships had gathered along the bay, as if they might hear the coronation from a thousand feet below. The sun was low in the sky, casting long shadows from the vessels' masts and bathing the city's mass of stone in golden light. A final flash of Lusánt's signet, and they were brought through a side door of the Spring Throne.

The colonnade was a wonder of Arregalt. In every measurement, a twin of the great Winter Throne that rested under the Spire, but this one an enormous courtyard under an open sky. At its entrance, two huge doors of ivory, forty feet high, were intricately embossed and worked through with a fortune of gold. Up the colonnade's center, a slender path of tile ran arrow-straight, and hemming this path was a long line of free-standing marble pillars. Beside each pillar, an ancient cherry tree grew, and all were now in full bloom, their petals raining down in a constant flow of fragrant white.

Between these pillars and the walls, broad lawns of green were choked with a press of nobility and servants, religious authorities, officers, and foreign dignitaries. There were crowds of common men as well, no doubt carefully selected and groomed for this occasion. Vast tables of dressed quail and puddings, of venison and other game, of steaming bread and garnished wheels of cheese, were prominently displayed and jealously guarded by their proud makers. The twisting odors flowed overhead in competition with the blooming trees.

A large group of musicians were cordoned off near the far wall opposite the doors, straining to hear their harps and cornetts over the din while they prepared for some great fanfare to come. Even chambered drone flutes were brought in from the Far Marshes with their players—an unusual sight in the city. The mass of humanity was broken up only by a well-manicured selection of ponds and fountains. Gamad's soldiers were everywhere in ordered ranks, atop the walls and along their base, and ringing the great throne that sat at the end of the tiled path.

The Spring Throne was perched atop a dais of twelve marble steps, impossibly old. Veins of gray ran through shining white, polished so fine that Voldigar suspected he would see his reflection were he standing near. The throne itself, like the door, was ivory embossed with gold. Once the seat of his friend Olwis the Shield, it now stood empty, save for a golden scepter that awaited the prince's hand.

A woman, dressed also in black, crossed over to Voldigar and Gwenyth where they stood searching for a familiar face.

"Lady Gwenyth! What a pleasant surprise. I didn't expect to see you."

Gwenyth curtsied in return. "God save the Emperor, Lady Veysara. You look lovely this evening."

Veysara simpered sweetly. She was an older woman with a severe face, but a practiced bearing. She looked the sort who'd spent half her fortune clinging to a last vestige of her youth.

"Who's this fellow?" She rested a hand on Voldigar's arm and smiled coyly. "So rustic!"

"This is my husband, Voldigar—"

"Ooh! House Anteres?" she interrupted. "Hmm, I don't think there's an area set for you."

"Thank you, Lady Veysara. There wouldn't be," he replied with a nod.

"But I think your friends are over there." She pointed to the right of the throne where his brethren stood in red cloaks looking uncomfortable. It was surprisingly close, almost to the foot of the dais. "Hopefully nothing *too* exciting, this time around," Veysara finished with an exaggerated raise of her eyebrows.

"Let's hope," Voldigar replied.

"Well, come on, Gwenyth. House Sispérus is right there." She pointed to the left of the throne, no more than a stone's throw from where the brethren were. A crowd of nobles in black and gray stood there with a much more convivial demeanor.

Gwenyth looked questioningly at Voldigar. He nodded with a shrug of his shoulders and an apologetic smile. "Have fun," he mouthed silently as Veysara whisked her away through the crowd.

The brethren's faces brightened to see him, and they saluted as Voldigar squeezed his way into their midst.

"You almost missed it," Taro mumbled through a mouthful of cake.

"What?" Voldigar said over the din. His stomach growled, and he wished he'd had the sense to raid a table before he'd pushed so deeply into the crowd. On cue, Taro offered a morsel which he accepted gratefully.

"You look hungry, Elder."

"I am. How'd we end up so close to the throne?"

Taro shrugged. "I don't know. An officer told us to stand here, so we did."

Lutz called up from below. "Doesn't matter where I stand. I'll be staring at backsides all night. Wake me up when it's over."

Voldigar looked to Medellai who stood quietly between Soris and Urias. The former whispered to him from time to time, but Medellai kept his eyes closed and face flat. Voldigar did not have long to consider or further strain his voice over the noise of the crowd. From high above, a clear trumpet rang, followed by many more across the walls, and then a long low blast from the great, curling horn mounted where the fortifications gathered behind the throne. The ivory doors groaned, and the crowd fell silent.

Every eye was turned to the entryway as a dozen soldiers strained to pull the huge panels apart. At the moment they were wide enough, two standard-bearers entered side by side, obscuring whatever was behind. They held identical tall banners of House Sispérus with huge, gray sigils upon them. In unison, they split apart, and there was Lusánt, striding down the narrow tile path with his head held high and the gravity of an empire on his face.

He wore ornate lacquered plate from head to toe, all in black. It was edged in silver and articulated over shining mail beneath. His hair was as unkempt as always, clearly no attempt had been made to prepare him from the neck up.

Behind flowed a long black cape, the hems of which were held on either corner by Diocesan Ragat and Master Hyrodan, garbed in the traditional ceremonials of their respective cults.

The crowd cheered and applauded as he strode along the colonnade of the Spring Throne through a downpour of cherry blossoms. Behind him and his train, young men of his inner circle walked, as well as the Xerimadi warrior who was always near. General Gamad with a company of soldiers entered last, and the doors closed behind them.

As Lusánt passed, every knee bowed in a rippling wave of his subjects. The brethren stayed standing but dropped their heads to their chests. This was the old tradition of Aramon. *A Brother does not kneel, save to God only.* With his head low, Voldigar could not see Lusánt's reaction, nor of any others around him. He could only hope the prince and this crowd of nobles remembered these traditions. He did not recall any controversy at Eleanora's coronation, save for a momentary frown. As he lifted his head, he caught nothing more than a glance and a smirk from Lusánt. *So far, so good.*

As the last light of the evening sun fell beneath the walls of Arregalt, Lusánt Sispérus ascended twelve marble steps of the Spring Throne and grasped the Golden Scepter of Tymicha which lay across its arms. With his back turned, he hesitated a long while in silence while the wind whispered through his cape. The dignitaries watched and blinked. General Gamad shifted his weight from foot to foot, and a low murmur stirred among the people. Still, Lusánt's head remained drooped toward the scepter which he clutched. His body gently swayed. Just when Gamad looked as though he would step forward, the prince finally turned about. There was a tempest on his face, but it melted into a broad smile, and he held the scepter high. The crowd erupted in deafening cheers.

Lusánt reveled in their roar for some time but finally raised his hand for quiet. "My people. My friends. This day has come too soon and cost us too dearly," Lusánt spoke in a loud but somber voice. "Your Empress, my mother, our beloved Eleanora Sispérus, departed from us but two days hence. We wished that she might live forever, but the gods did not agree." Lusánt took a shaky breath and stared at his feet for a moment. "As my first decree under this scepter, I call for quiet remembrance of my mother, until the last rays of the sun vanish behind the Spring Throne."

The crowd obeyed and a hush fell. The bells had stopped and no sound came into the colonnade, save for a rustling breeze and the distant waves of the Wending Sea. *Appropriately done.*

After these few solemn minutes, darkness settled, and the many torches and lamps of the great courtyard flickered off the faces of the crowd. Ragat and Hyrodan stood unsmiling behind the prince, surveying the people. Lusánt took a deep breath and spoke again.

What followed were many greetings and welcomes to the noble houses. Customary words and well-worn oaths were next, platitudes and promises. Voldigar glanced down at Lutz who rocked quietly on his feet with his goggles dim. He was ready to shake him if a snore escaped. Looking across the path, he caught Gwenyth's eyes and they shared a brief smile. A mundane coronation would suit him just fine.

Voldigar's attention was brought again to the dais as Lusánt descended a stair and entered into his personal remarks. There was an energy and intention now in his eyes and the forward lean of his head.

". . . and thus," Lusánt went on, his voice rising, "the crown shall pass to me, but not without ambition. Under my reign, Aramon will change. I know men fear when they hear that word, 'change,' yet what is progress but change? Where is greatness unless we step forward to take it? Why should our future labor under the weight of our past?" He paused and waited for nodding heads, his arms becoming animated.

"Aramon has been the light of the world near to a thousand years, and we shall have more light, not less! A new reign brings a new age, but will you join me at the forefront?" Lusánt scanned the faces before him as though he expected an answer. He held his hand out and rubbed his fingers together.

"Can you feel it, my people? Can you see it? There is thunder on the air. Gone must be your old prejudices and narrow thinking. Gone must be the chains of your past. Tymicha threw off your bondage in antiquity with a single flicker of light. I will throw it off tonight!"

His eyes were growing wide and his gestures more wild. Urias caught Voldigar's glance with a raised eyebrow and a frown. Where was the boy taking this?

Lusánt descended one more shallow step. "I am not afraid, Aramoni. Are you afraid?" He pointed into the crowd and scowled. "Will you shrink back at this moment . . . or will you *trust* your Emperor?"

"Theatrics," Lutz muttered from below and shook his head. Voldigar returned his attention to Lusánt in time to see him raise a long hand to the sky.

"I swear to you, I will excel all my forebears in wisdom, in strength, and in power. Will you excel with me?" He flung his arms wide. His voice had grown a dangerous edge. "Do you offer me cowardice or loyalty?"

Stiff silence settled over the courtyard again, save for a muffled murmur. Lusánt's eyes came briefly to rest on Voldigar before he peered down the center of the colonnade and took a deep breath. "It is time!"

Lusánt raised his wide eyes to the ivory doors as they creaked open once more. All heads turned to the back of the colonnade where a lithe woman stepped through the doors in a gown of deep emerald. At the very moment her feet touched upon the tiled path there was a pulse of light, and the rising moon emerged, brilliant and green. It looked twice its normal size and peered down over the walls of the Citadel as it climbed the shoulder of the Spire. The torches shrunk from its presence. An audible gasp rose from the crowd.

The woman held the Silver Crown of Aramon in her hands and walked forward steadily with the unmistakable gait of the *Miridas*. It was cat-like, subtle and hypnotic. Her people were often seen below in the Undercity, coming and going from their ships that plied the Wending Sea, but they never came here, never above in these halls. Her steps passed noiselessly along the path. Hyrodan and Ragat looked on in shock and silent horror.

The long train of her dress followed behind, yard after yard, and upon her brow was a shimmering circlet from which hung strings of spinning pearls that obscured her face. Only a vague smile was visible on her faintly turquoise skin. All about her, the cherry blossoms continued to rain, but now glowing in the green light of Mirvánè.

She ascended the steps gracefully where Lusánt stood, eyes closed and arms still stretched wide. Slowly, she raised the crown and placed it upon his head, then stepped backward down the stairs, staring up at him. All was silent for a long breath.

"Behold!" she cried in a high clear voice and raised her hands. "Lusánt. Emperor and Lightbringer! Long may he reign!" She knelt upon the lowest stair.

There was no response at first, but General Gamad cleared his throat and swept one huge fist into the air. "Lusánt!" he roared. "Lusánt! Lusánt!"

The crowd was swept up in his chant and roared along with him, thrusting their fists into the air as well. "Lusánt! Lusánt! Lusánt!"

The brethren stood in silence, eyes wide in flickering light while the chant went on around them. Voldigar blinked and looked across the path. Gwenyth was there, as still as he, face pale and drawn. They held one another's gaze and let silent words pass between their eyes. *What madness was this?*

———— ❖ ————

The Tower of the Sea was not so much a tower as a many-tiered gazebo that stood in open air on the farthest tip of Arregalt's promontory. It overlooked the Wending Sea in a breathtaking panorama. The lights of many ships twinkled in the darkness below, larger violet-colored lights for the great vessels of the Miridas. The moon's long glow stretched across the bay. There were few places in the capital Voldigar had never been, and this was one of them.

Musicians had struck up amid the roaring crowd and allowed Lusánt his escape from the coronation through an unremarkable door that led on to the Tower of the Sea. A group of soldiers whisked Voldigar away shortly thereafter and sent him through alone while the crowds erupted into a swirl of revelry. The muted sound of their mirth and of the instruments now drifted through the walls.

To his surprise, Voldigar found it was only Lusánt within. The ground floor of the tower was ringed with red-cushioned benches along its edge. On these, Lusánt perched upon his knees, leaning dangerously over the railing. The tower reached within inches of the promontory's lip.

"Can you believe Undercity is just below us?" Lusánt asked. "Have you ever wondered if one of them might try to just crawl up here into the tower? I can almost smell it! You?" He pulled himself back over the railing, and now seated, he brushed his black gloves aside.

"No, Your Highness, I can't say that I have. I smell only the sea," Voldigar replied.

Lusánt smirked and flicked his hand. "Bah. You lack imagination. What did you think of my coronation? Wasn't it magnificent?"

Voldigar stood stiffly in the door. "From your messenger, I understood I was to bring my brethren. Should we wait for them?"

Lusánt frowned and rolled his eyes. "Lanathor's not even here, Sword-Lector. Why is that?"

"He had urgent business across the pass and was unable to return in time. I am sorry for his absence."

Lusánt suddenly jumped to his feet and crossed the room to stand only a few inches from Voldigar, examining him like one might study an insect. His breath smelled of liquor.

"In the future, I'd prefer your men not have 'business' more urgent than my instructions. You look tired, old man."

Voldigar resisted the urge to rub his eyes as Lusánt wandered across the room to a cellarette. "It's been difficult to find sleep, my lord."

"Yes, well I can only imagine. You've kept yourself very, very busy." He poured wine into two cloudy-looking goblets and held one out to Voldigar.

Voldigar took it with a short nod of thanks, and Lusánt downed half of his in a gulp. He seemed to be considering what he next would say.

"I hear you let Lord Commander Caliras go," Lusánt finally said as he swirled his wine and stared into the cup.

"Caliras was slain near Westfort."

"Was he? Do you have a body?"

Voldigar held his glass still and swallowed on nothing. "I do not. But two members of my order bore witness. His body was washed into the river."

"That doesn't fill me with confidence," Lusánt said. "Why was he allowed to flee all the way to Westfort? No less than the mighty Brotherhood of Aramon were personally assigned by their Emperor to find him."

Voldigar opened his mouth to reply, but Lusánt held up a hand and continued. "I know why, Voldigar." He downed the rest of his wine. "You were busy hunting ghosts again."

Voldigar frowned. "Forgive me, Emperor, but I must speak plainly. The creature that assaulted you presented a terrible and urgent danger to Aramon."

"It did not assault me," Lusánt said loudly. "Do you have a body?"

Voldigar blinked at the sudden question. Lusánt crossed over to him but did not meet his eyes. "Is. The. Orun. Dead?" He emphasized each word with a stab of his finger in Voldigar's chest.

"Where did you hear that word?"

"Oh come on, Voldigar. I am the Emperor. I know a lot of things." He took Voldigar's glass and used the same finger to swirl the wine. "I'm not a child. You confided these things in my father, did you not?" Lusánt sat back down on the cushions and continued to drink.

"I did."

"I understand that a creature like that must be put into some kind of prison . . ."

"Yes."

"And? Are we speaking plainly or not? Did you . . . imprison it?" Lusánt gazed into the bottom of the wine glass again.

"No," Voldigar replied. "But we have reason to believe it was destroyed. We continue to watch."

"Watching," Lusánt said. "Waiting. Sounds riveting. What were you doing in my vaults?"

Voldigar tried not to flinch. "Our investigation led us there, Your Highness.

"What a strange place to look for Caliras." Lusánt frowned. Voldigar started to reply, but the young Emperor continued. "For an order sworn to do my will—you have a very curious habit of defying me. Is an oath to your Emperor not important to you? Is it not an oath to your people? What could be higher?"

"Only the will of God."

Lusánt sat in silence for a moment, staring out over the bay. "You still haven't told me what you thought of my coronation."

"I pray you will long defend and protect Aramon's people," Voldigar replied. "I don't think it was wise to have a Priestess of the Moon place your crown."

Lusánt threw his head back and laughed. "There it is. Of course. Voldigar the Wise! How shall I rule Aramon without you, Teacher? Did you see the nobility? Did you see the soldiers and the common men? They *loved* me. They united behind me—and what a show it was! What good is it without a twist?"

"The people are fickle, Lusánt, and I pray you would appeal to their principle, to their wisdom, and to the truth God has given us."

Lusánt rolled his eyes again. "What do you care about moon priestesses anyway? What's it to you? You don't even believe in the gods." His words had begun to slur.

"My belief or no, it is dangerous to meddle with that cult. Olwis outlawed it with reason."

Lusánt stared unblinking at the cushion beside him and absently picked at its upholstery. A disturbing flicker of pain flashed across his face. The young man flinched, almost imperceptibly. "My father was so fond of your superstitions," Lusánt said wistfully, his voice growing distant.

"And I respect your religion, Voldigar. I really do. I admire your . . . principle? Convictions?" He shook his head and then stared into Voldigar's eyes as he rose to his feet. "It's just the practical realities of what you said. . . . Loyalty, old man. In the end, that's all it is. That's all anything is." He waved his hand behind him, and another twitch crossed his jaw. "My kingdom is full of sycophants and cowards, treachery and reckless ambition. Why do you think I gave *you* my ring? I need men of principle and skill. I need *you* and your order."

"Aramon needs justice, Lusánt." Voldigar's words sounded strangely remote in his own ears.

A cold wind was blowing through the open sides of the tower now, and as thin as his own voice seemed, the young Emperor's had become oddly present. He approached Voldigar slowly while his words echoed dully from all sides, a gentle, sibilant whisper. "I know your history, Voldigar Anteres. I know about Gwenyth's . . . illness. Is she not my cousin? I know about your deep poverty." He smiled but his eyes looked sad. "I know the good news you received today, and I even know about Rory."

Voldigar narrowed his eyes and stepped back involuntarily. Lusánt took the last few steps toward him.

"Did you know that I can make *all* that pain go away, Voldigar? And who would deserve it more than you? Who has sacrificed more than you? Who has been more faithful? Your name restored, your lands restored, your reputation restored—and The Brotherhood of Aramon standing tall again in the power and respect they deserve. . . . I just need to know I have your *loyalty*."

Voldigar remembered his weariness again, the strain of the last two days, the emptiness of his strength. He let his eyes fall to the floor but then blinked like he'd just awoken from a dream. His skinny student stood before him again, nothing more.

"Don't answer yet, Voldigar," Lusánt said with a smile. "There's one more piece to my coronation. Tonight we must make our own great light, and secure my realm."

CHAPTER SIXTEEN

LOYALTY

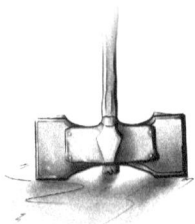

T HE SEVEN BRETHREN WALKED in wary silence, following their
new Emperor along the Citadel's long circuit. Lusánt held a
flaming brand high above his head and moved with purpose at the
front. General Gamad and no less than two hundred soldiers had
joined as Lusánt's escort and struggled to match his long strides.
Voldigar squeezed Gwenyth's hand and did all he could not to simply
turn aside, leaving the city and this strange night behind. He felt as a
man marching to his doom, but duty drove him on.

It wasn't long until their destination became clear: the fortified barracks of the Stonepike Guard. It was a huge structure of rough-hewn
wood, concrete, and quarried stone. Five stories in height, it extended
from near the wall of the Citadel all the way to the edge of the southern
sea cliffs. By daylight, a huge inner wall and aqueduct would have cast
their angled shadows on its face, but in darkness, it was nothing more
than an ominous monument, quiet and dead. There was no sign of
stirring within.

All about the barracks was a hastily constructed camp, filled with men
in Dantic's blue and Gamad's maroon. The cordon was indistinguishable

from a siege, and there must have been two thousand men at least encircling the barracks.

Commander Dantic emerged from a tent, and catching sight of Lusánt's troop, he hurried up a wide flight of stone steps to meet them. His face was worn and hard.

"Emperor," he said as he bowed. "To what do we owe the honor?"

Lusánt ignored the question and instead surveyed the barracks in quiet contemplation.

"Stay here," Voldigar whispered to Gwenyth. "No matter what happens, do not come down these stairs." Gwenyth bit her lip and nodded. Voldigar flexed his fingers and rubbed his eyes. Rest was only distant memory, and he wondered how little of his strength and of his Chanting remained. He shouldn't be here. Every fiber of his experience and intuition urged him to withdraw.

"Where were you at my coronation, Commander Dantic Banari?" Lusánt asked.

"With my men," he answered. "I am sorry to have missed it, my lord, but I believe we are near to concluding negotiations with the Stonepikes. They're not prepared for a siege and Lord Caliras is dead. It's only a matter of time before they surrender—on our terms."

Lusánt smirked and repeated the word as though he were tasting a lemon. "Surrender . . ." he said. "Too gentle a fate for Lord Caliras, don't you think?"

Dantic squinted at the question, but Lusánt did not explain. Instead, he signaled for all to follow, and they made their way to the bottom of the long steps and into the encampments below. Gwenyth stayed behind.

"Gamad, please proceed," Lusánt said with a knowing nod at the old general.

Gamad smiled and stepped forward at a trot. He stopped as he passed Voldigar and let out a low growl. "My key, whelp."

Voldigar met his gaze but felt a sudden warning and hesitation, as though the gesture meant something more. Nonetheless, he pulled Gamad's key from his pocket and dropped it in his meaty paw. Gamad smiled triumphantly and continued on, barking orders to his men.

"I suggest you place your soldiers on alert, Commander Dantic. There may be action soon," Lusánt said.

Dantic's eyebrows shot up, and he looked as though he wished to speak. Instead, he hurried off, and in a mirror of Gamad, passed a flurry of orders among his soldiers. No sooner had he left than dozens of Gamad's legionnaires surged forward with sloshing buckets and huge bales of dry hay. The latter they placed all along the walls, and the former they splashed again and again against every surface of the barracks. Soon after, squads of soldiers ran forward with huge crossbeams. The largest of these, ten men wedged against the two-paneled front gate. Smaller beams were pressed against a handful of other doors along the wall. There was a flash of motion behind the small windows of the barracks, but the legionnaires then hurried back to their lines without further incident. All was quiet again.

"What are you doing, Lusánt?" Voldigar asked. He felt his hands begin to shake as the smell of oil streamed through the air.

"I," the Emperor replied, "am preparing my first lesson for you—my fellow king, and former teacher." He waived Gamad over and whispered something in his ear.

"Kings must make difficult decisions," Lusánt continued. "Bring forth your men." Voldigar did not react, but the other brethren soon joined him at his side.

"Which of these is your Skeltemist, Voldigar?"

Urias bristled with an audible snarl. Medellai, blind as he was, placed a calming hand upon his shoulder.

Voldigar stayed the others with a glance and answered. "Skeltemeny is outlawed. This you know, Emperor."

Lusánt waved his hand dismissively. "Your Fireweaver then, whatever. I see I have my answer." He examined Urias from head to toe. "You, and your lord, come with me. The rest of you, back up the stairs." Lusánt stepped to the edge of the siege lines and stood with his back turned.

The brethren looked from face to face in confusion. "It's alright," Voldigar said. "Don't intervene." There was a moment of unspoken argument, but the others soon relented and led Medellai up the stairs. Voldigar and Urias made their way alone to the Emperor.

"Give your man the command," Lusánt said.

Voldigar set his jaw firmly and said nothing.

"Oh, don't play coy with me, Sword-Lector," Lusánt said as he looked over his shoulder. "You know exactly what I mean. I set the fuel, but this bonfire needs something more potent than a match." Lusánt laughed as he turned away again. "It needs loyalty."

"Emperor, you heard Commander Dantic. The Stonepikes are near to surrender."

"Stop dithering, Voldigar!" Lusánt yelled.

"I'm not dithering, Lusánt. These men are soldiers, nothing more. They have homes, wives, families."

"Do they? Would you teach me compassion too, Elder? These traitors chose Caliras. They chose their loyalties poorly. And now they pay their due!"

"They enlisted, that is all. They serve in what they know. Give them another day, for God's sake. There are a thousand men in there!"

"Don't appeal to your god with me, old man! Do as I say."

Voldigar's hands trembled as he lowered his brow and mustered what strength he had left into his voice. "No."

Lusánt whirled and rushed to within an inch of his face. He spoke in a hissing whisper. "Remember what I said to you. Remember who I am." Lusánt searched his face, expecting a reaction that never came. "I will *not* extend my hand to you again, Voldigar Anteres!"

Voldigar stood motionless. He had said all he could.

"I suspected as much. The Kings of the Thirteen Provinces bow to their Emperor, but you, little king, you dare not!" Lusánt shook his head as he backed away. "What a shame." He motioned with a hand to Gamad and into their midst the old general dragged a wiry man in rags on the end of a chain. His eyes were wild, and his limbs moved as if he had no joints. He shook and staggered, and his fingers twitched like the legs of a spider.

"As it happens," Lusánt went on, "I've brought my own Skeltemist."

From the top of the stairs, the brethren cried out and reached for their weapons. A thick row of soldiers gathered to bar their way. Voldigar too lurched forward, but Lusánt's escort closed around him in an instant.

"Whatever stupid thing you think you're about to do," Lusánt shouted, "don't!" His hand was stretched out to the brethren in warning. Soldiers grasped Voldigar about his arms and chest, pulling him backward. Lusánt nodded to Gamad.

Gamad marched the chained man ahead and snapped the binding from off his neck. The prisoner stumbled onward, gibbering mad words and waving his arms at invisible phantoms. He stopped and stared at the ground a moment before he leaned his head back to the sky. A light flickered from his eyes, and broiling flame vomited from his mouth, cascading over his shoulders. He stood frozen in this pose for a few seconds, then arched his back and lunged. His feet came fully off the ground, and he hovered there a foot above the cobblestone.

In a blinding flash of light, a huge plume of flame erupted from his hands and crashed against the barracks' walls. The man flicked it side to side as it licked along the surface. It seemed at first like nothing would happen, flame deflecting harmlessly off the stout stronghold, but a moment later the oil and hay caught in a massive conflagration. The Skeltemist went on, and a raging inferno sprang to life combined of fire both natural and sorcerous.

Voldigar's weary mind raced as he watched in horror. What could he do? What could he say? If he broke free, he would surely only add the deaths of seven brethren to those of the Stonepikes. If he managed to open the door and the Stonepikes poured out, it would be a bloodbath in the streets as the armies fell one upon the other.

"Stop!" Voldigar cried out. "Stop!"

"Stop?" Lusánt laughed and held his hands up high like the conductor of an orchestra. "I'm just getting started! It's too late now, King Voldigar. Too late! Look at my bonfire! Look at my justice!"

It was true. The flames rose up a hundred feet into the night sky, taking on a life apart from the Skeltemist or the fuel. From a high narrow window, Voldigar saw a man lean his head, coughing and tearing at his eyes. The figure vanished for an instant, only to reemerge and squeeze through the tiny gap. Like a ghastly comet, he plummeted ablaze through the night air and crashed into the pavement below. Voldigar's chest and shoulders convulsed, his eyes stung with the smoke of the fire, but he could not look away.

"Illegal sorcery! Illegal sorcery!" Lusánt shouted and danced side to side. "But no!" He stopped. His eyes were wide in wicked delight. "We can't have illegal sorcery, can we, Brothers of Aramon? Gamad!"

Gamad smiled and yanked a long knife from his belt. Walking behind the mad Skeltemist, he wrapped his thick arm around the wiry man's head and drew the blade across his neck. He slumped to the ground in a steaming heap.

"See!" Lusánt shouted and laughed, even as he coughed in the vapors. The flames grew higher. "Aramon is pure again!"

Voldigar could bear it no longer. There was no more consideration. No more fear of consequence. No more rationale. He would not let a thousand men die unaided while fire consumed them, come what may. He searched for the brethren upon the stairs and saw that they were now bodily restrained. He spotted Gwenyth too, standing a little further off, and gave her one more glance. He smiled softly and hoped he had seen the same upon her distant face. With a great heave, he swung one arm and then the other, scattering legionnaires like toys. He lowered his head and charged forward with his shoulders low. He felt the edge of a sword bite deeply into his chest and a spear pierce him below the arm. Heedless, he continued his mad charge.

In an instant he was at the huge crossbeam, pulling with all his might. It budged a little. The wood groaned, but it did not give way. He was so tired. He pulled again, and the flames licked at his arms and face. It was so heavy. With a great cry he leaned, but there was nothing left. Smoke blinded him and filled his lungs. A few seconds more and the legionnaires were upon him, pulling from every side—kicking and cursing and batting at the flames.

They dragged him into the square, pinning every limb. Merciless blows rained down, one after another. Lusánt leaned over him and shook his head in mock remorse. Through blurred vision and streaming fume, Voldigar could see him only dimly. "So much lost, old man. So much thrown away. Give me my ring!" The blows ceased and he reached into Voldigar's pocket. He pulled the signet ring out and placed it on his finger. "The Emperor speaks for himself again!" He leaned low over Voldigar and whispered where only he could hear. "For you, Brother Voldigar, this life is over. Go home, and die a peasant." The world reeled, the earth seemed to open beneath his back, and all became darkness.

PART TWO

Chapter Seventeen

Ghost Light

THERE WAS NO TIME to flee, for the ghost light upon the horizon gathered like a falling star and crashed into Dizghizádè. Lanathor shrank back, but Liadov stepped to the terrace's edge and spread her arms wide. There was a blinding flash, and she was enveloped in a roaring inferno. Lanathor could only shield his eyes. He was knocked upon his back, and his priceless telescope careened off the roof. Instead of the searing death he expected, he found himself surrounded by a brilliant radiance. He caught his stolen breath and crawled to his hands and knees.

There Liadov stood, a strobing light doing battle with the pale green fire against her. It stretched in a wide arc around them. Swirling blackness licked between the billowing flames of these two beacons. Lanathor inched his way forward and saw Liadov's face, frozen in her dread. Her teeth were bared, and the whites of her eyes shone around great blue irises. She trembled terribly but otherwise did not move. The green fire slowly drove her back, her delicate slippers tearing against the roof's surface.

"Liadov!" Lanathor cried out, but she did not hear. His voice was a distant echo in an endless stream of light. Powers too terrible to comprehend were only inches from his body. Through the maddening clamor, fear took him, the sort which he had not known since before the Brethren rescued him so long ago. He was powerless to act, no less frozen than the brave face of his dear friend before him. He was a child again, a victim and nothing more. He tried to reach for the last piece of root within his robes, but his hand would not move. His gaze was fixed on Liadov, watching her slowly falter. A sun of gold, flickering into the abyss.

It was then he saw a curious thing. One of the little blue fireflies of the oracle lazily fluttered past his face and landed there on Liadov's outstretched hand, uncaring, unafraid, its glow untouched by the horror before them. Almost imperceptibly, he saw Liadov's mouth move, trying to form a word. A tear streamed from her eyes and into her golden hair that whipped behind her. He found the root within his hand, bit, and swallowed it whole.

Like the flame of a torch suddenly snuffed out, darkness overtook him. The earth vanished, and a great field of starlight sprang into brilliant array. Before him, Liadov hovered in silence, locked in battle with a force he could no longer perceive. All about him, the threads of the Song flowed and rippled against his body in an undulating weave of shadow, a great thick mane of resonating filament.

Lanathor reached his hands forward. No longer a network of jagged fissures, they were all aglow in the violet light of a deep well of power. There was no spell upon his lips, no Teller's weave, no arcane memory that he could form within his learned mind. He tottered there upon the precipice, his being a great constellation collapsing in upon itself. He could not grasp the threads, but to his own astonishment, felt himself pour into them like rain into the sea. The end had come, mortality uncoiling in a bloom of unimaginable beauty.

The stars spun, and the roar of searing lights washed over him again only to reverse and rupture with a rush of air. The world flickered into sight where he and Liadov hung weightless for a wavering moment in time. The great flames were gone, and Lanathor heard only the sound of life-blood pulsing in his ears. The moment passed, and they both fell to the earth.

Lanathor groaned and rose again upon his knees. The green light rapidly receded like the obscene leg of a massive spider, dying and curling back to its ghastly body somewhere over the horizon. All about him, he could see the twisted and broken marble of the once beautiful gardens. There were terrible gashes in the ground and huge stones upturned and cast about like leaves. The glow of more natural fires flickered all around, but shimmering sparks of green still dropped like snow.

Liadov lay several feet away upon one of the few remaining patches of grass. Her eyes were closed. Lanathor scrambled to her and tried to grasp her arms, but he found to his dismay that he could do so only weakly, for his hands were stiff and burned. "Liadov!" he cried. She was sleeping, as peaceful as the firefly folding its wings upon her brow. Her chest gently rose and fell.

<hr />

"Help!" Lanathor called out again and again. "Can anyone hear me?" He turned his head from side to side, but rubble and fire obscured his view. He tried to wake Liadov again but only confirmed it was hopeless. With agonizing effort, he uncurled his charred hands. Blood oozed from them and though the motion brought tears to his eyes, he soon managed to rip long strips of cloth from his cloak, wrapping them about his palms.

A spreading fire crept closer, licking up what remained of any greenery in the oracle. Lanathor lifted Liadov into his arms and rose to his feet. He could see now over the rubble, twisted bodies of the garden's faithful servants. It was quiet, save for crackling flames. Across the field, he hurried with Liadov's light frame and laid her upon a low-hanging bough from a huge juniper tree at the head of the trail. He rushed back into Dizghizádè.

Smoke was gathering fast. He choked through the sleeve of his robes, searching in vain for survivors as long as he dared, darting between fires and leaping over toppled pillars. He called out without answer until his voice was hoarse and the flames finally drove him back. He swept Liadov up in his arms again and descended coughing down the trail, leaving the ruin of the gardens behind.

Despite the powerful dose of Falam Root, unbidden tears streamed down his dark face while he carried her along, weaving to keep the overhanging branches from striking her. Had he brought this doom upon Dizghizádè? Had his coming led to the deaths of all these souls? What malevolent power had he awoken? The thoughts were too terrible to bear.

Whatever had happened, the attack centered on Liadov herself, and yet she lived. He had to keep moving.

The light of the fires above receded, and Lanathor slowed as darkness set in about him. Narrow sections of the path ran along treacherous drops into the forest below. At length, he placed her gently in the elbow of a switchback and stopped to rest.

Beyond the blackness of the forest floor, the moon reflected off the wide snowplains of Danek below. It no longer looked so swollen as it did upon its rising, but the moon was full and soared into the sky far earlier than it should, illuminating a massive gash across the land. Such a thing was impossible, he knew, but Liadov herself prophesied these signs many years before. He had thought her words symbolic but now laughed bitterly to see them with his own eyes. He wished for anything that he might wake her and ask the meaning.

He glanced down at her, still peaceful in her rest. Black soot and his own blood marred her white garment, but she was unharmed. He'd rested long enough. Lifting her lightly, again he disappeared into the deep gloom of the forest trail.

The dangerous drop-offs were now passed, but sight became hopeless in the deepening forest. He moved slowly as the cold grew about him. A light layer of snow that had passed through the canopy mingled with needles upon the ground and crunched under his feet. Liadov's garment was thin, and Lanathor stopped again to blindly wrap her in his fur cloak. Bitter cold swept across his body, but in this at least, the root did its work. He cared little and took up his march again.

The ground soon leveled, and a thin glow of moonlight penetrated the darkness. Lanathor was glad of the light, but without the descent of the mountainside, he feared he might lose direction. There was a village not far from the head of the trail, and he realized he would have to beg upon the hospitality of its people. The same cold indifference he'd been glad of in the day might now prove fatal in the night. What a thing it would be to see the same wandering Azkushan at your door at midnight, covered in blood and bearing a sleeping Daneki woman.

Lanathor's thoughts were broken by the sound of swift-moving feet, running and stumbling through the forest to his left. He laid Liadov softly beside him again and crouched low to watch and listen. He could hear the sound of labored breathing and the whimpering of a man's voice in fear. In a moment, a shadowy figure appeared, scrambling through the underbrush.

Closer now, Lanathor could hear a second sound—a snuffling, grunting wheeze, like that of an animal. He crept closer still and with a searing pain, allowed the purple light to emerge upon his left hand, though he hid it in his robe. With the other, he grimaced and drew his short sword. He was nearly upon the fleeing man.

Out of the darkness, something leapt upon the runner with a snarl and a squealing, pig-like shriek. Lanathor burst from the bushes and flashed the light of his hand into the night. There he expected to see a man in the brush and an animal in pursuit. The man he saw, but what attacked him was something entirely different.

Under the violet glow, from the chest up was the form of a boar with matted brown fur, furious red eyes, and even two hoofed forelegs in the place of arms. From the chest down it was the body of a man in ragged garb, covered in congealed blood. Lanathor had only a moment to gape in horror, for the creature caught sight of him too and spinning, leapt from its victim with a howl.

In his surprise, Lanathor was sent flailing onto his back. He tried to catch himself and cried out as pain shot through his hand and arm. His sword he still clutched, as tightly as he could in his other fist, and this he thrust into the neck of his attacker. It shrieked and gurgled, and its eyes went wide. It clawed or perhaps kicked at its neck in desperation. "Hold still," it croaked in a guttural tone as it writhed. "Hold . . . still . . ." And then it fell limp on top of Lanathor.

Lanathor lay breathless for a moment before he rolled the foul corpse from his chest and stood, shining the purple light of his hand over its face. Expecting some sort of hood or mask, he was astonished to see that the creature was indeed just as ghastly as it seemed. He had not considered long when the man, a Daneki farmer by his look, tried to scramble to his feet and flee again over tangling roots.

"Wait!" Lanathor called after him. "Wait!" he repeated in Daneki. "I'm a friend."

The man paid him no heed but continued to squirm. "Daneki!" he said as firmly as he could. The man hesitated.

"The creature is dead," Lanathor went on in his language. "I'm not going to hurt you. I'm a traveler, in flight myself. What happened here?"

The man was young, and he had the weather-beaten face and hands typical of his people. Sweat-soaked blonde hair was swept across his forehead. Trembling, he stopped, leaned his head against a tree, and wept.

"Are there more?" Lanathor asked.

The man nodded through his sobs.

Lanathor lowered his voice. "You must be quiet, young man." He placed a bandaged hand on the farmer's shoulder. The young man flinched but tried to control his crying. Lanathor listened into the darkness, glancing nearby where Liadov lay. It was still, other than the shaky breaths of the Daneki man.

"Are you a wizard?" the man finally said, staring at Lanathor's glowing fingers. Lanathor let the light fade out, and the two stood in darkness.

"No. My name is Lanathor. I am a lector—a reader." He struggled to find the Daneki term. "A teacher, from Aramon. Please, lower your voice,"

The man caught his breath and tried to match Lanathor's whisper. "Who is your woman, lying in the darkness there? Is she dead?"

"No, unconscious. What's your name?" Lanathor asked.

"I'm Survii. Just a farmer. I'm from the village—over there."

Lanathor held up his finger. Though the man could surely not see it in the darkness, he seemed to perceive Lanathor's purpose. They both held their breath and listened into the night. All was calm.

Lanathor's eyes adjusted a little to the faint moonlight. He could see the farmer backing round a tree. "Survii, tell me what happened." He let a little of the light return to his fingertips.

Survii's face twisted in fear, revealing a pair of missing teeth. "The village was attacked," he finally managed to say, staring in wonder at Lanathor's hand. "These things, they beat down our doors and dragged people away. They took our animals. Some men tried to fight, but . . ." Survii shook his head, unable to continue. His breath was growing shaky again.

Lanathor stared at the corpse by his feet and turned his light to it again. "Did the attackers all look like this?"

Through clenched teeth, Survii nodded his head. His whole body shook. "That was my brother, Alazi." He closed his eyes. "And my pig."

Chapter Eighteen

A Man for the Job

Two days had passed since the coronation, and Tepic stood on a desk, resting on his elbows to look out his turret window into gathering evening gloom. Other than the strange woman who'd crowned Lusánt, it was a boring event. His mother had hardly allowed him to see anything and then whisked him home right after. His father had not allowed him outside since, not even for sword lessons. All he could do was daydream about the city below and friends he wished he had. Not for the first time, he considered how he might tie sheets together and climb down the wall of the Citadel like the hero in some fairy tale.

Sword lessons, he recalled, were probably canceled anyway. He couldn't get his parents to answer any questions, but when Father had come home late on the night of the coronation, he'd woken up and overheard them talking in urgent tones about things he didn't fully understand. It seemed the old sword-lector had gotten himself into a lot of trouble.

Tepic lay on his bed and closed his eyes. There in his imagination was the leering face of Caliras. He could feel the hilt of a dagger in his hand and a coiling fear in his stomach. Something else lingered there as well, like late frost on spring fruit. He wanted to hide, to be alone forever. He flashed his eyes open and absently rubbed at his throat. The man was dead and gone, he reminded himself. The sword was safe, out of his reach, and whatever wicked plans he had were foiled. Perhaps the villain really did deserve to die.

The Brothers of Aramon had all seemed very impressed with his fight, but Tepic felt only misery. He'd always wanted to be in an adventure, but his kidnapping and the battle in the mines left him numb—and those were the better moments. He had nightmares about his fall both nights since. He wished the old sword-lector were there to talk to. It seemed like Father didn't want to speak about anything ever again, as if the words alone would steal Tepic and Lyrusia away once more into terrible danger.

A knock came at his door, and Lyrusia walked in. She never waited for him to respond. "Are you coming to eat?" she asked.

Tepic rolled over on his side.

"Oh come on," Lyrusia continued. "You can't starve yourself."

"Yes I can," Tepic said. "And why do we eat together anyway? Nobody says anything."

Lyrusia crossed the room and rolled him over, wagging a finger in his face. "You have to eat, and try talking about something normal. Mom and Dad are just scared. The last time Dad talked to you about monsters you went off and got captured by one."

"You got captured too!" Tepic said and turned back to his side.

Lyrusia huffed in exasperation and stomped out of the room.

Tepic lay there a few minutes more while his stomach growled but finally slid out of bed to wander down his spiral stairs. Passing the den, he glanced at the empty rack where Grandfather's sword once hung. Dantic had let Tepic hold on to the sword all the way home, but then locked it away in his own chambers the moment they returned.

In the dining hall, his family was already seated, and servants were standing in the shadows near the entryways. He sat in silence and watched his mother and father do the same. Lyrusia stared at Tepic for a long while with her eyebrows raised and her thumbs pressed together. She coughed.

"These are good potatoes," Tepic managed.

His mother swallowed and nodded. "Yes, very good."

Dantic clinked a spoon on his dish and raised it with a grunt of approval. Tepic waited several moments for someone to say something else and then glared at Lyrusia.

"What did Sword-Lector Voldigar do wrong?" Tepic asked.

Lyrusia groaned. Dantic finished chewing and wiped his mouth. "Sword-Lector Voldigar, as I've said before, Tepic, did not see eye to eye with the Emperor's decisions at or after the coronation."

"But what does that mean?" Tepic said.

Dantic looked to his wife and gestured. "Claras."

"It means," Claras said, "that we're looking for a new instructor for you. Lector Voldigar will not be coming to the city anymore."

"But why?" Tepic protested. "Father said it's *good* that the Readers teach me!"

"Yes, but things are a little bit strange right now," Claras replied.

"Why can't I just go visit his farm?"

"That's enough, Tepic," Dantic replied.

"Are you just going to keep me locked up forever?"

Dantic started to reply, but Tepic scraped his chair away and stormed off to his room. He was thirteen now and had fought a man in a secret passage all the way in Westfort. He'd seen things nobody else had seen, but they still thought he was just a child.

He flopped back into his bed and covered his eyes with his hands.

<hr/>

Tepic awoke to the muffled sound of voices below. He could not tell who was speaking, but it didn't sound like anyone in his family. He crept from his room and tiptoed down the spiral stairs to the edge of the den.

The fire was low, and his mother stood in the arch between rooms with her arms crossed. His father was at attention with a concerned look on his face, and Lyrusia sat quietly in the shadows across the room. In the center was none other than Emperor Lusánt himself, sitting casually in a chair someone had dragged across the floor. Beside him stood a tall Xerimadi warrior, sleeveless and dark-skinned. He had a heavy mustache and knotted muscles. The latter glanced up the stairs the moment Tepic had come into view. He looked away, pretending not to notice.

"What if I'm asking your opinion?" Lusánt was saying. "You are a commander of my military, are you not?"

Dantic replied. "Of course, my lord. I misunderstood. It was effective, of course. As a matter of morale and conscience though, I would not have advised it."

"Conscience?" Lusánt said with a warning brow.

Dantic licked his lips. "Yes, my lord."

"Explain your meaning," Lusánt said.

Dantic shifted his weight. "It is my military advisement, Your Highness. The Stonepikes are—were—soldiers, and many were no doubt still loyal. They were caught up in confusion."

"So you would take traitors into your ranks, Commander Dantic?"

"No, my lord, not at all. I—"

"You're full of contradictions, Lord Banari. No matter. I will take your opinion under advisement. Here." Lusánt held an envelope out to Dantic.

Dantic accepted the letter with a look of surprise and a bow.

"Open it," Lusánt said.

Dantic tightened his brow as he read, dismay spreading across his reddening face.

"This is a demotion . . ." Dantic said quietly.

"Yes!" Lusánt leaned forward. "Yes, it is. Not only am I unhappy with the security of Arregalt, I had to personally intervene against the Stonepikes." He rose to his feet.

Dantic's mouth hung open as he read further. "Eastfort? I'm to be a field officer again?" he asked.

"And Westfort," Lusánt said as he paced and stared at the floor. "You already command the Eastfort, but I was also quite unhappy with one of Gamad's men who I understand lost the Westfort without a drop of blood." He looked up. "Be glad you did not receive his punishment."

Dantic began to protest but Lusánt cut him off again.

"It's not up for discussion, *Captain* Dantic. I'm replacing command of the City Guard with one of Gamad's more capable officers. As for you, I'm assigning you to guard the pass in *both* forts. A high honor, really. Four cohorts for a single captain is unheard of." Lusánt looked Dantic in the eyes with a thoughtful expression. "I can't think of a more brave and loyal soldier to hold the border—but you're not the right man for City Guard."

Claras had gone white, and she chewed her trembling lip. Lusánt went on. "You will have to leave this house behind, of course. We'll have porters here in two or three weeks to help you with all the arrangements."

"Your Highness," Claras cried out from the archway. "We've been here fifteen years. Please!"

Lusánt's expression went flat, he blinked a few times as though the wall had just spoken.

"Claras," Dantic said sharply. "Please."

Claras muffled a sound into the cuff of her dress and backed into the room behind.

Lusánt inhaled. "As I was saying—the porters will help you carry everything to Eastfort, my expense. It's the least I could do. There are two exceptions though."

Lusánt waited for Dantic to tuck the folded letter into his pocket and went on. "Firstly, I understand there is a dangerous object in your household, a sword of some antiquity. My bodyguard here will be taking it back to the Spire for examination." Tepic's heart leapt into his throat.

Claras stepped back into the room. "No, m'lord, please, that sword was my father's. It's all I have left!"

Lusánt jerked his hand into the air. "Captain! Would you please get this woman under control?"

Dantic's face twisted in a rapid series of unreadable emotions. "Claras, please. It's alright." He led her a few paces into the next room where she continued on, her sobs disappearing through a further door.

Lusánt waited for Dantic to return. "We can return it to you, of course, after we confirm its safety. Please, go and fetch it for my man here."

Dantic hesitated. His cheeks were drawn and cold. A glance at the floor, and he slipped across the den through another set of doors. Tepic could hardly stifle his cry and looked wide-eyed to his sister.

Lyrusia still sat motionless in the corner, coolly regarding the Emperor. Lusánt stared casually at a painting while he waited, a fanciful scene of the mountain at the center of the world, but he soon looked up the stairs and smiled.

"Hello, fellow student," he said. "No hard feelings I hope from our training the other day. You were very good for your age." The Xerimadi grunted and grinned.

Dantic returned a moment later. In his hands, he held Grandfather's blade, still wrapped in cloth.

"My lord, I would ask you to return this soon. My wife has nothing left of her house, save this heirloom."

"Of course," Lusánt repeated. "As long as it's safe to do so, she'll have it back. There is a second matter though." He pointed up the stairs at Tepic. Lyrusia sat up in her chair. "I have need of new retainers. Your son, Tepic, he will be staying with me in the Spire for a while."

The blood drained from Dantic's face, and he jerked his gaze up the stairs. "My lord—"

Lusánt held up his hand. "It's already decided, and I will accept nothing to the contrary."

Tepic's mouth hung open. He felt dizzy. His weight rolled forward, almost toppling him down the stairs while he gripped the cold stone. Dantic's mouth moved again but no sound escaped into the muffled room. Tepic felt every set of eyes upon him and wanted nothing more than to bolt, but there was nowhere to run.

Chapter Nineteen

The World Fell Quiet

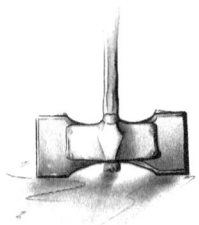

A S VIVID AS IT was, Voldigar knew he was dreaming. Still, he could not wake himself. The barley was ripe, and he and Gwenyth raced through the fields harvesting with frantic hands. Her face was set in concentration, and no matter what he said, she did not seem to hear. A great flood of water was rising rapidly, first over his toes, then over his ankles, and soon upon his knees. Back and forth he sped as the waters rose. He tried to carry more and more barley in his arms, but the fine stalks were soon submerged and waving in the turbulence.

The water was up to Gwenyth's neck now, and Voldigar cried out a warning. She continued to cut at the stalks and then hold them dripping above her head. He kicked his legs and swam to her with all his might, but a current had picked up. He was too weak, and it dragged him away. "Gwenyth," he shouted again and again. "Run!" But still, she did not seem to hear. Farther and farther he drifted away until she was only a speck on the horizon of a vast ocean, rising above the thatched roof of his meager home.

"I'm here," Gwenyth said. Voldigar opened his eyes. "I'm here," she repeated and placed a cool hand upon his forehead. He was breathing heavily.

Voldigar blinked in the candlelight. Gwenyth turned her head over her shoulder and called out. "He's awake again." Someone pulled the curtain back, and Voldigar shielded his eyes. Shivering, he gathered a blanket to his chin. "Gwen?" he asked weakly.

Vasherk crossed the room and knelt. "Really awake, old man?" he asked.

"Yes, what else would I be?"

Vasherk laughed. "Good. Very good."

Another man entered. Voldigar's own bedroom, he gathered. The familiar thinness of his old mat betrayed the location. His eyes soon adjusted and he saw Taro too, crouching beside Vasherk.

"Awake, awake?" Taro asked.

"Would someone mind telling me what's going on?" Voldigar tried to sit up and a cold fire tore through his chest. He grimaced.

"Easy, old man!" Taro said. He propped a pillow behind his back and eased him against the wall. "Here, drink this. Slowly now." He handed Voldigar a bowl of warm broth.

Voldigar drank it eagerly. He was famished. "How long have I been sleeping?"

Taro looked to Vasherk a moment before the elderly healer wiped his hair from his eyes. "Almost three days, Brother. It's the third morning since coronation."

Voldigar's brow shot up. A dozen anxious thoughts poured into his mind. The Orun. The Sword. The Emperor. His eyes darted around the room, and he tried to push himself to his feet.

"Whoa now, Voldigar. Careful," Vasherk said. His face was dark and earnest. He raised one of his hands from Voldigar's shoulders and laid it on his forehead instead. "You're still feverish."

Vasherk's eyes were black-rimmed, and for once the indefatigable old rogue looked tired.

"Your wounds were deep, Elder," Vasherk continued. "Those, I was able to care for. It's the fever though. I was never much good at it. Maybe Liadov could help, but . . . you get Taro's broth for now—and rest."

Voldigar groaned and drained the last of the bowl. "Where's Lanathor?"

Taro inhaled. "Late, unfortunately. Our hope is that Gardoric's already gone looking for him, but we sent Wulf off this morning too." Taro frowned and laid a gentle hand on Voldigar's arm. "You just rest though, Brother. Don't think too much."

Voldigar closed his eyes and concentrated on his breathing. His head ached and his stomach turned, but he decided he was feeling stronger by the moment. "How's Medellai?" he asked.

On cue, the Elder had just entered the room. "I'm fine."

"Can you see?"

"I can, a little, but only natural sight," Medellai said. His eyes still held the strange yellow tinge. "It started at the Stonepike Barracks. It's like looking through a cloud, Brother. All's in gray, but yes, I can see."

Voldigar sighed. "Thank God. What happened at the barracks?"

"God's honor, " Medellai said. "We made it out alive."

"Barely," Taro added. "We saw you break free, Elder. We weren't about to let you die down there alone."

"I know," Voldigar said. "Rash fools."

Vasherk laughed. "Medellai held us back. Taro was halfway down the stairs, but the Elder bid us hold. He said Lusánt wouldn't kill you. It was touch and go, Voldigar, but he was right."

"Thank you, Medellai," Voldigar said. "I was afraid you'd all follow me. I couldn't act—"

"I know you were," Medellai said. "You were too tired old man. Seems we all have our limits. We're lucky Gamad didn't finish you off. He's hard to predict, but Taro was able to help."

"How'd we get out?"

"At the point of a spear," Vasherk said. "You, we had to carry, and you're not light."

Voldigar laughed painfully. "And the Stonepikes?"

Vasherk shook his head. "Dead to a man. They had to open the aqueduct to keep the fire from spreading."

Voldigar fell silent and leaned his head against the wall. An image of the flaming soldier plummeting from the window flashed in his mind. All dead. One thousand men of Aramon, burned alive. "I need some air."

Against their protests, he stumbled to his feet and steadied himself against the wall. When he stepped into the next room, Soris, Urias, and Lutz rose to their feet with a flurry of salutes.

"Have you all been waiting for me?"

"Three days, Elder," Soris said.

Voldigar shook his head. "A whole flock of mother hens. I'm going outside."

"You're welcome," Lutz called after him.

Hobyn waited on the bench by the front door. "Young Master Voldigar, you're awake," he said as he too rose to his feet.

"Barely."

Hobyn furrowed his brow. "You know, you should be more grateful to your friends," he gently chided.

He was right of course—it wasn't the time to be irritable. He thought to lean his head back in and give a *thank you* to the brethren, but all he could do instead was prop himself against the door frame with a trembling hand.

Unexpectedly, Hobyn embraced him. "You had us so worried, and you talk so much in your sleep."

Voldigar laughed and winced, immediately remembering he shouldn't. "Bad dreams."

Hobyn nodded somberly. "Let me show you something."

He slipped an arm under Voldigar's and led him around the house where a fresh mound of dirt was raised. "Wulf helped me dig it," Hobyn said quietly and folded his hands.

The five stones Gwenyth had dug up from the field were close at hand, but one lay at the head of the grave. The rune for "R" in Daneki was carved into it.

Voldigar squeezed Hobyn's shoulder. "You're one of the good ones, Hobyn." He stood at the grave for a long while before he limped back inside.

"What news from Dantic?" Voldigar asked.

"Nothing, unfortunately," Medellai replied. He sighed heavily. "We're barred from the city."

Voldigar ground his teeth. "But what of Tepic's sword?"

Medellai shook his head. "Nothing."

"The Orun?"

The brethren shook their heads as one.

Voldigar glared. "The Emperor cannot just banish us from Arregalt—"

"Seems he can," Lutz interrupted. "I tried to enter this morning." He held up his hands in dismay.

Voldigar was overcome with a fit of coughing, and he steadied himself on Gwenyth's rocking chair. The room spun. She rushed to his side.

"You need to lie down again, Elder," Vasherk said. "You're burning up. We'll handle things, we'll search out the sword, and Lanathor, and all of it. You just rest."

Voldigar held up his hand. "No."

"You're no good to us half-dead. Don't be daft." Vasherk put his arm under Voldigar's and pulled. He relented, and they led him back to his mat.

Voldigar closed his eyes. It was the only way to stop the room from spinning. He could feel cold sweat pooling on his skin. His mat was soaked. Gwenyth was by his side again and put a small hand under the back of his head.

"Here, drink this," she said.

Voldigar blinked his eyes open. The smell of cloves and cinnamon wafted from her cup.

"Your Falam Root!" he said. "No, Gwen, we don't have that much."

"I feel fine," she said. "It's already mixed. Don't let it go to waste."

Voldigar meant to look her in the eyes, but his own stung and refused to focus. He had to close them again. She lifted the liquid to his mouth, and he reluctantly drank.

"You need to sleep a little more, Vol. Sometimes that's what the work is." Her voice trailed off.

Voldigar tried to capture the many thoughts that scurried over his mind, but the world was falling quiet around him. There was some other question he wanted to ask, something important, but he couldn't quite remember. He felt Gwenyth's hand upon his head. He heard the rush of blood in his ears, but the voices had gone silent. Soon he fell into a deep and dreamless sleep.

Voldigar shuffled his feet over the last few yards of field and dropped a final handful of seed. Hobyn was on the far side hitching Mack to the harrow. No dreaming, this time. Once the seed was in, they'd comb the field, cover what they'd sown, and wait for rain. Tomorrow, Hobyn's nephew would arrive to collect his tools and complete his own fields, just as planned.

Despite their protests, Voldigar had decided not only to do his own work but to help the young man with his planting too. He argued loudly that he wasn't an invalid, but in the end, relented. It was all he could do to convince them he was able to get out of bed at all. He was certain they were near to mutiny and to forcing him back to sleep with a double dose of Falam Root.

A day after Taro was last to leave and rejoin the Brethren in Maghaltani, Voldigar could stand it no longer. They'd made certain he knew that he was *not to intervene* and not to exert himself. They'd handle things without him, and his job was to rest. It was torture.

Hobyn and Gwenyth had completed the plowing and half the sowing without him when he finally stumbled his stiff legs across the field to take the seed grain from Hobyn and finish the job himself. They weren't entirely wrong, his fever had broken, but a profound weakness lingered in his limbs. He'd slept the greater part of five days and had not Chanted at all. His walk up and down the rows left him breathless.

Voldigar made for the bench by his front door and sat heavily, watching a lazy cloud roll across the horizon, slowly following the Ekhebiri where they drifted. It had been a dry few days, and he did his best to will the solitary cloud toward his farm. Gwenyth squeezed in beside him and offered a tasty-looking barley loaf.

"You look hungry," she said.

Gratefully, Voldigar raised the warm bread to his mouth. She leaned her head on his shoulder.

"Why so sad?" she asked. Gwenyth looked up into his eyes.

"Sad?"

"Yes, my love. You'll wilt the grain with that frown."

Voldigar chuckled. "Won't be any sprouts to wilt if it doesn't start raining again. Was I frowning?"

"Yes." She nuzzled closer and pulled his hand to her belly. "You're the cheerful one, Vol. I'm the sad one. Our son needs your smile."

Voldigar pressed his head against hers. He did smile. "So it's a son now, is it?"

"If you wish it, m'lord."

Voldigar stroked her cheek. She looked tired, but perhaps more well than most days. "I just wish us good health, Gwen, boy or girl. You are cheering me up."

"Good," she said. "We'll get rain. We'll get a good crop too. Maybe being a farmer isn't the worst thing, old man."

Voldigar nodded. "All I ever wanted."

"You're not worried about your Order? About your dragons?"

Voldigar rolled his jaw and thought a long while on her words. "No," he finally answered. "I can't be anymore. I slept a week and the world didn't end. The Order will get along without me."

Gwenyth searched his face carefully. "Will you get along without the Order?"

Voldigar sighed. "I won't live forever, Gwen. I'm just worried about you now." They sat in silence with their heads together, gazing across the field. Voldigar ran his hand across Gwenyth's belly. "How soon until he kicks?"

It was Gwenyth's turn to chuckle. "Another month or two at the very least, or so Lyrusia says. You'll just have to wait."

"How do you feel learning child-rearing from a seventeen-year-old?"

"Happier than I ever have in my life."

Voldigar smiled. "Fair enough."

Hobyn had finished preparing Mack, and slowly now, he worked the harrow across the field. They watched him quietly as seed disappeared under the churning earth.

"Your cousin said something to me in the capital," Voldigar said at length. Gwenyth turned her face toward his again with a quizzical look. He went on. "Go home, and die a peasant." Voldigar let the words hang in the air a moment while Gwenyth frowned. He shook his head. "I'd like nothing more, Gwen. Nothing more. Just give me a gray head and full years with you."

Her frown softened and she smiled. "With us, old man."

Voldigar kissed her head and began to softly Chant into her hair. There they stayed and held one another until the sun had crept down in the west, and the long shadow of the Spire was cast upon their field.

CHAPTER TWENTY

FOREIGNER

L ANATHOR LAY TREMBLING UPON his stomach, just below the crest
of a snowy knoll, rubbing his eyes and peering between squat bushes into a moonlit field. A pack of *Wyrna* were gathered in front of a
fire-blackened barn near a mangled corpse. Crouched upon their haunches, they grunted and jostled one another while they shuffled round the
body. Streaks of blood marred the trampled snow. In the ruined village
beyond, no less than a hundred more of the fiends picked at the ruins,
pulling at crumbled walls and tearing at the flesh of their victims. Lanathor
could not will himself to move.

'Wyrna,' Survii called them—a crossing of man and beast that had
stepped out of Daneki folklore and into their waking nightmares.
Lanathor remembered an encounter many years before with a sorcerer
who convincingly proclaimed himself to be a wolf walking on his hind legs.
It was a solitary madman then, and Survii too spoke of the Wyrna as lone
mythical hunters that haunted villages on a full moon. In the last two days,
they'd seen thousands.

Survii, for his part, had proved himself a doughty ally, far different than
the panicked serf he first seemed to be. On the night of their meeting, they
found a wide row of tracks leading away from his village, but no Wyrna
and no survivors. Smashed doors and grizzly remains were all that greeted
them. They barricaded his home and stayed there until morning.

Survii was insatiably curious about Liadov and had the shifting eyes and lingering gaze of a man accustomed to the night. Lanathor did not answer his questions. Instead, he placed himself between Liadov and Survii, taking first watch and sleeping with one eye open thereafter. To Lanathor's relief, Survii did not avail himself of banditry but slept fitfully instead, whimpering behind an upturned table.

The next morning, Lanathor had been eager to continue on to Aramon. Survii would not be parted from him, and after gathering warm clothing and supplies, he insisted on accompanying him to the border. The man wept and muttered witlessly as he tried to bury frozen corpses in the hard ground, but the earth would not yield, and Lanathor's wounded hands prevented any help. In the end, they could only hastily cover the victims in fresh snow before they fled together to seek the next village along the southern road and hope it was untouched by Wyrna. Lanathor crudely constructed a sled of sorts and used it to drag Liadov's sleeping form over the snow.

Far from untouched, the second village was overrun. Like a swarm of locusts on a field of carnage, a herd of Wyrna blackened the earth and sent a noisome fume into the air. The two men narrowly avoided detection and spent the day trying to find a way round only to see the Wyrna suddenly gather and depart in a rumbling stampede when evening fell.

As before, they thought to likewise fortify themselves in the village overnight, but when they finally entered with sleeves over their mouths, a straggling Wyrna stumbled upon them. To Lanathor's astonishment, Survii calmly dispatched the creature with a hand sickle, and the two settled in for another long cold night. What should have been a half day journey back to Aramon's border had become an ordeal of terrified plodding along the long valley floor of Danek.

And so it was, they reached this little knoll on the third night. Lanathor should have been in Aramon by now and prayed the Brethren had been able to hold off the Orun without Liadov. He tried to control his breathing, shaking while he sucked the cold through his teeth.

Clutching his sickle, Survii crawled to Lanathor's side and squinted into the darkness. "What are they doing?" he whispered.

Lanathor held his finger to his lips and glanced behind him down the knoll. Liadov still lay there upon her sled, wrapped in furs, peacefully exhaling little puffs of condensation. He turned his gaze to the Wyrna again just as a door opened beyond them. Out stepped an immense man, covered in coarse black fur with the living face and horns of a goat upon his neck. In one hand he too held a sickle, not unlike Survii's. In the other, he dangled the severed head of a dog.

The goat-man kicked and snarled at the other Wyrna. They scattered a few paces and gnashed their teeth in return. One swiped a clawed hand at the newcomer and took a booted strike to the face for its reward. It crumpled with a gruesome crunch and lay still on the snow.

The goat-man crouched over the corpse and worked at it with his blade. The others gibbered and howled. Lanathor could not help but look away, but he forced himself to watch again. To their noise, the creatures added a writhing dance of sorts, gyrating round the body and throwing refuse in the air.

A minute more and the goat-man's work was done. It stepped back and tossed something wet and heavy on the ground. The crowd of Wyrna shrieked and scattered toward the barn while a ghastly thing stood upon its legs. The mannish arms of the new beast tore at its own face while a snout snapped and barked at the twitching fingers.

Survii's mouth hung open in horror and Lanathor suspected he looked much the same. They inched back down the knoll.

"There are so many," Survii whispered breathlessly.

"And more in every village," Lanathor replied.

"What do we do?"

"Wait for them to move on, like the others. What more can we do?"

Survii looked up to the crown of the knoll again and closed his eyes to listen. "What if they don't move on?"

Lanathor had thought of this often in the last two days, never arriving at any satisfactory conclusion. The Wyrna seemed to be gathering, more and more, and always southward along the path that he must travel. They were in the wake of a swelling army of these creatures, and their danger festered with every passing hour.

Quietly, Lanathor crept to the crest again in search of some answer. His breath caught in his mouth, for now perhaps only twenty yards ahead, the dog-headed man stood, snout raised, sniffing into the air. Lanathor choked off his cry and shrank into the cover of the bushes as low as he could. Instinctively, he reached out for the threads of the Song, but they were faint, nothing more than a ringing in his ears. "*Concentrate, Lanathor,*" he told himself.

The last hint of Falam Root upon his mind had faded to a sputtering candle. A bewildering tangle of fear or perhaps disgust pounded in his chest. It didn't matter what it was, it had to be quiet. *Concentrate, Lanathor!* The dog-headed Wyrna seemed to catch a scent. Its ears stood straight, and it turned its head in his direction. A glow of light flickered on Lanathor's fingertips for an instant, and a thread of the Song rippled before him like the passing shadow of an owl. He grasped and pushed it forward.

There was a shudder, and the near corner of the barn buckled and lurched forward with a groan. A second later there was a tremendous crash of splintered wood. As one, the Wyrna wailed and descended in fury upon the surprise. The dog-man spun too and dashed down the hill toward the barn, running on all fours.

Lanathor whirled himself around and slid down the hill to Survii. "Come on," he hissed. "We have to go now!" With trembling hands he tied the long rope of Liadov's bier back around his waist and ran low behind the cover of the hill, dragging her along behind him. The loathsome clamor of the Wyrna faded as Lanathor prayed they would not follow. He was headed east now, away from Aramon, but what could he do? They had to find a way round.

⸺◆⸺

Lanathor soon realized the cover of the knoll continued eastward into a deepening depression much longer than he wished. Each step put Aramon further behind. They'd gone on for an hour in silence before he was finally satisfied they were not being followed, at least not imminently. There was little tree cover, and the light of the setting moon shone brightly here. He was glad he could see, but felt exposed, like Mirvánè was staring across the plains at them, watching their course through the snow. He checked on Liadov again, peacefully resting on her sled, and then dared a short climb out of the wide furrow.

Confirming his suspicions, he found they had been traveling in a gully nearly parallel to an ever-widening river. The gully must have once been its old watercourse. Despite the chill, the river was unfrozen and broad. Even in Danek, Spring would soon arrive. It flowed steadily and quietly in the direction they traveled. Lanathor hurried back down the embankment.

"There's a river to our right."

"I know," said Survii. "The Vedkorya."

"You knew it was there the whole time?" Lanathor asked.

"Where else would it be?" Survii replied.

Lanathor waved a hand dismissively. "We're traveling the opposite direction from Aramon. I have to get turned round. The river looks deep. Is there anywhere to cross?"

"It is deep, *zizechi*," Survii said, "but why turn around? More Wyrna back that way."

Lanathor did not know the word in Daneki but gathered that 'zizechi' was something akin to *foreigner*. "I have to get my friend back to Aramon," Lanathor said. "Wyrna or not."

Survii shrugged. "There's a keep a few hours ahead, Fort Dromvedya. I thought that's where we were going. You can cross the river there and take the road to Kurath. Don't know where you go from there."

Lanathor searched his mind fruitlessly for the charts he knew of the Thirteen Provinces. Their recent conquest would no doubt improve things soon, but there were surprisingly few such maps in Aramon, and all of low quality. Another failing of the drunkards and sycophants in the capital. All the same, he could envision another valley that ran perpendicular to the main course of Danek. He might have to travel through the corners of Kurath and Tituria to return, but that detour seemed a better chance than turning back toward the Wyrna. The safety of a nearby fort was also appealing.

Survii stood frowning with arms crossed and one eyebrow raised. "Wizard?"

Lanathor blinked from his thoughts. "I think I know the way from here. Thank you, Survii."

Survii shook his head while Lanathor shouldered the harness of the sled. They set off down the valley again, breathing heavily.

They'd gone some miles, and dawn was showing on the horizon. A gentle snowfall had come in and began to blanket their hoods. Survii broke the silence. "I could help you with that sled, *zizechi.*"

"No, I'm fine . . ." Lanathor replied. His words trailed off when he spotted an oblong shape bulging in the snow cover along one side of the gully. Veering off course, he brought the sled to rest by the object's end and flipped a knife from his belt. He gently cleared the snow away from what was indeed a fallen log and sighed with relief.

"What are you doing?" Survii asked as he came alongside him.

Lanathor did not answer but finished wiping snow away from a wilted plant with a woody base. He busily worked the point of his knife into the log. His hands ached, but it didn't matter.

Survii tried again. "What is that?"

"Falam Root," Lanathor muttered in Aramoni.

"It's dead."

"No, these are perennial."

Survii peered closer, coming within inches of Lanathor's hands. "Pavka flower!" he exclaimed. "So you are a wizard!"

Lanathor popped the root bulb from the wood and quickly slipped it into one of his empty capsules.

Survii stepped back and waggled a finger. "Pavka is not for eating. I knew you were magic! 'Teachers' don't have torches for hands."

Lanathor sighed. "I am a teacher, Survii. I teach Rhetoric. Other than that, it's better we leave things unsaid."

Survii laughed. "Thought young Survii was just a stupid Daneki, eh, wizard? Where are you really from, and why do you have this sleeping Daneki girl?"

"I told you, I'm from Aramon. This Daneki girl is a priestess and my very dear friend. We need to move on."

Survii stood with his chin raised. "I can see she's Daneki, but you're not Aramoni. You think Survii is blind?"

Lanathor was tempted to take a nibble of the root, just to cure his rising irritation. Instead, he held his hands out and rolled up his sleeves. Survii stepped backward.

"What are you doing, zizechi?"

"I understand your meaning, Survii. Have a good look," Lanathor said. He stepped closer with his scarred black arms raised. "My father was Azkushan, but I am Aramoni or I am nothing. Were a host of Azkushan to descend on Aramon, I would fight them to the death. Were Azkushan in flames, little would I care. I don't know where your loyalties lie, Survii, but mine are with my home, and with my people. I need to end this foolish conversation and get back to Aramon. You can follow me to the fort or freeze to death in this ditch. Is your curiosity satisfied?"

Survii swallowed hard. "Are you going to cast a spell?"

"No," Lanathor said and pulled his sleeves back over his wrists. "I'm going to walk."

The snowfall grew more heavy as the afternoon set in. The sled held up well, gliding along the surface, but Lanathor found his feet dragging through the snow as it gathered about his shins. Survii had gone on ahead and often had to stop to allow Lanathor to catch up. At times he was barely visible in the blinding white.

"We shouldn't be out here, zizechi," Survii said. He had stopped to allow Lanathor to come near again and was eyeing Liadov's sled. The tip of her nose was red, but she continued to rest peacefully.

Lanathor waved him off. "I'll speed up."

"I can help," Survii said.

Lanathor shook his head and trudged past.

Survii let out an exasperated sigh. "Don't make me leave you to be a wizard icicle."

Lanathor realized he'd hardly slept in the burnt-out villages they'd passed the last few nights. All the same, he redoubled his efforts. If Survii was right, Fort Dromvedya was perhaps only a mile or two ahead.

They soon came out of the gully onto a flat plain, and were the skies clear, they might have seen the fort already. Lanathor's eyes were heavy and his hands ached, but he tried to focus on Survii as the farmer passed him again. Without the lip of the gully for reference, movement over the snowfield was imperceptible, a hypnotic swirl of twirling flakes.

Lanathor leaned against the harness and let his gaze droop to the ground. In contrast to the cold, his hands were an inferno of pain. He wondered if one or both had become infected. He dared a look at his left, peeling the bandage back. The effort made his eyes water, and he gave up after reviewing no more than an inch. He closed his eyes and let the pain subside.

With eyes closed, the momentary focus on his hearing revealed a subtle noise. Lanathor caught his breath and listened. It was no more than the whisper of an echo, but somewhere over the plains behind, he heard an unmistakable sound: the baying of dogs.

Lanathor flashed his eyes open and charged ahead. Survii was gone. He'd been still too long.

"Survii!" Lanathor yelled into the vast nothing. He could hear and feel the blood pounding in his ears as he bounded through the snow, the sled bouncing and jerking behind him. With Survii's figure vanished, the sense of running in place was maddening. All he could do was keep rushing forward, looking for Survii's tracks and praying that he'd not lost the direction. "Survii!"

In his terror, the Falam Root capsule bouncing in his pocket came to mind. He might drop it in the snow with his tortured, trembling hands, but the snuffling sound of animals was growing in the distance. He'd have little time to prepare, but what else could he do? Just as he was about to stop and face the sound, Fort Dromvedya loomed over him, peering through the blizzard. It was a huge pine structure, its outer palisade no less than four times his height. Inner fortifications and watchtowers showed dimly beyond, receding into the haze.

Falam Root forgotten, Lanathor made a mad dash for the walls. The sled careened wildly and nearly tipped but soon righted itself. Survii was ahead, and Lanathor caught sight of him just as the farmer slipped through a stout gate that closed behind.

"Survii!" Lanathor shouted again as he ran on. He hazarded a look back and could now see a pack of swift figures in pursuit. He had a good lead, and if he just kept moving, he could make the gate. "Survii! Open the gate!"

He ran on with all his might, but the gate did not open. He crashed into it with a dull thump. The momentum of the sled carried it on, first scraping along the dirt and gravel before the gate, and then adding a second bang against the wooden planks. The creatures were nearing, two dozen Wyrna at least.

Lanathor pounded on the gate, wincing at the pain. Its cold face did not reply. He spun round and thrust his shaking hands into the folds of his robe to grasp the capsule of Falam Root. In his haste, it fell to the dirt and rolled into a snowdrift. Lanathor crouched to retrieve it, but the snarling beasts were upon him. He closed his eyes and tried to focus, tried to hear the Song—but there was nothing, just the roar of his terror.

A whistling sound erupted from above him, followed by the rapid wet thud of arrows. He opened his eyes to see several of the Wyrna fall and the others shrink back. He did not have long to gape at his sudden fortune, for the gate swung open and many strong hands pulled him inside. Several more raked the sled in after. The gate slammed shut just as another salvo of arrows whizzed overhead.

For a brief moment, Lanathor saw a wide and muddy courtyard with dozens, no hundreds, of scared-looking Daneki commoners. The next moment he was on his face in the mud, gasping for air as feet and elbows buffeted him.

"He's a wizard! A wizard! Watch his hands!" a voice called out. It was Survii.

Lanathor tried to call the Daneki's name, but only an anguished groan emerged.

"Bind his hands. No! In the back, in the back!"

The blows finally stopped, and Lanathor weakly worked his way to his knees, staring into the wet earth beneath him. Blood poured from his mouth. One eye was covered in mud. Cord dug into his aching wrists.

A rough hand tore Lanathor's hood off and pushed his forehead back. Before him, a man menaced with a broad steel blade. One half of his face was completely obscured in black tattoos. A long, blonde beard swept off his chin, and piercing blue eyes that reminded him of Voldigar observed him coolly.

In a quick motion, the man thrust his blade down and severed the harness that connected Lanathor to Liadov's sled. Wordlessly he gestured to the side with his chin and several men collected the sled while others dragged Lanathor across the courtyard.

He struggled and called out. "Liadov!"

One of the men struck him hard on the side of the head. "Shut up!"

Lanathor's head swam "You don't understand, we have to get to Aramon," he moaned weakly.

Survii was standing by the door of a nearby building.

"Survii . . . I helped you . . ." Lanathor managed.

Survii's face was set in a hard line. "Never trust a Daneki in winter." He shook his head ruefully. "And never trust a wizard at all."

Lanathor struggled to maintain consciousness. The last thing he saw was a door above him shutting out the light. They dragged him down cold earthen stairs.

Chapter Twenty-One

Birds of a Feather

TEPIC LOOKED AROUND HIS room in the high turret of Arregalt's citadel and sighed. How oft he'd dreamed to be a man upon his own, but all he thought of now was how he wished to stay. The morning sunlight peeked through the little window over his desk, setting the dust aglow again while he stuffed hastily folded clothing into a trunk. The porters would be here within the hour to take everything away. His desk, his bed, his dented brass pitcher . . .

He bent down to pick up his sword training gloves and caught sight of Lyrusia walking through the door.

"Shouldn't you knock, Ru?" he muttered and tossed the gloves in his trunk.

"Not your room anymore, Tep," Lyrusia said and stood beside him.

Tepic glared. "Thanks for the reminder."

Lyrusia set about refolding things he'd already crammed into the trunk. She matched his sigh with one of her own. "Sorry, little brother. Moving's not that bad, you know."

"How would you know?"

"It's not my first time."

"Weren't you two or something?"

"Three. But I can remember. We lived in watch housing near the front gate. Dad was just an enlisted man. Mom was only a little older than I am now."

"I'll bet it was horrible."

"The watch housing?" Lyrusia stopped folding and put her arm around Tepic. "Not at all, Tep. It was the same. Maybe even better. I was so sad when we had to leave."

Tepic glanced at her for a moment and compacted the contents of his trunk to test the lid. It was too tight. He opened it again to consider what he might pull out.

Lyrusia leaned her head on his shoulder. "You can't be so sad, little brother. You're the sunny one. Wherever we're going, it will still be happy. Think of all the adventures!"

Tepic puffed his cheeks out and exhaled. "But it isn't 'we' anymore. . ."

Lyrusia stepped back with a curious look on her face, then opened her eyes wide. "You're getting taller!" She moved a flat hand from her forehead to his. "A little. Still shorter than me."

Tepic balked. "You're moving your hand up." She made the motion again and Tepic laughed. "I'm much taller than you."

"There's a smile!" Lyrusia said. She rested her hand on her chin. "You know what happened right after we moved in here?"

"What?"

"You got born, little man, and I was happier than ever before—even though you took the best room. Sometimes change is good."

Tepic didn't know what to say. He grabbed Lyrusia for a hug and stood there a long while.

"Why do we have to move to different places though?" Tepic whispered and closed his eyes.

Lyrusia wiped a tear from her cheek. "I don't know," she said. "But I'm going to keep an eye on you."

Tepic thought they were just nice words at first, but there was a strange edge to her tone. "What do you mean, Ru?"

"Lusánt isn't a good person, Tep."

Tepic looked at the floor. "I know."

"You're not going to be anything like him." She grasped his shoulders. "Nothing like him. You understand?"

Tepic nodded. "Of course not. He's a bully." They both smiled while the wind rustled the last curtain against the wall.

"I'm staying here in town," Lyrusia said.

Tepic's eyebrows shot up. "What? How?"

"I'll sleep in the apothecary."

"Dad won't let you!"

"They can't stop me. I've made up my mind."

"Ru, you'll be all alone!"

"I don't care." Lyrusia lowered her chin. "I'm grown now, and you're not going to disappear into the Spire without me. I'll be right down the street. I'll check on you every day. I promise. Do you hear me?"

Tepic nodded and felt tears welling up in his eyes. He hugged Lyrusia again. "I'll be fine. You better be careful."

A knock rang out from the front door below. "They're here," Lyrusia said.

―――――◦―――――

Lyrusia was first to the door, weaving through crates and trunks, rolled rugs, and sheet-covered artwork strewn about everywhere. When she opened the door, much to Tepic's surprise, there stood Emperor Lusánt again. Today, he'd shed his black cloak and wore burgundy in the theme of Aramon. Loose-fitting clothes gave him an almost casual appearance. The ever-present shadow of his Xerimadi warrior blocked out the morning sunshine behind him. No sooner had the door opened than an army of porters streamed into the house.

Dantic hurried across the room and bowed low. His voice was a lonely echo in the hollow room. "My lord, we're honored."

Lusánt stepped in. "Everything's prepared then, I trust?" It was more of a statement, but Dantic nodded anyway.

"Where is the newest member of my court?" Lusánt asked.

Tepic stayed in the den overlooking the front door and eyed the Emperor warily. Several porters pushed past.

"Sitting shyly at the top of some stairs again I see." Lusánt frowned and nodded to Dantic. "Time for goodbyes."

Tepic's family gathered about him with many tearful hugs and farewells, cheerful promises, and hurried instructions. Tepic missed the majority of it, his mind and eyes fixed mostly on the haughty-looking boy who stood in his front door. The little wisp of beard that clung to his chin was growing longer.

"No need to dally, Tepic Banari," Lusánt called up the stairs again. Two porters pushed past with Tepic's trunk. "I'm a busy man, but I chose to come see you today. The porters will set up your room before we even get there. Come, walk with me along the wall."

His legs felt like lead. For a moment, Tepic considered running again but was sure he'd simply fall if he dared. Lyrusia watched him with a brave face and a nod. He took one step, and then another, trying to stop his hands from trembling. His mother wiped her eyes with the corner of her garment.

Lusánt seemed to read their thoughts. "I should think you'd be honored, House Banari. I suppose it's hard to see your only son out the door. I assure you, no harm will come to him. Please, visit us soon." Lusánt gave the sweetest smile he could manage across his sunken cheeks and closed the door behind them.

Once outside the Emperor held his arms wide and let out a long sigh that sounded halfway between disgust and a stretch. The porters hurried along the top of the citadel wall before him. "Fine morning, isn't it?"

Tepic chewed his lip but did not reply.

Lusánt blinked a few times. "I was asking you, Tepic. Fine morning, isn't it?" he repeated.

"Y-yes, m'lord," Tepic mumbled.

Lusánt laughed. "It speaks! Come along then."

Along the curve of the soaring wall they strolled, listening to awkward silence. Many more of Lusánt's bodyguard trailed behind, while only the Xerimadi kept pace.

"I understand this is all very uncomfortable for you, Tepic. I would feel the same at your age."

"You're fifteen."

Lusánt laughed again, and this time the Xerimadi chuckled too. Tepic didn't understand what was so funny. "Sixteen, Tepic. I'm sixteen."

"My sister's seventeen," Tepic replied.

Lusánt rolled his eyes. "You're a fine conversationalist, aren't you?"

Tepic's face flushed red, and he locked his eyes on the wall's paving, slipping along beneath his feet. Each guardsman they passed knelt low. Lusánt didn't seem to notice them and instead stooped to pluck a pebble off the ground. He sent it soaring over the edge of the wall to tumble two hundred feet below.

"You shouldn't throw things off the wall," Tepic said reflexively.

"Oh?" Lusánt asked. "Your dad tell you that?"

Tepic looked back at his house and forgot to reply. The four-story turret was rapidly shrinking. He thought he could still barely make out Lyrusia's face, watching them through a window.

Lusánt sighed and continued on. "I don't know what kind of nasty stories people tell you about me, but they're not true. You and I could be friends. Aren't you glad to be out of the house?"

"Sorry," Tepic managed to say.

"Don't be sorry," Lusánt said. "I don't care. You just seem kind of dull." He threw another pebble off the wall. "I guess you'll warm up. I heard you climbed this wall with your bare hands. Is that true?"

Tepic eyed Lusánt suspiciously. "Who told you that?"

Lusánt stopped and blew his lips like a horse. "I'm the Emperor. It's my job to know things. Well, did you?"

"I did."

"Ha! That's amazing," Lusánt exclaimed. "Show me!"

Tepic blinked. "What?"

"Show me, right now. I want to see you climb this wall—with no ropes."

Tepic's skin ran cold and his mouth hung open, searching for a reply.

Lusánt stood with his eyes wide and a flat expression on his lips. He watched Tepic squirm for a long moment and then waved a hand dismissively with a grin. "I'm just joking. Relax!"

Tepic blinked again and tried to smile. It didn't touch his eyes and only half his mouth.

"I think being cooped up too long made you lose your mind, Banari-boy." He chewed on the nickname he'd just invented, clearly pleased with himself. "I'll bet your parents thought it was too dangerous for you to even go outside, what with rumors of demons running around."

"They're real," Tepic said.

"Pfft. Maybe," Lusánt said. "But what do we care? I think you're a bird like me, Tepic, and birds need to be free."

They started walking again, and for a minute, Lusánt was finally quiet, staring off at something to the north. Tepic thought back to his mad escape not long ago and all the fear and danger he'd gone through. He pictured Taro's face, and Lutz, and old Lector Voldigar. It made him feel a strange mixture of bravery and fear.

"What did you do with my sword?" Tepic asked.

Lusánt turned back to Tepic. It took him a moment to register the question. "Your sword? Nothing."

"My dad let you borrow it—weeks ago. What did you do with it?"

"Well, it's not your sword. It's your grandfather's." Lusánt erased a frown. "It's in my palace. Do you want to see it?"

Tepic was startled by the response. "What?"

"I said, do you want to see it? You are a strange boy."

"Yes," Tepic hurried to add.

"Well good. We'll get something to eat and then go sightseeing. We're going to have lots of fun."

———◆———

The muffled hiss and rumble of the lift worked its way through the walls as Tepic tried to smooth the wrinkles out of his new shirt. It was much too long and a little too tight. He suspected it belonged to Lusánt before. The burgundy hue was a near match to the tunic Lusánt was wearing. Tepic wanted nothing more than to tear it off and put his comfortable old clothes back on. They weren't half as fancy, but at least they smelled of home.

They'd spent the better part of the day wandering around the Citadel and the Spire looking at things Lusánt seemed to think were important. It felt more like bragging to Tepic. They'd stop occasionally to eat something that was always much too rich, reeking of garlic or dripping with butter. Tepic tried his best to clear his plate, but Lusánt always seemed more interested in playing with his food. He never stopped talking. Tepic had given up trying to be polite hours ago.

The motion of the lift made him feel sick to his stomach. Tepic stopped tugging at his shirt and scratched his collar instead, ignoring whatever Lusánt was talking about. Lost in his own thoughts, he wondered not for the first time if the Emperor would actually show him the sword. Lusánt hadn't mentioned it again during their long, boring tour, and Tepic had been afraid to ask.

"Are you listening to me, Banari-boy?" Lusánt asked.

Tepic blinked. "Sorry, the lift makes my stomach hurt."

"You'll get used to it."

Tepic felt the lift accelerating, and he tried peeking past the Xerimadi warrior and out the small foggy window instead. "Why am I here?" he asked.

"I told you already. I need new retainers," Lusánt said. "My court is full of old men with boring ideas. My Aramon has new ideas."

Tepic considered Lusánt's statement for a moment, wondering what ideas he could possibly have. "I'm just a kid."

"Exactly!" Lusánt replied and poked his index finger into the center of Tepic's forehead. The lift came to a stop, and Lusánt opened the door.

All about was a blood-red room with an impossibly high ceiling. It glowed with golden trim on every surface. Several long stairways swept up in all directions. Thousands of glittering lights lined the walls and hung from the ceiling in long chandeliers.

"My great hall!" Lusánt announced.

The room was empty, save for a dozen bored-looking sentries that wandered about in the long tabards and burnished greaves of General Gamad's legionnaires.

"I've seen it before," Tepic said as he pointed at the causeway a hundred feet above. "From up there."

Lusánt frowned. "Well, it's better up close. We'll have feasts down here. Come on, there's something I want to show you."

Lusánt led him up one of the long curving stairwells to a balcony that soared over the great hall. A few moments later they stepped outside onto a dizzying terrace overlooking all of Arregalt below. The Xerimadi was left inside.

The elevation here was twice that of Tepic's bedroom in the turret of which he was so fond, and the edge was guarded only by a dangerously low railing. The sun was setting and a strong sea breeze whipped Lusánt's hair about his face. Tepic froze by the door.

Lusánt laughed. "Come on. Don't be so scared." Lusánt grabbed the rim and leaned far over the perilous drop. "See? Come look at this!"

Tepic inched toward Lusánt who suddenly thrust a hand out and pulled him against the edge.

"Stop acting like a little girl, Tepic. Look!"

Tepic's head spun, and he gripped the railing with white knuckles. Lusánt's other hand was pointed stiffly to the city below.

"Do you know what loyalty is, Tepic?"

Tepic nodded his head.

"Well, a lot of people don't. I'm glad. Look at that building."

In the distance where Lusánt pointed was the burnt wreckage of a huge structure, barely visible over the lip of the citadel wall.

"Isn't that the Stonepike barracks?" Tepic asked.

"Not anymore. Everything down there is mine," Lusánt went on. "That's a monument now. A symbol of my coronation. Do you know what they call me?"

Tepic shook his head.

"Lightbringer! I burn old things away, and I make new things in the fire." Lusánt smiled widely. "It's a monument to loyalty!"

Tepic frowned and stared at the barracks, wondering what Lusánt meant.

"The Stonepikes betrayed me, Tepic, and they kidnapped you. I'll bet you felt helpless. Well, they won't hurt you anymore, or me."

A creeping dark uncoiled in Tepic's stomach, an awful sense he'd last known when Lord Caliras pushed him through the mines beneath the pass. "Did you burn their house?" Tepic asked quietly.

"I did more than that!" Lusánt said as he laughed. "What do you think of it?"

Tepic lowered his eyes to the stone tiling under his feet. "I don't know. . ."

Lusánt frowned. "You're smarter than your dad at least. The Stonepikes were old, just an old idea." He crossed his arms and looked intently at the burnt building for another long moment before he stabbed the air with his finger again. "That was disloyalty. Do you understand?"

The charred barracks loomed silent in the dusk while Tepic tried to swallow his growing dread. His hands were trembling. "Can we go back inside?"

Lusánt sighed. "Oh, Banari-boy." He shook his head. "You and I are a lot more alike than you know. You won't be afraid much longer."

Tepic was glad to be free of the blasting wind on the high terrace of the Spire. At any moment, he'd thought he might be swept away like a loose feather. The hush over the red carpets within was welcome relief, and his eyes grew heavy as he walked. He'd had enough tours for one day.

Leaving his bodyguard behind, Lusánt led Tepic past his own apartments with their double doors and on around the inner balcony to a patch of bare stone. There, they entered through a heavily recessed door into a round chamber beyond with a vaulted ceiling. There were many windows along the far wall, but night had fallen, and the room was lit by flickering braziers instead. A great stone chair stood beneath the windows, and eerie shadows were cast upon intricate paintings that graced the four domes of the room.

Tepic expected another grandiose announcement of whatever this room was, but Lusánt instead crossed silently to the chair and flopped onto a fitted cushion. He looked small slouching between its oversized arms, and there he picked up a golden scepter, twirling it absently. His other hand rested under his cheek.

Tepic stood at the door in his best "at attention" imitation of his father that he could. He wasn't sure what he was supposed to do, and Lusánt

remained quietly examining him, lost in a long stare of thought. At
length, he cleared his throat and pointed the scepter off to his side.
"Tepic, this is my advisor, Kyriana."

Unnoticed before, Tepic saw that there were several large, colorful
cushions and long, low velvet settees along the walls and scattered
between the braziers. On one of these, a woman in emerald garb was
lounging. At Lusánt's voice, she rose to her feet and inclined her head
courteously. Her eyes were completely obscured by dangling rows of
pearls. "How do you do, Tepic of House Banari?"

Her voice was youthful and airy, yet clear like a ringing bell. Tepic
flinched in surprise as she rose and he stood dumbfounded. She pulled
the circlet bearing the pearls from her brow, and he was astonished to see
a youthful face to match the voice. Her skin had a pale hint of turquoise,
even in the orange glow of the braziers. She could not have been any
older than Lusánt, and Tepic thought her the most beautiful girl he'd
ever seen, like a maiden of the sea stepped from the page of a storybook.
His breath caught, and he looked at the floor while heat rose in his face.

Lusánt laughed and knocked his knuckles on the stone chair. "Going
to say hello, or just stare at your shoes?"

"Hello," Tepic managed at last. With a determined effort, he tightened his jaw and looked her in the eyes.

"You remember her from my coronation, no?" Lusánt asked.

Tepic nodded.

"Good. I've been eager to have you two meet. Kyriana has some
questions for you."

Tepic blinked and was arrested again by a subtle smile from Kyriana.
Lusánt twisted to his back and tossed the scepter at the ceiling.

"The Emperor speaks true," she said. "I understand you are a very
special young man."

Tepic's mouth hung open. He wasn't sure if he was supposed to
respond. "Questions?"

She continued. "Indeed. If my lord would grant me an audience, I
would very much like to understand some things about an heirloom of
your line."

Lusánt stopped his tossing and smirked.

"Please sit with me, Lord Banari," Kyriana said. She extended two graceful hands toward a couch.

Tepic hesitated, but then warily lowered himself to the seat, crossing his arms. Kyriana sat near and softly folded her hands into her lap. She smelled like a garden of spices.

"It's said that you traveled from Arregalt not long ago with a beautiful sword, crystal hilt and gems upon its blade."

Tepic nodded again, still struggling to look at Kyriana. At the mention of the sword, his weariness left him. "I did, but it wasn't really traveling. I was just trying to take it somewhere safe. I got captured."

Kyriana smiled. "That was brave of you, and I perceive that you are an honest friend. Why wasn't the sword safe?"

Lusánt sat up at this question and leaned forward to listen.

Tepic eyed the Emperor but quickly looked away when he noticed. Too late.

Lusánt rose to his feet and crossed over, laying a hand on Kyriana's bare shoulder. "Still having trouble talking, Banari-boy?"

Kyriana subtly swiped Lusánt's hand away and glanced at him with a strange look. A flicker of irritation crossed Lusánt's face and then something silent passed between their eyes.

"I'll leave you two alone," Lusánt said and walked to a tapestry. He examined it briefly before pulling it aside and passing through a narrow door. Tepic glimpsed a balcony beyond, jutting into the night air, but Lusánt pulled the curtain back into place and the door thudded behind.

"Here," Kyriana said, "let me set your heart at ease."

She rose to her feet and walked behind the great stone chair. Her steps were strangely lithe, as though her joints were different. Stooping down, she quickly returned bearing a bundle in white cloth. This she laid on Tepic's lap. He stared down at it questioningly.

"Please," she said and sat down again.

Carefully, Tepic unfolded the cloth and to his amazement, saw his grandfather's sword within.

"I thought—" he began.

"Your emperor is no thief," Kyriana said. "And nor am I. Pardon my impertinence, my lord."

The sword was immaculate and looked more lovely than ever, glowing in the light of the braziers. There was an artful gradient between the gems along the cassolke.

"Please, grant me to know. What is in your heart?"

Tepic didn't know what to say or even what to think. The blade reminded him of home—the reflection of the fires like the hearth-light in his den. What of Mother and of Father? What of Ru? He just wanted to hang the sword back on its two pegs and curl up under the floating dust in his turret. He wished he hadn't lost the beautiful scabbard.

"I'm just lonely, I suppose," Tepic said. "I miss my family. I don't understand why I'm here."

Kyriana watched him with her almond eyes. "Are you afraid?"

"No," Tepic said. "I'm not afraid."

"May I ask you again then, my lord. Why wasn't the sword safe?"

Tepic felt a quiver in his lip and tamped it down with an angry thought. "It put people in danger," he said at last. "Evil creatures and evil people want it."

Kyriana gave a gentle nod. It looked sincere, like an expression his mother might give.

"How old are you?" Tepic asked.

Kyriana laughed musically. "You've spent very little time at court I see. Shouldn't ask such a thing to a lady." Now she looked almost mischievous, like Ru.

Tepic smiled. "You're not very old. I can tell"

"Can I tell you a secret?" she asked.

Tepic shrugged. "Sure."

She leaned in and whispered. "I haven't been at court very long either, and I'm lonely too."

Tepic nodded.

Kyriana leaned back again and took on a more serious face. "I also heard you know how to use the sword."

Tepic shook his head. "Not really. I'm just a student. I can sword fight, kind of. I just learn the same things from Lector Voldigar that Lusánt does."

"Not that," Kyriana corrected him gently. "I mean *this* sword. It's magic, isn't it?"

"It is! But no," he quickly added. "I don't know any magic."

Kyriana looked disappointed. "Did you not demonstrate your magic only a few weeks ago, in a duel with a young guardsman?"

Tepic remembered Sergeant Galomar and his friendly smile. The guardsman was kind to him, and he still felt bad about knocking him down. He began to answer, but a warning touched his heart. He swallowed his words. "Kyriana . . . er . . . Lady Kyriana. Thank you for talking to me. I'm very tired. Can we talk again tomorrow?"

She smiled and bowed her head. "Of course, my lord." Rising to her feet, she stood with hands clasped just as Lusánt reentered from the balcony.

"All acquainted now? A couple of best friends?" he asked.

Tepic nodded.

"The young lord is weary," Kyriana said.

Lusánt frowned and raised an eyebrow. "I see." He turned to Kyriana. "You can go."

Kyriana dipped her head swiftly and left the room. Tepic and Lusánt were alone again.

Lusánt sat and tapped his scepter against the stone chair. "My servants will show you to your chambers shortly, but there's one more thing I must show you before bed, Banari-Boy. Bring the sword." He leapt to his feet and hurried onto the small balcony again. This time he left the tapestry drawn and the door open. Tepic followed pensively behind, clutching Grandfather's sword in both hands. He could sense its sharpness even through the thick white wrappings.

This small balcony at least had a high stone border, and the wind was not so fierce. It was nothing more than a little turret with an open face. The moon was rising swiftly on their right, shining green and brilliant. At this, Lusánt silently gazed for a long while. For his part, Tepic was glad to simply watch the stars in the quiet and forget where he was.

"Can you keep a secret, Tepic?" Lusánt finally said.

Tepic didn't like Lusánt's tone, but he was always curious about secrets. "Sure," he said.

"No," Lusánt replied tensely and moved in close. He continued in a hard whisper. "I mean it. A real secret."

Tepic nodded.

"Swear it." He held out his hand to shake—a common gesture amongst the boys who learned from the lectors. It seemed so odd here on the balcony of the Spire with Lusánt, but Tepic took his hand all the same.

Lusánt sighed. "I like you Tepic, in your own dull way you're a nice boy. It's time you grew up though. You need to learn things."

Lusánt was clutching a velvet bag that Tepic hadn't noticed before. He held it up dramatically, and his eyes went wide before he thrust his hand in. From the pouch, he pulled the most curious object Tepic had ever seen. It was a perfectly round ball that looked delicate but heavy at the same time. Lusánt held it awkwardly in his hand, and a green light glowed first between his fingers and then even through them, illuminating the Emperor's face in a haunting ghost light.

Tepic was struck by just how much the light reminded him of the Orun and his harrowing nightmare a few weeks before. A stifled cry rose up in his throat.

"Don't be scared," Lusánt said hurriedly. His eyes grew wider still. "Don't worry."

"Put it away." Tepic tried to say loudly, but it only came out in a whisper.

"No. It's frightful at first, but you don't have to be scared. You just have to control it." A bead of sweat formed on Lusánt's forehead and ran down his nose. "Watch this," he said and turned around to face the moon.

Tepic thought it was a trick of the light at first, but Lusánt repeated the gesture again and again. He would press his thumb against the base of the orb, and a pulse of light radiated outward. To Tepic's amazement, as he did so, the surface of the moon above subtly echoed its own shimmer across its face.

Tepic's hands began to shake. "What are you doing?" he whispered.

"I said don't be scared."

"You shouldn't do that."

Lusánt spun around, an angry light in his eyes. "Why not?"

"You shouldn't," Tepic said again. "It's wrong."

Lusánt thrust the orb back into the bag and its light vanished. He seemed to struggle to pull his hand out, and once he did, he rubbed his palm with his fingers and wiped it on his shirt. He licked his lips, then spoke in a hushed tone. "That's the problem with you, Tepic. You're scared. You're always scared."

Tepic set his feet and tightened his face.

"You can't just act brave," Lusánt said. "You have to do brave things."

"I am brave," Tepic said.

"We'll see about that" Lusánt pointed at Tepic's sword. "Take that cloth off."

Tepic looked down at the bundle in his arms. He loved looking at the sword, but once again, a warning in his heart bubbled up. He hesitated.

Lusánt shot his hand out and ripped the cloth away. "Stop dithering. I haven't even told you the secret yet." Lusánt smiled wickedly and dropped the cloth on the ground. He stood still and let Tepic squirm. Once satisfied, he leaned forward and whispered. "You . . . can do what I can do."

Tepic's eyes went wide, but before he could respond, both he and Lusánt flinched together. Kyriana was standing in the open doorway.

"The young lord's chambers are ready," Kyriana said.

Lusánt did not try to hide his irritation. "I thought I dismissed you."

"You gave me permission to leave, Your Highness. Then I came back."

Lusánt let out a short derisive laugh and looked back to Tepic. "Don't forget to keep your secrets, Banari-boy. I'll call for you again tomorrow."

———◆———

Tepic followed Kyriana to a steep stairwell past the red gallery overlooking the great hall. He was struck again by her strange gait.

"You're miridas, aren't you?"

Kyriana laughed as she lifted a small brass candlestick from a shelf over the stairs. "Yes. You are observant, my lord."

"Why didn't you just send servants for me?"

"The servants are afraid of our master Lusánt," Kyriana replied with a shrug. "I can move freely in the palace." She started to descend the steps. "But I don't tend to roam far. Some find me startling."

"I don't think you're startling," Tepic said. "Well, I mean you are, but not, well I mean . . ." He stopped, flustered, only to be given another of her musical laughs. He wished he could peel the red heat from his face.

As they emerged on the landing below, Kyriana pulled a key from her garments. Tepic froze.

"What is it, my lord?"

The door before him led to the officers' hold that his father once owned. It was here he had witnessed the Orun when it slew the guardsmen. Tepic's face withered under the heavy air of his memories.

Kyriana's eyes softened. "Is this not to your liking, Tepic? The Emperor selected it for you himself."

Tepic inhaled deeply. "This was an office for my father's men." He considered stopping at that but went on. "The evil creature I told you about, it attacked them here."

Kyriana frowned and glared up the stairs. "I'm sorry."

"Why do I have to stay here?"

Kyriana sighed and opened the door. "A room is just a room, my lord. Let me show you." She disappeared past the door. Tepic swallowed and followed after.

The room had been fully renovated. Gone were any trappings of the officers, lockers and bunks removed. In their place were furnishings more akin to his old room in the turret, only bigger and more richly adorned. There were carpets and furs and a fine four-post bed. Carved chairs, a circular table, and a studious-looking desk with many small drawers filled the rest of the space. High above the desk, a small window with open shutters captured a hint of moonlight. Neatly trimmed oil lamps set a tranquil mood, casting shadows on his own overstuffed trunk.

Kyriana sat gracefully on the edge of the bed and beckoned Tepic join her. She spread her hands open. "Forgive my forwardness, but look around. I believe this room is quite nice. Peaceful even." She looked Tepic in the eyes and continued. "Fear . . . is in here." She poked him in the chest. As quickly as she'd sat, she rose and placed the pearl circlet over her eyes once more. She held out her hands. "The sword must be kept elsewhere at night, my lord. I trust you understand."

Reluctantly, Tepic handed the bundle to Kyriana. She bowed her head graciously and swiftly exited the room, handing the key to a guard on her way out. The guard, a heavy-set balding man, flashed a crooked smile, and with a "'night-'night, little lord," he shut the door. There was a click, and Tepic could see there was no mechanism within and no other doors.

To confirm what he already knew to be true, he tried the handle. Locked, of course. A quick search of the room showed it had all he needed. There were cakes and cheeses sitting on a countertop, water in a large pitcher and basin, and even a selection of books. These he perused for a while, but soon lost interest. He was left only with his thoughts, memories of the men who'd died here while he hid and distant echoes from the mines below Westfort.

Tepic closed his eyes and sighed. There was no one to talk to. He wished Kyriana would come back. He wished he really were a free bird and could fly out the tiny window over the desk. He wished a lot of things, but in the end, he could only snuff his lamps and lay down in the cold darkness. A profound sense of loneliness forced aside his pervasive fear, and he drifted off to a fitful sleep, imagining himself to be nothing more than a tiny leaf, floating on an ocean with an endless, black horizon.

CHAPTER TWENTY-TWO

DO YOUR DUTY

V OLDIGAR STOOD BY HOBYN'S shack under an early morning
sun, working busily at his bent and rusted tools. He'd never used
them so much and marveled at how quickly they degraded. Hobyn
himself was in the house across the field putting finishing touches on
a baby cradle he'd made with his leathery hands. Voldigar smiled. He
could picture the old man showing it off to Gwenyth while she rocked
in her chair. Hobyn would be proud enough to die on the spot, the
world's happiest codger, his life's work achieved.

Dry as it was, there'd been a little rain at least, and tender sprouts
filled Voldigar's small field. Hovering over it and tending it obsessively
kept the weeds at bay, but it failed to still his mind. Instead, it gave him
time to think. What of the Orun and Tepic's sword? What about his
missing friend? It didn't help that messengers from Maghaltani came
every two or three days with fresh news and anxious questions. Last
he knew, Wulf and Gardoric were also missing. There was no word on
their hunt for Lanathor, and Vasherk too would soon head off into his
native Danek in search of them all. *Am I a farmer, or a field marshall,
holding council in my camp?*

Voldigar finished oiling his trowel and spied a patch of clotbur in the corner of his field. *A farmer, apparently.*

Many lengthening days had gone by like this, thoughts of farm and family doing battle with a shadowy host of worries. He told himself other men would tend to these. He told himself that his brief return had been enough. Others could shepherd the Brotherhood while he faded back into obscurity. No more harrowing days of fear, no more long recoveries, no more intrusions. He'd raise a hedge between the old life and the new.

For her part, Gwenyth suggested Voldigar find some courteous way to affirm trust in her brother—simply tell Medellai to stop sending messengers. A reasonable request, but one he could not bring himself to carry out. 'I'm just a farmer now,' he was supposed to say, but he could hardly say it to himself, let alone his half-blind counterpart. What harm were messengers anyway?

Gwenyth's health had been declining again, and their stock of dried Falam Root was running low. It was God's mercy that he had now mostly recovered, working his field by day, and Chanting over the Scriptures by night. He felt almost himself, save for the anxious thoughts and a deep ache where infection had ravaged his body. For neither the first time nor the last, he was grateful for his brethren, meddling as they were, and regretted that he did not express it more.

Voldigar looked up from the dirt to see a rider emerging on the crest of the hill at a slow trot. He thought it another messenger at first but soon perceived the blue livery and rust hair of Commander Dantic. He tied his horse to one of the red-leafed aspens and waved a greeting to Voldigar. He was alone.

"And hail to you, Commander. To what do we owe the pleasure?"

Dantic held a somber look on his face as he approached, and wariness touched Voldigar's heart. At least it wasn't the middle of the night.

"It's Captain now," Dantic said.

Voldigar squinted, but Dantic went on.

"I wanted to stop by and give my greetings. The rest of my train is back at the Trakast Bridge."

Voldigar tried to look as though he understood and gave a polite nod. Dantic had a way of not explaining himself, a man too long in command. Voldigar wondered how often he did the same.

"I've been reassigned," Dantic said, "and demoted."

"I'm sorry, friend. More foolishness from our new sovereign, I don't doubt." Voldigar brushed soil from his shirt.

Dantic looked into the wood, as though he expected the trees to scold Voldigar's comment. "The guard of Arregalt has been turned over to Gamad. My command now is that of both West and Eastfort. We're on our way to Eastfort now, with all of my possessions."

Voldigar nodded again. "Well, I'll be glad to have you at our border, Dantic, and if you ask me, the demotion is petty." Voldigar remembered his oil rag and tried fruitlessly to wipe his hands. "It's only a couple of miles to the bridge," he said. "Please, bring your family up. We can feed you before you move on."

Dantic shook his head. "No, I want to make Westfort by nightfall so we can climb the pass early tomorrow. It's just me and Claras anyway, and the servants." Dantic tightened his jaw and swallowed. "Tepic's still in Arregalt. The Emperor has taken him into his household."

Chill fingers brushed over Voldigar's skin. "What? Why?"

"I couldn't say, friend. He sent us all away but demanded Tepic—and his grandfather's sword—come into the Spire."

Voldigar's eyes widened. "The sword? Dantic, no, how could you allow this!"

Dantic spread his arms out. "What was I supposed to do? Reason with him? Refuse? Better this than the gallows!"

A murder of crows broke from the aspens at the sound of their raised voices. Voldigar ran a hand over his head.

"Look," Dantic said. "I didn't come here to be scolded. What's done is done. It's awful and I know it. We're allowed to visit often, and my stubborn daughter has stayed behind to look after him. She's living in the apothecary."

Voldigar shook his head. "This can't stand, Dantic. You have to bring him home."

Dantic sighed and looked at the ground, his eyes flitting from pebble to stone. "I know. I know I do."

There was helplessness in the man's eyes, the raw gleam of defeat already taken. Voldigar ground his teeth. "Just . . . let me know if you need anything, anything I can do to help." The words came out with effort, even as anger rose in his chest.

Dantic met his eyes again. "I know, friend, and I will. Just take care of your family." He swept a pouch from his belt and tossed it to Voldigar. "Compliments of Lyrusia. She told me all about your good news."

Voldigar caught the pouch and stared down at it in his grimy palms. "Dantic, I can't keep taking gifts from you. Please, let me pay for this."

"No," Dantic said firmly and held up a hand. "It's not like that, Vol. I don't expect anything. You . . ." He drew a deep breath and looked away. ". . . You just keep doing the right thing."

Voldigar nodded and Dantic snapped a salute. A moment later, the captain was kicking up dust as he sped back to Trakast Bridge.

<hr />

When Voldigar came inside, Gwenyth was resting in her rocking chair with one hand on her belly, smiling at Hobyn. Her shawl was draped over her shoulders. The old fellow was eagerly demonstrating how the cradle could swing or be locked in place with a little round peg. He looked every bit as pleased as Voldigar imagined.

". . . and just like that," Hobyn said with a flourish and a popping noise. "Safe as an egg in mother's nest. I've got some linen to stuff with goose feathers too. The little lord will live in luxury!"

Hobyn chuckled and caught sight of Voldigar. He stood up and brushed sawdust from his hands. "It's off to the well with me. Don't forget to eat, young master. Farming's hard work." He waggled his finger and slipped out the door.

"I think Hobyn's happier than you, Gwen," Voldigar said with a grin. "And see, he says it's a boy too."

Gwenyth shrugged and held out her hands. "What did Commander Dantic want?"

"Heard us talking?"

"A little."

Voldigar held up the small pouch and smiled. "More presents."

Gwenyth raised an eyebrow. "The Commander came all the way here to personally deliver medicine?"

"No. As it happens, he's moving to Eastfort." Voldigar sighed and looked into the hearth before he continued. "And Tepic's not with him. Lusánt has taken the boy into his household." He wanted to gather the words back up the moment he'd said them.

Gwenyth gasped and sat up in her chair. "No . . . no, why?"

Voldigar shook his head. "I don't rightly know, but he's taken the boy's sword too."

"It's mischief. You know it is, and—" Gwenyth began, but the words caught in a string of coughs.

Voldigar walked to the corner they called a kitchen and began to prepare her medicine with a shake of his head. "We can't let the world keep pushing in here, Gwen. No more of this. I shouldn't have brought it up."

She caught her breath. "No more what?"

"No more anxious visits. No more urgent news."

"What are you going to do?"

"Nothing!" Voldigar said, more loudly than he intended. "Nothing."

Gwenyth was frowning with arms crossed when he turned around. "How long is the boy there?"

Voldigar shook his head again. "I don't know."

"Forever then?" she asked.

Voldigar opened his mouth to reply, but let out a long exhale instead. He sat against the counter and stared at the wall for several long moments. At length, he tried and failed to wipe the worry from his face with a brush of his hand. He spoke quietly into his fingers. "The Emperor will drip poison in that boy's ears until he's a shell of who he was."

"Maybe he's stronger than that," Gwenyth said.

"Maybe. He's so young, Gwen . . ."

Gwenyth searched Voldigar's face with her knowing green eyes. "I don't believe you."

"What?"

"That you'll do nothing. I don't believe you."

Voldigar set his jaw and looked at Gwenyth sidelong. "The next messenger," he said. "They'll be here soon, sometime in the next couple of days. I'll send word to Maghaltani. That's all I'm doing."

"What word? You're all banished from the city," Gwenyth said. "What will the Brotherhood do?"

"I don't know, but more than a hundred took the Oath. We'll find an answer," Voldigar said. "*They'll* find an answer." He moved alongside Gwenyth's chair where he sat on the ground again and held her fingers.

"I'm staying home, Gwen. I'm not the only Brother in Aramon. I'll tell Medellai everything and then . . . wash my hands of it."

Gwenyth's brow was furrowed, and her face was filled with doubt. "Wash your hands, Voldigar?"

"What?"

"You sound like a trouper, playing at his lines." She lifted her palm from her belly, grabbed his chin, and glared into his face. "Don't lie to me."

Voldigar closed his eyes. "I just want it to end, Gwen. I'm so tired. Isn't it time to let go?" He opened his eyes and pulled her hand fully into his own. She was still watching him intently.

"You're sure about this?" Gwenyth asked.

"I have to be."

She took the medicine from him and drank, then shut her eyes and leaned back to rock again. They sat quietly while the wood creaked. "Maybe it is time, Vol." She curled to the side and pulled her shawl more tightly as the root took hold. "Smells like rain is coming . . ." she muttered before she passed into sleep.

The rest of the day, the night between, and the morrow were miserable. After Gwenyth nodded off in her chair, Voldigar proceeded to break his only spade, knock a mallet into the depths of his well, and shatter a wooden bucket. The latter had some deliberate assistance from the man himself. After finding a small leak in the bottom and reflecting on his two prior mishaps, he sent it careening against the side of Hobyn's hut into an explosion of splinters. Hobyn emerged in a panic and then a huff, complaining loudly that he could have fixed the bucket.

That first night, Voldigar turned from side to side so many times that Gwenyth had to move to her chair by the hearth again, not for warmth, but just to get some sleep away from his flailing. He awoke the next day in a hazy stupor that no attempt at napping could resolve. Hobyn and Gwenyth hardly said two words to him, staying well clear of his palpable frustration.

He finished the day smoking his pipe in the aspen grove but found the exercise no less vain than his other diversions. He wished for all the world that he could throw a stick and watch Rory chase it for the next hour, but instead, his companions were the crows, staring down from tree limbs with mocking croaks. A mist was rising from the ground, and a swift-moving sheet of gray flowed overhead.

Gwenyth was already sleeping when he crawled under the blankets and drifted off to another fitful night. He dreamed of crows. They swooped into his field by twos or threes, and he drove them off with his broken spade, shouting and cursing. Back to the aspen grove they flew and perched. Their numbers grew until an army of cawing, screeching fowl drowned every other sound. Defeated, he fled into his house, batting wildly at the birds as they beat their wings and pecked his face. He slammed the door behind him and leaned against it, but all around, upon the hearth, in Gwenyth's chair, and even clinging upside down to the ceiling beams, the crows watched him with knowing eyes and took to their squawking again. Voldigar sat up with an arrested shout. His knife was already in his hand. He could feel eyes on him.

"Vol?" Gwenyth asked into the dark.

Voldigar could only sit and focus on his shaking breaths. He slowly lowered the knife to the floor and let the nightmare subside. "I . . . I can't do this, Gwenyth."

He felt her arms wrap around him and her head against his chest. They sat wordlessly for a long time and listened to the wind and rain buffeting their home.

Gwenyth finally broke their blind silence in a hopeful tone. "A messenger will be here in the morning."

Voldigar shifted his weight and groaned. "It doesn't matter, Gwen."

"Why not?" Her voice was small and hollow.

"I can't spend the blood of my brethren on something I'm unwilling to do myself."

Gwenyth let out a quiet whimper and buried her head more deeply against him. The sound broke his heart. Voldigar reached up in the dark and held her cheek in his hand. "I'll be back tonight, Gwen, I promise. I'll tend the field again tomorrow. I just have to—"

She cut him off with a gentle press of her hand against his lips. He could feel hot tears flowing from her eyes and in between his fingers. "Do your duty . . ." she whispered.

The rain was strangely warm that night, and Voldigar could see, or rather feel it coming down sideways, blowing the folds of a drab old cloak across his face. It was pitch black, and a southerly wind carried heat and fog up from beyond the bay. He was glad of the cover of darkness, and though he could hardly see his hands in front of his face, he moved swiftly and steadily over the folds of familiar land. He splashed over the wide ford on the northward arm of the Adionel, and the glow of Arregalt emerged ghostly in the mist.

He made for the postern gate he'd so often used to report to the old training grounds. Standing a long way off, he crouched in darkness and watched. High above, he knew the battlements protruded in a watch of sorts, but this was only a dim island of light floating in blindness over the murk. He considered finding a way to scale the wall and avoid the gate altogether, but the risk of sentries along its top was too high. His passage would have to be upon the ground. Of most concern would be the pool of light he expected to lie before the narrow gate itself. Instead, he found the torches snuffed in the driving rain, and the same thick night he sat in was gathered about the foot of the door.

Lightning crashed through the night sky, momentarily illuminating the walls and battlements above. He made up his mind. He knew by custom that two guards were on the other side of the door. These were his only real obstacle. If he'd rightly judged the time, they'd be early in their watch. With luck, they might even be sleeping, but he would not count on fortune of that kind. Were they to somehow miraculously slumber through his breaching of the door, it would not be long until a hue and cry arose and the Emperor sent a host of soldiers to his farm and to Maghaltani to find out what man had pulled a gate from its hinges in the middle of the night.

When the lightning subsided, Voldigar ran low across the open space and knelt by the door. He slipped a pack from his back and opened it. Then, he simply knocked.

There was no response at first, but every few seconds he would knock again until at length, a panel of the solid gate slid open.

"What do you want?" a voice called out from within. "Gate's closed until daylight. Sod off."

Voldigar stayed low and out of sight against the door, but called up in a scratchy wavering tone, "I'm hungry master, a bit to eat." It was the best impression of Hobyn he could manage. The slide slammed shut. He knocked again.

The war of attrition was short, and on his fifth or sixth set of knocks, he heard the bar of the door lift, and one guard stepped through, followed by another. Voldigar was huddled low in the darkness and waited only as long as it took for the two of them to emerge. One held a cudgel and the other a torch.

"Listen here, grandfather—" the one began to say, but it was too late. Voldigar sprang like a coiled adder and caught them both under their chins with broad hands, impossibly strong. With his fingers, he clamped shut their mouths and gripped their jaws. He swung them about like sheaves, and in a moment had them around their necks, side by side in the crooks of his elbows. Their implements dropped to the mud as his huge arms stopped the flow of blood and air. Noiselessly, they both fell limp.

A few seconds more and they were tightly gagged. He bound them hand and foot and laid them against the wall as they regained consciousness. He thought to mutter a word of apology but realized one of them he recognized. Better to be scarce. He slipped quietly through the door, careful to keep his face in shadow, and barred it behind him.

With his head low and his pack swung to the front of his body, he strode swiftly through the most ragged parts of Arregalt where a man in a dirty brown cloak wandering the night might look less out of place. He went mostly untouched, hurrying through alleys and only once feeling the hand of a disappointed pickpocket slip into his belt.

The rain picked up as he marched, and he was soaked from head to toe by the time he emerged into the quiet district where Lyrusia's apothecary stood. Few citizens were out at this late hour, and the spare patrols were simple to avoid. He had only to lay in the shadows near a sad-looking flower bed and play the part of beggar again when the one unavoidable group of watchmen wandered by Lyrusia's door. They passed him without a word, and when they'd gone out of earshot, he crawled from the soil and gave a gentle knock, praying Lyrusia would hear within.

The apothecary was a narrow three-story building, pressed between a wheelwright and a soothsayer. The rest of Arregalt divided its businesses along the same lines as its guilds, but a random collection of shops belonging to the well-to-do, and unburdened by the pesky need of profit, were crammed along this row against the wall of the Citadel. Voldigar hoped the other owners were in proper houses and not sleeping on the upper floors of these nearby shops. The guard would soon change at the postern gate. Voldigar rapped on Lyrusia's door more loudly. He heard movement inside.

"Lyrusia," he called out in a hurried whisper. "It's me, Voldigar."

The curtain of a window with hazy glass pulled back a hair. He quickly flicked the hood off his head and turned his face to the light shining within.

Lyrusia unlatched the door with a "What do you want?" but Voldigar hurried inside and shut it behind her with his finger to his lips. She had a hard look on her face, maybe a touch of fear, but it quickly softened with realization.

"You're here for Tepic, aren't you?" she whispered.

Voldigar nodded and made sure the curtain was shut. Lyrusia stood with a candle just starting to drip wax into a brass tray.

"I am," Voldigar whispered back. "As best I can."

Lyrusia nodded. "We knew you'd come."

Voldigar sighed. "To be fair, Lyrusia, I did not."

A moment of confusion touched her eyes, but restless determination flowed from her like smoke in the flickering light. "You'll snatch him from the tower then! You could bring him here."

Voldigar shook his head. "I'm afraid it may look much different from that. If the Emperor suspects anything, you can be sure he'll be looking for all of us—your family, mine, and my order."

He expected disappointment, but she nodded resolutely. "What can I do?"

"I just need information. What do you know, have you seen him?"

"Yes," she said, "today."

Voldigar sighed in relief.

"The Emperor is keeping him close," she continued. "Very close. They let us speak—in the courtyard—but one of his men was there the entire time. Tepic looked scared, Lector."

Voldigar furrowed his brow. "I don't doubt it. Did you talk about the sword?"

"Only a little. Every time I brought it up, he looked at the guard. They wouldn't let us be alone. They're keeping him in father's old officer quarters, the snakes."

"Oh?" Voldigar asked.

"Where Tepic saw the demon," Lyrusia added.

Voldigar frowned and nodded. "*The* Snake," he gently corrected. "This is no doubt a device of Lusánt's making. I know where it is."

"Why would they do that to him?" Lyrusia asked, her face twisting with emotion.

Voldigar placed a hand on her shoulder. "I don't know. There's much I don't know, but we'll find some answers—tonight. Pray for your brother, Lyrusia."

She chewed her lip and nodded.

"I won't return here," Voldigar continued, "and I cannot tell you all my errand. Please, do visit us soon though, Gwenyth and me. I may need for you to pass messages to Tepic. Can you do this?"

"I can."

"Good. I was never here."

From his pack, Voldigar produced the incredible tharmskolp that Lutz had given him weeks before. This he studied carefully, placing his eye to the viewport and flicking the angle back and forth to confirm his route. Once satisfied, he stowed it away and vanished into the night again.

Not far from the apothecary, a high stone barrier formed a narrow enclosure, pressed against the Citadel and hung with ivy. By the distant glow of lamplight, a single bolted door showed dimly in its face. Crouching in the shadows, he stole over cobblestone and leapt high to grab its lip. As quiet as he could, he hoisted himself up and over and lowered to the ground.

It was mossy and slick in the tiny courtyard beyond, and here Voldigar laid the heavy cover of a sewer drain aside. Descending the ladder, he propped the disc on his fingers, returned it silently to the hole, and vanished like an earthworm into complete darkness. In a moment, he stood in waist-high water that tugged at his dingy cloak.

Thankfully, the smell was only mild. This section of the sewers under Arregalt was not connected to any indoor plumbing deeper in the city. It caught the normal refuse of the streets and whatever filth the tenants tossed into the gutters, but most of the water that went about his hips was nothing more than swollen runoff from the rainstorm that rang against the metal cover above his head.

He'd been careful to keep his tinder dry within his pack, and this he used to spring a tiny lantern to life. The long tunnel looked the same before and behind in an endless, round gloom of gray stone and black water. He waded carefully for a long while, often turning far out of his way to find a safe crossing through the depths and then to continue on in the direction he intended. In one broad intersection, the water gathered into a swirling vortex to disappear into a deeper channel invisible below. Pulling his cloak from the water, he was able to free himself of the river in a mighty leap, narrowly avoiding a strike of his head against the low, arched roof.

Lutz's map had proved reliable thus far, and he knew his jump put him past the lower edge of the Spire. Many passages spread away to his left and right where the water grew more shallow. He wondered what strange life might carry on here underneath the great stone edifice, but was glad to encounter none of it. Soon he came to a tumbledown bit of masonry over a platform that jutted from the water. Squeezing through a gap near its top, he plopped down on the other side, hands first into a few inches of frigid water. He was greeted by another ladder.

If the map stayed true, this one would lead him into a cellar in the Delvings beneath the south end of the Spire, only a hundred feet or so from the entrance to the Vaults. At this hour it was unlikely, though not impossible, that a servant might be within, fetching this or that for his master above. The hatch at the ladder's top would also be locked, or worse, covered in crates and barrels.

Voldigar feared this moment of his stealth more than all the others to come and spent a long while with his ear pressed to the hatch. No sound or light came. He confirmed it was locked or otherwise covered and began to lean his weight against it. The wood bent and groaned, but it held fast. Something behind was even more firm. He closed his eyes and dug his heels into the ladder until sweat poured over his brow. The door finally gave way with a loud pop and clang.

He stood on the ladder a long time with the hood pulled over his lamp, listening. All he could hear was the heartbeat in his ears. Cracking a small sliver of the hood, a dusty cellar showed round about, his own head peeking through dead center. Hastily, he hid a broken iron bar and covered the hatch with a dusty rug that must have been there before. Still quiet.

Voldigar breathed a little easier as he soon found himself moving along passages that Lutz had led him through only a few weeks before. Going from these memories and the study of the tharmskolp, he moved like a shadow from one stairwell to the next and through one dripping, dilapidated passage to another, always ascending by the deepest and most unfrequented way he could discern.

At one point, a servant passed an intersection directly in front of him. His breath caught but he kept moving forward as though he belonged. She was singing a quiet tune to herself and did not even look to the side. Voldigar shook his head at his good fortune and continued on.

By a long and weary way, he reached a dry passage far up the great height of the Spire. It was so unused that a thick layer of dust caked the stone floor. He lamented the prints of his shoes as he trekked through it and dragged his feet to obscure them, but the dust soon gave way to a true dirt floor in a high-ceilinged, slender chamber with a vague light descending from above. A tall wooden ladder lay against the wall, leading upward into gloom. Voldigar examined the map and placed himself on the south side of the great red hall that lay a hundred feet below the royal apartments. In a sense, he was inside the very wall that enclosed it. The sliver of torchlight, he realized, was from a thin crack in the side of the hall above.

Carefully, he removed his shoes and pack and laid them on the ground. He kept only the wondrous map and four stout nails in his pocket. Then, barefoot, he began to climb, slowly, praying that the rungs of the ancient ladder held and did not betray him with a creak.

He emerged on a high shelf where he could just make out the shadow of his shoes and pack below. There were dark scaffoldings that led from the other wall over perilous drops. The construction was perhaps an abandoned project from long ago, walkways for when the hall might have been used for playacting or music. Lutz's map proved correct once again, and along the ledge, Voldigar found a hard layer of crumbling plaster, about the size of a small door.

It was now that he dug more richly into his Chanting, even daring to let the words tumble softly from his lips in a tuneless roll. He pressed his fingers into the plaster and pulled, careful to let none of it fall into the open space behind. It gave way like dry dough in a baker's hand and was soon peeled and piled into a small heap at his feet. A wall of brickwork was revealed behind and this Voldigar covered with his cloak, driving the nails silently into the stone border with his thumb at both upper corners and one of the lower.

The bricks came free easily but with more noise than the plaster. These he set aside. The buffeting of the wind and rain outside he hoped was louder to anyone listening within the inner walls. He could feel the breeze and sense the spattering of raindrops against the cloak as the hole grew bigger and bigger and the cloth shivered in the wind. When it was cleared, Voldigar crawled onto a tiny terrace with a rough stone wall. He pinned the last corner of his cloak as best he could and prayed no light shone through.

He was now some fifty feet below the officers' quarters where Lyrusia had told him Tepic slept.

Voldigar had made many mad climbs in his decades as a Chanter, but none so foolish as this. He was over four hundred feet above the streets of Arregalt in driving rain and a pitch-black night, staring at a smooth wall above him. He let his Chants grow a little louder.

In truth, the wall was not perfectly smooth, and here and there, tiny fissures and joints could be felt. Some of the great stones had nearly imperceptible bumps on them, remnants of their construction in antiquity. To these bumps and fissures, Voldigar dug his fingers deeply and gripped with the unimaginable strength of his gift. He moved by feel, mostly with his eyes closed. He did not look down and imagined by the long habit of tired watches, that sentries below never looked up. Even if they had, they would have seen little in the foggy darkness.

He'd made it less than ten feet when a flash of lightning lit the back of his eyelids in shimmering white. Unconsciously, he pressed his body against the stones, picturing what his splayed limbs must look like against the great tower. Slowly, he opened his eyes and peered over each shoulder but there was nothing more than a swirl of mist and vague lamplight below. If he'd been spotted, there was nothing he could do. He dared a little more speed.

When he'd gone twice as far again, the little bumps along the base of the stones thinned and the fissures grew infrequent or invisible altogether. He considered reversing course but spotted one small nob several feet above. He'd have to leap, but then he'd be more than half the distance. The old man dug his toes into the joint beneath his feet and vaulted. For a breathless moment, he was in open air, a shadow flying in the rain above the great city. His hand met the nob in a wet terror, but his grip found purchase while the rest of his body dangled there.

Whether by fear or cold, Voldigar began to tremble terribly, but his strength held and he inched along the final stretch of wet stone until he came to a small pair of wooden shutters, no wider than his palms. The effort of holding in place again while he shook was more excruciating than the terrifying climb, but he managed to free one hand and rap against the shutters.

"Tepic," he hissed as loudly as he dared.

No response came, and he knocked a little louder. He was about to announce his own name when the shutters suddenly swung open, narrowly missing Voldigar's face. With a heave, he gripped the lip of a small, paneless window—now open—and pulled himself up to peer inside.

Tepic stood below, blinking, a candle held aloft in one hand and the shutters' long cord in his other. "Who's there? What are you?"

Voldigar could only imagine what his face must look like in the candlelight ten feet up, filling the tiny window frame with his nose peering over the edge. "It's me, Voldigar."

"Sword-Lector?"

"Yes."

"Sword-Lector!"

Voldigar held his other hand to his lips and nearly slipped. "Shhh. I don't have much time."

Tepic gasped and hurried to grab a chair. He placed it on the desk below the window and clambered up to stand upon the tips of his toes, his face now a foot below his old teacher, where the wall subtly sloped inward.

"What are you doing in my window? How did you get here?"

Voldigar smiled. "It's quite a view up here, Tepic. I'll have to tell you some other time. How are you?"

"I'm alright, Teacher. Well enough I suppose—but I don't want to be here."

"As well you shouldn't. What has Lusánt done to you?"

Tepic looked confused a moment and shook his head. "Nothing, I think. The sword, they want to know everything about it. They think I know how to do something with it."

Voldigar nodded. "Who's 'they,' lad?"

"Lusánt, and his advisor. A miridas girl."

"Girl?"

"Yes, from the coronation."

Voldigar switched hands and then tried to wedge them both in the window. "Listen to me, Tepic. I don't know what they want either, but you must swear to me, never, ever, under any circumstances do what they ask you to do with that sword."

Tepic looked away and shook his head in dismay. "Teacher, Lusánt has something—something he shouldn't. He showed me at night. It's a ball, a glowing ball, green like the creature you fought!"

Voldigar narrowed his eyes but otherwise tried not to react. "Did he say what it is?"

"No, but he can do things with it, things to the sky and the moon! He says I can too." Tepic set his jaw and glared. "He made me promise not to tell."

Voldigar nodded. "Sometimes you have to tell, Tepic. You did the right thing. Do nothing they ask, and be wary of everything they tell you."

"Are you going to rescue me, Teacher?"

"I'm afraid I can't fit you through this window."

Tepic's lip began to quiver. "I'm scared, sir. You told me to learn what courage is, but I haven't. I'm always scared."

Voldigar's hard face softened for a moment, and he let his voice rise ever so slightly. "Tepic Relius Banari. Look at me. You are the bravest boy I have ever known in my entire life. You've done things the sternest soldier wouldn't dare. Courage is not the absence of fear, Tepic. It's doing the right thing, even when you are scared."

Tepic considered his words a moment and smiled as he did. "You really think so, Lector?"

"I know so, and never let anyone tell you otherwise—including yourself. Listen, lad, soon you may have to do something very brave, something well within you, but you have to be ready." Voldigar squeezed his arm through the window and dropped a heavy object in Tepic's hands. "Take this, Tepic. Never let anyone know you have it. Look into that little hole on the side."

Tepic gasped when he peered into it, and Voldigar watched as he curiously pressed the buttons and realized its function.

"It's a 'tharmskolp.' The whole Spire and more is inside. Anywhere you visit, you come back here at night and you study that map. Know it like you know swordplay. Learn it better than anything you've ever learned. And Tepic . . ."

The boy looked up.

"When the time is right, you find a way to run where no one can follow. Do you understand?"

Tepic nodded as he clutched the device in two hands.

"Good."

Voldigar winced as another flash of lightning flickered behind him. "I have to go, lad. Trust Lyrusia only, and stay strong." Voldigar stared at his face a few more moments and then began his descent while thunder rolled across the bay.

"Lector!" Tepic called after him.

Voldigar popped his face back over the edge of the window. "What?"

"I did learn what faith is."

"Oh?"

"Yes, in the river. I prayed, Teacher. I prayed."

"And did God answer you?"

"He did!"

Voldigar smiled. "Good, very good." He paused a moment. "Do you know what to do when he doesn't answer?"

Tepic shook his head. "No."

"Keep praying, and keep doing the right thing. An answer is on the way."

Voldigar gave a final nod and dug his toes into the stone. It would be a long, weary march back home.

———◄O►———

It was an hour before dawn when Voldigar finally returned to his humble home. He left his filthy garments by the well and poured a few buckets of water over his head. Standing alone in the darkness, he let the icy cold wash over and through him, pondering the events of the night. He couldn't shake the nagging sense that somehow his deeds would be discovered. He'd done all he could to cover his tracks, but the two guards at least might bring suspicion down on him once they were found. What's more, Lusánt seemed to have an uncanny knowledge of all that went on in Aramon.

Voldigar sighed and shook his head, looking into the well water below. The rain had let up, and a tiny reflection of the green moon shone in its depths. He'd done what he had to, and tomorrow he would just be a farmer again.

Voldigar tiptoed into his house and stirred the coals of his fireplace back to life. For several minutes he crouched with his back turned, drying himself by the flames. Hobyn's new baby cradle sat still in the dark, and on this, Voldigar fixed his gaze while he Chanted in a whisper. At length, he slipped into bed to enjoy a half hour of rest before the sun rose.

As gently as he could, he wrapped an arm around Gwenyth's waist and closed his eyes. She awoke all the same and reached a hand back to stroke his cheek.

"You've returned . . ."

"I have, Gwen," he said. "I made a promise."

Chapter Twenty-Three

Through the Void

I F Lanathor had known day from night, one would have bled into the next on the cold dirt floor of his basement cell under Fort Dromvedya. It was always dark, but even so, he marked each crack of light that shone when a guard arrived bearing a bowl of noxious gruel. They expected him to eat upon his knees like a dog—with hands still tied behind his back. This he refused many times until hunger broke him. The guard had laughed on the first such occasion but ignored the humiliating ritual thereafter.

Sometimes they dragged him blinking from the basement to sit before the man with a tattooed face. The men of the fort called him *Veyli*, and whether it was name or title, Lanathor could not guess. His face and words were hard and stern, and Lanathor could see no soul in the void behind his eyes. The interrogation never changed. Why are the Wyrna stirring? Who is the sleeping Daneki woman? What are you? Lanathor told them honestly all he could, but it was evident they did not believe—and held him responsible, both for the Wyrna and for Liadov's long sleep. They demanded that he, the "wizard," break both curses. Having done neither, it was then the torture began.

His body was a sheet of bruises and cuts, but these he bore without complaint. They had burned and pried, scraped and crushed, but Lanathor never gave them the answers they sought, nor could he. They grew more desperate and cruel as time went on. Lanathor discerned from broken words that the teeming horde without the fort had swollen beyond all measure, and supplies were dwindling within. It was clear their belief that he might somehow end the curse of the Wyrna was the only thing that kept him alive with the occasional sludge of wretched porridge.

The torture he could bear, but darkness and solitude wrought heavy shapes upon his mind. For the first long stretch of days, he could hear the voices of two men in cells down the hall. He tried to speak to them when the guards were not present to beat them for their "racket." One of the men would respond to Lanathor and was sometimes kindly, but the other only cursed and berated them both. One night, or so he believed it was night, the two had somehow come together, and the sounds of terrible struggle ended only with the kindly man's whimpers, more and more quiet until he fell silent. Lanathor never heard the voice of either man again. From then on he was alone.

When he slept, nightmares tormented him, and when he awoke, dark memories of childhood that he had no root to blunt. The tortures his jailers devised could not compare with the horrors of his cruel master from bygone days, long before he was Lanathor. He tried many times to manifest his magic but found that any control of his emotion was impossible. He wept bitterly until he could weep no more and soon wished day by day that he might join the kindly man in his end.

The Scriptures became his comfort then, and he read the pages in his mind, clinging to the words of God and the promises he knew. Surely, his desperate captors could not afflict him much longer. He would soon be just another mouth to feed, and they would then discover if a wizard's death might end the curse. He would enter his long rest, but what would become of Liadov? To what terrible fate had he summoned her?

Days sped on like waves on the Wending Sea, and he could feel the ridges of his ribs against his skin. His mind would soon follow his body. Sometimes he paced within his cell, to stave off atrophy, but his constant gnawing hunger, both for food and for the root, always strode ahead. In time, he could no longer will himself to walk or even stand, but only to lay upon the packed earth and dream fitfully. He passed in and out of wakefulness, and the same image filled his nightmares again and again.

"*Why did you drop it, you fool?*"

He could see the wooden capsule of Falam Root lying in the snow, larger than it ought to be. Beyond it lay the smoking bodies of votaries, gray ash mingling with gusting white.

"*Pick it up!*"

Snow piled upon it as the grunting and scraping feet of the Wyrna grew in his ears. His hands were closed in scabbed, oozing fists—arms pinned to his sides. Why was he lying down? Why couldn't he stand?

"*Fool!*"

There was a burning in his chest, an auger, twisting and grinding. Bone was giving way. He cried out, but the Wyrna only laughed. "*Hold still,*" one said in its guttural speech, "*hold still!*" A rough hand thrust the capsule into the hole, even as it grew. He could see it now, as though he were a specter, hovering over his own stiff body. The capsule grew too, until it had consumed most of his chest. Lanathor knew he had to tear it from his body, that he would soon be dead, but the desire to open it drowned every other thought.

"*Open!*" a voice cried out. Was it his own? "*OPEN!*"

His blood was pouring underneath him in a widening pool, soaking his robes and leeching into the snow, but the capsule stayed firmly closed.

"*OPEN!*"

He somehow took hold of it, digging his fingers into its lid like a vulture's talons. He pressed until the skin folded back and splinters dug under his nails.

"*OPEN!*" he cried, but the sound echoed from the walls of his cold cell. He lay sightless in the chill air. He could feel wet tears along his cheeks, streaming to his parched and cracking lips. There was no capsule, no blood upon the snow, no Falam Root—but the aching phantom in his chest remained. The last thought he had before losing consciousness again was of terrible thirst.

Thankfully, in passing weeks the nightmares ceased, and his rest was marked by blackness—not of terror, but of nothing, like the long quiet breadth between the stars. On one such night, the black of his dreamless sleep was interrupted by a vision of his own cell bars. To his surprise, Liadov stood just beyond them, staring into his eyes. He called out, but whether he was silent or she was deaf, it was plain to see she did not hear. He soon awoke in dismay and fruitlessly tried to fall asleep again. He found his voice in waking and called her name once more, but the dream had passed. Liadov was not there.

Many hours later, he was glad to fall asleep again, for once more, he dreamed of his dear friend. This time she spoke. Her voice was distant, like words through water, but the music of it was a balm on Lanathor's weary soul. "Take heart . . ." she said, ". . .take heart . . ." and nothing more. He tried again to speak to her, but as before, she did not hear.

From then on, the dream repeated every time he slept, and though she could not perceive him, her words of comfort grew more and more, and the clarity of her voice became such that he could hardly distinguish whether he was awake or no. He soon believed with certainty that these were not merely dreams. Liadov was speaking to him across some immeasurable distance, through the ether of another world he did not understand.

"I cannot wake, Lanathor. I am still here. Come, and free me from the keep," she told him one night. He shot awake in clammy sweat—or rather thought he did, for once again a vision met his eyes. Crouched outside his cell, Brothers Vasherk, Gardoric, and Wulf knelt low and peered like ghosts through the bars.

"Lanathor?" Vasherk asked in a whisper.

Lanathor blinked at the sliver of light emerging from a lantern Wulf held and watched the apparitions in silence.

"Elder?" Vasherk asked again

"Liadov . . ." Lanathor croaked.

"No, Elder. It's me, Vasherk."

"You can hear me?" Lanathor asked weakly.

Vasherk raised his eyebrow. "I'm two feet from your face, Brother. I'm not that old." Wulf brought more of the lamplight to bear, and Lanathor heard all three take a sharp breath.

"We've got to stop meeting like this, friend," Vasherk said.

Overcome, Lanathor leaned his head against two bars and found that he once again had tears to weep. His brethren sat in stunned silence until Vasherk reached through and placed a hand upon his head.

"It's alright, Brother, we're here, we're real, and quite a chase you've led us on. What are you doing all the way out here?" Vasherk said.

Lanathor blinked through wet eyes and looked from face to face. He could not yet speak. Gardoric's expression was locked in anger, and Wulf looked much the same. They stared at him with a mix of apprehension and disbelief.

"What did they do to you?" Wulf growled. "I hardly recognize your face—and how have they kept you locked away?"

Lanathor shook his head and found his voice. "I . . . can't . . . Brother. I can't feel the Song. I'm . . . broken."

Wulf glared and grabbed hold of the bars. "Then let's be rid of this place." Wedging a foot against one, he gripped and strained at another. Sweat dripped down his face as the bars began to bend.

"What's happened outside the fort?" Lanathor asked, gingerly testing the movement of his legs. "Did you see . . . the Wyrna?"

"See them? It's like the end of days," Vasherk said ruefully. "From the pass, to Vlacha—everything is overrun or near to be. Dizghizádè's burned to the ground. We walked the length of Danek and came here by the edge of Wulf's axe—and no small fortune the beasts pulled back by day. They were thick against the walls ere sunrise. I fear we cannot return the same way."

Gardoric looked nervously down the hall. "We've got to move, soon. There are sentries making rounds outside. Can you walk, Elder?"

Lanathor nodded and slowly squeezed through the widening gap between the bars. The effort left him breathless. He rose unsteadily to his feet. "How did you enter the fort unseen?"

Vasherk grinned as he cut Lanathor's bonds. "Gardoric's gift, Brother—Third Virtue. He can imbue now. Very useful."

Gardoric did not match Vasherk's smile. He squinted at Lanathor, now standing in the torchlight. "You're near invisible already. You're sure you can walk?"

"Unless you want to carry me." Lanathor stumbled a few steps while Vasherk steadied him.

"It only lasts a few seconds," Gardoric continued. "We have to move fast."

"Wait," Lanathor said as he rubbed his wrists. Having his arms free after so long felt alien, like his appendages weren't his own. "Liadov is here."

His three rescuers froze. Wulf's mouth hung open.

"Yes. In the keep," Lanathor said. "We cannot leave without her."

Vasherk narrowed his eyes. "There is no prison that can hold her. Have they hurt her too?"

"She's asleep again, and a long while I judge, longer than ever before. Terrible things have happened here in Danek," Lanathor said. His head swam. He closed his eyes and leaned against Vasherk.

"So we've seen," Wulf said.

"How long have I been here?"

Vasherk frowned. "It's been months, Lanathor. You're lucky we found you."

Lanathor swayed in mute dismay. *Months?*

"It will be more months for all of us if we don't go now," Gardoric interjected. He straightened Lanathor with a hand and looked into his eyes. "Listen. When I give you Virtue, you'll know it. We've got to get outside and cross the courtyard. Don't delay. Liadov complicates things and we'll have to move in segments. There's a lumber pile on the left side of the keep. The shroud should hold until then. Make for it the moment you're outside. You're not strictly invisible, so stay to the shadows. Do you understand?"

Lanathor nodded.

"Wait for my signal from the top of the stairs."

With his final instruction, Gardoric closed his eyes. In a blink, the shadows shifted. There was a shimmer in the air and a heaviness. Gardoric vanished from view. Wulf waited a few beats and then closed his lantern. By feel, they followed to the foot of the stairs and watched. The door above moved ever so slightly, and a thin line of torchlight appeared. As quickly as it showed, it vanished again, and Wulf let his lantern shine once more.

Gardoric was at the top of the flight, waving his hand. Like a train of mice, each man sped softly up the steps. "I'll go last," Gardoric whispered.

Lanathor watched in amazement as Gardoric touched each in turn and they vanished like candlelights. He could not wonder long, for Gardoric touched him next. The feeling was in some ways akin to the Shifts of his own power, but more subtle. He could not see his limbs, and though it was disorienting, at least the world did not spin.

Wulf's lantern light disappeared again, and the door swung open. It was night, and a spare number of smoking torches flickered through the courtyard in a gentle misting rain. Two sentries passed near the front gate with their backs turned. On Lanathor's left, further into the fortress, a large stock of lumber sat on pallets near the stout keep's rough-hewn wall.

He could not see the others but trusted they moved as he did. Low and fast as his aching limbs allowed, he stumbled to the lumber pile and worked his way between two wet stacks. He felt himself bump into something he could not see and soon realized it was Wulf, for the huge man popped back into sight a moment later. The others appeared in like manner.

Wulf's massive shoulders easily cleared the woodpile, and a wide-eyed Vasherk pulled him down in a splash of mud.

"I don't know why I'm on a stealth mission," Wulf complained in a whisper. "When do we bash heads?"

Vasherk grinned, but Gardoric ignored the question. "There's no way we make it through the gate. We've got to get over this wall. We'll use the lumber piles," he said.

Gardoric looked tired, far more so than the others, and Lanathor wondered how long he could keep sharing his gift. He wondered too how long he himself could continue. His body trembled uncontrollably.

"Wulf," Gardoric went on. "You've got to get over first, and then you can use your strength. Wedge yourself above and pull us over." Gardoric pointed to a spot on the wall and frowned. "We have to do this by feel, don't lose sight of that spot. Me, then Vasherk, then Lan. Then we trust to fortune. Find cover on the other side."

The men nodded, and Gardoric again closed his eyes and touched each one in turn. Lanathor waited anxiously, listening to Wulf scramble over the wall. After he thought he heard the other two men clear, he clambered atop the wood and felt blindly for a hand. Again, the exertion stole his breath, and the ache in his shoulder left his arm only partially extended. He lunged again and swept at air, nearly falling from the pile. This was taking too long.

Just as he despaired, he felt a huge hand sweep against the back of his neck and pull him limply over the wall. The carved tops of the rough logs tore at his sides and legs, but he did not cry out. He was numb to pain. Of far greater concern was the loss of precious seconds. Wulf more or less carried him to the dirt below the battlements, and in that instant, both men reappeared.

A group of sentries stood near the inside of the gate, but Lanathor did not have time to see if they were noticed. Wulf plucked him from the ground and whisked him round the base of a square watchtower. In the dim light, he could just make out the dread on Wulf's broad face. Both men held their breath as they watched and waited for sentries that never came.

Lanathor let out a shaking exhale. Before him were sloping grounds that led to a keep of darkened wood. It was intricately carved with many roofs and trusses in clever angles, reminiscent of his mountain home. The back of the building abutted the inner palisade beyond. Crouched behind a nearby oxcart, Vasherk and Gardoric huddled in the rain, obscured from the sentries' view. Gardoric held his hand up in warning, but then quickly waved them over.

Lanathor half limped and was half dragged by Wulf in a stumble through the shadows. Wulf did not bother crouching his huge frame behind the cart and instead lay upon his belly. Gardoric drew their heads together and spoke almost inaudibly but with many careful gestures.

I go in myself. You, wait.

He did not pause for reply but vanished again. Lanathor watched a side door open and close on its own, and then all he could do was sit quietly in the dark.

In the silence, he could make out the sound of the night sentries jesting coarsely in Daneki. One was scraping a stone along his axe. Another strolled passed the oxcart but did not look to where they were. Lanathor flinched when Gardoric reemerged in their midst.

She's inside. Two Lefts. One guard. Wulf.

Gardoric delayed no further but enshrouded each in turn and they were on their feet again, Vasherk bringing up the rear with a gentle hand on Lanathor's back. They moved swift and silent in the darkened hall, guided by the light of low, red sconces and the sightless sense of Gardoric ahead. Two left turns and they came upon a broad chamber before a reinforced door. A single guard sat upon a stool, whittling a figurine with his pocket knife. Lanathor did not see what the figure was, for a moment later the guard slumped from the stool and his knife and wood clattered to the floor. Wulf appeared next to him with his great hand balled into a fist. "Sorry," Wulf mouthed.

The noise of the knife echoed against the high ceiling, and all four men hurried to open the heavy door. It was locked, but with a shoulder, Wulf quickly overcame it. The room within was dark, and having lost his lamp vaulting the wall outside, the huge man wrenched a sconce from the wall and thrust it forward.

The chamber was larger than Lanathor would have guessed and mostly empty. Across from the door on a frame of quartered timber, Liadov lay peacefully, still wrapped in Lanathor's fur-lined cloak. With renewed strength, he rushed across the room and laid his hand upon her forehead. The others gathered round.

"I've come to wake you, Liadov," his voice rasped. "I heard you." He wasn't sure what to do, and as the seconds passed, he closed his eyes and held her hand. He reached into his memories and tried to still his heart, searching for the threads of the Song, but it was a tangle of confusion. The silken strings he'd run his fingers through as a master of his craft felt like some unspeakable texture, a twisted mass of coarse hairs woven with inscrutable geometry. Even if he could touch his magic, what would he do then?

"Please, Liadov. You have to wake up," he whispered helplessly. "We have to leave."

"There's no time, Brother, we'll carry her," Gardoric said.

Vasherk cocked his head in doubt. "We're on the edge of a knife, Gardoric. It was hard enough to get in. Let me try."

The old Chanter placed his hands on Liadov's arms and closed his eyes. His mouth worked silently, and his brow wrinkled in concentration. "I can't tell what—"

The door burst open and several watchmen rushed in, clutching torches and glinting axes. Veyli was at their head, bearing his broad blade.

"Thieves! Throw down your arms!" he cried.

As one, all four brethren whirled to face him, drawing weapons of their own. Lanathor sought frantically for an implement to use. His body, weak as it was, would not last a second in pitched battle—but there was no other choice. He'd fight them with his bare hands if he must. He would not go back into their cage.

Sensing their resolve, Veyli stepped forward and his body tensed to leap and strike. But as he coiled, his weapon fell from his hand. Likewise, the mass of men beside him did the same, their axes and lights clattering to the stone floor. They briefly looked to each other in confusion, closed their eyes, and then collapsed. They were fast asleep.

"You heard me," Liadov said warmly. She was sitting up in her bed, skin pale and her hands outstretched and trembling. "What is this place?"

Lanathor rushed to Liadov's side, tripping on his faltering legs. Her warm smile melted to concern. He cut her off before she could ask and grasped her hand in two of his own. "I know. I look like death. We've been here a long time, Sister."

"And we can't stay a moment longer!" Gardoric called out.

The sound of many rapid feet echoed from beyond the open door.

Wulf sprang to the heavy bed, and with a grunt, hoisted its edge to drag it across the floor, rolling sleeping men aside with his foot. He slammed the door closed and let fall his burden, driving it against the door. "Sorry," he muttered as Liadov spun her legs over the side and stood unsteadily.

Though the lock was broken, a heavy wooden bar stood by. This, Vasherk snatched and dropped into place. "Now what?" the old man asked. Ceaseless pounding and dull thuds erupted against the door.

"Stand back," Liadov said. The brethren moved to the edges of the room, but instead of to the door, Liadov turned and walked to the far wall where the bed had once stood. With eyes closed, she placed a shaky hand against the surface and otherwise fell still. Nothing happened for precious seconds while the others looked on nervously at the shuddering door.

A network of red embers spread in a smoking hiss beneath her hand. The glow wove in a spiraling pattern over the wood. The tendrils soon terminated a few feet out in every direction and formed into a perfectly round halo upon the wall. The thin circle of fire grew brighter until it was a searing, brilliant white.

"Close your eyes," Liadov said firmly.

They did as she said, but even with eyes shut, Lanathor winced at a sudden blinding flash. When he opened them, the circle had grown dark, and a deep smoldering gouge held its place.

Wulf opened his eyes and assessed her handiwork for only a moment before he rushed forward toward the wall. He grinned wildly as his legs left the ground and smashed into the circle with a flying two-footed kick. A huge section of the wall came free and burst outward. The palisade against it crumbled too, and a gaping hole now showed the outer courtyard beyond at the rear of the fortress.

"Come on!" Wulf cried as he scrambled to his feet. "Quiet time is over!"

The open space here was narrow, and to their left a small postern door stood unguarded below a single wavering torch. A setting moon gave off the only other light. The rain had let up, and there was no sign of any sentry. With luck, every conscious guard was now behind, bashing at the barred chamber door.

The group ran forward as swiftly as they could. Lanathor's body screamed. He felt like a newborn deer tottering on spindly legs, but he would not be the cause of their recapture. He went on, sometimes aided by one or the other of his fellows and other times flailing and stumbling on his own.

They were quickly through the postern gate, then racing down a treacherous cleft of loose stones toward an open field. Far in the distance, a dark forest rimmed the horizon. The first thing he realized as he ran was that the snow was gone. The seasons had changed while he lay in darkness under Dromvedya. Secondly, he found to his dismay that though they'd covered a fair stretch of ground, Liadov moved as poorly as he. For all her strange power, she was merely human too. She'd lain still a long while and awoken to a panic. The delicate slippers she'd worn in the gardens of the oracle were already in tatters, and her feet were red and bleeding as they struck upon the rocks. A look of profound weariness hung over her face.

"We have to stop," Lanathor gasped as he brought Liadov to a halt and tried to steady her on sliding stones. The others slowed and looked back.

"I can run," Liadov protested. "I just need . . . a little time to recover."

"We have to keep moving," Gardoric said. "They'll set dogs on us the moment they see we're gone."

"Gardoric's right," Vasherk said. "Daneki love their dogs more than each other."

Lanathor stayed still. "We'll never make it to that forest." The rest of the party came to a stop. "If the dogs don't catch our scent, the Wyrna will."

"I'll carry you both!" Wulf shouted.

Liadov pulled from his hands and limped forward again. Vasherk started to move with her, but the resolute look of the adventurer was suddenly replaced with a physician's gaze. He placed a gentle hand on her shoulder and spoke with the firm tone of a grandfather. "A moment, young lady."

He stooped down to look at Liadov's feet and took another long look at Lanathor as well. He shook his head. "What did they do to you two?"

"There's much to discuss," Lanathor said darkly. "But there's no time. We have to make our stand here."

"Nonsense," Vasherk replied, "and we don't have time to tend to you either. What you both need is rest, real rest, and good food." He smiled. "Taro and a warm fire would be better than me right now."

The old Chanter stood up and peered into the night sky, lost in a moment of thought. Gardoric was glancing nervously back at the fort and looked like he was about to say something, but Vasherk spoke first. "There's a river just to the south of here," he said. "The Vedkorya, much closer than that forest. It flows east to Kurath. If you can't run, can you cling to something?"

Lanathor squinted. "You mean for us to use the river?"

Vasherk nodded. "Solves two problems at once, Elder. No dogs, and no running."

Liadov's eyes brightened. "The white pines!"

"Yes," Vasherk said. "You remember. They're all along the river here, and they float like corks."

Wulf unslung the great axe from off his back. "They float good enough for me?"

Vasherk chuckled. "Even for you, old ox. Quickly now, follow me!"

CHAPTER TWENTY-FOUR

AN HONEST FRIEND

DAYS AND WEEKS PASSED in the Spire of Arregalt while Tepic dreamed of home. Ru was right—he was growing taller. It was uncomfortable. His legs hurt, and his voice cracked when he spoke. He found it better to be silent most of the time, and it suited him just fine. The Emperor had not called for him as often as he said he would, but when he did, their time together was always the same. Lusánt talked and talked, complaining of old men, complaining of young women, and cursing the many duties that an emperor apparently had. They were rarely accompanied by any others, save Kyriana or the Xerimadi bodyguard. Conversation always turned to the sword.

Lusánt tried many things to convince Tepic of how he might bring out the magic of it, as he'd once done so long ago in his old house with Galomar the guard. Tepic found he could do no such thing, and in truth, he did not try, neither by his will nor by his hand. He could not forget the strange midnight meeting with Voldigar, and Lyrusia gave the same warnings as clearly as she could whenever she was allowed to visit under the watchful eyes and prying ears of the Spire guards.

While Lusánt was often cross and growing more jaundiced over time, Kyriana remained respectful. She spoke with disarming warmth. How Tepic longed to make a friend and break the loneliness of the Spire, but even with her, he chose his words carefully—if he spoke at all. She too seemed fixated on the sword. Tepic found another boy near his own age amongst Lusánt's entourage, but the young man was cruel and wicked and more interested in dismembering insects than friendship. The older boys dismissed Tepic out of hand and had taken to calling him 'Emperor's Pet.' He retired to his empty chamber each day, muttering to himself, and unable to sleep despite a weariness he could not explain.

Mother and Father visited once, but they also were closely watched and listened to. He was glad of their company, but the gathering ended all too soon. He was left with his one pastime: exploring. This Lusánt allowed him—without the sword—and with a trailing guard at all times. Whenever he was left alone a day, he wandered the long halls of the Spire while a silent sentry stalked behind, smoking or spitting seeds.

The structure was massive beyond his wildest dreams, and on every level, there was something akin to a city of its own, with residents unique from those above or below. He was not allowed to speak long to anyone, for the guards always moved him along if he lingered. For their part, they too were often surprised at the strange corners and lost places of the Spire that Tepic led them to.

True to his word, when alone at night he would quietly take up the little map that Voldigar called a 'tharmskolp' and study the places he'd gone until he finally overcame his restlessness, and fitful sleep took him. The ritual kept his mind busy and stayed his despair. Within the map, he found many things, deeper secrets around the places he had visited. Hidden passages were his favorite. He longed to search them out, but a guard was always close in tow, and he thought it better to keep his secrets to himself.

Late one summer evening, after a lengthy excursion, Tepic sat upon his bed studying the tharmskolp. A gentle knock rapped on his door. It was locked from the outside as always, so he wasn't quite sure how to respond. He quickly hid the device and jumped to his feet.

"Uh, hello? Come in?" he said.

The door clicked and swung open, and other than the guard, Kyriana stood there alone holding a candle. It was odd to see her by herself, especially at night.

"May I come in, Lord Banari?"

He remembered his manners. "Please," he said and stepped aside.

"Thank you. I understand that you must be very lonely," she said in her lyrical voice as she strode into the room.

"I suppose," Tepic said, pulling his collar about his neck. "It's not so bad though."

Kyriana frowned. "I know you've not gotten on well with the other young men of the court—and His Highness is very busy."

Tepic scratched his head. "Sure."

Kyriana sighed but replaced her frown with a sweet smile. "You've grown so quiet, Tepic. Will you walk with me?"

Tepic raised his eyebrows. "Alright." A light overcoat lay carelessly on his desk. This he grabbed along with a pair of boots and wandered through his open door. Kyriana gestured ahead while the guard locked the room. Tepic began to walk, and to his surprise, Kyriana slipped her arm into his.

"We'll be taking the lift tonight, almost to the lowest floor," she said.

To reach the lift they had to descend a long staircase into the great hall. She walked arm in arm with him for the length of it and on through the brass doors of the lift. "I have a surprise for you," Kyriana said as the doors shut and she pulled a silver cord.

They stood in silence as the lift descended, save for a quiet song that Kyriana hummed to herself. Tepic watched the floors speed by in foggy windows while he drifted on her voice. The sound was beautiful, and he wished for a blissful spell that the lift might descend forever. All too soon the doors opened in a puff of steam, and they walked into a corridor of yellow-brown stone, very unlike the rest of the Spire.

Kyriana was careful to let him lead her by the arm, but she subtly controlled their direction. After a few turns, they stood near a heavy, riveted door guarded by a man in the new imperial purple of Gamad's palace guards.

"Please, open the door, guardsman," she said and flashed a large ring upon her left hand.

The man nodded and obeyed without a word. It was darker within, and many heavy doors were evenly spaced along the walls. There were no furnishings over the worn stone, and a stale air lingered in the hall. Tepic's apprehension grew as they passed several more guards.

"Why are we in a prison?" he whispered.

"This is the Imperial Reformatory," Kyriana answered with a smirk. "It would be most unwise to enter a prison."

Tepic's heart leapt into his throat. "A reformatory? Why?"

"Patience," she said as she stopped before a door with a long gash in its planks. She repeated the gesture with her ring, and another guard hurried to assist. For a split second, Tepic thought to flee, but curiosity drew him on. A light flickered from beyond the door.

He peered inside, and to his amazement, a familiar face peered back through iron bars. Sergeant Galomar, with his long bangs and wispy mustache, raised his eyes and grinned. "The boy who beat the Emperor!"

Kyriana smiled. "I understand you two know each other. I'll be outside."

———◆———

The door shut behind him with a clang, and Tepic let his eyes adjust to the dim light. Galomar was still grinning behind the bars and looked well enough for an incarcerated man. Out of uniform, Tepic could see just how young he was.

On his own side of the barrier, Tepic found a low stool and a small table with a tray of plain but wholesome-looking food. Tepic sat. "How old are you?" he asked.

Galomar laughed. "Came all the way here to ask me that, did you?"

"Sorry," Tepic muttered around a mouthful of bread.

"It's alright," Galomar said. "I'm seventeen. Going to give me any of that?"

Tepic's eyebrows shot up. "Of course, sorry." He scooted closer and held the tray to Galomar who eagerly grabbed a wedge of cheese.

"No need to be sorry for everything, my young friend. What are you doing here anyway?"

"I don't know," Tepic said. "Kyriana just brought me down."

"Who? No, the Spire I mean. What are you doing here at all?"

"Oh!" Tepic said. "Emperor Lusánt has taken me into his service. I don't really know why."

Galomar whistled. "First you beat him in a duel, and now you're his right-hand man. What a tale."

Tepic frowned. "I never beat him, remember?"

"Not even with my expert instruction?"

Tepic began to answer when a sinking realization followed a handful of berries down his throat. "It's my fault you're in here, isn't it?"

Galomar laughed again. "Not at all, Lord Tepic of the Spire, though you did get me in some trouble. That was a merry chase you led us on in the Citadel, and I'd love to know how you knocked me off my feet like a wet rabbit."

"Sorry," Tepic mumbled.

"There you go again with the apologies. Don't worry, friend. I found some trouble all my own to end up here." Galomar pointed at the rest of the berries, and Tepic held the tray out again. "No, as it happens, there are certain people you shouldn't insult and certain people you shouldn't speak near. As it also happens, there's a special place for young noblemen who get themselves into trouble."

"You're noble?" Tepic asked.

"Yes. House Veskelti. How else do you make Sergeant at seventeen?"

Tepic twisted his face.

Galomar waved it off. "Never mind." He took a breath and raised his eyebrow. "Why do you suppose we get special midnight meetings and food trays?"

Tepic pondered the question a moment. It was rather odd. Even more odd, he realized, as this was the first conversation he'd had unmonitored since his arrival in the Spire. Galomar of course was the only person who'd ever seen Tepic use the magic of the sword. For a fleeting moment, he thought to speak plainly with the friendly soldier, but the words caught in his throat.

Tepic shrugged. "I don't know. The food's good though."

"That it is," Galomar replied.

They rambled on another half hour or so, and Tepic was delighted to have his first normal conversation in a long while. It turned out they had much in common and many humorous stories to share, not only of Commander Dantic but also the simple pleasures and joys of a young noble in Arregalt. He was sad to go when the door swung open and Kyriana led him away with a smile. He could come back again, "soon," she said.

That night, Tepic slept a little more easily, glad to have at least one real friend in the Spire.

The next few weeks were much the same, but every handful of days, Kyriana would visit his room and bring him on a late-night visit to Galomar. There he would find the same stool, the same tray of wholesome food, and the same smiling Galomar. They took to playing at words, sharing riddles, and even carving out a board game of sorts on the back of the wooden tray. Most surprising of all, after these visits Kyriana never asked what they spoke about, not even of the sword.

Many hot, dry days passed in Aramon, and Tepic kept his shutters open morning and night. He often ruminated on Voldigar's visit while he looked up at the tiny window. The sword-lector had somehow scaled the Spire in driving rain, just to speak to him. Nothing made sense, but he would keep his promise, no matter what. He poured over the tharmskolp every day and added Galomar's 'Reformatory' to his research. Like everywhere in the Spire, there were curious passages near it and in it, and they filled Tepic's mind with wild fantasies of escaping with his friend through a secret door.

One night, the dry air stopped, and a furious storm battered the sides of the Spire outside his room. Tepic closed his shutters and sat listening to thunder as it echoed from the bay and rumbled through his wall.

A loud knock at the door and Tepic leapt from his bed, slipping on his coat. Before he could speak, the lock clicked, and he quickly hid the map in his pocket. A frowning Lusánt walked into the room. The unmistakable hilt of Grandfather's sword peeked over his shoulder. Tepic's smile evaporated, and he stood quietly before the Emperor.

Lusánt regarded him coolly for several long seconds before he sniffed. "Expecting someone, Banari-boy?"

Tepic stood blinking. "I thought—"

"I am disappointed in you, Tepic. It seems you haven't been honest with me."

Tepic's brow tightened and his mouth moved, but Lusánt went on.

"Yes, not mad but . . . disappointed." He nodded to himself. "Come with me."

Tepic's feet were lead, but he had no choice. The Xerimadi loomed over him with a scowl and crowded him from his room and down to the lift. It shook to life and plummeted noisily until they reached a floor near the lowest level. They stepped into the familiar halls of the Reformatory. Tepic's heart began to pound in his ears. Lusánt marched them through the doors with his chin low, elbowing guards aside.

They stopped at a door with a long gash across the wood, and here Lusánt finally turned to glare at him. The Emperor shook his head while his hand rested on the planks—but he said nothing. He pressed upon the door.

Inside, the huge figure of General Gamad towered in the shadows with his eyepatch and meaty hands. The door of the iron cell hung open, and Galomar sat on Tepic's stool with his wrists bound behind his back. Both his eyes were swollen nearly shut, and blood trickled from the corner of his mouth. The food tray they shared was splintered against a wall. Tepic gasped. "Galomar!"

Lusánt grabbed Tepic by his shirt and jerked him into the room. "Since you have nothing to say, Sergeant, I've brought your friend."

Galomar cried out. "Leave him be!"

Lusánt turned back to Tepic. "It's time for us to speak plainly." He wrenched the sword from off his back and thrust it into Tepic's hands, still stowed inside a new scabbard. "I hate liars, and I hate cowards. You *know* how to use this sword!"

Tepic's head spun, and the weapon trembled in his hands. "I don't! I don't! I promise!"

"Promises, promises, promises," Lusánt mocked. "Enough! This is the guard you used the sword on before, and you'll do it again." Lusánt gathered Tepic's collar tightly in his fist.

"Don't hurt him," Galomar gasped.

"Don't worry," Lusánt said and gestured to General Gamad. "We won't."

The giant man lowered the torch he held and pressed the flame against Galomar's arm. Galomar flailed and screamed and fell to the ground. The general wrenched him back to his seat and held him in place to burn him again.

"Stop!" Tepic cried. "Stop!" His eyes welled with tears.

"It stops when you decide to be honest, Tepic!" Lusánt shouted.

Gamad lowered the torch again, near to Galomar's neck.

Tepic was blind with terror as he cried and his whole body convulsed. He ripped the sword from its scabbard and held it out with two hands. Lusánt leapt backward, and Gamad swept a short blade into his hand like a bolt of lightning.

"Good!" the old general bellowed. "Good! Show us!"

The sword shook so hard in Tepic's hand he thought he might drop it, but he could hear the voice of his sword-lector behind his stinging tears. *Do nothing they ask.* He let the sword point fall level.

Gamad growled and strode forward, knocking the sword from Tepic's grip with a ringing strike. "Pick it up, whelp!"

"Do as he says," Lusánt cried. "Do it!"

Tepic grasped the sword again and held it out. "Leave Galomar alone," he managed in a shaking whisper.

"Don't listen, Tepic," Galomar groaned from behind. "Don't do a thing they say!"

Gamad whirled and struck Galomar with the back of his fist, sending him and the stool crashing to the floor with a wheezing grunt. Galomar managed to turn painfully to his stomach and force himself onto his knees.

"Stop!" Tepic cried again, helplessly.

Lusánt turned to Tepic with sad and distant eyes. "This is your doing, Tepic. Look what you've done." He turned back to Gamad and nodded.

With his free hand, the old general grasped Galomar by the back of his shirt. Tepic's friend hung there limply with a spooling stream of blood pouring from his lip. Gamad gave Tepic a pleading look. His knife hovered in the air for a tortured second, frozen like the cruel edge of winter, and then plunged between Galomar's shoulders.

"No!" Tepic cried out and rushed forward in his anguish. Gamad's blade rose and fell again, and then he whirled on Tepic. The deflection should have been easy for such a veteran, but he was far too late. Tepic's sword flashed through the air like the glimmer of a mirror and cleanly severed Gamad's arm at the elbow. A bright golden light erupted all along the weapon's length and even up to Tepic's shoulders. The general roared like a wounded bear and staggered back against the wall where he crumpled to the floor and held the ruin of his arm. A few feet away, a pool of blood rapidly spread under Sergeant Galomar where he lay sideways on the floor. The blood began to vibrate and dance upon the stone.

Lusánt drew a sword from beneath his cloak and backed into the corner with a wild gaze, holding the point of the weapon before him. "Your friend is dead, Tepic. Dead!"

Tepic stood in shock, clutching his grandfather's sword as though he might crush the hilt in his shuddering hands. He stared at Gamad, whose blood gushed between the fingers of his other hand, and then at poor Galomar's still body. Their blood began to mingle and pool and flow in currents. Hot tears poured down Tepic's cheeks.

"You can save him, Tepic!" Lusánt cried fiercely. "You can bring him back to life. You can do anything! Anything! Just try!"

Tepic's gaze lingered a long while on his friend who lay upon the floor and then on the mad Emperor, scrambling into the corner. The light pulsed ever brighter upon the blade and upon his arms. It called to him like the most beautiful song he'd ever heard, more lovely than Kyriana's voice as they walked together. He did feel strong. He felt like someone else—like he could do anything.

"Do it, Tepic," Lusánt said again.

Tepic ground his teeth and blinked away his tears. "I won't," he said at last. The light flickered out of the world, the blood stopped moving, and once again, he was just Tepic, standing in a gruesome cell with a trembling blade.

Gamad stirred, and he grasped his knife from off the floor with slick fingers. Lusánt's face twisted in rage. Tepic thrust the sword into its scabbard, backed two steps through the door, and fled across the stone floor, running as he'd never run in all his life.

Chapter Twenty-Five

Head and Heart

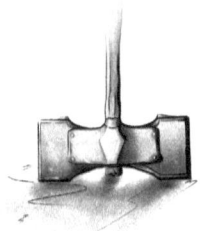

B Y SOME MIRACLE OF the weather, Voldigar's field had been doing
well. Heavy rains punctuated long dry spells just in time and managed to bring up rank upon rank of waving green stalks, half a yard high.
Hobyn claimed the grain would head soon, early for Aramon and more
akin to the warmer weather of Tituria and Kurath beyond the mountains.
The old man was optimistic, and the field was healthy from lying fallow
for so long. It was then the weather changed.

The timely rain ceased, and they grew more worried day by day. Voldigar
took to watering the furrows by hand with two huge buckets Hobyn had
made for the well. It was grueling, maddening work that took the greater
part of each day to complete. His hands were rough as shoe leather, and
his skin had gone to bronze in the relentless sun. He had to keep going.
They no longer had the income he'd provided as Sword-Lector, and all
their hopes were in this field. Half its produce would be their staple for
another year, and the rest would be replanted or sold. Barley did not grow
near Maghaltani, and Wulf promised good coin for however many bushels
they could spare. Voldigar had even planned to acquire some adjoining
land.

Gwenyth had grown weaker, and she could no longer aid them in the field. Her garden behind the house she still kept, and the home was tidy, but she slept more and more, and the sickness they'd been warned of early in her pregnancy had not relented, deep into its middle. Lyrusia came often with advice and medicines, steeply discounted. She brought news of Tepic too, but it was always spare. As far as Voldigar could discern, the young man had held to wisdom. The sword remained a curiosity of his new house and nothing more. In his heart, the old man knew it wasn't so, but he allowed a thought to take root that maybe the danger had passed.

The sun was high overhead on a summer day so warm and quiet that Voldigar's ears hummed in the wavering haze. His back ached and his feet likewise rebelled, but he had begun to think of himself as a farmer in truth. The concerns of each day were of field and tool, weather and water. Of dirt in his hands and dirt in his nails.

He'd just lowered himself to the bench before his front door and covered his face with his forearm when the sound of hooves punctuated the stillness. Another messenger from Maghaltani, no doubt. Voldigar kept his eyes closed and waited. They came often, but it never amounted to much. Many weeks before, he told one of them about Tepic's entry into Lusánt's household—though he kept the details of his midnight climb to himself. He didn't know what they'd done with the information, but the Order seemed to be getting on well enough without him. Maybe he could sleep for two minutes under his sweaty arm before he had to entertain more meaningless talk.

He waited until the hoof beats stopped and the breath of a horse was nearly in his ear before he peeked his eyes above his arm. Before him was not one horse, but two. Sure enough, a red-cloaked messenger sat on one, but the other was empty.

"Head and Heart, Eldest." The man saluted. He held the reins of the other horse in his hand.

Voldigar returned the salute and squinted one eye as he leaned forward and balanced his hands on the edge of the bench. The rider was Eadom, an Initiate, and the most recent pupil of Vasherk, if he remembered right. The young man was as somber and flat as Vasherk was charming.

"What news from Maghaltani today?" Voldigar asked.

"You are summoned to council, sir," Eadom replied and tugged on the spare horse.

Voldigar raised a brow and felt the skin of his weathered face crease. "Am I?" He rose to his feet and took a deep breath. "Well, I'm sorry you had to come all this way, Initiate." He wiped his hands and gestured to his field with a shake of his head. "Send my warmest greetings to all, but please let them know I cannot attend. Voldigar Anteres has a farm to work." He took a few steps into his barley.

"Sir?"

"Please also tell Medellai, there is no need for so many messengers, meaning no offense to you. He has my full trust. Good day to you, friend."

Eadom cleared his throat, but Voldigar took no notice. He stooped to bury a root that had somehow worked to the surface.

"Lanathor has returned," Eadom said.

Voldigar stopped and swallowed his surprise. "Did he? Thank God."

"God's honor. Yes, sir. Yesterday morning."

Voldigar stood and shielded his eyes from the reflection on Eadom's harness. The initiate had taken a few steps forward to the edge of the field. "It's just Brother, or Elder," Voldigar said.

"Pardon?"

"Honorifics, young friend. There are no 'sirs' in the Order. And I thank you for your news of Lanathor. I perceive that by it you mean to convince me to go with you. Please, tell him to visit soon."

Eadom pulled on his reins to prevent his horse from an opportunistic nibble on the barley. Despite his unchanged expression, there was urgency in his voice. "Forgive me, but Elder Lanathor cautioned me that you might not wish to come. There is more. The woman called 'Liadov' is with him, and she will not tarry long. It is she who summoned the council."

This time, Voldigar could not hide his shock. He'd not seen Liadov since King Olwis passed, not through all the years of Eleanora's reign, and not since he and Gwenyth made their home in a tiny shed built into the hill of Maghaltani. Liadov had been unequivocal—she would not return. Voldigar stared quietly into his field. How could Lanathor have possibly changed her mind? Did he plead with her all these many days?

Eadom stirred side to side on his horse. "Sir?"

Voldigar blinked. "You are certain?"

"I saw her myself."

"But . . ." His mind spun. He'd lost all grasp of his thoughts. Council? *It isn't my business anymore . . .*

Voldigar was loathe to leave his field. His feet were planted there like two old fenceposts, driven into bedrock. He stood in doubt to meddle with the Brethren again, to let the world push in on him, to push in on Gwenyth. Hobyn needed help with the storage he was building. There would be more irrigation tomorrow—but how could he disregard this summons? *I don't have to meddle.* Perhaps he could go, just to see them, *just to talk.* It was a day he'd long forgotten that he hoped for. *Liadov.* His field could wait.

"Stay here, Eadom."

Voldigar hurried inside and swept his dusty pack from off the floor. Gwenyth opened her eyes and looked on with wariness from her chair.

"Where are you going?" she asked. "What's wrong?"

"Maghaltani. Lanathor's back," Voldigar said as he stuffed a few provisions into the satchel and thrust his knife into his belt. "Liadov too."

Gwenyth narrowed her eyes and opened her mouth to speak again, but Voldigar went on. "There's nothing wrong—it's just talk. They've asked for me."

Gwenyth frowned and shook her head. "Asked for you? Vol . . . don't get yourself in trouble."

Voldigar stopped, his bag held in both hands. "I never thought we'd see her again." He crossed the room to kneel by Gwenyth's chair. "You should come with me."

Gwenyth shook her head. "I can hardly walk across the house." She frowned again. "Voldigar, you know where this leads."

"No, Gwen. I'll be firm. No more messengers, no more dangers. I just want to see them, that's all."

Gwenyth's face twisted with doubt, and she looked like she might push herself to her feet. She dug her fingers into the strap on Voldigar's bag, but her expression softened a moment later and she sagged back into her chair, her eyes in her lap. "I understand. Do your—"

"No," Voldigar interjected. "My duty is here, Gwen, at home. I'll give your regards to Lanathor, to Liadov. I'll give them my advice, and that's all."

He stood up to kiss her quickly on the forehead. "I'll stay out of trouble, I promise—and I'll be back tomorrow." From a peg, he reached for his red cloak last of all but drew his hand back instead before he sped out the door.

<hr />

By late afternoon, Voldigar and Eadom emerged from the thick forest at Maghaltani's foot and ascended her hill. It was somehow even hotter here than on his farm, but many shady trees continued up the slope, and they kept to these as they approached. The gate was all of wood and flanked by two stone structures that tapered above them. On one of these Lanathor stood, watching their arrival.

"Head and Heart," Lanathor called out.

"Head and Heart," replied Voldigar as they came to a stop and dismounted.

Lanathor grinned and shuffled gingerly down the stairs behind the tower to let them in.

Voldigar caught his breath at the sight of his old friend. "Did you eat in Danek?"

Lanathor frowned. "Less than I might like. I *knew* you'd come."

"Just for talk."

"Of course."

With a nod, Eadom hurried away to tend to both horses.

Voldigar caught Lanathor in an embrace and felt the bones of his shoulder blades beneath his hands. "It's like someone stole half of Lanathor."

"They tried."

Voldigar held him at arm's length for a better look. "You look miserable, Lan. How many more lives do you have?"

"Taro agrees with you. He's cooking for us now at Medellai's house."

Voldigar's stomach growled at the thought. "You can have my portion, Brother. What happened?"

Lanathor laughed grimly and gestured for them to walk. They first passed the thatched roof stables and squat smithies at the lowest levels of Maghaltani, whereafter the ground rose steeply. Long years of work had created many terraces, and a bubbling river weaved and tumbled cheerfully through the village with its narrow two and three-storied wooden homes and shops. Many were adorned with balconies, and short bridges passed between their upper floors.

There were few new structures since Voldigar had last been there, a fine high windmill rising among them, but there were many newly built channels of irrigation dug into the terraces. Compact and orderly fields of wheat and beans, radishes and garlic, occupied every angled space they could, and in these, dozens of the Brethren and their families worked and waved or saluted to the Elders as they passed. Families were once rare in Maghaltani, but it seemed half or more of the Brothers now had wives and children gathered around them.

"I was captured in Danek," Lanathor said. "But that's the least of our troubles."

Voldigar raised his eyebrows. "Captured?"

Lanathor nodded. "Yes. A darkness has come upon that land, and the people thought me responsible. We can tell all when we gather at Medellai's house. Strange things, Eldest."

"Strange indeed," Voldigar replied with a wary eye. "I have tales of my own to share."

They turned sharply west past Wulf's Tavern at the village center and headed through another gate into a thick wood of beech and oak growing so closely that their huge trunks often intertwined. Ferns grew upon their shoulders, and the forest smelled of rich earth. Moss was heavy over the shaded ground, tumbled boulders, and rippling roots bulging from the hillside. Thin columns of sunlight cascaded in shafts to pool beneath their feet.

"Is it true that Liadov is here?"

Lanathor smiled. "It is, and I hope for good. We learned many things from her in our return to Aramon, but she's withheld most, awaiting council with us all, you especially. I'm glad you've come so quickly."

Voldigar sighed and nodded. Lanathor stopped with an even broader smile. "I heard your good news, Brother."

Voldigar indulged a grin and looked away at a mossy stone. "Did you?"

"Of course! Taro still walks the earth, and between him and Vasherk, no rumor goes unspoken."

"Gwenyth felt the child kick this morning," Voldigar said. "He pushed his foot against my hand too when I searched for it."

"Amazing," Lanathor said. "It took you long enough, old man. God blesses you in your autumn years."

"His honor," Voldigar replied.

"Honor God." Lanathor's smile dropped. "In honesty, I did not *know* you'd come."

"Oh?"

"Indeed. They told me you'd finally done it, Vol. Not just a child but a field full of barley."

"You're my friend, Lan."

"And you mine, but you have more important things to worry about now."

"I'm just here for Liadov's council, Brother. Then back home." *Just talk.*

Lanathor tilted his chin. "I pray God that's true, but you may find this darker than you expect. Come on."

The trunks of many trees gave way to a broader and flatter bowl of land, nestled above a dark pool fed by trickling waterfalls. It was no less shady, for the canopy of a single massive oak overshadowed the water and a meadow blanketed with purple flowers. Nestled against the trunk and cleverly built into the elbows of its roots and huge winding limbs was a rustic home with lamplight glowing in its windows. It was Medellai's house, and the door stood open.

Within, a dozen of the Elders, Justiciars, and Guardians of the Order were gathered in quiet conversation, and a fine, savory smell filled the house. As Voldigar adjusted to the light, they stood as one and saluted. Medellai crossed the room to offer an embrace. His eyes were focused, and the yellow shade had mostly fallen away.

"Your eyes!" Voldigar said.

Medellai smiled. "The wisdom and skill of our sister. She has returned."

Liadov rose to her feet with a gentle smile and a small dip of her chin. She was as radiant as ever. "Even the Wilding can be stayed," she said. "Elder Medellai is strong of spirit, and the prayers of his brethren have been effectual, but there is still much to be done for him before he is restored. How do you fare, my father?"

Voldigar allowed a wide smile to cross his face and wordlessly saluted Liadov with a dip of his own chin. There she stood, unchanged but for a keenness hid behind her gaze. "You honor me," he said. "I fare well, Sister, though the days grow dark about us. I'm glad you've returned."

"I would that it were in lighter days," said Liadov. "I know not yet if I am glad to gather here, only that we must."

Taro and Vasherk emerged from a room further inside, bearing trays laden with meats and summer fruits. The Brethren gathered round and faced one another in a mixture of formality and comfort, sitting at a few low tables, upon the hearth, and along benches they'd dragged from the walls. Amongst a few others, Gardoric, Wulf, and all the brethren who'd joined in the Spire at Voldigar's summons some months before were present. It had been many years since Voldigar sat with an assembly of so many leaders of The Brotherhood of Aramon at once. He was glad to take his seat in a quiet corner of the room and gladder still when Medellai took his place at the head of the assembly. *Just talk.*

"Let us begin," Medellai said.

------◆------

The assembly conversed for long hours until night fell and their shadows flickered in the warmth of Medellai's hearth. Many spoke while Voldigar kept silence. Liadov too held her peace.

Medellai and Taro went first, and to Liadov they recounted all the tale of pursuing the Orun across the hinterlands of Aramon, destroying it at Westfort, and rescuing the boy Tepic and his crystal-hilted sword from Commander Caliras in the mines below.

Lanathor told of finding Liadov, of her battle and her long sleep, and of all his terrible ordeal in Danek. While he spoke, Taro kept loading Lanathor's plate higher and higher until the Elder had to turn the disappointed Brother away. The Brethren listened with dark faces while the plague of the Wyrna was described. They gasped and whispered prayers when they heard of the destruction of Dizghizádè. Voldigar lowered his brow but gave no response through all this long account.

Wulf and Gardoric told next of finding Lanathor, how they first worked their way north through Danek as the snows melted, searching fruitlessly for Dizghizádè along its slopes. They'd avoided the light-shy Wyrna by day and hid from them at night, sometimes narrowly escaping notice, and other times cutting their way through a pack of them to flee for their lives. They made it all the way to Vlacha, the ancient capital of Danek at the uttermost end of its long valley, without any sign of Lanathor, and they despaired of ever finding him. Gardoric, they learned, had discovered his Third Virtue along the way.

"Fair news, drowned by stormy weather," as Soris put it.

Vasherk had traveled alone at first, surviving more by his wits and connections to the people of his homeland than by the point of his rapier. Here and there, he found pockets of survivors and fortifications not yet destroyed. The locals helped him along his way until, overjoyed, he found Wulf and Gardoric. He led them to the secret path of Dizghizádè, and together they too saw its smoldering ruin. From there, they found remnants of Lanathor's ruined cloak in a village at the mountains' feet, and Gardoric's keen skill at length brought them to Fort Dromvedya.

Gardoric then described how they made their escape with Lanathor and Liadov downriver, clutching to bobbing white pines, navigating by foot over the waterfalls above Kurath, and then in a wide circle through the hills of Tituria. No less than Danek, the two lowland provinces were themselves overrun by creatures from their darkest legends. They had no reprieve there, for the golemic Odomo covered Kurath, and the shades of Tituria he called Bashevi now haunted its moors. The Brothers had barely escaped through the gates of Eastfort, pursued by a whisper and a shadow that now covered all the lands behind them.

They warned Dantic at their passing, and the Captain was incredulous, though not wholly ignorant of trouble. Along with his own scouts, a few other survivors had fled to Eastfort, bearing tales of nightmares too terrible to believe. Dantic sent to Arregalt for aid a dozen times, but to his dismay, no reply had come.

At word of the Emperor's inaction, a coiling fear grew and tightened in the pit of Voldigar's stomach. Dantic was alone on the edge of Aramon while devils gathered on their doorstep. *Just talk.*

The Brothers had not lingered long at Eastfort but made haste to Maghaltani. In the short time since, there was still no word of any help sent from Arregalt, and they looked nervously to the east. The horde was as real as the Orun, and it was only a matter of time before it found its way into the pass and crashed against its fortresses.

Lanathor remarked that many long days, weeks, and even months, had gone by since he first set out from Aramon in search of Liadov. He shook his head bitterly at their misfortune, and it was plain to see—he wondered with a doubtful eye at the tale of how the Orun was slain before the gates of Westfort.

At length, the room fell silent under the crackling of Medellai's hearth.

"Do you have counsel for us, Eldest?" Medellai asked.

With a blink, Voldigar realized all eyes were upon him, and he rose heavily to speak. His throat was dry and a great weight pulled at his heart. This was worse than he could have possibly imagined, and try as he might, the image of Gwenyth rocking weakly in her chair filled his mind while he tried to gather his thoughts. Medellai handed him a little wooden bowl of wine that he accepted gratefully. He looked from one dark face to another but directed his words to Liadov most of all.

"As many of you now know, the Orun we faced, was . . . not the same creature we locked away those many years ago. Lutz and I examined its Kishket. We found it untouched, secure as the day I concealed it. Not only this, there was another tomb we found, open—disturbed, but this matter of its prison, and of its escape, remains a great riddle."

He continued more firmly. "Whatever we destroyed before the gates of Westfort was another. I've wondered at our fortune, to have crushed that nameless thing without a greater craft—wondered and hoped with the hope of a fool that it is truly dead. There's been no word of it, no further sign or rumor, but how could that be? The purpose for which we first sought you, Liadov, is long past, but now I wonder if you might answer this riddle instead."

Liadov stood and Voldigar retook his seat. Her face was young, more so than any man or mokja who sat in Medellai's dark room, but he was struck again by the depth in her eyes, unveiling the wisdom of countless years. How strange to see his pupil, passed beyond the ways of the Order and now its teacher. Her face was troubled, and she spoke in a quiet voice that all leaned in to hear.

"There was no Kishket, Brothers. And this was no Orun."

A murmur arose in the room until Medellai held up his hand for quiet.

Liadov went on. "The creature you struggled against at Westfort was Brelabbus, *Fly Father*, and I pray none of you repeat that name, for the creature above all else watches and hungers for this world with hatred and envy. It has somehow been freed to roam about and devour what it may—and to seek after me."

There was a dark silence among the Brethren. Even the fire ceased its noise, and spreading cold seemed to breathe along the rafters of the house.

"It is cousin to the Orun," Liadov said, "but older and fouler by far. That it found a way into our world is a perilous mystery indeed. It is now contained, after a fashion, but that is more dangerous still. I suspected it upon the mountain in Dizghizádè. I suspected it when I learned the Wyrna arose, but now there can be no doubt. The power that sought me there was beyond anything we have known."

Liadov looked from face to face with an expression of pity and regret. "Brothers of Aramon, you did well to delay and weaken it. Better still to prevent it from acquiring the sword, but no, it is not dead. It has given birth, birth to the Oruni, and you do not know just how close your danger was and is."

"Birth?" Lutz asked with a hard swallow. He'd been sitting in silence by the fire, but now the gears over his eyes clicked and spun.

"Yes," Liadov answered. "The Wyrna, the Odomo, the Bashevi—they are Oruni, its . . . children, mad dreams it thinks are its own creations, but they are nothing more than mockery and defilement, the outflow of its jealous brooding. Mourn the people of those lands, for they are lost. But be certain of this, the malice of our foe is fixed on Aramon."

Lanathor leaned forward and spoke in a low voice. "The mystery of its coming—we must search it out. If there was no Kishket, how did the demon emerge?"

"From a different prison, Brother Lanathor, deep in the discordant heart of Mirváne. Someone has let it out, and *that* is the mystery. Someone has a key, a Prism of the Heavens, an old thing that should have been destroyed a long time ago."

Her words hung as fog in the air for a long while as the coiling fear unraveled into something else in Voldigar's heart. The restlessness of a tree, waving in the wind. A weary work he thought was done now crept into his aging bones. The room faded from his view as he tried to picture home, but all was smoke and shade. Many anxious eyes blinked back at him in the dimness. So much toil and so much pain, but rest could not be found. It sped away behind him while he was carried on by dark waters. *Just talk.*

Voldigar rose slowly to his feet again. His words came out in a choke while he tapped his fist on his thigh. "I know who let it out, and I know who has the key." All eyes were fixed on him, and Liadov sat again. The shadows of the room had grown deep and cast themselves against the walls and ceiling. They danced on Voldigar's face. "It is another of our students, none other than the Emperor, Lusánt Sispérus."

There was another long quiet while the Brethren ruminated over his words and shifted nervously in the growing dark. Liadov closed her eyes and whispered something to herself.

Medellai squinted. "How could he be capable of this? Why would he do such a thing?"

"I know not," Voldigar said as he shook his head, "and I should have told you more before. He's taken Tepic into his household as hostage, this you know—and that I visited the boy in secret. But Tepic also confided in me, that Lusánt possesses an unusual object, an orb with a strange magic that can touch the moon itself. I thought it a work of petty sorcery, mulled it in my mind, but now it becomes clear. It is far deeper. Lusánt himself has somehow freed this evil, and he seeks to do it again. That is why he has the boy. That is why he constrains upon him daily—to force the use of the sword. For if I perceive it rightly, this weapon is a second key, is it not Liadov?"

Liadov opened her eyes and took a deep breath. "It is, and though I have not seen it, I know it in my heart. By now, our enemy has a terrible grip on Lusánt's mind. Where this creature is contained, it whispers in his ear. The Prisms must be destroyed, or turned against the horde through some miracle—but I fear we are too late. The enemy will not stop until its brothers are freed and fed as well. The boy, Tepic—he is in great peril."

"I've brought this on him," Voldigar said as he shook his head and stared into the hearth. "I've delayed too long." The Eldest sagged back into his chair.

Urias stepped from the shadows where he'd been leaning against the great trunk of the oak that pushed into the room, his face bent in a grim scowl. "Not so, Eldest. The Order still draws breath, and if these Prisms are within Arregalt, why do we delay a moment more? Our purpose is clear and our lives are forfeit. We may all perish in the effort, but they cannot stop the entire Order—if that is our will. Away with banishment, and away with foolish boys. We enter the capital. We take both orb and sword—or destroy them where they lie."

"That would be rash, Brother Urias," Liadov said, "for one Prism feeds into another, and there is a third. They must be destroyed together, else we would only deepen our peril."

Brethren gasped, shook their heads, or buried their mouths in the palms of their hands, but Urias pressed on more loudly. "Where is the third then? If all hangs in the balance, we'll melt a mountain of these things."

"I know not," Liadov said. "It is beyond my sight."

"Then we start with the two. Who goes with me?"

"I do," Gardoric said and rose to his feet.

A chorus of brethren echoed the same reply. Voldigar watched the flames and thought of Tepic, trapped in the high Spire of Aramon, twisting under the hand of Lusánt, twisting under the whispers of the Prisms, wondering if his old sword-lector would ever come back. A red ember at the heart of the fire pulsed and then went black. He turned from the hearth. *Just talk indeed.* "I too will go."

Medellai looked sharply at Voldigar with the green eyes of his sister. Lanathor raised his head from his two skeletal hands with his brow tightly drawn. "Hold," he interjected. "Hold! We get ahead of ourselves. Be wary of your words! And until we examine it . . . how can we even be certain that Tepic's sword is one of these keys?"

Liadov gazed silently at Voldigar, lost in thought before she finally turned and answered Lanathor. "I told you, Brother Lanathor, that I am certain, for that key is the same that set me free, and the only thing Brelabbus would have sought across the hinterlands."

The room broke out in argument once again, and Lanathor shot to his feet. "You? But . . . what shall we do then! If we destroy it . . . what would happen to you?"

"I don't know . . ."

Voldigar ground his teeth and looked again from face to face. There was weariness and despair plain to see among the Brethren, doubt and fear flickered in their eyes. He rose from his seat. "Grave judgment should not follow weary council," he said. "Let us decide our doom by daylight instead of darkness. Meet here again, at first light tomorrow. Sleep, pray, Chant, think. We have deeper need of wisdom now than ever." He felt old, his body ached, and he wished nothing more than to will himself awake from one of his foolish nightmares, but he could not.

"Voldigar," Liadov said. "Walk with me before you rest."

The assembly went their separate ways, and Voldigar sat staring at the joints of Medellai's wooden floor. Disaster loomed like the hush before a thunderstorm. For all their struggle and for all their suffering, the earth grew only colder. Was his quiet life nothing more than mists and dreams? He had little time for contemplation, for Liadov soon rose and led him to the dark pond's edge where she stood with her back turned.

"I'm sorry, Voldigar," she spoke across the water.

"For what?" he asked as he descended the last few steps.

"I'm sorry I wasn't there for Gwenyth."

Voldigar stopped short behind her. "That wasn't your fault, Liadov."

"Wasn't it?"

"You can't save everyone."

"I could have saved her."

Voldigar's hands trembled. He wasn't sure what to say. It was pain long buried. Dead seed in hard-packed earth. He stared into the water.

"What happened to her?" Liadov whispered.

"I thought you knew."

Liadov shook her head.

"Gwen . . . she got caught up in things when the crown passed to Eleanora. It was I who should have been there, Liadov. They came for her at home." Voldigar inhaled sharply. "We found her in a flooded field, did all we could, but the infection broke her. She never recovered."

"I'm sorry," Liadov repeated, "I'm so sorry." Her shoulders sagged and she wiped a hand across her eyes. "You should not have come here, Voldigar. Nor should I have returned."

Voldigar walked quietly to her side and placed a hand upon her back. "Perhaps not, Sister, and I am surprised you did."

Liadov turned her face to his, uncertainty in her eyes. "You would not persuade me otherwise?"

Voldigar shook his head. "What would it matter? There is a fine green sea of barley in the field before my home, Liadov. Soon it will go from green to brown and droop its tired crowns to the harvest. My wife is with child and my heart is with these, then to rest in the breeze of my aspen grove."

Voldigar smiled and looked into the pool again. "A pleasant dream, no? But what is my life, Sister? If I am to suffer again, will I refuse it? Medellai and Lanathor, for their part, they've done all they can to give me rest—and I thank them for it. But whatever we intended, whatever we reasoned, let persuasion be silent. You and I stand beside the pool of Maghaltani now, contemplating the doom of Aramon. There is no dream . . . if I will not fight for it."

"You would die like Qasimar then?" Liadov said and met his eyes in the reflection of the water.

Voldigar flinched at her reply, but it was not wholly unexpected. He sighed. "You still blame yourself for Qasimar?"

"Blame myself? As sure as night follows day, his death was my doing. Don't steal my guilt from me, Brother."

Voldigar stooped to pluck a stone from the ground and skip it across the water. "I won't, that isn't my job. But if you are to blame, then so am I."

"You?"

Voldigar's hand had unconsciously gone to his chest, to grip the little key that hung beneath his shirt. "Yes, me." He pulled it free where it shimmered under the moonlight. "I think of Qasimar every day and dream of him nearly every night—how I might go back for him, where I *left* him, Sister."

"You're wrong, Voldigar. The fault was mine and he knew it."

Voldigar shook his head. "No. He would blame neither of us, Liadov. Not in a thousand years. He took the oath."

Liadov laughed ruefully. "Oaths?"

Voldigar gave her a hard flat look. "You can have your guilt, but Qasimar loved you. The oath of the Brethren is forever. Don't withhold him his honor."

For a moment the deep age of Liadov's eyes faded, and Voldigar saw a flicker of the scared girl he found a score of years before. Her mouth worked in protest, but Voldigar tucked the key back into his shirt and went on. "Qasimar sought to serve God with his life and in the path that he was given. God is good. He will redeem, whether we can see the end or not."

Liadov sighed and shook her head. "Lanathor questioned my faith as well, Eldest. But of all people, do I not know God's purposes will be done? I could sooner close up the pipes of heaven, drain her of her waters, or move the stars from their course than defy God—but I do have one choice. I can choose whether to bring pain to my friends again, or not."

"You would withhold honor from us all then?" Voldigar asked.

Liadov's voice rose. "Honor? I would hold you back from your deaths, Voldigar. God's will shall be done, whether you all perish in its doing or not. Do not think overmuch of who and what you are."

"I think nothing of myself, Sister, and I trust my brethren do likewise. It is God's honor that we seek."

"Fire is spreading, Voldigar. Do not take hold of it, do not even touch it. Shall you and all your brethren be consumed? Is that what you desire? The wheel turns but you are not the axle. Why crush yourself beneath? Let this wash away. Go home to your wife. Let Lanathor return to his books. Let Medellai rest here under his oak." Liadov breathed deeply. "I can do this alone."

Voldigar shook his head. "I don't presume to know the depths God has placed in your heart, Liadov. But do you not assume overmuch? What if he has raised the Brethren up for this very time? Should the Order shrink back when good can still be done? Will you fly to the Spire and beyond the mountains to face the enemy yourself?"

Liadov's eyes welled with tears, and silent anguish twisted upon her face. "The enemy is fixed on me, Voldigar. For once, let me save you. Let me erase you from the pages of this tragedy."

Voldigar sighed again and wrapped his arms about her. "Ah, my daughter. I would sooner cast myself into the Wending Sea than send you against the enemy without me."

Tears now flowed down Liadov's face. "If I cannot dissuade you, then what would you have me do?"

Voldigar narrowed his eyes. "Take up the cloak again. Fight beside us as you once did. Though the heavens fall and the Order pass from memory, we will enter the Spire, we will find the Prisms, and we will end this nightmare. There is no other way."

"You're wrong, Voldigar, there is another way," a voice rang out from behind them. Lanathor, slender as he was, slipped from the shadows like a ghost and staggered down the path. His hands shook and his lip quivered, but his low voice resonated with resolve and clear eyes shone like stars in the dark. "Yes, I was listening. And no, I will not ask forgiveness. I have heard enough to know you both chase the wind!"

"Lanathor—" Voldigar began, but the Elder jerked his hand up.

"Hear me, Voldigar, while you speak of oaths and redemption. Remember who Lusánt is."

"He is the Emperor."

"No! He is Olwis's son, your dear friend's boy, and you promised to look after him." Emotion rose in Lanathor's voice. "Do you think he'd hand you the Prisms while you stood on the bodies of his guards? Would you kill him, Voldigar?"

"Lanathor—"

"Would you kill him!"

Voldigar rolled his hands into fists as frustration welled in his chest. He breathed several sharp breaths as he stared at his friend upon the path, but no words came to his lips. Liadov placed a gentle hand on his shoulder and stepped forward.

"What then is your counsel, Lanathor."

"My counsel is for truth, Liadov. Give us truth. Give Aramon truth and nothing else. Let us obey God and fulfill the words of *all* our oaths, come what may. Let us serve while strength remains." Lanathor took a deep breath. "If you will have it, there is a part that you still can play alone. We are banished, yet you are not. What I ask of you is to stand before the house of Olwis once again, to warn and to prophesy while time remains."

Voldigar found his tongue again, but the words came out in a dry whisper. "Lusánt burned a thousand men alive . . ."

"To his shame, and may that be the end of his great sins," Lanathor said.

"The boy will not listen to me," Liadov said. "He will blame me for Olwis as surely as his mother did. It will only fuel his hatred and lead to further mischief, I am certain of it."

"He may, and the fire may grow. But shall we abandon hope? Will the Brethren dash themselves against the Spire? Will you immolate yourself for your guilt? Why throw your lives away?"

"My life is nothing. Why speak, if he will not hear?" Voldigar asked.

"Because it's the right thing to do, Brother—and you know it." Lanathor held Voldigar's gaze in silent struggle, their eyes balanced on the edge of a knife. "If we don't try to reason with him, to warn him of his danger, then we've been derelict, we've rejected hope. I know he won't listen to the Brethren anymore, but Liadov is different. She *must* try!"

Lanathor's words echoed across the pond, and they stood in silence.

Liadov shook her head slowly and warily. "I cannot see a happy end to this . . ."

Voldigar still clenched his fists until his arms shook. Half his heart wanted to rush away—to batter down the walls of the Spire while the iron was still hot within—but the other half could only picture Olwis, dying in his cold chambers, taking comfort in a final promise. *I'll look after him, friend. I'll look after your boy. Just rest.* Voldigar opened his hands.

"He's right, Liadov."

"What?"

"He's right . . ."

Lanathor seemed to breathe for the first time.

Voldigar went on. "It's the right thing to do. Lusánt *is* Olwis's son. How can we believe that he's beyond the reach of truth? He must have a chance to give up the Prisms, to send forth his armies and undo the harm he's unleashed."

"And if he does not?" Liadov asked.

"Then we have deepened our peril," Voldigar replied.

"A fool's hope then . . ."

"Aye, and let us be fools, until all hope is gone. If he will not listen . . . then, we do as we must."

Chapter Twenty-Six

Disarmed

T HE FIRST GUARD BY the open door of Galomar's cell was easy to avoid. By the time he'd heard the Emperor's shouts, Tepic was well past his flailing arms and running free. The second was not so easy and stood at the end of a narrow block of cells, square in Tepic's path. Tepic planted a foot and tried to conceal his direction, but the guardsman was quick and caught a fold of his shirt. It tore in a long strip of tattered cloth, and the man lunged forward to grasp him with his other hand. Tepic brought the sheathed sword down on the back of his knuckles with a crack, and he was free once again.

On he ran, aiming for a low dark opening in the wall ahead. He'd seen this small archway on his tharmskolp and dreamed of one day escaping through it with poor Galomar. A steep flight of stairs should be just beyond, and though it was near pitch dark, he flew through the hole with head low and raced down the steps heedless and sure-footed. He could hear the heavy footfalls and cries of Lusánt and his guards behind.

He soon emerged on a broad square landing where his eyes adjusted to a sliver of orange light showing through a crack ahead and far below. It came from a tall set of double doors that led to a courtyard beyond. There was a huge cistern to his left, but before him only a perilous drop. A wooden crane overhung the blackness, but its rope vanished into nothing. Swift moving torchlight flickered, and the yells of many guards echoed from the opening behind.

Tepic slung the sword over his back and leapt into the dark where he caught the rope and clambered down as quickly as he could, rubbing his hands raw as he went. Men were emerging from the stairwell above and calling for a ladder. His feet touched the floor, and only a moment later the heavy clunk of a ladder's feet thudded next to him.

Tepic spun about wide-eyed, searching for his planned escape. The tall gates were heavily barred and out of the question, but in the wall at the high platform's base was a little door, no higher than his chin. Finding it secured with a stout padlock, he swept his sword from its scabbard. The ancient blade sheered through the metal as though it were paper. He rushed into smothering black and now moved entirely by feel, stooping as he fled.

Right, right, left, right, left, left, right—then down the stairs. He struggled to keep the map in mind as he hurried along and dragged his hand against the wall. Its surface opened many times in voids that were not other passages but large alcoves in the stone. It was disorienting, but he could not slow down. He'd rehearsed it all a hundred times, yet in his panic, he feared he'd made a mistake and would be lost forever in a mokja maze.

The sound of voices and feet far behind faded and Tepic dared to slow. Closing his eyes, he tried to recall what the tangled web of halls had looked like on the wondrous tharmskolp. *The tharmskolp!* It was then he remembered that he'd thrust it in his pocket when Lusánt surprised him in his room. The tiny, heavy device still bounced against his leg. He stopped to peer inside.

Sure enough, even in the dark, it maintained a faint blue light. The view was still fixed near his location, and as best he could tell, he'd made only one wrong turn. He pressed his hand against the wall again and retraced his steps. Soon he found an opening and then the top of the flight of stairs which he sought. A bare mote of light reached up from below.

Tepic listened for a moment and then charged down the stairs, glad for the distant glow that shone upon them. As he burst through the opening at their foot, he saw a channel of water to his left, flowing into darkness. The glow was from his right.

"Tepic!" a voice whispered sharply.

Tepic jolted to his side and nearly rolled into the water. There on the wall was a row of tightly spaced iron bars filling a round opening in the stonework. Kyriana stood behind the bars, bearing a torch in her hand.

"Be gone!" Tepic cried out in alarm and scrambled to his feet.

"Tepic, wait!"

"Go away!"

Kyriana stepped forward against the bars. "I had nothing to do with Galomar!"

He hesitated. "You're lying."

"No!" she cried.

"You made us friends, just so you could kill him."

"No! Tepic, I gave you a friend because you were lonely. I wanted you to feel safe." Her face was earnest and pained.

Tepic shook his head bitterly and moved away. "You just wanted me to use the sword. You're all liars!"

"I'm not a liar, Tepic. I wanted you to use the sword, but I didn't want to hurt anyone. I wanted you to use it willingly. Please, believe me."

"I don't believe any of you."

"I'm your friend too!"

"No, you're not! You're a snake!"

"Please, Tepic, don't make an enemy of me. Why am I here alone?"

Tepic hesitated again.

"My lord, you cannot run forever."

"Maybe I can."

"There's nowhere you can go that I won't find you, but I want to let you go. You don't have to use the sword anymore. I'll find another way."

Tepic narrowed his eyes. "What do you mean?"

"So long as you have it, Lusánt will never stop looking for you, and he will command me to do the same, but I don't want him to find you. You've done enough."

Tepic backed away.

"Give the sword to me, Tepic. Just hand it through the bars, and you can be free again. I'll tell them you got away, I'll lead them astray."

"I thought you weren't a liar."

"I'll lie to protect my friends."

"You don't understand, Kyriana. You can't let Lusánt have it."

"No, you don't understand. He's the *only* one who can have it. Let it go, and just be a boy again."

Tepic chewed his lower lip and stared into Kyriana's eyes. "Goodbye, Kyriana."

Tepic sped away from the glow of the torch, drawing his hand along the tunnel wall as blackness swallowed him again. Kyriana's voice called after, "Don't make an enemy of me, Tepic! Don't be a fool!" but he ran on until he could no longer hear.

⸻ ❦ ⸻

Hours passed as Tepic wormed his way through the sewers and tunnels below Arregalt. Frequently, he stopped to look into his map and reorient himself. The only lights he dared go near were dim shafts of lamps and torches that sometimes pierced tiny openings to the streets above. After a while, even these occasional glimmers ceased and he was buried in a never-ending gloom.

Through dripping culverts and echoing shafts he heard, or thought he heard, the sounds of other life scraping and skittering in the dark. As he turned a corner, he was certain a slimy shape brushed against him and then stopped to watch him noiselessly with huge, hateful eyes. He could bear it no longer and fished the tharmskolp from his pocket once again. This time, he held the eyepiece out and thrust it into the dark. It gave only the barest hint of light, but after so many hours underground, it was welcome relief. Nothing was there, before or behind. A low, damp tunnel ran on forever.

He soon realized he had no real plan of escape. Somewhere in the foolish dreams he'd made of breaking free with Galomar, he imagined he'd bring them to Lyrusia's apothecary, or maybe to Lector Voldigar's farm, but how could he do such a thing? Would he bring danger upon his sister or his teachers? And where else would the Emperor be looking for the sword? *"No,"* he resolved, *"I cannot go to my family, nor to my friends."* He had to keep going, deeper and farther away from everyone and everything.

Perhaps if he could get outside—he could run forever across Aramon and hide in the woods or in cracks below the mountains. Maybe he could swim the canal again and slip through the city's wall unseen. He stopped to sit and stare into his map.

With weary effort, he deduced the patch of cold stone where he sat. Not long ago, he'd passed an intersection where five passages met and he'd taken one at random. That particular structure seemed more or less unique and would place him a long depth below the northwestern edge of the Citadel. He flicked the view left and right, up and down, and noticed nearby several long, straight shafts that led from above and cut through countless layers of the Delvings in which he hid. The shafts descended a long way down and emerged in what could only be the Undercity—a sprawling tangle of caves, platforms, and rickety constructions assembled on the ruins of older things by Arregalt's less fortunate. A plan began to form in Tepic's mind.

He'd heard of Undercity—a little. Polite company simply didn't bring it up, his mother said, and that of course only piqued his curiosity. Tepic had brought the question to his father, but Commander Dantic didn't seem interested in long discussion either. He gave a dry description of a chaotic city sprawl filled with poverty and violence that clung to the sides of Arregalt's promontory or dug into its stone below. For her part, Lyrusia had simply told him people who went to Undercity were never seen again.

Outside his own family, he'd only ever heard the occasional rumor of whole pieces of Undercity falling tragically into the sea, or companies of soldiers charging heroically into that den of thieves to put down one revolt or another. The shafts all led down to it.

He doubted the tharmskolp meant much in the city itself—if chunks of it were resting on the ocean floor and its poor souls held the rest together with ropes and driftwood—but surely the mokja stonework above was correct? He found one shaft, the shortest of all, near the very edge of the map. If it was true, somewhere ahead of him, the floor and ceiling would simply give out to gaping holes above and below.

Tepic moved ahead slowly. The passage angled upward ever so slightly and curved a little to the left. In a few minutes, it came to an end, and there before him, as surely as the map had shown, a round, black hole about two or three feet wide stared up at him like the mouth of a dragon.

He put the tharmskolp to his eye again and judged the hole to be perhaps a hundred feet deep, with a ledge beneath that overlooked the bay. Holding it out again for a little light, he stood a long while at the shaft's lip. A rotten odor wafted from the hole but so too did the subtle smell of the sea. He stowed the map away and squinted into the darkness until his eyebrows hurt. Somewhere, off in the long expanse below, he thought he saw a spot of dim gray-blue light, but he couldn't be sure. *People who go to Undercity are never seen again...*

Tepic felt for the inner edge, and then, with a deep breath, he swung his legs over the side and began to descend. Like a crab abandoned by the tide, his limbs sprawled and pressed against the stone. Inch by inch he squirmed his way down the breach and tried to remember to breathe.

It seemed like a whole day had gone by while his legs and arms ached and shook. The hundred-foot hole might as well have been a thousand. He had no sense of movement but knew a treacherous and endless drop was below. He had to hold firm, twisting at times to rest his arms with his backside pressed against the wall. At length, he dared to look down and was now certain of a light shining up at him, the glow of dawn and the world outside.

He couldn't judge how far he had to go, nor how much longer he could press against the walls. As he lowered his foot, it slipped against a slimy patch, and he slid several inches before he caught himself against the stonework. Whatever skin on his hands the crane rope had not harmed was now scraped raw by stone. He kicked his legs wildly to regain his hold but only swiped against more slick surface. His arms were growing tired, and he couldn't push himself back up again. In a moment, his hands gave way and he fell.

Terror struck and he wrenched his arms painfully as he tried to dig them against the slimy walls, but it was no use. It was a filthy scrape against the shaft, and then he was plummeting in open air. With a rush of wind, he crashed breathless into a tumbling pile of rubbish and reeking sludge. The dim of morning glowed about him. His body trembled in the cold, but he was alive.

—◆—

In all his mad flight through the darkness, Tepic had not dwelt upon the harrowing events of the night now passed. Here on the stinking mound, it all came rushing back. He lay with eyes closed, but hot tears seeped from the corners. Everything had gone all wrong. It was his fault Galomar was dead, and he'd let everyone down. He swore to his teacher he wouldn't use the sword, but he had—and more than once. He'd been a fool and let Kyriana's kindness disarm his wits. He cut the old general's arm clean off, and he'd probably died in a pool of blood . . . just like Galomar. He was all alone.

Tepic's chest shook, and his sobs came out in great moaning cries. "What have I done?" he whispered through his weeping. "What have I done?"

He opened his eyes and saw there a great overhanging mass of stone with a black hole staring down at him. All about was a giant pile of rubbish and stench. Carved stone enclosed him behind and partially beside, but before him, the open face of the ledge looked out over the bay. The garbage reached its edge and spread over the entire shelf. Some tumbled over the side as he shifted.

"I'll be rid of it forever," he said angrily and wiped tears away with the back of his dirty hand.

Tepic worked his way down to the very rim and balanced there on his knees overlooking the great drop. Hundreds and hundreds of feet below, the face of the sea rippled slowly in the morning breeze. His sobs continued unabated, and bloody images of the prison cell worked through his mind. He closed his eyes. His head spun until he vomited on the little edge of stone. He looked again and held the sword out in two hands over the vastness. The blade seemed to look back at him, whispering through its gleam.

Tepic imagined it spinning end over end, its crystal hilt glinting with each rotation, falling until it sliced through the waves and disappeared forever into the Wending Sea. His hands trembled no less than his mouth as he spoke silent words to himself. Surely no one would find it there. Surely it would be lost for all time in the endless water.

"What 'ave we 'ere. You lost?" a nasal voice called out from behind.

Tepic clutched the sword to his chest and whirled about. Atop the pile, a stick-thin boy with red hair only a little darker than his own stood brandishing a rusty dagger. Two more were tucked into his belt. A heavyset girl stood behind him with a large, crude blade like a butcher's cleaver, and another boy was pulling himself up and over the far edge, knocking refuse into the sea. The hilt of a weapon showed over his shoulder too. All three were pale of skin, but it was hard to tell through layers of filth.

"Stay back!" Tepic shouted and held the sheathed sword before him.

"Easy, lil' muggy."

The other boy had worked his way over the lip and pulled a pitted sword from off his back. "Let's batty-fang 'im, shut that dirty box."

The skinny boy held up his hand. "Easy on you too, Fish. He's not even got his lil' pricker out. He draws it, an' we batty-fang 'im." He turned back to Tepic. "You, muggy, what's it called?"

"Leave me alone," Tepic said.

"Look 'ere, muggy, I'm trying to gab polite-like. I 'aven't nicked nuffin' off you—yet. What's your name I says?"

"Don't 'fink he wants to says," the girl called out from behind.

The skinny boy regarded her a moment and then turned back to Tepic with a grin missing many teeth. "That pricker's fruit-in-a-basket. What say we 'and it over, then I don't have to nick it." He took a step toward Tepic, held out his free hand, and wiggled his fingers while he stared at the sword.

"Don't come any closer," Tepic shouted and set his feet.

"Shhhh," the boy hissed but it came out more like a whistle through his missing teeth. "Don't start bleating."

"I 'fink his time's up, Ferret," the other boy called out. "Ain't got minutes for jib-jab. Shank 'im, an' send 'im to fly."

The boy with the knife turned back to respond, but Tepic had heard enough. The lectors had always taught: *Don't wait for violence that's sure to come.* Act. He lunged forward with his sheathed sword and knocked the knife from the boy's hand, then swept his legs out from under him. He collapsed with a grunt on his back, and the other two rushed forward.

"Wait, wait, wait, wait, wait!" the skinny one shouted and held his hands up where he lay. The others stopped. "I 'fink we got off on the wrong foot, love-boo. How 'bout we give our names first and proper?"

Tepic hesitated but still held the sheathed sword out in front of him.

"I'm Ferret," the boy continued.

Tepic raised an eyebrow.

"It's 'cause I find 'fings. And this one's Fish." The other boy let his rusty sword droop and made an exaggerated bow that showed a round spot of soot and grease on his bald head. "'cause he's slippery. An' this one," he twisted his head over his other shoulder to jab his thumb at the girl, "this one's Pig, 'cause . . . well . . ." The girl snorted a laugh. Her nose was remarkably flat and upturned. "Now what's your title, love-boo?"

"I'd rather not say," Tepic replied.

Ferret let out an exasperated sigh and raised himself up on one arm, his other hand still held forward in surrender. "Fine then. Your name's Dove, little love-boo, Lovey Dove."

"That's 'cause you's up 'ere cryin' on a ledge," Fish interjected with a short laugh.

"It's a good name," Ferret said and glared. "Nuffin' wrong wif' it. How'd you get 'ere anyway, Dove? You wif' Chub's boys?"

"Take me into Undercity," Tepic said, "and then leave me alone."

Ferret laughed. "You's in Undercity, muggy. You a soufy or sumfin'?"

"Look at 'is skin," Pig said. "He's a soufy or I'm a donkey."

"You is a donkey," Fish said, and Pig cuffed him.

"I don't know what you mean," Tepic said. "I'm not from around here."

Ferret narrowed his eyes as he got back to his feet and looked at the hole above their heads. Realization spread across his face. "It fell 'frough the poop-shoot, din'nit?"

The words were hard to follow, but Tepic understood them well enough. He didn't want to answer and wasn't sure what to say.

Pig's eyes widened. "He did fall 'frough it! You's not a soufy. You's a topper!"

"I did," Tepic finally said. "I did . . . come out of there. But it wasn't an accident. I came here on purpose. I . . . I need your help."

Ferret's small dark eyes widened so far it looked like his brow would slip over his forehead. "Help? What's a topper come down 'ere and want 'elp for?"

Fish started to laugh uncontrollably until Pig cuffed him again.

"I want to disappear," Tepic said.

"You serious, muggy?" Ferret asked.

"I am."

The three youths looked at each other, passing some signal between their eyes until Ferret turned back to Tepic and crossed his arms. "Alright, Dove. Let's make a deal. 'Fink you could show us how you nicked that shank from my 'and right quick?"

"What?" Tepic asked.

"What, what?" Ferret mocked and tapped his finger on the side of his head. "You'll 'ave to get that nugget as quick as yous 'and if you want to disappear down 'ere, Dove. Now show us the goods."

⸺⬦⸺

Tepic spent the next couple of hours on the ledge showing Ferret, Fish, and Pig how to disarm someone, even with their own crude weapons. It was simple stuff that any half-wit could avoid if they knew what they were doing, but Tepic felt good passing on his training to the three. It didn't take him long to discern that all of them were a little younger than he. When he asked, they lied about their ages of course, but despite their precocious air, he was certain of it.

Fish he liked best, maybe because he'd been told he was "slippery" too, but also because the boy had a matter-of-fact way of speaking, a soldier's brevity and wit that reminded him of Galomar. Ferret was too long-winded but seemed to have a conscience of a sort. Pig was a mystery and looked as likely to laugh as strike someone on a whim.

"I think you've got it," Tepic said as Pig twisted her cleaver and jerked it back. "I think the choil makes it even easier."

She stood proudly and smiled. "The child?"

"No, the *choil*. It's that notch by the heel."

Pig squinted.

"'Fink you could show us more, Dove?" Ferret interjected. "Mop-man's not 'ere 'til tomorry, an' it's good an' private 'ere as any."

"Mop-man?" Tepic asked.

Ferret pointed to a wrought-iron gate, covering an opening dug into the wall. Tepic was surprised he hadn't noticed it before. Stairs ascended from it further than his eyes could see.

"Aye, mop-man. Comes down wif' a few tin-heads from top-side and runs this treasure trove off the cliff like drum-beats, Dovey. We gotta grab while the grabbin's greased."

Tepic nodded and thought uncomfortably of soldiers coming down the steps. "I'd like to get going, into Undercity, if that's alright."

Ferret tapped his chin thoughtfully. "You's asking a lot, topper. Don't 'fink a quick lesson pays all. What's says you run wit' us for a peck. Watch our backs an' suchas."

Fish nodded. "He's a 'fick chum says I. Look at 'is pipes."

Pig concurred with her chin and Ferret went on. "You show us more pricker-tricks too, 'an we'll help you disappear, Dovey. Pinned and struck?" Ferret spit in his hand and held it out.

Tepic thought he understood the deal and tried his best to respond. He spit in his own hand and held it out, "Pinned and struck."

Pig snorted in laughter and Fish let out an "Ewwww."

Ferret frowned. "Come on, Dovey, that's disgusting. I offered the deal, so's I spit."

"Sorry," Tepic muttered and wiped his hand on his shirt.

Ferret gave a quick nod of approval and they shook hands. "Punctual." Then he stood back with an appraising look. "Won't do, Dove. You need new spindles an' a shave." He waved Pig over. "Have a seat."

Tepic sat warily, and Pig grasped her cleaver in two hands. He gripped his sword so hard his arms shook, and he peeked over his shoulder twice.

"You 'ave to 'old still," Pig said. "Or you'll get sliced up, muggy."

"Don't shake so much," Ferret said. "We're norfies, an' we don't break deals. Find 'im another shirt, Fish."

The blade was surprisingly sharp, and it rang with every stroke. Tepic watched his hair float past his eyes, waiting for Pig to nick his head or ambush him, but it never came. Her hands were steady, and in a few minutes, he was apparently totally bald. Fish hopped forward and presented a stained threadbare shirt with holes and mildew.

"Always one or two, sure as rain," Fish said.

"Last bits that pricker," Ferret said. "Everybody's armed down 'ere, but not like that." He tore long strips from Tepic's discarded tunic and held them out. "Wrap it up."

Tepic did as he was told and wound the strips around the hilt and the scabbard until any hint of its wealth was covered. The other three all stood back with their arms crossed and nodded.

"Looks a proper norfy, I says," Pig said.

"Punctual," Fish and Ferret agreed in unison. They all laughed.

———◈———

The gang were disappointed to have no more sword lessons on the ledge, but they quickly turned to the "grabbing" Ferret had described. He thrust a thick empty sack into Tepic's chest with a leather belt sewn firmly into its edge. Then they set about rummaging in the huge pile of refuse. It was the most putrid thing Tepic had ever done, but once he was past the initial shock, there was a strange freedom about it, and he forgot his misgivings and even the smell.

They didn't have an extra sack, so Ferret stood with his arms crossed and instructed Tepic while the other two thrust their arms elbow-deep into filth and rooted around for whatever they could find. At first, Ferret kept shaking his head until Tepic finally deduced that it was metal they were after. Every bit, down to the tiniest scrap, was fair game. They tucked little pieces of wood away too and textiles that had even the sparest value. It wasn't long until each sack was bulging and heavy.

"Now you gets to see our plucky lil' nursey, Lord Dovey." Ferret stepped aside and ushered them toward the lip of the ledge. "Have a look-see."

Dug into the northern side of the shelf were a pair of thick metal pitons. Leaning over the edge, Tepic could see a long rope ladder dangling above the sea to a wooden platform below. It was entirely concealed if one were not looking for it. The climb looked perilous indeed, but he slung his heavy sack over his shoulder and knelt to begin the descent. He'd done worse, if not so high.

"Oi' there, not like that," Ferret said.

The other two were fastening the belts around their waists and letting the sacks dangle between their knees.

Ferret went on. "Those sacks is 'eavy, love-boo, and the wind's a spitter. Just as soon to send you flying as not. Tie on."

Tepic followed their instructions and then the other two down the ladder. He soon understood why. The heavy sack bounced against the rungs, but every several feet a gust of wind blew him in a wobbling toss that set the world to spin. Fastened as it was, he felt heavy with the sack but balanced. It wasn't long until they plopped one after another onto a creaking wooden platform and detached their sacks to hoist them over their shoulders once again. Ferret dropped down last of all. What Tepic saw next took his breath away.

Spread out before him were arcing miles of the north face of Arregalt's jutting promontory, rising massive from the faraway sea below. Even wisps of cloud clung to its towering heights. Instead of the smooth rock he'd imagined, the soaring face of the cliff was covered in thousands upon thousands of doors and windows of innumerable shapes and sizes. Huge beams of wood thrust out over the ocean, and winding paths and platforms of salt-bleached planks were stacked one over another in an endless maze of scaffolds and terraces that led down to the bay whereupon hundreds of impossibly long quays extended into the water. Over the whole edifice swayed a subtle sense of shimmering motion.

Tepic stood in silence with his mouth open while Pig grinned like she'd built the whole thing herself.

Fish gave him a hard slap on his back and puffed his chest in pride. "Toppers 'fink they own the world," he said, "but they doesn't."

"Gape all day if'n you wants, muggy, but I got grobblets that need grobbin'," Ferret said.

Tepic could guess well enough what "grobblets" were and followed the others into a short cave through an outcropping of stone. He noticed for the first time in many hours just how empty his stomach was and how dry his tongue.

Emerging from the cave, he was no less astonished than he was standing upon the platform. As he walked forward, the sense of motion he'd seen revealed itself to be a mass of humanity, one jostling against another in crowded streets over which billowed endless rows of colorful sheets and plumes of steam that belched and rolled from countless pipes. Ropes and chains hung everywhere and crossed one another in a bewildering network.

Everything moved and shuddered under milling feet or even swung where structures were entirely suspended.

Ferret marched with a determined, weaving stride and led them swiftly through many streets and walkways. No one seemed to pay them any attention at all as they moved steadily downward, sometimes over shifting bridges and sometimes through more stony caves. At length, they turned sharply into a torchlit passage that delved deeply into the side of the promontory. Ferret knocked a pattern on the door and it opened a second later.

In a crack crossed by chains, the ugliest warted face Tepic had ever seen stared through with a long nose and a scowl. The door slammed shut, then opened wide again, and a twisted mokja even shorter than Lutz hurried all of them across the threshold.

"Who's this poncy lil' prat?" the mokja asked.

Ferret collected the sacks and laid them heavily on a countertop. The room was dim and dusty, littered with barrels, odds and ends, smoke-stained jars, and piles of nameless, broken contrivances.

"Cozi meet Dove. Dove, Cozi."

Cozi crossed to Tepic and sniffed him with a long inhale. "This one's a topper. He a podge?"

Ferret and the other two were now unloading objects while Tepic stood uncomfortably.

"He's no podge," Fish said. "He's just a kid. Runnin' wif' us a peck."

"Chub's boy?" Cozi asked.

"No," Ferret said.

Cozi poked his finger in Tepic's chest and glared up at him. "What's a topper doing in my city?"

Ferret began to answer, but Cozi cut him off. "Let the prat answer for his self."

"I'm . . . uh, just trying to disappear down here," Tepic said.

Cozi snorted. "Down 'ere?" He laughed. "Oi, you'll disappear all right." He somehow seemed satisfied with the answer and crossed to the counter to rummage through the contents of the sacks. "Buncha' dog-flesh," he muttered. "You tryin' to skin me, Ferret?"

"We takes what we find. 'Sides, you always say that."

Cozi scoffed and wandered into a back room. He emerged a minute later with a tray that held something like four biscuits. He slapped it down on the counter with a large pottery pitcher beside, and last of all, he cast a penny to spin before Ferret who flattened it under his fingers with a frown.

"One tif?" Ferret complained.

"You gave me another mouth to feed, chum, and that haul was poxy."

"Double nuggets!"

"Fine," Cozi said.

Ferret spit in his hand and held it out. They shook on it, and Cozi soon came back with four more biscuits. The children set into them ravenously. Tepic hesitated a moment and then tore into his as well.

The biscuit was firm and a little bit spongy. He was surprised to find it tasted like a savory potato with a touch of crispy oiled bits and a heavy dose of sea salt. It was delicious, though difficult to chew with his parched mouth.

"What is this?" Tepic asked.

Fish stopped and raised his eyebrows. "You what?"

"This biscuit."

"It ain't biscuit. Toppers don't 'ave pacho?"

Tepic shook his head and the others laughed.

Cozi was listening in and interjected. "Pacho's like a potato, boy, Dove, whatever your name is. Grows good in the dark—doesn't need no light at all." He'd produced one of his own and was munching away as well.

"Listen to ol' Cozi," Ferret said around a mouthful. "If he wasn't 'ere, the whole shack would snap and plop into the sea."

"You built Undercity?" Tepic asked.

It was Cozi's turn to laugh now. "Sure I did, leastwise some of it."

"He's modest," Pig said.

"My pimpled backside," Fish said and picked up the pitcher. Pig cuffed him, but he didn't spill a drop.

They passed the pitcher from hand to hand until Tepic grabbed hold. He knew at once that it was beer.

"Mind you don't chug it all, Dovey," Pig said.

"Do you have any water?"

"Water?" Pig asked. They burst into laughter again.

"Sure," Cozi said. "I got plenty—if you'd like to 'ang your bum over the bay for a week."

Tepic knew he was the butt of a joke once again, yet he allowed himself a wary laugh. The pitcher tasted and smelled like the inside of a shoe, but he quaffed a healthy pour until Pig made him stop. He smiled and felt the pacho and beer settle in his stomach.

The room was dark and the air hazy. Whether by the long hours or the strong drink, his weariness finally took hold. The sound of the others' laughter slowly muffled into flickering light while he sat and leaned his head against a rough-hewn wall. His body ached and his heart more so, but to jest and feast on simple fare seemed to right an upturned world. Some part of Tepic drifted off to another place. Perhaps that boy could just be a memory, and Dove, the free bird, could really fly away.

CHAPTER TWENTY-SEVEN

THE BEST OF HIS LIFE

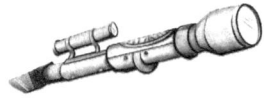

T HE NIGHT OF THEIR council, Lanathor found he could not sleep. Never before had he so boldly challenged Voldigar, let alone Liadov. The effort left his wasted body shaken, and still he breathed heavily, even as he lay upon his old bed in the tower of Maghaltani.

They had come so close to disaster—open rebellion! Even oath-breaking. All the suffering of his long journey to find Liadov would have been squandered in fire and fury, yet somehow he had turned their minds. Somehow there was hope of dawn. How often had his own words failed, but surely, Liadov's would not. At some far hour of the night, rest finally overtook him, and Lanathor drifted into deep and quiet peace.

Voldigar was silent again when the council reconvened, other than to give his firm assent when Lanathor told all. There was an ancient injunction against capital punishment for The Brotherhood of Aramon, but as near as could be said, the Brethren were barred from Arregalt on pain of death. Liadov, not truly of their order, did not face this same banishment.

She, Lanathor reasoned, might stand before the Emperor and convince him not only to relinquish the Prisms but to send forth his legions to check the horde beyond Eastfort. They would propose this audience by letter. It was perhaps a madman's hope, but it was the right hope, and the deed duty demanded.

Many brethren were loathe to stand down when their hearts had been steeled to action, Urias most of all. Careful argument and even the support of Voldigar and Liadov were not enough to sway them. Lanathor arranged for two dozen brethren to immediately make for Eastfort, and as one who had not been there the night of the coronation, he agreed himself to write and deliver the letter to Arregalt's gates. In the end, he was forced again to appeal to the Brethren by their oaths to King and country, to call them to the promises they'd made.

For all his wicked foolishness, Lusánt was their sovereign, and the brethren admitted that he must be warned, even rebuked. For centuries, the Order had served in this manner, countering their ruler gravely whenever there was need. For centuries, Kings and Emperors had listened. Though few had any hope the impudent boy who wore Tymicha's Crown would hear, they would try—with Liadov as their voice.

Lanathor helped Voldigar to collect the armaments he'd sent to Maghaltani months before, and so, together with Liadov and Medellai, the four of them returned to Voldigar's farm with quill and parchment to draft a desperate letter to the Emperor in the dim light of the old man's lamp. Lanathor set off in the gloom as soon as it was done.

As surely as he suspected, he was challenged at the gates. They did not let him in, but a captain of the guard whisked the letter away. The deed was done. Their hopes in paper and ink. He could only turn to wander down the road again, a solitary Azkushan with empty hands but hope in his heart.

<hr />

For his part, Voldigar started well and seemed happy of their company. He worked his field with vigor and spoke little of their peril. Perhaps at first he was even relieved to be given leave to stay on his farm. Gwenyth was gladder still with the womanly attending and healing hands of Liadov—but it was clear to Lanathor that the Eldest grew more agitated by the day and struggled to conceal it from his wife.

They'd sent their two dozen brethren to Eastfort and received messengers from there and Maghaltani twice daily. The reports of what they scouted beyond the pass were dire, but as yet, no wicked horde had poured into the mountains and no brethren had been harmed. The fifth day of waiting came, and Voldigar no longer spoke at all. On the seventh day, a messenger informed them that Urias and Gardoric had finished constructing a daring plan to raid the Spire and reclaim the dangerous artifacts by force—if the need arose. They only awaited Voldigar's command.

Lanathor doubted the old man would have waited even one more night when on the eighth day, the letter bearer finally came, decked in imperial livery. He brusquely handed a parcel to Voldigar and departed. Voldigar leaned upon his new spade on that hot and humid summer evening and wiped his brow. He did not open it. Rather, he gave it to Lanathor and beckoned that he follow him inside.

"Well," Voldigar asked, "what does it say?"

"He's agreed to an audience," Lanathor replied. His eyes widened, but a lump formed in his throat. "He's demanded my presence as well."

Voldigar leaned with arms folded and his back against the unlit hearth. "I'm not surprised. You were the only one who missed his coronation. Fine. When?"

"A week from today."

Voldigar shook his head and groaned, gesturing into the air. Medellai stood and buried his red beard in a nervous hand.

"That's too late," Voldigar said. "In a week the hinterlands may be overrun."

"Why does he delay?" Medellai asked. Liadov was sitting quietly in one of Hobyn's chairs.

"He's toying with us," Voldigar replied.

"No," said Medellai. "Lusánt is impetuous. There's some other reason he doesn't want this audience—yet."

Voldigar stared out the door that stood ajar to let the evening air flow through. "We have to act. We made the wrong decision."

Lanathor regarded his friend quietly and watched his hands as they trembled, clenching into fists and releasing. "The Brethren are there, in Eastfort, Voldigar. We'll have warning if anything goes wrong," Lanathor said.

"Will two dozen brethren stop a horde?" Voldigar asked.

"Then send them all," Lanathor replied.

Voldigar shook his head again, but Medellai interjected. "All one hundred brethren wouldn't stop it. Delay them yes, maybe even for a long time. But it's all the more reason we must speak to the Emperor. He has to send the legions, and the Prisms must come into our care."

Lanathor nodded. "Medellai is right. All our hopes lie with Arregalt. Lusánt will see reason. If he does not, we all perish in one fire or another. Wait the week, and if hell empties on our doorstep before then, we all go forth to meet it. Stay the course, old man."

Voldigar groaned his displeasure once more and abruptly strode through the door. The sound of an axe on wood followed. Lanathor rose to follow after, but Liadov held up her hand. "Let him go."

"What do you think he'll do?" Lanathor asked.

"He'll wait," Liadov said. "Just let him be."

Lanathor swallowed any further words and turned his eyes and ears to the door. It was as though he could hear the ticking of the great clocks in the Spire, even where he stood. *Just wait a little longer, old man.*

There was little speaking over the next week, and Voldigar split enough wood for ten winters. He could do nothing else for his field as he waited for the harvest that an unrelenting heat would soon surely bring. He smoked his pipe in the aspen grove. He yelled at crows, but Liadov was right. He did nothing more and never sent the command to Urias and Gardoric.

By day, Lanathor helped Hobyn plan and construct three wooden granaries, about the height of a man, tightly jointed and raised above ground on short stilts. They could be filled from the top and grain let out the side. It felt good to help his old friend prepare for what was promising to be a once-in-a-generation harvest. They ate well too, and he could feel the flesh slowly returning to his cheeks and ribs. Yet all the while, doubt gnawed at him as he pondered what his words might be before the Emperor.

By night, Lanathor and Liadov stared at the stars and wondered at the strange moon, sliding more and more from its course as the calendar slipped by. Medellai and Voldigar would join them sometimes, but he confessed to himself that he loved it best when they were alone. Her mind was an artful maze, and he had no greater pleasure than wandering its halls or gazing silently upward in her company. A withered piece of root sat dryly in his pocket, forgotten while he passed the days with his companions.

It was a rare overcast morning over browning grass and still air when he and Liadov finally departed Voldigar's farm for the gates of Arregalt. He would long remember those two weeks in his friend's humble home as the best of his life.

Chapter Twenty-Eight

Grubby Hands

Dove sat against a wall in the shadows of a narrow alley overlooking a long dock in the glare of the setting sun. He'd once been known as 'Tepic,' but no one had said that boy's name in a long time. He wondered if he might forget it and hoped everyone in Arregalt would too.

Even in this isolated edge of the wharf, the vast number of ships and crew coming and going were a dizzying dance. Having only seen them from a thousand feet above, Dove had never realized just how massive the miridas vessels were. Their great engines hummed and throbbed under the surface of the water with a violet glow, and even the huge galleons of their human counterparts looked like toys bobbing in a bathtub next to them. It would be many hours past sunset before business settled on the piers.

In the last half month, he'd met a host of other children in Ferret's crew like Snake and Goat and the more creative, though appropriately named, Oxtail. A coarse tuft of hair hung from the boy's otherwise bald and leathery scalp. At first, Dove had hardly slept in the burnt-out tannery they called their hideout. Firstly from the lingering odor of the place, but mostly for fear that one of the sharp-eyed youth or another would *nick* his grandfather's sword or *shank* him in the middle of the night. After a few days though, it was clear that he was just another dirty boy on the streets, and no one paid any particular attention to him or the linen-wrapped hilt he hugged against his chest while he slept.

He quickly determined that he was likely the oldest boy who slept in the tannery. From Oxtail, he learned that older youth were pressed into other work and not ignored half so well as all the rest. If he had no one to protect him, it was common most of all for a stray lad to end up on a miridas ship by twelve or thirteen and never to be seen again. There was a fence-straddling art in Undercity of being barely useful enough without being only another mouth to feed. Ferret had taught him all the ways to remain unseen, to slouch and lurk, to blend in, and hide in plain sight.

Dove could hardly keep up with it all and was glad now to simply sit in the dark shadow of the alley and watch the bustle of the quays from his quiet perch. No less astonishing than the ships were the Miridas themselves. Kyriana was the only one he'd ever seen, but on the docks were many. They all had skin in one shade or another of subtle green or blue, but while Kyriana could nearly blend in with the *toppers* in Arregalt, the mariners here were far more exotic, vaguely feline, and spoke in their rapid, resonant language.

One of these was directly across the street, speaking instead in heavily accented Aramoni to a drunken peddler sitting precariously atop a stack of small wooden crates. The peddler was their mark.

"We're nearly full. Not worth the weight," the miridas said. "Captain may wish some in his personal effects. Ten pennies for five."

The merchant swayed a little and slid off the crates, steadying them with two hands. "Ten tif wouldn't pay for the wood! This is fine citrus, muggy. 'free a box."

"I'm not negotiating, and you're drunk. If you want to make any money today, don't waste my time."

The peddler cursed and flicked his hand. "I got fitty boxes to sell. Don't grease me!"

The miridas spit and turned to walk away.

"Wait, wait, wait!"

The miridas didn't wait, and the peddler could only sputter and curse again. When he'd expended his salvo of expletives, he unsteadily walked round the pile of crates and stood bow-legged to relieve himself into the ocean. This was their chance.

"Muggy who drinks like that's gonna fill the sea, soon as not," Fish had said. Like rats from a hole, Ferret, Fish, Pig, and Oxtail streamed across the street and discretely lifted one box each. They were back in the alley as quickly as they'd gone. Dove sat watching while Oxtail worked the box open to reveal a few rows of plump orange fruits wedged into straw.

"Stop gawking, Dove!" Ferret hissed. "Do a runner."

Dove hesitated at the mouth of the alley and rubbed his fingers. He'd never stolen anything from anyone, and while he hadn't given it a second thought on the way down to the docks, a flood of doubt now poured in as he stood dumbly in the setting sunlight. Fish shoved him from behind.

Dove stumbled forward but then stopped again. The peddler was returning from the edge of the water. He halted when he caught sight of Dove.

"Having a nosy?"

Dove didn't register the question and stood still.

"Sod off, noblet!"

A flicker of realization crossed the peddler's face as he looked between Dove and his boxes. "You . . . you pinched me. Didn't you?" He took a step toward Dove, but suddenly Ferret was at his side.

"Oi, Guvvy. Easy now. That's my bruv. He's soft in the 'ead."

"You pinched me!" the peddler repeated.

Ferret opened his mouth to respond again but then snapped it shut and bolted. Dove followed hard after him.

In a moment all five of them were sprinting through the alley with armloads of fruit while the peddler tripped and cursed behind, shouting for guards. They didn't look back but went swiftly at their course, chosen out before they'd ever sat a moment to watch their mark.

Breathless minutes later, they were on a small landing halfway up a steep and narrow stairway covered in ivy. All sound of pursuit had stopped. Dove exhaled in relief, but Ferret was on him in an instant.

"You 'alf-wit lump!" he cried as he shoved Dove against the wall with his forearm. "You want to get us copped up?"

Dove didn't like being called a "lump," much less being thrust against the stone while he was already tired. He pushed back. The other three stood with arms crossed and dark expressions.

"I can't steal!" Dove yelled.

"Bags you can't!" Ferret yelled back. "We can't pick muck piles every day. If ye don't wants to work, then you don't wants to eat." Ferret collected his fruit crate from the ground in an angry swipe and stomped up the rest of the stairs. The others quickly followed while Dove took up the rear in silence.

It was a quiet and awkward walk back to the tannery, and then hours passed while Dove's stomach growled and the others gorged on fruit. Night had fully fallen by the time Fish finally came and sat by Dove in the darkness. He was now feeling very much like Tepic again as he stared blankly at his open palms.

"You can 'ave one of mine," Fish mumbled. He was holding an orange out to Tepic.

"What?"

"I says, you can 'ave one."

"I don't deserve it," Tepic said. "I'm a coward." He could just make out a grin on Fish's face in the dim light.

"Fine," Fish said. "But why be a 'ungry coward?" He pulled half the flesh from the orange and pushed it into Tepic's hands, then he reached up and patted Tepic's bald head with his sticky fingers. "You need another shave soon, muggy. Won't be pretty as Fish."

"Why doesn't your hair grow back?" Tepic asked.

"Dunno," said Fish, "never did. Leastwise this way I don't 'ave to worry about Pig chopping me up." He shrugged.

"She cuts your hair too?"

"Yep. Just once though, when I was new."

"My mom always cut my hair before," Tepic said.

"What's that like?" Fish asked.

Tepic shrugged. "Better than a big knife I guess."

"No, I mean 'aving a mum."

Tepic blinked. "Oh . . . I—"

Fish went on. "If I had a mum, I wouldn't be in Undercity. I bet she wouldn't let me nick any'fing either. Is your mum pretty?"

"I suppose so," Tepic said and scratched his head "I guess I never really thought about it."

"Is she good at sewing or dancing or sumuch?"

"Both," Tepic said.

Fish nodded in approval. "I 'fought so." He handed Tepic the other half of the orange. "You know Dove, you's not a coward just 'cause you's got a conscience. Problem as I see it—I'm not gonna give ye 'alf me grobblets forever."

Tepic laughed. "Don't you ever feel bad about it?"

"'Bout wut?"

"Stealing."

"Oh . . . 'spose I do," Fish said. "But don't 'fink about it much anymore. Guess I don't really want to nick 'fings from a sloshed up old peddler." Fish twisted his face and gave Tepic a punch on the shoulder. "Don't go makin' me feel bad about it."

Tepic stared at his grubby hands in what little light remained when an idea popped into his head like candlelight. "What if I could show you secret places? You could be a . . . a treasure hunter instead of a stealer."

Fish raised an eyebrow. "You daft?"

"How do you think I got to Undercity?"

"You fell 'frough a poop-shoot."

Tepic sighed. "No, but how did I find it?"

Fish held his hands up. "Chums if I know."

"I know my way through the Delvings," Tepic said.

Fish scoffed and let out a long puff of spit and air. "Not even Cozi knows his way 'frough. Door's locked and stay out."

Tepic gave Fish a stern look.

"You serious, Dove?"

Of course," Tepic said. "What would you say if I could show you secret places? You wouldn't have to steal anymore, at least . . . not from old drunk merchants."

Fish narrowed his eyes. "What I'd says is you just earned some supper, that's what I'd says." He stood up. "Hey, Ferret, come 'ere. Dove's got somethin' to tell you."

CHAPTER TWENTY-NINE

TRUTH

L ANATHOR AND LIADOV STOOD silently before the great bronze
doors of the Winter Throne, looming over them some forty feet in
quiet eminence. Upon the polished floor, the one cast a dark finger of
reflection, the other all of flowing white. The Emperor had removed his
court from the outdoor colonnade long before and hid within from the
relentless blast of Aramon's strange heat.

Lanathor mulled his words over in his mind again and again. Their
purpose was clear: to appeal to Emperor Lusánt plainly that he must face
the encroaching threat with all the might of his realm, and also, to abandon
the Prisms of the Heavens which they were now certain he possessed. He
yet doubted himself and wished that Liadov might speak every word, but
he knew Lusánt would directly address him also. Without thinking, he
reached into the fold of his robes.

Liadov touched his arm gently. "Sixteen days," she whispered.

Lanathor flinched and looked inquisitively to his friend. "What?" he
whispered back.

"You've not touched Falam Root in sixteen days, Elder, and you went
months before."

"I must have it for my magic, Sister."

"Must you?" Liadov turned her face to his. Her eyes were obscured by
the crystal beads that hung from the circlet upon her brow, but he knew

that she was peering intently into his own. "Telling does not require Falam Root, Lanathor."

"Mine does, Sister, it always has." A tension was rising in his chest that surprised him. "Every Teller must have memories, but mine are all of pain. Were I to sleep, I must have nightmares. What others forget, I must hold in perfect meditation. What should drive me mad, I must balance on the edge of a knife." Lanathor's face was tight and sweat was forming on his brow. He never spoke so plainly of these things, least of all to Liadov.

She let her hand drop to his and squeezed his fingers. "You asked me once if I believe in God's goodness."

He opened his mouth to answer, but she went on. "Give excuse no longer, Brother. I know what you think you need. If we are to speak plainly to the Emperor today, let us begin with ourselves. You must learn to be more than you are. There is no more time to delay." She turned her face back to the doors.

Lanathor swallowed the swelling anger and let slip his grip on the tiny capsule, allowing it to roll back into his pocket where it now hung like an anchor. He blinked in stunned silence but could not consider longer. The massive doors before them groaned to life, breaking the dread stillness as a long colonnade was revealed beyond.

Before them, the way ran straight over a fortune of marble, hemmed by mighty columns extending into the gloom above. Between each was a low-burning brazier and many soldiers to watch them pass.

No one welcomed or announced their entrance, and the Emperor sat at an angle, far away in a great stone chair, worked through with iron and gold, and raised upon a dais. Their feet echoed as they walked, the only sound along their narrow path. All about the Emperor, his advisors and bodyguard stood. Doctor Challeric, Diocesan Ragat, Master Hyrodan, General Gamad, and most strange of all, a woman in flowing emerald garb who wore pearls upon her eyes. They stopped at the foot of his throne, and both dropped their heads in deference, waiting first for the Emperor to speak.

Lusánt tapped his scepter in a covered hand and regarded them, noiseless and unblinking. A great flowing heap of robes obscured his arms and legs and draped over the sides of his throne. "Welcome to my hall, Elder Lanathor. Why were you not at my coronation?" Lusánt asked at last.

Lanathor lifted his head. "I am sorry, Your Highness. I was trapped in Danek and could not return."

"And why were you there at all?"

"I sought our sister, my lord. This is Liadov, Seer of Dizghizádè."

"I know who she is, Lector. I don't need your lessons anymore." Lusánt raised himself straight in his seat. "As it happens, I was very disappointed in the brethren you left behind, your *titular head*, as you say. Do you know what happened?"

Lanathor swallowed hard and considered his words. "I am to understand that my order were banished from the city. I—"

"As though it were a whim?" Lusánt interrupted. "You think me a capricious child?" He paused while Lanathor searched for a reply, then held up his hand and snickered. "Don't answer, Lanathor. I have acted with cause, Learned Teacher—as I always shall." He relaxed back into his chair. "Now answer my question. Why were you in Danek . . . and why do you bring this troubler of Aramon before my throne?"

"We would not bring you trouble, but grace, and counsel, and warning, my lord."

Lusánt raised his eyebrows. "Warning?"

Lanathor bowed his head again and went on. "Evil has arisen in the east, of a kind unseen in our lifetime. A horde crouches at your door, and the hour is growing late."

Lusánt looked to Gamad in mock surprise. "General? Have you heard of this? A horde?"

Lanathor noticed for the first time that Gamad was missing his right arm below the elbow and a black prosthetic stood in its place with a painted hand carved in a frozen grasp of deep-stained wood. The general shrugged and gestured with the false limb.

"We'll look into it. There were some rumors among my low-ranking officers. Is that all you've come to tell me?" Lusánt asked.

Lanathor licked his lips and went on. "As you know, Emperor, Commander Dantic has sent word for many days, and as yet, no aid was sent to him. There is an army of many thousands amassing beyond the pass, tens of thousands, and without help, the forts will soon be overrun, then the hinterlands, then all of Aramon. Send forth your legions and check the foe, before it's too late."

"*Captain* Dantic," Lusánt corrected. "And I did not ask for your military advisement, Lanathor. Would you have me empty Arregalt? Odd wouldn't you say that the men whom I have banished would seek to drain my seat of its protectors? Very odd. What evidence do you have of a horde? Are these not just stories? Perhaps our poor neighbors are risen up in fruitless revolt? Starving refugees from Azkushan or Suramn? Lock the gates. Keep them out, but why trouble me?" Lusánt rose from his seat.

Liadov stepped forward and cried in a loud voice. "Emperor!" Her word rang from the walls and sent a ripple through the air.

Lanathor took a deep breath. Lusánt froze and fixed his eyes upon her.

"You know why we are here," she went on. "Let us no longer speak in the dark what should be plain in the light."

Lusánt frowned and lowered himself again to his chair. "The troubler speaks!"

Liadov took another step and went on sharply. "I speak of what I know. You mock the Elder's plea but you are not blind to the evil which has arisen, Son of Olwis. The Oruni are upon you. Wyrna, Bashevi, Odomo—a darkness from the cold nightmares of your forebears. We have seen it with our own eyes, and the enemy which calls them forth now whispers in your own ears. Why do you not send aid?"

A murmur arose in the colonnade, and Lusánt's eyes lit white with fury. "Clear my hall!" he cried. He pointed his scepter at Lanathor and Liadov. "You, stay."

Within a pair of confused minutes, the hall was drained of soldiers and courtiers and all others, save the three of them and Lusánt's small cadre of advisors and personal guard. The doors pulled shut again. Lusánt stared at Liadov with lances in his eyes.

"How dare you—" Lusánt began but Liadov replied more firmly.

"How dare *you*, Emperor. Your realm is in peril while you toy with things that you should not. But I perceive you may not yet be wholly taken in your folly. Send forth your armies and fill the gap of Aramon."

Lusánt grimaced. "I should have you flogged and thrown from my presence, but you are the Seer and Prophetess of Aramon." He spat the words. "Go on, Prophetess, tell me what you know."

"Give back what you have stolen, Lusánt Sispérus, and let The Brotherhood of Aramon destroy it."

A hush fell over the room while silent battle worked between their eyes. At length, Lusánt blinked and looked away. For a moment, he looked every bit the teenage boy he was, but it soon passed, and a subtle sneer spread across his face.

"You speak in riddles as though we ought to be ashamed. Do you think I cannot see your purpose? Do you think I only work in secret?" Lusánt gestured to the servants about him and then, with strange effort, unfolded his robes. There upon his lap, a glistening orb radiated with green light. His other hand was stuck fast to it, knuckles pale in his clutching grasp. "Behold, the symbol of my house, and no secret to my friends! This is the treasure you *thieves* would take from me."

Lanathor gasped and moved to Liadov's side. Gamad and the Xerimadi bodyguard that flanked Lusánt stepped forward to match his movement.

"Do nothing foolish, Teller!" Lusánt hissed through clenched teeth. "You would be very disappointed at the result."

"Emperor!" Lanathor cried, "You cannot use that thing!" Liadov now stood by, searching the pulsing light in silence.

"Can I not?" Lusánt lifted the orb from off his lap, and in both hands held it menacingly before his flickering face. "Do you adjure me by your strange god? And what shall happen to me if I do? Prophesy to me!"

"Live forever and do all that is in your heart!" Master Hyrodan called out from behind his shoulder.

"Bring light upon us, Emperor!" Diocesan Ragat echoed.

Lusánt chuckled. "Do you hear these flatterers, Sister Liadov?" He did not take his gaze from off the orb. "My father said that you spoke only words of truth. Is that really so? He told me as much—before you let him die." He took his eyes from off the orb as his face sank and he gave a hard look at Liadov. "Oh yes, I have learned many things—many hidden things. Would you tell me truth now, Prophetess, and only truth?"

"Emperor Sispérus, God grant that you rule justly forever," Liadov said flatly.

"Did I not say truth?" Lusánt spat. His glare deepened while a hollow sound reverberated through the chamber.

Lanathor could see the smallest tremble in Liadov's lip beneath the crystal strings. She pulled the circlet from her brow and stood quietly a long while. Then she began, softly at first.

"I would speak, but you would not listen," Liadov said.

Lusánt leaned forward to object, but a look of realization crossed his face, and he sank back into his chair to cradle the orb in both his hands.

She went on. "I would cry upon the highest peak, but you would not hear. Will a man defy his creator, will a mortal curse his God? Yet this you do to me, Aramon."

"Ask the truth, Sons of Tymicha, and receive a bitter wine, for your God utters knowledge as a wind upon the pines and breath over the sea. It passes by, but you do not understand"

"Forever have I loved a wayward folk, but you sought the sun, and moon, and stars. I spoke only truth to you, but you wandered far from me. Aramon, exalted beyond the measure of all your brethren, brought low to lick the dust. Though you rose to touch the heavens, your folly leads you on the roads of hell."

"A tide is flying far to sea while lying prophets sigh. 'Light,' they say to you, but there is no light in them, for as surely as the Wending flows, I will scour this land and wash away its filth. If they would listen, I would soon restore them, but they do not."

"The day is coming when I will strike the one who leads them and give to them the harvest they have sown. Then will I redeem. Then will I have mercy."

The blood had drained from Lusánt's face while she spoke, and at the corners of his mouth hung a withering frown. "Enough!" he cried at last and stood, bent and stooping over the orb. "I knew you would speak like this. 'Troubler,' I called you rightly. Are these the words you said to Olwis? To bring his gray head down to the grave?"

"Turn to your God, Lusánt, while there is still time," Liadov said.

Lusánt shook his head bitterly. Tears pooled in his red-rimmed eyes. "For all your 'truth,' you lie to me even now. Hypocrites! Prophesy me this: Where is that sniveling betrayer of yours, your little student, Tepic Banari?"

Lanathor widened his eyes in surprise. "He is with you, Emperor. You have taken him to your house!"

Lusánt raised the corner of his mouth. "You think yourself subtle, don't you, Lector? Subtle indeed." He sat again. "Tell me to where you've stolen him away. Where has he taken the sword? I know he's gone to your precious Order!"

Lanathor moved his mouth to reply but Liadov gave him a wary glance. They stood in silence while despair gathered like a starless night about his heart.

"Be gone from my hall," the Emperor cried, "before I defile it with your blood!"

CHAPTER THIRTY

SMOKE OVER THE BARLEY

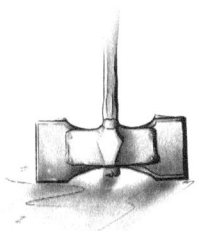

I T WAS DISHEARTENING HOW quickly Gwenyth's health declined when Liadov was absent, even for a day. Her brother worried over her while she rocked in her chair with eyes closed. Medellai held one of her swollen hands and was in the midst of recounting some story from their childhood. Perhaps it would at least distract from her discomfort.

Voldigar stood by an open window, scraping the last of the ground Falam Root into a wooden cup. Night was falling fast, and this simple ritual was short respite from his troubled thoughts. What of the border? What of his two learned friends appealing to the Emperor in the dark halls of the city? What would he do for Gwenyth once Liadov left them . . .

For her part, Liadov had a low opinion of the root, but she had not forbade it, and thank God, it still let Gwenyth ignore her suffering while it lasted. That was enough. He crossed the room with cup in hand and let Medellai give it to her. She took it gratefully.

". . . and I say, that's why mother never let you hunt again," Medellai continued his tale. "For all my promises, you looked more like a mokja forgeman than a noble's daughter."

Gwenyth smiled. "And you looked more like a noble's daughter than a mighty ranger." She drained the cup in one long gulp.

Medellai laughed and stroked his beard. "It's true! I had not yet completed my uniform with this massive mane upon my chin. I perceive that you are jealous?"

Gwenyth laughed and slid a hand over her bulging belly. "Don't make me laugh!" She closed her eyes again. "It hurts to laugh." She sighed and stretched her feet out as far in front of the rocking chair as she could. "Why do my feet always hurt?"

"Why do the spirits jape and pull the wind?" Medellai said. "You're old, that's why."

Voldigar stooped down and worked Gwenyth's slippers from off her feet. Like her hands, they were swollen and discolored. "Just put your feet up a while," he said.

"How's the harvest?" she asked in a distant voice.

"Very fine," Voldigar replied. "Not long now. We'll have a fortune in grain. Give it no thought, my love."

The root was taking hold, and Gwenyth was soon fast asleep. He watched her chest gently rise and fall. Somehow, even as she dozed, she held the same brave face, the same gentle curve at the corners of her mouth, though her brow was knit with pain. Voldigar felt a tremble travel from his arms and over his neck. Unconsciously, he wiped a hand across his eyes.

"Come get some air, Vol," Medellai whispered.

Voldigar tiptoed with his twice-made brother to the front stoop and there produced a pipe. They watched the barley sway in a gentle moonlit breeze while the embers glowed to life. He felt Medellai's eyes on him.

"Are you al—"

"I'm fine," Voldigar replied quickly.

Medellai pursed his lips and gazed over the field again. Voldigar let the silence linger until his thoughts had grown quiet. He drew a long breath through the pipe.

"Your mother always sounds so severe in your stories," Voldigar said and blew a plume of smoke at the clear night sky.

Medellai smiled and cocked his head. He looked relieved. "She was," he said, "at least until Gwenie got sick."

Voldigar nodded. "I don't think she ever liked me much."

"Sons and mothers-in-law. What can you do?" Medellai chuckled. "But she liked you well enough. At least before you gave up title. She might have lived ten more years without that little chestnut."

Voldigar returned a smirk, and they sat quietly for another stretch. "She'd have been less astonished if she could see it today. It was no great loss. Did you know the Anteres lands are now fully submerged?"

Medellai raised his eyebrows.

"Yes," Voldigar went on. "Another swamp came off the river and swallowed them up. A good Artificer could drain it into the Haroel, but it's just a dead well now, peeking up over a stinking bog." Voldigar puffed again and handed the pipe to Medellai.

"Sounds . . . pleasant."

Voldigar tilted his head and added a concurring nod. Despite everything, his brother gave him some comfort. "Quite, if you're Gardoric—or enjoy flies. I'll take our little farm any day, thank you. And look at my barley." He spread his hands wide and smiled smugly.

"Magnificent," Medellai replied and ashed the pipe. Liadov and Lanathor were walking past the aspen grove bearing a small lamp. Even in the dimness, it was plain to see on Lanathor's face that things had not gone well.

———◆———

Lanathor's scarred head drooped over his sagging shoulders. He subtly swayed, and his words came out in rasping groans. "The Emperor did not hear us, Brother."

Voldigar stood with a quiet frown and flexed his fingers.

Lanathor swallowed and went on. "We saw the key—the Prism—with our own eyes. He bears it openly amongst his aides, an orb of green light, just as Tepic told you."

"Did he use it?" Voldigar asked.

"No, at least not in our presence," Lanathor said. "But he threatened us and would not abide any suggestion of its surrender or of its hurt."

"And what of Eastfort?"

Lanathor shook his head and dropped his eyes to the ground.

Voldigar sighed heavily and looked out over his grain.

"He may yet send men to reinforce the border," Liadov added, "but I would not look for it, and he will not respond in the way we hoped."

"Then all has been for naught," Voldigar said.

"No, not *all* for naught," Liadov replied. "In his anger, the Emperor bid me prophesy. And I did, Voldigar, I spoke the truth as Lanathor asked me."

Voldigar narrowed his eyes.

Liadov went on. "He did not listen, as we feared, but he did give one response that is of use to us. Tepic Banari is missing . . . and the sword with him."

Though doubt still gripped it, a sudden hope leapt upon Voldigar's heart. "What? How?"

"The Emperor thinks we've secreted him away," Lanathor said. "But we told him true."

Voldigar flicked his eyes about the dirt at his feet as he considered. He nodded. "The boy's escaped then. Good. He did as I asked, and far more. He was wise enough to hide himself, even from us."

"No good will come of this," Medellai said. "How long can he elude the Emperor?"

"Not long, but perhaps it buys us time. For now, the second key is out of Lusánt's grasp," Liadov said.

Medellai shook his head bitterly. "If I had my sight, I could find the boy. We could help him."

"Of that, Medellai, there is more that I can do," Liadov said. She straightened. "I am going home, and you must come with me."

"Home? What do you mean?" Voldigar asked. "Why now?" Lanathor's eyes shot up in dismay.

"To the old shrine, Voldigar. It isn't far, but there are answers there—my books, my prayers . . . my memories. Tepic has changed our course. We just need time."

"We don't *have* time, Sister!" Voldigar objected. "The shrine may not even be there anymore. We should act with this opportunity Tepic has given us. We've waited too long already."

"Then what do you propose?"

Voldigar's mind raced, but only the smoke of old fires kindled. "We gather all the Brethren. We do as Urias said and take the orb by force. We scour the city for Tepic. Then we turn to face the horde. What else can we do?" His voice was rising now, and he glanced sideways to where Gwenyth slept behind his low stone wall. He knew his plan was folly, even as the words tumbled from his mouth.

Liadov shook her head. "Please, Voldigar, do nothing rash. Just a little longer. I'll restore Medellai's sight. Then we'll find Tepic safely, but I must learn where the third key is hidden. I have to go home, to pray. I will find an answer there. Let me do this."

Voldigar grasped for further words, but nothing came. Despair bent him like a whithered bough. A nightmare was unfolding in the Spire to the west, a formless terror in the fortress to the east, and he stood immobile, an old farmer in a barley field, dithering while all the world came crashing down.

"No," he said. "No more delay."

Lanathor stepped forward. "I'll go to Eastfort myself. I'll bring the rest of the Brethren and hold the wall. We can stay the horde. Please, Brother, listen to Liadov."

"Just until harvest," Liadov added. "Give us until then. You bring in your barley, and if you do not hear from me, do as you think best. Take care of your wife, Voldigar. Let her rest here in the life that you have chosen, and hope for better days."

"Don't throw it all away, friend," Lanathor said with another hard swallow.

In all his frantic musing, Voldigar had thought of Gwenyth most of all, but he'd been loathe to speak it. Now they'd thrust their hands into his thoughts and pulled. How could he clutch at mists and dreams while others risked their lives? "Shall I let shadows creep into my windows when I could fight them far away? Do you think to protect me?" he said.

"There is still a chance, Voldigar. Tepic has given it to us, if he can but hide a little longer—if you can stay your hand."

Voldigar felt his anger rising, but a sliver of their words worked into his mind. He fought and cursed himself inwardly and ground his teeth while he stared into the barley again. "She isn't well, Liadov. What will she even do while you are gone?"

Liadov reached her hand out and gently held it to Voldigar's face. "Gwenyth will be alright, Voldigar. Help will come to her from other hands. Let me take Medellai with me, and I will return. Not long now."

Voldigar had no more words to say and finally let out the breath that he was holding. "We've waited too long already . . . but what choice do you leave me? If I am alone in this, then I am twice the fool." He felt their eyes on him, but he could not meet their gaze.

"Go Liadov, go Medellai. Go Lanathor to Eastfort." He motioned with his hand. "But do not empty Maghaltani. Choose brethren to leave behind—men that would go into the Spire with me."

Lanathor nodded.

Voldigar's fists clenched again, and he lowered his eyes to the ground. "I will not listen to you again," he said. "The barley heads are filling fast, and I will soon gather them. But see that you return swiftly, for I soon become a fool. When I lay my sickle down, I swear it, I will take my hammer up."

CHAPTER THIRTY-ONE

PODGES PODGING

TEPIC HAD NEVER BEEN more proud of a black eye. In truth, he'd had very few. More than one, to be sure, as any self-respecting swordsman in Voldigar's training yard must, but this one was special. He was feeling like Dove again.

The boy they called *Whale* came back the day after Tepic told Fish and Ferret about the Delvings. Came back, that is, because Whale had apparently been running a few weeks with "Chub's Boys," a gang of "Soufies" they sometimes did business or battle with. The exact reason why was hard to piece together, but it sounded like a great ruse that the youth found unbearably funny.

Whale was popular, and had his nickname for good reason. He had huge fat hands and a huge fat body and spat when he talked. He had a curious habit of repeating himself or others in a whisper after they spoke, and he did not like *Dove*.

First, because he *'talked smart.'* Second, because he wouldn't steal and thought he was *'better than everyone else,'* and third—and most important—because he was *'a grimy weasel liar who couldn't gets into the Delvings, let alone find 'is way 'frough.'* The boy they actually called Weasel took offense, but Whale didn't care. He'd keep an eye on Dove, and *'batty-fang 'im if he felt like it.'*

It only took another day. While Tepic looked for an opportune passage through the Delvings, Whale's patience ran out. Tepic was eating pacho that Whale said he had no rights to when the larger boy gave him a shove and the biscuit rolled in the dirt and broke apart. Tepic opened his mouth to object, but one meaty fist and then another knocked him to his back. It was the last straw.

The next few seconds were a whirl of dust and flying fists. Tepic was a fair wrestler and found that despite Whale's impressive size and rude ambush, he didn't stand a chance. With an arm around his neck and a flurry of socking, Whale began to blubber and cry, and finally concede.

Tepic felt horrible, but the Norfies cheered and he became an instant folk hero. Strangest of all, Whale's pride didn't seem to sting at all, and they were somehow now the best of friends. The rituals of Undercity were too dense to pierce, but they spit and shook on it. Whale and Dove were chums, pinned and struck. *'No 'ard feelings.'*

Now, Whale and Dove, along with Ferret, Pig, and even old Cozi the Mokja stood in a cellar near the surface, marveling at a long row of crates, all filled with expensive-looking shoes. The latter had insisted on *'seeing for his self.'*

"I can't believe it," Cozi muttered for the tenth time. "We could pop 'frough that door and be topsy."

"... and be topsy ..." Whale whispered quietly. Everyone could hear it, but he had a word of his own too. "I tolds you Dove-boo could do it. Punctual savage!" A great spray of spit left his mouth on the last exclamation, and he whispered it again.

Ferret was pleased too and couldn't hide a smile behind his glare. "Best get quiet or we'll all be in a box. Get to nicking," he hissed. He held the only lamp they had and hoisted it up so everyone's face floated in the dark room.

Tepic had made up with him after the nearly-botched heist at the docks and was glad this contribution had only taken a few days to come about. If socking Whale didn't impress their leader, this surely would.

"I can't believe it," Cozi said for the eleventh time. "I'd know all 'bouts this if'n they'd let me finish schooling. It's a bleeding miracle." He eyed

Tepic with a shake of his head. The others were all busily filling their sacks with shoes. They froze with the sound of feet overhead.

Ferret covered the light in a split second, and the cellar went quiet. It was a long, tense spell until he finally let out his breath and the others followed suit.

"Time to break a fiddle," Ferret whispered, and they poured out of the room on hurried feet, back the way they'd come.

Tepic didn't carry any stolen shoes or any sack at all. Somehow in his mind, he'd decided showing his friends around the Delvings wasn't quite the same as taking things himself. At any rate, his hands were empty, and Dove, the Whale-punching, treasure-hunting folk hero, thumbed the little tharmskolp in his pocket. Thus far, no one knew he had it, and he didn't expect he'd need to glance at it at all on their way back. Cozi could remember every turn once he'd taken it, and Tepic let his thoughts drift while the warted mokja led a long descent back to the tannery.

—◆—

The mood in the tannery was festive. Cozi stuck around long enough to leave a flask of something potent and black that children passed from hand to hand. Every member of the gang now wore a pair of excellent shoes. The clean black leather looked ridiculous against the rags they wore, but they took the occasion to fetch whatever colorful things they owned and put them on. The day would be forever known as Newshoes Day in the annals of the Norfies.

It was almost always shady on this side of Undercity, nestled and overhung as it was on the northern face of Arregalt's promontory. Tepic did not count himself particularly clever but was pleased nonetheless to deduce that the universally pale skin of the Norfies was no doubt due to their particular geography. Lector Vasherk would have been impressed. He smiled to see that Newshoes Day had started right on cue with the few hours of sun they received at the end of the day.

"Gonna get dishy wif' some new shoes, Dove?" Whale asked around a mouthful of Pacho. He pointed at Tepic's bare feet.

"I'm fine for now, Whale. Good to warm my toes in the sunset, you know?"

". . . warm my toes . . ." Whale repeated under his breath. He shrugged. "Suit ye'self." He took another bite and wandered off.

Fish was standing behind him and now stared at Tepic with a grave face. Ferret saw it too and shuffled over with a suspicious look. He wore brand new high-laced boots that gave him the air of a very small sea captain.

"Oi then," Ferret said. "What's brewing in your kettle, Fish?"

"We 'ave to talk, private-like." Fish eyed side to side. "Bof' of yous."

Ferret frowned. "Come on then."

Tepic was sad to leave his sunny perch but followed inside the tannery through a tangle of cobwebs. They huddled their conspiracy behind a huge rotted barrel.

"Out wif' it," Ferret said.

"Been on the prowl all day and learnt sumuch. Podges," Fish said in a low voice. "They's out podging."

Tepic opened his mouth in confusion but Ferret answered first. "Tin-'eads, Dove, you know—soldiery types."

Fish nodded seriously. "They roughed up sumuch of Chub's lads. Pressed 'em good."

"Fer what?"

"Fer a red-haired kid . . . wif' a fancy sword."

Tepic's skin went cold as both boys looked at him. He didn't know what to say but was suddenly overcome with the familiar urge to bolt.

It seemed like Ferret read his mind. "Now look 'ere, Dove. Don't get all rabbity. Not even a dirty soufy's gonna cooperate just 'cause some podges are bashing 'eads. That's not punctual in Undercity."

Fish agreed. "Not punctual at all. And Norfies would sooner give up they mums than get afeared at tin-'eads."

"There's a rub though, " Ferret said.

Tepic raised his eyebrows but kept quiet.

"They start wif' 'ead-bashing, but then the smart ones bring the tif out."

"Coppers," Fish clarified. "Bribes and such. If they want sumuch, they got tif to pay for it." He tapped the side of his head.

"An' that's when it gets dicey, Dove. Tif get involved, and smart lads go soft in the 'ead."

Fish and Ferret fell silent. Tepic realized it must be his turn to speak.

"What do I do then?"

Ferret shook his head sadly. "You 'ave to go to ground, bruv. Hide somewhere good."

Fish narrowed his eyes. "What'd you do anyway? You nick sumfin?"

Tepic lowered his eyes to the ground. "I suppose I did." He looked up again. "But they nicked it first."

Ferret sucked his lower lip and stuck out his chin. "My boy Dove's an honest chum, an' no one tells me different. You can trust me an' Fish." He shook his head. "And we don't want to know nuffin' else about what you nicked. Better that way."

Fish nodded in agreement. "Say goodbye to the tannery, bruv, and soon. Don't want to be 'ere when the podges come podgin'."

Chapter Thirty-Two

Threshing Fate

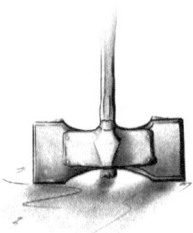

THE HARVEST CAME MORE quickly than even Hobyn's optimism would allow. At first light one breezy morning, he showed up pounding on the door. The old man was more excited than Voldigar had seen him in fifty years, when his hand was quick and his head full of hair. "It's time!" was all Hobyn said and eagerly handed out short sickles to Voldigar and Gardoric, whom Lanathor had sent to the farm before he set out for Eastfort.

The heads of barley listed heavily to one side, *'but not too far'* as Hobyn said. They were dry and thick, and every hint of green had long since faded. The kernels were rigid, and with a firm press, they cracked between Voldigar's fingernails. Gardoric knew nothing of agriculture, but he was a quick mind and a quicker stroke. With Hobyn's instruction, they made fast work of the field while the crinkled gaffer nearly danced through the stalks in his excitement.

In the end, there was so much grain the bundles filled half the house and all of Hobyn's shack, not to mention every hasty shelter they'd erected near the barrel-shaped silos. As they brought in the last of it, they sang silly songs of folly in the barley, and even Gwenyth propped herself in the doorway on aching feet to clap her hands above a great round belly.

The sun-soaked grain required little drying, and Hobyn needed only a few days to voice his satisfaction. Voldigar was wholly in his hands now, like Hobyn's woodland student once again, hanging on every word lest he stumble in the way. In the flurry of a rapid harvest, he forgot his troubles and hid them in a silent forest while he fixed his mind to the task at hand. He would see to the care of every seed.

On another breezy day that smelled of sevenbark, Voldigar was inside, hiding from the mid-day heat. It was a rare rest, and he sat in Gwenyth's rocking chair with eyes closed while she snored in the other room. His mouth moved silently, forming well-worn Chants as he half slept. That was when Wulf showed up unannounced.

The man pushed his huge head through the fragrant sevenbark, growing over the open windows. He looked like an ox intruding on the cart. "Hullo Elder," he said. "I've come to check on my investment."

Outside, Voldigar was surprised to see that Wulf carried a bundle of flails and huge canvas rolls. They had planned to use simple poles and his own bedsheets for threshing, but Wulf's tools would make the work considerably less difficult. Within a few minutes, the farm was all abuzz again. The rhythmic thumping of the flails kept time with another day of simple harvest songs while Wulf regaled them with boasts of the amazing beer he was going to brew.

Winnowing was a more muted affair as they poured grain from bucket to bucket and watched the chaff blow away in the wind. The day had been much cooler, and for once when Voldigar reached to wipe the sweat from his brow, he found there was none. Darkness was near to settle over Aramon by the time they'd dumped the last bucket of grain into the third and final hopper, filling it nearly to the brim. Hobyn closed the hatch with a satisfied grin, a look of finality, and the offer of a firm handshake. "Well done, my boy," he said.

Voldigar took his hand and, nodding his thanks, looked over the stooped man's shoulder. There upon the road, a small, solitary figure was stumbling toward the farm, silhouetted by the setting sun.

Lyrusia was inconsolable. The others had stayed outside while she sobbed into Gwenyth's shoulder and Voldigar looked on with furrowed brow.

"It isn't right," Lyrusia wailed. "Father built every cabinet with his own hands. They gutted it—*gutted* it!"

Gwenyth stroked her hair and spoke softly. "It's alright, Lyrusia, it's alright."

"That brute!" Lyrusia cried and buried her face again.

Through her sobs and broken tale, Voldigar gathered that Lusánt had visited the apothecary—or rather his henchmen had—and had done considerable damage. He looked on in simmering silence until he judged that she had collected herself. She looked every bit the child huddled against Gwenyth's comforting arms. In her great competence as an apothecary, Voldigar never realized just how young she truly was. It made him angry.

"Tepic is missing," she said. Her face twisted in pain. "They think he's hid with me. I knew something was wrong! Last week they claimed he was sick, the week before, they said he was traveling with Lusánt. It was lies, all lies. I haven't seen him in over a month!"

"I know," Voldigar said. "I know he's missing."

Lyrusia's eyes widened in surprise.

"We found out only recently ourselves."

"Why didn't you tell me?" she cried.

Voldigar responded as gently as he could. "We have to wait for you to come to us, Lyrusia. My order is banned from the city. But no matter, please hear me, it's good that your brother is missing."

Lyrusia opened her mouth to object but Voldigar went on. "He's escaped with the sword that's brought so much trouble to your family, and Lusánt is looking for it with all his evil will. But my order is searching too. We will help Tepic." He narrowed his gaze. "What did they do to your shop?"

Lyrusia's eyes looked distant for a moment, but she dropped her gaze to the floor as her hands shook. "They wrecked it, Lector Voldigar. Broke every door and pulled up every floorboard. Destroyed my herbs." She held up a satchel. "This is all I have left. I'm ruined."

Voldigar noticed now that her wrists and neck were covered in bruises, clear marks of rough fingers and struggle. Her garments were torn too. A trembling rage built in his stomach, red and boiling. He'd always had a temper, but the twisting knot that curled within was of a nature he'd not known before. He had to consciously restrain it and could only choke out his next question. "Do you know where Tepic might have gone?"

Gwenyth looked at him warily a moment, then back to the girl.

"I don't," Lyrusia said. "Maybe Eastfort. Maybe to find Father?"

Voldigar clenched his jaw until his teeth ached. "You can stay with us, Lyrusia, as long as you need."

Surprise flashed across her face, but she quickly looked at the floor again. Of all people, the supplier of Gwenyth's medicine knew their deep poverty. "I couldn't," she said. "I'll go on to Eastfort."

Voldigar shook his head. "No. No one should go to Eastfort right now. The danger is even greater there. Stay with us."

Gwenyth nodded and gave a motherly look to Lyrusia. Voldigar could see that his wife needed desperately to lie down, but she stood firmly on her feet and continued to comfort the girl. "I'd be happy of the company," Gwenyth said, "and we have more than we can eat. Let me show you my garden."

"What will you do?" Lyrusia asked Voldigar.

"Something I've put off far too long," Voldigar replied.

Wulf and Gardoric stood in silence in the aspen grove, watching Voldigar while he gripped his maul and stared into the west. Darkness gathered while they waited for him to speak again, and the vanished sun left only a faint glimmer on the horizon.

A disturbing image had arisen in the old man's mind of crashing his great hammer into the wicked device and straight through to the wicked youth that held it, not stopping until he'd split the stone throne on which Lusánt sat—not stopping until Aramon's nightmare was over.

'*Revenge is a baser thing than justice,*' Liadov once said to him. The clawing grip it now held on his heart frightened him, and the rage that undergirded it was untamed. He was ashamed to have let it take hold at all, now or ever. But this white-hot lance was different, focused, a dense mass in the center of his chest. He wondered if this was how the Tellers felt as they fixed their emotions and summoned their magic.

A second fury did battle with the first, this one centered on his own inaction. He'd waited too long for what he knew he must do—while he pretended to be a farmer. He'd let counsel of discretion cloud his mind while hope dwindled away. He hoisted the great hammer over his shoulder as the last light of dusk went black.

"I'm going to Arregalt," Voldigar said at last, "and I may not return. The harvest is over. My promise is fulfilled."

"The time is come then," Gardoric said darkly.

Wulf nodded and took a deep breath. "Lanathor kept men in Maghaltani, ready at your word. I'll gather them and return with horses. Won't take long."

Voldigar shook his head. "No. No more delays. I'm going now and I'm going alone."

Wulf raised his eyebrows. "Alone? What will you do alone?"

"Much, and more than you know," Voldigar said.

"We're going with you," Gardoric said firmly.

"No. The sins are mine, and the curse is on me."

Wulf lowered his brow. "You don't have a choice, old man."

Voldigar searched both faces and exhaled. "I won't try to stop you."

"What's your plan?" Wulf asked.

"To enter by stealth," Voldigar said. "I suppose Gardoric may help in this. We make our way to the Spire. I know a way to the top. We force our path to Lusánt and take the orb. If there is too much resistance, we destroy it on the spot."

"Liadov warned against the destruction of only one key at once," Gardoric said warily.

"I know," Voldigar said, "but we have no choice. The Emperor is turned against his own people. Brelabbus was his doing. The horde was his doing, and now he hides while his people die. We may never have all the keys, and while we hesitate, his evil spreads."

Gardoric nodded and thumbed his hatchets nervously.

"Getting out will be harder than getting in," Wulf said.

"So it will," Voldigar said, "but there is hope in speed." He met their eyes. "And in courage."

Voldigar turned and strode to his farm. What could he say to Gwenyth this time? The words turned over in his mind, but all was smoke and ash. They'd begun to believe their dreams, their mists, and this was not how he wished to wake her. He took a wavering breath before he grasped the handle of his door.

"Don't be rash, Voldigar!" a voice rang out from the field behind.

Voldigar jumped. It was Medellai.

"Don't be rash," Medellai repeated breathlessly. He was bent over double in the headless barley, breathing hard.

Voldigar blinked and narrowed his eyes. "Will my friends forever gainsay me!"

"Head . . . and Heart . . . Brother."

"Your timing is impeccable."

"No . . . I heard you," Medellai said as he stood upright and caught his breath.

"Heard me?"

"Yes, talking to Lyrusia, and talking to the others."

Realization sprang upon Voldigar's face. "Your senses!"

Medellai grinned.

"I'm not sure how I feel about you listening through my walls," Voldigar said.

"All the way from the shrine no less," Medellai said with a laugh. "And it's a good thing I did, before you went off and got yourself killed. I ran all the way here."

"My course is set, Medellai."

"I don't think you understand, Elder. I can hear Tepic too. He's still in Arregalt, and there's still time to change your course."

———— ◆ ————

Gwenyth had finished showing Lyrusia her garden behind the house and left her outside cutting herbs by lamplight. She was now sitting in her chair with a grimace, wrapping her shawl about herself. Medellai leaned against the hearth, his arms crossed and his folded brow a mirror of his sister's.

"I have to go into the city again," Voldigar said to Gwenyth. He was crouched before her chair, holding one of her swollen hands in two of his. Gwenyth did not respond except to tighten her trembling lips.

"I might be gone a day, or two. We know where Tepic is."

"I'm not well, Voldigar," Gwenyth said. Her voice was thin.

"I know." He gently squeezed her hand. "I know, but Lyrusia's here now. She's going to help."

"Her medicine's destroyed."

"She'll find more," he said as cheerfully as he could.

"Rosemary, Voldigar?"

Voldigar swallowed. "In the forest I mean. You'll be alright, Gwen. You just need rest. Remember what she told you."

Gwenyth nodded.

Voldigar forced a chuckle. "We're a little old for this. Not long to go now, and you'll be alright."

"Why do *you* have to go, Vol?"

Voldigar glanced at Medellai briefly. "We can't delay, Gwen, and there cannot be mistakes. The others don't know their way round the city. I do only as I must."

"We'll bring him back, Gwenie," Medellai said. "I won't let him do anything stupid."

Gwenyth rolled her head to the side. Her eyes were still closed. "I don't want to be alone again."

Voldigar bit back sudden emotion working up from his chest. He made his mind up quickly. "I'll leave Wulf here again."

"What if Lusánt comes?"

"We won't bring Tepic here. Lusánt won't have any reason—"

"What if he does anyway?"

Voldigar was silent a moment. "Then let him have a look around. He won't find anything."

"I think I'm going to be sick."

Voldigar nodded but then realized she meant *right now*.

He led her gingerly outside to a quiet corner of long grass where Gwenyth heaved upon the ground. Tears were in her eyes and she swayed on her feet. Lyrusia came softly near holding a bundle of rosemary.

"I can help you with your nausea, m'lady," Lyrusia said with a cheerful smile.

Gwenyth nodded and wiped her mouth with her sleeve.

Voldigar began to speak again but Gwenyth cut him off. "Just go, Vol."

The words stung like a slap. He couldn't think of what to say, but the air shifted as quickly as it came. Gwenyth wrapped her arms weakly around his neck. He could tell she meant to embrace him firmly, but in her weariness, she could only hang limply. He pulled her in and squeezed as tightly as he dared. "I'll be back soon, Gwen. We'll have barley cakes and beer with Wulf. We'll sing songs and scour the woods until Lyrusia's rich again. Just a little longer. Just a little longer . . ."

Gwenyth nodded her head against his shirt and wiped her eyes. She pulled away. Voldigar watched her go, Lyrusia helping her inside once more. Medellai passed them by in the door with a furrowed brow and shut it behind them.

"How sick is she?" Medellai asked.

"Very," Voldigar said. He pulled the hair back from his forehead and stared over the aspens.

"I suppose I should have known."

"She doesn't let on."

Medellai nodded somberly. He glanced at the house again, but his eyes were far away. Voldigar interrupted his thoughts.

"What has Liadov learned?"

Medellai blinked and stroked the corners of his beard. "I'm not sure. It's prophecies again, day and night—when she wasn't helping me. A lot of writing, praying."

"The third key?"

Medellai shook his head.

"We need answers, Brother."

"I know," Medellai said. "If we cannot find the third, and they must be destroyed together, we are at an impasse. I still wonder if she might use the sword herself instead. Or, God have mercy, teach Tepic."

Voldigar's eyes widened. "Use it?"

"Yes. You heard what she said. It set her free, and Tepic is its Wielder. I've thought much on those words since. She speaks of it more in prophecies. A mighty artifact, and to it they are bound."

Voldigar worked his hand and stared at his fingers. "But look what Lusánt has wrought with his."

"Lusánt is a petulant tyrant. Liadov is the greatest living adherent of Aramon's most sacred truths."

Voldigar shook his head in disbelief. "Listen to us. To think the Brotherhood would ever speak of the sovereign like this."

"It's not without precedent," Medellai said darkly.

Voldigar let out a long sigh. "Too many mysteries, Brother. Whatever we do, we do with haste, or all our plans are for naught. First Tepic and the sword. We'll send them both to Liadov."

Medellai nodded, then licked his lips and thought a moment. "You know, you don't have to go with us, Brother. We can solve this without you."

Voldigar shook his head. "I won't see you burned up again—and the city is crawling with Gamad's men. I will lead you on the fastest path. That is my duty."

Medellai held Voldigar's gaze a moment longer. "You have a lot to lose. Gardoric can get us through without you—even if it takes longer."

"Medellai, I'm going."

The two fell silent until Medellai shook his head and gave a defeated sigh. They rejoined Wulf and Gardoric in the aspen grove.

"Wulf, I'd like you to stay here," Voldigar said.

Wulf looked like he'd eaten a bogberry, and he sent a great breath out of his nostrils. For a moment, Voldigar thought the man might strike something or someone, but as quickly as it came, the expression was replaced by an amused smile.

"To be honest," Wulf said, "I'm tired of stealth. I'll watch your cabbages, old man. Don't get killed."

Voldigar searched for a word of apology or thanks, but Wulf slapped his back and was trudging to the house whistling before he could reply.

"Well," Voldigar asked. "Where's the boy?"

Medellai walked off a space to the edge of the aspen grove and closed his eyes. The breeze picked up a bit, and Voldigar was surprised at an unfamiliar sensation. Cold. Through the long withering heat of Aramon's most remarkable summer, the intrusion of chilly evening air was unexpected.

"The sound is faint," Medellai said. "He may be sleeping. But he's . . . below the city, I'm certain of it."

Voldigar nodded. "Undercity. I'm not surprised he went there, only that he stayed."

"Quite a spot to hide. Just as soon to end up dead in a gutter," Gardoric said. "No place for a boy."

"He's more clever than he seems. We have to hope he's done well for himself," Voldigar replied. "Let's be off, while his luck holds."

The docks of Arregalt ran for miles all about the base of its great promontory, most numerous near its point, but with vast gaps of nothing where rubbish was pushed into the sea from high above. While they could be accessed from Undercity, merchants and porters from above did not go that way. Instead, there were long roads that descended along the southern and northern sides. At first, they switched back again and again near the curtain wall, and then ran straight on huge causeways, well clear of the shanty towns that clung to the cliffs.

It was to the northern road, not far from his farm, that Voldigar chose to lead them. While the southern road was heavily trafficked and had no less than a dozen guard posts and tolls, the northern had fallen into disuse long ago. In the shadow of those cliffs, crime and filth overtook guards and tolls, and like the inner roads, tradesmen no longer traveled it. Only the entrance was now guarded, if only to keep Undercity out. Voldigar knew the road itself was now a pitted waste, crumbling into the sea. It was the perfect way into Undercity.

The night was dark and the moonlight pale, but they moved easily through the brush toward Voldigar's ford. His two companions were experienced woodsmen both and kept pace or even walked ahead as Gardoric did now. Voldigar let his thoughts wander while they marched.

"She didn't say the words," he said quietly to himself. Medellai was at his shoulder.

"The words?" Medellai asked.

Voldigar looked up. "Yes. 'Do your duty.' She always says that."

Medellai sighed and reached a hand out to pat Voldigar's shoulder. "You think too much, Vol, and that's coming from me."

"Or not enough, Brother. It was dark musing before you wandered into my barley patch."

"I know," Medellai said.

"You know what I said," Voldigar replied. "But not my thoughts, unless Liadov's given you a new gift."

Medellai chuckled. "Alas, no. I'll leave that to Taro. I do have limits."

Voldigar shook his head. "It wasn't good, Medellai. All I could think of was avenging us against the Emperor, that I could solve another problem with a swing of my hammer."

Medellai nodded. "It's alright, Brother. I think we've all fantasized a bit at this point."

"No," Voldigar said quietly. "It's not alright. He's just a boy, a foolish lost boy, and running headlong down a wicked path."

Medellai sighed. "I'd contend that he's a man now, Voldigar. But maybe there is hope for him yet. He had the best teachers after all."

They passed the next hour in silence until they'd reached the northeastern tip of Arregalt's wall that jutted out over the sea. There was a guard tower there that ostensibly overlooked and barred the entrance to the road, but this they evaded easily. Gardoric wished aloud for his ropes and hooks, but the night was dry, and with deft downward climbing, or horizontally at times, they were soon clear of the tower and descending the switchbacks in rapid turns.

The condition of the road was worse than Voldigar remembered. In places, great pieces of it were not only crumbling but simply gone, tumbled into the sea in some bygone year. Here and there, they resorted to climbing again, and the crescent moon was high in the sky by the time they'd reached the bottom. It was here they saw a confounding thing.

In all their long descent, they'd not noticed—for who would look for such a thing—but the sea was simply gone. Or rather it was far away, and a sloping beach now ran for a hundred yards where the ocean ought to be until it finally sunk beneath the distant waves. Gardoric had spent a fair time at sea, and the others watched him while he blinked and gaped.

"The tide?" Voldigar asked. He knew he was wrong.

"No," Gardoric said, "not the tide. I . . . I don't understand . . ."

Farther away, where the docks began and water should have been, there were a few vessels wedged in the sand and rocks, and the huge blocks of the quays stood exposed in the moonlight, bristling with barnacles. Of the docks which had previously floated, they now stood at wild angles leading to the uncovered seabed below. Many vessels had been drawn further out where they bobbed in the waves, far below the lip of the docks.

Medellai shook his head. "Something has drained the ocean."

"Men will be upon the quays tonight, no doubt," Voldigar said. "Let's keep moving."

The brothers pulled plain hoods upon their heads and went along the endless causeway, marveling at the sand below. They had to leap over broken sections, but it was better than sinking into the wet seafloor. To their left, many rickety bridges extended out from the lowest structures of Undercity to touch and overlap the causeway. On the southern road, these would have been violently cleared away, but not so here on the north. It was like a jungle crawling outward to reclaim a ruined city.

The brothers watched these paths warily for any that might come across to interfere. The tower guards were far behind, but thousands of windows looked down on them from Undercity. From these, they could surely be seen, but they reached the more numerous docks near the western end before they encountered another soul.

Here, a man in a threadbare coat trying very hard to look official demanded tolls from them. Medellai paid without complaint. The trickle of souls soon grew into a lamplit press upon the wharf, where man and miridas mixed freely in a jostling crowd of sailors and peddlers, merchants and beggars, and colorful persons of every sort. The pungent air of the sea, so long uncovered, had grown to a nauseating reek. Many voices complained loudly of it while hapless ocean creatures rotted in the dark.

As they shouldered through the throng, Voldigar gathered snippets of conversation. Apparently, the tide had gone out that day, then gone out some more, and then simply never came back. Ships were beached, vessels tipped, and cargoes lost. In a word, disaster—and the frantic crowds were gathered late at night for this very reason, still scrambling to recover what they could and respond to the mess while they shivered in the unexpected cold. There were many soldiers from above here too, and Voldigar was glad for the chaos. With their eyes fixed firmly toward the bay, no one noticed three more wanderers slipping along the docks.

At length, Medellai stopped and gathered them close.

"He's moving," he whispered and pointed. "Upward."

Voldigar peered at the glowing lights of Undercity above them and pulled his cloak against the chill. "The Delvings," he said. "He'll be somewhere in the caves." They hurried from the docks and left the mystery of the missing sea behind. Their only hope lay ahead, a lost boy with the fate of them all in his hands.

CHAPTER THIRTY-THREE

MOONLIT HEIGHTS

I T WAS A CHILLY night under the crescent moon, and Lanathor was ascending a flight of steps to Aramon's highest and most eastern wall. The great mass of stone called Eastfort stretched from one sheer mountain to another, barring the way from lands beyond. The air was always colder here and the pass only briefly cleared, yet a blazing summer had reached even to these peaks. It was a shame it ended so soon. For tonight, frigid wind gnawed at his bones, whistling from a cloud that hung over ominous moonlight heights.

Lanathor emerged under a starry sky, clear save for the gray mantle upon the mountains ahead. He was carrying a tray with two mugs of fragrant tea. One for him and one for Vasherk. Since he'd arrived at Eastfort with seventy of Maghaltani's brethren, he assigned three to join Dantic's watch nightly along this wall overlooking the long slope to Kurath and Tituria. Vasherk sat humming near the center by an open-faced turret with a huge bell. His feet were propped on the parapet and his hands folded behind his head. A solitary brother often sat here, but tonight, Vasherk was joined by a broad-faced soldier in Dantic's blue livery.

"Evening, Elder," Vasherk said. He and the soldier gratefully took the tea and warmed their hands. "Pull up a chair."

Lanathor did and sat quietly with them, staring alternately at the stars or the pine-wooded land below. His red cloak was lined with fur again, and

Vasherk looked the twin in his own, though his hung open to show a rapier and a broad short blade on his other hip.

"Elder Lanathor, meet Corporal Rul."

"Reverend," the man said with a duck of the chin. His eyes widened at the sight of Lanathor, but he quickly hid his surprise.

"A pleasure," Lanathor replied. "Rul is not a name I've heard before."

"Titurian," the man said with a chuckle and a heavy accent. "Got in a little trouble back home and joined the guard here. You know how it is."

Vasherk laughed. "Lanathor knows all right."

"What was your trouble?" Rul asked. "Never seen a Daneki with wizards for friends."

"Wizards?" Vasherk smirked and blew a puff of misty air. He took a sip, then handed his cup to the Elder. "Stay warm and help us watch for ghouls. Every province has their own fairy-tale nightmare now. It's bets on which one shows up first."

"Bashevi is not a Titurian word," Rul said. "Back home we call them *Varpan.*"

"Varpan?" Lanathor tested the word on his tongue. He spoke some Titurian but this word was unfamiliar.

"Yes," Rul went on, "and to think I'm on a wall waiting for a horde of them. Suppose I should count myself lucky. Can't imagine what it's like back home."

"Worth your prayers—and your vigilance," Lanathor said.

Rul nodded. "You're a reverend, right? Are the Varpan, er . . . Bashevi actually real?"

"Close enough to the mark, and yes, they are very real."

Rul shook his head in wonder. "It's just tales to scare naughty little boys."

"Blooddrinkers," Lanathor said. Vasherk raised his eyebrow but the Elder went on. "They start small, a drop of blood and little more than a mouth. They seek more after that, growing strong as they may. The Wyrna and Odomo are their cousins. The first are cruel crossings of animals and men. The other are spirits that search for broken things and gather them upon their bodies."

"Fine conversation for a cup of tea," Vasherk said.

"A man should know what he's fighting," Lanathor replied.

Rul nodded. "Can they be killed? You know, spirits?"

"Indeed they can," Lanathor said. "Their forms are flesh, of a sort. You can destroy it as you destroy a man's."

Doubt still rested on Rul's face. "Where do they come from?"

"Awful burrows and cruel places, bred in shadow."

Vasherk shifted uncomfortably and passed the tea to Lanathor again. "Have some more tea, Lan."

Rul's questions ceased, and he seemed lost in thought, a somber mood settling over his face as he stared into the dark. Lanathor thought of Liadov, as he often did, and wondered if she'd found the answers that she sought.

"Is it true that The Brotherhood of Aramon only believe in one God?" Rul asked at length.

"Don't get him started, Rul," Vasherk laughed. "We've only got one watch."

"I'm curious," the young soldier pressed on. "Why would you want just one? There's star and moon, mountains and sea."

"Because it's true, Rul, that's why. It was all of Aramon that once believed as we do."

Rul's eyebrows shot up. "No . . ."

Lanathor pointed up at the stars. "Do you know which one is Patradavi? The Pole Star?"

Rul pointed.

"Right," said Lanathor, "and all of these have names. But did you know there was a time when none of them wandered and all were as constant as he?"

Rul was attentive now, and even Vasherk looked over for the tale, familiar as it was.

"Yes," Lanathor went on, "in a great liminal expanse of the sky, they rested still as stones, suspended in the sea above. They stretched across a band of the heavens right over the center of the world and looked down upon a glistening field of living snow. It was their domain, and life flourished beneath them in a cold that did not bite."

"And on either side, a mild sun and a warm moon did not wander either but shone great and bright over the lands that God had given them. A clear night of joyful silver under the one, and for the other, an endless day of golden peace."

"But they learned their names, Rul, and shared them with men. Glory that belonged to their creator, they stole for themselves, and in their pride, they sought to make their own song. God had played every perfect melody upon the instruments he made, and even let them sing their own harmonies. The pillars and structures of that great Song were life itself, all that exists, perfection. The filaments of creation and the vibrations of that great work. But they would have it not, and men followed them to their discordant doom."

"Only Patradavi did not join them in their madness, for that name is one given by men, and he never shared his secret. For this, I love him best. He drew those wayward ornaments into his orbit, save for a few. He is faithful to this day and grieves the twisted worship of foolish men. His light honors God alone, as should we all."

Rul blinked while his tea steamed. Lanathor held him in his gaze a little longer. "Men have followed on in their rebellion ever since, my friend Rul. We have one God because he made all things." Lanathor turned his eyes away and sighed. "The people of Aramon once knew this, but men now worship the things that were made, rather than the one who made them."

"That's . . . quite a god," Rul said. "Just one to make all this?" He spread his hands wide.

"Yes," Lanathor replied. "And now you know the root of the Bashevi, the Odomo, and the Wyrna. That same wandering envy formed those wicked things."

Rul contemplated a moment while he resumed his watch over the pass. "It's a good story, Reverend. But I don't buy it. I just hope there's not too many of them."

"And that they don't like tea," Vasherk added.

Rul laughed but then took on a more serious face. "What do you think happens when we die?"

Lanathor lifted a brow. "Perhaps it's not the time."

Vasherk answered instead. "Judgment," he replied. "Before the almighty God."

"You believe all that too?" Rul asked.

Vasherk laughed. "These cursed *wizards* take all kinds, even old Vasherk."

"I suppose he only judges Brothers worthy then?" Rul asked.

Vasherk shook his head. "Not so, my friend. He judges no one worthy."

Rul scowled. "Your religion depresses me. What does he even want then?"

"Just trust, Rul. What else can we give? And then to trust his mercy, until the day of his redemption and the day we join the Song."

"Honor God," Lanathor added.

"God's honor," Vasherk replied.

The night fell quiet again for a while, but Rul soon stood. "What is that?" he asked.

Lanathor thought the inquisitive man was asking another question of theology, but glancing up he saw that Rul now leaned over the battlements, pointing into the darkness.

Lanathor hurried to his side on stiff legs and peered into the shadows where he pointed. There was movement in the distance, a flicker at first, but then of many shapes. Flitting shadows danced upon the ground and flashed on the trunks of pines. Hand over hand they were lifting something from the ground as more and more shapes emerged from the woods.

As it came into view, all three men gasped and recoiled. In the shivering moonlight, it was plain to see the body of a man, impaled upon a pike and hoisted high by a crowd of twisted forms. Countless more came forward, a growing wall of dark figures.

"They have come," Lanathor said.

A roar came up from the massing horde, a rolling wave of gibbering shrieks and maddening howls. The tormented cries of rank upon rank of hateful spirits, their glinting eyes gleaming in the night.

Rul sprinted to the bell and rang it furiously. The sound was drowned in the thunder of their foe.

———— ◆ ————

Whether by the booming toll of the great bell or the clamor of their foe, the quiet fortress sprang suddenly to life. The shouts of men and the ring of steel erupted all about Lanathor in a chorus of alarm. Rul was joined by a group of men who emerged from a nearby hatch. Lord Dantic ascended stairs three at a time with Urias just behind and leapt upon the huge gatehouse that was near at hand. He was still struggling to hastily secure a meager studded brigandine. There would be no time to fetch his mail.

A tide of dark shapes was surging forward already, heedless of any sort of discipline or formation. The garrison of Eastfort might have been surprised beyond remedy had the enemy used subtlety of any kind, but this charging mass was a rampage of noise and rage. Half a thousand men were upon the wall now with bow and javelin in hand. Dantic held his hand high and bellowed loud commands to his left and then his right. A bannerman whipped his flag from side to side, and the air was split by the whistling cry of innumerable darts.

The dreadful thump of piercing blows reverberated down the line, and Lanathor could now clearly see their obscene enemy. The Wyrna he knew well, with a veritable menagerie of hideous malformations displayed below. Besides these, there were ghastly constructs of dangling gore, alloyed with splintered stone and rotting wood. Blotched amongst the writhing mass were cowering hairless things of smooth gray flesh and cruel fangs. Countless eyes of red and ghost-light green burned spiteful in the dark. Hundreds fell and Dantic cried for more.

Lanathor dwelt in doubt for a moment only. He flicked the lid of a capsule with his thumb. The root was a familiar furnace in his chest and flushed to his fingertips as the foremost row of nightmares faltered and recoiled. There were not many bows among the horde, but there were many spears. A great flight of these hurtled thickly through the gloom.

Lanathor cracked the air like thunder and splintered a wide berth of the missiles into a harmless rain of dust, but he could hear the anguished cries of men as the violence hit its mark upon the wall to either side. A brilliant flash of light blinded him for an instant. Then, two long streaks of fire streamed down from the gate and licked the ground before they crashed into the creatures in an inferno of white-hot ash and fury.

The beastly throng howled in their chaos and smashed bodily into the gate, pressing with no implement save their crushing weight. They fell in steaming mounds of shambling revulsion, but still they came on as all the valley filled in rippling blackness. The walls shuddered. The gate boomed and groaned—but firm it stood against their madness. Many vile hands scraped fruitlessly at stone and wood, iron and earth, but the men of Eastfort kept them pinned below.

All sound became a formless drone as guardsman and Brother stood side by side, raining oblivion down upon the enemy, wave upon wave. Surely only minutes had passed, but Lanathor's arms and mind ached with the effort of hours as he focused all his will upon the battle. From deep within the ranks of the enemy, a new movement emerged of long things like snakes weaving through their swarm. It was soon apparent that these were trees, stripped of most their limbs and borne by many hands, rushing forward all across the valley floor.

"They climb! They climb!" Lanathor shouted. The trees were soon propped against the wall at perilous angles. Many were too short, and others were simply dropped as their bearers perished in a hail of arrows, but by their sheer number, all along the wall, the trunks of trees were secured in place. Men frantically pulled the logs aside and sent them careening back to the ground below, but the wall of Eastfort was too wide and its defenders too few to stop them all. In a breathless plunge of terror, the evil was upon the wall swinging wildly with axe and sickle.

The ring of swords echoed now from the snowy peaks, and the smell of hot blood and terror rushed upon the wind. To his side, Lanathor saw Taro swinging *Skullcrusher* in wide arcs, sending beasts flying from the wall. Vasherk he saw there too, but only for a moment as both were swallowed up in a flailing melee. Another flash, and a huge fireball arced high in the air before it came crashing like a comet into the heart of the horde that still pressed forward below. Urias remained above with arms stretched wide and red-gold fissures breaking open upon his wrists.

By some miracle, the melee was repulsed there on the center and north of the wall. Lanathor could not see the southern half where Soris fought and could only hope the man still held. A sudden fury of flying spears sped to the top of the gatehouse and was renewed again and again. Lanathor brought some of them down, then sprinted up two flights of narrow steps just in time to see a javelin rake across Dantic's brave face.

"Dantic!" Lanathor cried out, but the veteran soldier barely flinched. A wide line of red blood spread under his eye, but his face was stone. He motioned for Lanathor to come to his side, and they both ducked beneath the merlons.

"We can't do this forever!" Dantic shouted. "How many are there?"

Lanathor shook his head in wide-eyed doubt and buried the rising fear in his heart. Subconsciously he felt for more of the root in his pockets and found a few more capsules there. "I don't know, but they must have some end. Keep fighting!"

Lanathor looked north along the wall where he could again see Taro and Vasherk working side by side. There'd been some sort of breach at the far end where winged Bashevi whirled and leapt. He caught a glimpse of Vasherk pulling Corporal Rul to safety before the melee was drowned in chaos once again.

Near at hand, Urias was breathing hard and blinking in a daze. He stared into the dark below, fixed on some point of movement that came on directly toward the gate. Returning to his feet, Lanathor followed his gaze and to his horror saw a hulking shape pressing its way through the throng.

At first, he thought it was a bear, perhaps some hideous creation of the Wyrna, but it was far too big. Many limbs of oozing flesh and tarry debris rolled like a centipede bearing a head of twisted wood and crumbled rock. Lanathor had little time to wonder, for the volleys of spears renewed again and his hands flashed to bend the space before them and send the missiles clattering to the ground.

"The gate, Urias! It's coming for the gate!" Lanathor cried through gritted teeth.

Urias stood in a stupor, looking down at his smoking hands.

Lanathor too was growing weary and tried in vain to send some wave of force against the creature, but he could muster very little. His attention was divided, doing all he could to secure the men upon the gate. They returned fire in massive volleys, but it seemed all the fury of the horde was now fixed here.

Lanathor whipped his head to the south and searched frantically for Soris. From his vantage, he could see him now, battling among a host of men against a group of Wyrna that still laid fallen trees along the wall. "Soris!" he cried. "To the gate! To the gate!"

A moment more and Soris bounded up to the high tower, blue light already swirling between his outstretched hands. No explanation was needed as his eyes went wide at the sight below. The massive Odomo construct was charging on now like an avalanche moving uphill. Its allies were carelessly tossed aside as it gained speed and lowered its body to crash into the gate.

An arcing web of icy lances spiraled from Soris's hands and curled in on themselves in a vortex of shimmering glass toward the ground before the gate. Lanathor ducked and watched as power spilled over the bulwark. Soris's weave gathered into many points and thrust up from the earth while his eyes and mouth radiated a pale glow. The apexes of the frigid pikes slammed into the Odomo with such a tremendous crack that all other sound was numbed. The creature tumbled to the ground, slid, and then held still, mere feet from the door.

Tension dropped from Soris's arched back and he fell backward upon the stone where the beryl rings about his arms burst in a shower of shimmering dust. He lay still and gray, save for his heaving chest. Lanathor looked over the bulwark again and sighed in disbelief. The horde was melting away below. Dantic was soon at his side, wiping blood away from his wounded face. He rested his hand upon the wall to watch them flee. No one dared to speak, and Lanathor could only dimly hear their labored breathing through his ringing ears.

Vasherk found him there on the wall, a study in blood and sweat, but he looked unharmed. He stared off into the distance too and breathed deeply.

Lanathor examined the man. He seemed as hale as ever and smiled like he'd just woken up. "None of that blood is yours, is it?" Lanathor asked.

Vasherk smirked. "Doubtful." The sound came muffled, as though his ears were packed with mud.

Lanathor narrowed his eyes and tried to rub the dull roar out of his head. "Are you ever hurt, old man?"

Vasherk laughed and wiggled his fingers. "Fast hands, Elder." He looked out over the corpse-strewn field again. "Are they gone then?"

Lanathor smiled and peered into the darkness with him. The smile faded as quickly as it came, and his face twisted in grief and despair that no Falam

Root could hide. In the glowing light of many burning trees, another horde amassed on the edge of sight, much like the first, save only that it was twice as large.

"No, Brother . . . they've only just begun."

Chapter Thirty-Four

PINNED AND STRUCK

ON A COOL NIGHT after the tide went out and never came back, Tepic was in Cozi's workshop saying goodbye to his friends—and goodbye to Dove. It was pandemonium on the wharf and in the streets, and the folk of Undercity, mariners most of all, proclaimed it was the end of days. Ferret, Fish, and Pig decided this was the perfect night to disappear.

Tepic studied the tharmskolp in secret for many hours before he determined what to do. There was a cavern deep within the Delvings that was very hard to find from above or below and where, were he to have need, the nearest exit was right by the canal he'd swam through long ago. If he had to disappear into the hinterlands, he could. When he needed supplies from above, they were near. There should even be water available where one of the falls of Arregalt tumbled nearby through the promontory. It was the perfect hideout.

Not only was it obscure, but not far along the only path that led to it from Undercity, there was a curious rounded hollow. Tepic had described a few possible hideouts to Ferret, and this one the boy rejected out of hand. '*Too close,*' he said. But he also added, '*That room's full of coin, or I'm a dog-faced shrew.*' So convinced was Ferret, that he decided they'd travel that far with Tepic and be the richest lads in Undercity by the time they got back. Tepic would go on alone from there for two more miles into the enclosing darkness of the tunnels, and no one would know which way he'd gone.

He made himself a little song to remember the way, turn by turn. He even gave Ferret a charcoal-written map on a scrap of cloth to find his way back from the hollow, but the first step required passage through a door that sat right in the back of Cozi's workshop. Cozi stood beside it with his arms crossed and a sour face. "I's just gettin' used to 'avin' you around, Dove. You ever coming back?"

"I don't know," Tepic said. He was staring at his feet—new boots that Whale finally convinced him to take before he left. "You've been kind to me, but I don't want to bring you any more trouble."

Cozi scoffed and batted his hand. "I've dealt with podges longer than you four 'ave been alive—combined. You was gonna make me rich, Dove. Tha's all."

Tepic looked up and smiled. "My name is Tepic. Tepic Banari. If you ever need to find me, that's who to look for."

Four sets of eyebrows raised. Ferret scratched his head and stepped forward sheepishly. "My title's Roger, just plain Roger."

"I ain't 'ave a name," Pig said. "Just Pig."

Tepic laughed. The ritual felt strange but good, like letting out breath you've been holding too long. "What about you, Fish?"

Fish was spinning something on one of the many broken toys Cozi had stashed around the room and took a moment to catch up. "Oi?"

"Do you have a real name?"

"Oh, Ferret knows. I don't goes around tellin' no one."

"His name's Roger too," Ferret said with a grin. "Was a funny bit. That's how all this nonsense wif' animals got started. Guess we don't 'ave enough proper names in Undercity."

Tepic laughed again and took a deep breath. He'd made up his mind. "Cozi, I have a present for you." He took the tharmskolp from his pocket and held the device out to him.

He wished he could have painted the face that Cozi made. It was as if his chin and eyebrows fled from each other. He feared the old mokja might faint and even steadied him by the shoulder.

"Tym'cha's Teef'!" Cozi exclaimed. "How'd you get this? It's . . . but . . ." His eyes narrowed. "You nick this from someone?"

Tepic shook his head. "It was a gift, from a man who wanted me to do something important."

"Where'd *he* get it!" Cozi asked, incredulous.

"I don't know, but he's a good man, and I think you are too, Cozi." Tepic spoke as gravely as he could. "I don't know if you all know what happens topside, but there's terrible things going on there now."

Cozi took the map in two hands and held it like a mother with her first child.

"Awful things," Tepic continued, "and I'm afraid it's come to Undercity now too. You might have to do something brave, Cozi, if it all comes down to it."

Cozi grinned and let out a bemused laugh. "You really are one crazy seabird. Like an angel 'frough a poop-shoot. Wait 'ere."

Cozi disappeared and emerged from the back room a second later with a plump sack in one hand and a wineskin in the other. "This here's pacho, an' real wine." He shook the skin. "That 'fing you gave me's worf' every bit of pacho in Undercity—an' a ship to carry it all. If Tepic Banari ever needs old Cozi, he'll come running."

"He might. Goodbye, Cozi."

"Goodbye, Tepic. An' don't you fret about me. Tin 'eads is riled up, but it'll pass."

"I hope so."

Cozi unlocked the tiny door. Musty air flowed out, and the squat mokja extended an ushering hand. Tepic turned to say something but Cozi cut him off with a raised finger. "I don't wants to know nuffin' about nuffin'. Best that way."

Tepic nodded and led Pig and the two Rogers down a long stone path with a sputtering torch.

———— ◦◦◦ ————

Tepic held his breath while Ferret pressed his ear against the door. There wasn't supposed to be a door here, just a low arch, but the tharmskolp wasn't always current. Tepic had no idea how old the device was, but clearly, some things had changed since it was fashioned. He couldn't double-check since Cozi had it now, but it didn't matter—he was sure this was the spot. The round hollow, more like a dome, had to be beyond this little door.

"Nuffin'," Ferret whispered. This was his second listen, and Pig had tried too. "Get to it, chum."

The door was locked, but Fish was never without his picks. He'd assembled and maintained the crude kit for as long as Tepic had run with them, and surely many years before. Fish tapped the tip of his nose with his tongue and got to work. Tepic was surprised to hear the pop of a spring only seconds later.

"Pants!" Fish proclaimed, a little too loudly. "Too easy."

Ferret reclaimed his place at the front of the line. He signaled for Tepic to quench his torch and then slowly pushed the door open. They were surprised to see a thin glow of light emerging from somewhere ahead. All four of them froze and held their breath to listen again.

Tepic's eyes adjusted to the light, and he could see that they were surrounded by garments hanging from many racks and were crowded all about by haphazard boxes, stacked and sometimes spilling their contents upon a moldy carpet. The room smelled of long decay, and he saw that the source of light was from an ill-fitting door at the top of a precarious staircase. In the dark, it was just a glowing rectangle.

"Moldy blankets," Pig whispered. They were picking through the boxes and throwing handfuls of tattered textiles to the floor.

Ferret had given up his search through the crates and was staring at the door. "Treasure's up there, I says."

Tepic chewed his lip. "Why's it lit up?" he whispered.

Ferret considered a moment and then tiptoed up the stairs. They creaked awfully in the silence, but there were only a few, and Ferret was soon listening again while they held their breath. "Nobody 'ome," he said aloud.

Tepic hesitated.

"Better quick than quiet. Now's the time if you're coming, Dovey."

Tepic nodded and followed.

This door was unlocked and Ferret pushed it open. It caught after only a few inches. The others crowded round and Tepic reached through the gap to gently push a piece of furniture out of the way—nothing more than a small couch. They funneled into the chamber beyond, and Fish let out a low whistle.

The hollow was some thirty feet across with a low, domed roof and richly furnished. A set of double doors was across from where they stood, the only gap in a circle of ornate bureaus, desks, benches, and shelves of every kind. The floor was blanketed with furs and carpets, and the furnishings were draped with sumptuous cloths. In the flicker of many sconces, vessels of gold and silver shone all about. One sparkling urn was polished so smooth it glimmered like a looking glass.

"Someone lives here," Tepic whispered. "We have to go."

"A minute, love-boo," Ferret said with irritation. He was opening his sack and the others followed suit with hungry hands. "There's a fortune 'ere. Quick nick, an' then we break a fiddle."

There was an odd smell in the room that Tepic could not quite place, like a piece of memory he'd meant to tuck away. It reminded him of fish and metal and it made his skin crawl. There was a round stone in the center of the room, perfectly flat, and dark stains covered its surface. Tepic backed away toward the little door.

"That's enough loot," he said. "It's not safe here."

Ferret scowled. "'Course it's not sa—" The double doors opened and three stooped figures stepped into the room.

The youths froze only for an instant before a great clamor erupted and they rushed back toward the little door, metal clanging in their half-filled sacks. Tepic was closest to the exit and gave the couch a wild shove. It moved a foot or so before suddenly, and to his great amazement, reversing course and sweeping his legs out from under him. He hit the ground hard and looked up to see that the central figure had stepped forward. A long pendant dangled from her hand. The other she stretched out toward their escape.

Tepic scrambled backward wildly and found the couch pressed against the door. All four pulled fiercely at it, but it was stuck fast, some unseen force holding it where it stood.

"I told you that door would be trouble, Halma," the central figure said in the croaking voice of an old woman. Her two companions also dropped pendants to dangle from their hands and moved forward together, each with a strange, bobbing, predatory gait.

"*Sheyak beya nadooram,*" one of the others replied. It was the language of the Miridas. Tepic knew it from the docks but understood nothing of it.

"Speak in their tongue. It will increase their fear," the central figure said.

No matter how they struggled, the couch would not budge. Tepic grit his teeth and reached for the sword on his back, but found to his dismay that his arms would not respond to his will. A second more and his body took on another will entirely. Four sharp thumps and all four youths were lifted from the ground and forced against the wall to squirm like insects under the twisting hands of the three miridas crones.

The figure who had spoken first came within a few inches of Tepic's face. The pendant hung on a silver chain and was perfectly round, bearing a large marbled pearl in its center.

"Are these ones yours?" the third figure asked. Her voice was like the sound of a heavy brush against a sheet of tin.

"No," she replied. "Augur them."

Gently, almost motherly, the figures gathered about the children. One held her pendant in front of Pig's mouth. "Breathe child." The old woman held the pendant there a moment before she pulled it away and examined it. "Nothing."

They repeated the ritual dispassionately down the line. "Plain little goats then," their leader said at last.

They worked the weapons off of the children's backs and waists. Most they laid upon the couch, but the central figure flipped Tepic's sword over and over again in her free hand. "There's magic about this one."

"Augur him again," said one of the others.

She turned her eyes back to Tepic. They were green, as green as Lady Gwenyth's eyes, but there were no irises in them, just a pool of color in wrinkled pits. The miridas woman had the unsettling echo of long-lost femininity, replaced by a drawn, pale blue flesh, pulled into a tight mockery against the bones of her face. Her breath was putrid, and thick lines of blood framed her jagged white teeth. She held the pendant to his lips again and pulled it away to examine it once more with a squinting expression.

"What is this weapon, child?" she hissed.

Horror filled his heart, and Tepic pulled his head from side to side. His voiceless cry came out in strangled gasps.

"Answer me!" The crone's voice reverberated from the ceiling.

A dreadful compulsion arose in Tepic's mind to tell the old woman everything—his name, his home, all he knew of the sword. He bit his tongue and tightly closed his eyes. His limbs were pinned, and he could not struggle more than a pitiful twitch.

One of the crones behind inhaled deeply. "These ones are ripe."

"The girl first," said the other.

With great effort, Tepic turned his head to the side. He could see Pig there, squirming with only a little more success than he, her legs kicking against the wall where she was pinned. He could hear now too, labored whimpering from all of his friends.

In a moment, Tepic's memory came flooding back. The rancid smell was that of blood. The reek of it had sickened him in the officers' chambers where the Orun had attacked those months before. It seemed like years ago, but the smell had haunted him ever since, like a lingering nightmare.

They dragged Pig to the stone slab in the center of the room and laid her flat upon her back. Her mouth and eyes hung open. The woman with a voice like tin drew a long curved knife from her emerald-colored robes and held it high while the others looked eagerly on. The miridas, the green, the pearls—they were like a cruel shadow of Kyriana, as hideous as she was fair.

"Wait! Wait! I'll tell you!" Tepic cried.

The crone looked up. "You will tell us. You will tell us everything."

"Kyriana! I know Kyriana! She's my friend."

The old women stopped. A look of confusion passed between them. The central figure crossed quickly back to Tepic in her alien, stumbling gait. She gripped him by his chin.

"What do you know of Kyriana? Who are you?"

Tepic opened his mouth to answer, but in that very moment, the door beside him burst inward with an eruption of splintering wood.

Sword-Lector Voldigar, Tepic saw first, hurling a blade like a disc across the chamber as he vaulted over the couch. The old man caught the crone nearest Tepic by her torso in a hurdling tackle, and her hand wrenched free from his chin. As Voldigar drove the one to the ground with a crunch, his blade struck the other woman who held the knife over Pig. The miridas shrieked. Her feet left the ground and she careened against the wall.

The third woman hissed and backed against the far door, her eyes wide in terror and fury, her pendant held high. With a sound like a boiling pot, a sudden burst of light momentarily blinded Tepic. An arcing array, a stroke of green lightning, erupted from the woman's outstretched hand and flashed across the room.

Another man with auburn hair and white streaks in his beard charged into the hollow and thrust his arm forward in a violent gesture. The glowing beams coalesced onto his forearm where they were swallowed up like water into thirsty ground. A third man emerged a moment after and dashed toward the miridas who still held her pendant. A quick swing of his bone-blade hatchet and the battle was over. Tepic felt a pressure release under him, and he slid to fall seated on the floor.

With faces grim, the three men efficiently secured the bodies and searched the room. The auburn-haired man seemed familiar, but the man with the hatchet, Tepic recognized from Westfort as Gardoric. He watched as Gardoric slid a desk against the far doors, and then all three turned toward the children.

"Tepic," Voldigar said breathlessly. "Are you hurt?"

Tepic shook his head.

The old man exhaled and a smile crept onto his face. "You did it, Tepic. You really did it—and thank God we're here in time. These are brothers of my order, Medellai, and Gardoric."

Medellai looked up from the body of one of the crones with a frown. He glanced from Fish to Ferret to Pig. "It's alright, we're here to help."

Tepic blinked as though he'd just awakened from a nap. The hot danger of battle still hung in the air like smoke, and his friends were standing now with eyes firmly fixed to the ground. Pig had her hands crossed protectively in front of her stomach.

Tepic scrambled to his feet to echo Medellai. "These are my friends! It's alright."

He was surprised when the old sword-lector crossed the room and embraced him. "Quite a chase you've set us on, Tepic Banari. I fear all the world is catching fire looking for you. Who are your friends?"

Ferret had reclaimed his sack from the ground and was shuffling his feet toward the exit without making eye contact. Pig and Fish looked like rabbits about to flee.

Tepic put his hand on Ferret's shoulder and gestured to Voldigar. "This is my sword teacher."

Ferret stopped and side-eyed Voldigar. "Toppers don't understand," he muttered. "Best we get scarce. Fish, Pig." He waved his hand.

"What do you have in that sack?" Voldigar asked.

Ferret's face flushed. It was the first time Tepic could remember seeing him embarrassed. For a moment, he thought the boy would sprint out the door, but then his shoulders drooped and he held the bag out.

Voldigar peered into it and rummaged its contents with a clinking noise. A long angular gem he removed and tossed aside, then another, and then the shimmering urn that shone like glass. He took the sack and crossed to a bureau where he emptied a tray of polished stones inside. He turned back to Ferret. "This is a coven's burrow, young man. Not everything here is safe." He dangled the bag in front of him. "But the spoils are yours."

Ferret finally looked up from the ground, and his eyes widened. Gardoric laughed and shook his head.

"Don't ever come back here, son," Voldigar said.

"Title's Ferret."

"Don't ever come back here, Ferret," he repeated. "My name is Voldigar, and there are some places you shouldn't go. Do you understand?"

Ferret nodded.

Medellai called out across the room. "That goes for all of you."

Pig and Fish nodded too and eagerly offered up their bags. Voldigar quickly combed through both. Fish pointed across the room at the body near Gardoric's feet. "Those dangly bits wif' the pearls, can we nick them too?"

Gardoric quirked his brow and shook his head. The many piercings in his ears rattled together. Fish frowned and looked at the floor again.

"We have to go," Voldigar said as he tossed a silver mask from Fish's sack and turned the boy toward the exit. "There's no more time to waste." The old man ushered the youth down the stairs into the room that smelled of moldy carpets. "We'll be right behind you Tepic—" He stopped. "You should say your goodbyes."

Sword-Lector vanished back through the crooked door, and Tepic turned to face three sets of eyes blinking in the torchlight. There was a newfound wonder in their faces that he couldn't bear.

"You got some fancy mates, Dove," Ferret said.

Tepic nodded. He wasn't sure what to say. It had come to it at last and in the most unexpected way. Emotion rose in his chest, and he turned his eyes to the floor before hugging each of his friends in turn. He came last of all to Ferret.

"Why'd you ever come to Undercity anyway?" Ferret asked.

Tepic shrugged. "It was the right place for Dove . . ."

Ferret toed the bag of pacho that lay on the floor by Tepic's feet. "At least you got to try pacho," he said.

Tepic laughed then took on a more serious face. "You've done a lot for me, Ferret, all of you . . . you're the best friends I ever had."

Ferret furrowed his brow. "Come on now, love-boo."

"I mean it," Tepic said. Tears welled in his eyes as he looked at Fish and Pig too. "Things are different up top. I'll never forget you."

The others gathered round Tepic. Pig cuffed him softly, and Ferret awkwardly patted him on the head. Fish spit in his hand and held it out. "Norfies forever, Dove, pinned and struck."

Tepic took his hand. "Pinned and struck."

———◄○►———

Tepic sat alone in the dark and watched his friends vanish down the hall. They grew smaller and smaller, back the way they'd come, until their torch disappeared round a corner. He sighed heavily and wondered if he'd ever see them again.

Voldigar and the others emerged from the room behind with a torch of their own—and Grandfather's sword. They secured the door as best they could.

"You did well, Tepic, to have come so far on your own. How did you escape?"

Tepic had suppressed all thought of that awful night for a long time. With effort, he tore his eyes from the now-empty hall and let his memories flood back. He rubbed at his wrists and sought for his voice. His lips trembled. "I had to run," he said at last, "when Lusánt, he—" Tepic shook his head.

Voldigar laid a gentle hand on his shoulder. "It's alright. You—"

"He's crazy, teacher!" Tepic blurted out. "He tried everything to make me use the sword. He killed my friend."

Voldigar narrowed his eyes. "Here in Undercity?"

"No," Tepic replied. "Above, in the Spire. There was a guardsman, the one who'd seen the sword before. They let me talk to him, but then they—they killed him . . ."

Voldigar frowned and silence fell on the passage. Tepic felt his teacher's eyes searching his face, but he found he could not meet his gaze.

"I'm sorry, Tepic," Voldigar said softly. "It must have been awful."

Tears welled in Tepic's eyes again, but he swallowed and decided he wouldn't cry. "It was. But I won't let them have it. I'm taking the sword away." Tepic held out his hand toward the sword. It hung loosely in Voldigar's grip.

Voldigar watched Tepic quietly for a moment more before he sat down beside him. "Where are you going?"

"There's a cavern. It's closer to the surface and very hard to get to. I can hide there forever."

Voldigar nodded. "That's a good plan, lad, but we need to bring you somewhere safer. Lusánt is searching for you everywhere, even in the Delvings."

"No," Tepic said firmly. The word surprised even himself. "I'm going to hide here. No one will ever find me."

Voldigar glanced warily at Medellai. He and Gardoric were silently watching the exchange. "Tepic," Voldigar went on, "did you use the sword?"

Tepic hated lying, but the word blurted from his mouth again. "No."

Voldigar sighed. "Good."

"Well, not in the way Lusánt wanted," he added quickly.

"What do you mean?"

"I drew it—when Lusánt's general stabbed my friend."

"And?"

Tepic looked at the floor.

"Gamad's prosthetic," Gardoric said. "Lanathor mentioned it."

Voldigar's eyes widened. "Did you fight him?"

Tepic chewed his lip. "I did. I cut his arm off." The words came out bitterly. Voldigar looked down at the sword a moment. His face was unreadable when he looked up again.

"We have to take this to someone wise. She's a kind woman, Tepic, and in a very secret place. You'll be safe there—and the sword."

"No one's safe with it," Tepic said. A thought thrust itself into his mind. "Why don't we just destroy it?"

Voldigar blinked. "A lot of reasons, young man, but we need to get moving. Do you have the map I gave you?"

Tepic shook his head. "No, I gave it to Cozi."

"Cozi?" Voldigar asked.

"Cozi the Mokja. He built Undercity."

Voldigar's eyebrows shot up again. "Why did you do that?"

Tepic wasn't sure if the old man was upset. "You said I needed to be brave with it. Cozi does now. There's podges—soldiers—all over Undercity now. Cozi can help people. He helped me."

"How were you going to find that cavern?"

"I made a song. I know every turn."

"Did you?" Voldigar looked to Medellai again.

Medellai shrugged. "I could lead us up the way I led us here," he said. "Lots of retracing our steps, but if the boy knows the way . . ." He held his hands out and shrugged again.

Voldigar turned back to Tepic. "I need you to trust us, Tepic, and I need you to tell us everything. We'll talk as we go. Can you lead us on?"

Tepic nodded and they set off on their long weary march over miles and miles of cave. He often looked behind while he quietly recited his song, but it was only darkness that followed them. Time and again, he found his eyes lingering on the sword that Voldigar carried while the old man looked steadily ahead and stooped beneath the ceiling. He asked him once if he could carry it, but the sword-lector did not reply.

In time, they found the cavern Tepic sought and discovered that one of Arregalt's massive waterfalls plummeted through its very center in a roaring cascade. From there, he would have led them to his planned exit by the canal, but Medellai took the front instead. While the Brother often stopped to close his eyes and listen, they steadily made progress until they emerged blinking from a squat square tomb in the middle of a tumble-down graveyard.

This somber space was tucked into the corner of a neighborhood Tepic recognized as one of Arregalt's poorest. Despite the crumbling stonework, it looked civilized after so long in Undercity, a seat of wealth and development. However, what caught his eye most of all was the sky. It was snowing, and gentle snowflakes floated down to rest upon his head.

Chapter Thirty-Five

SNOWFALL

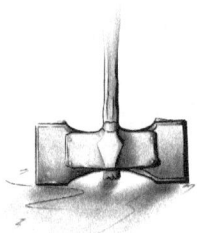

Voldigar watched the snow fall in dumbfounded silence, as though he expected to find a huge hand sifting it in some ridiculous prank. As far as he could see, in every direction the sky was a sheet of gray, and specks of white tumbled down at lazy angles in the earliest light of morning. Two days ago, he'd been wiping sweat from his neck beneath a relentless summer sun. Now, the sting of winter air crawled over his skin. Autumn had simply been forgotten.

Gardoric shook his head and glared at a snowflake on his thumb. "More of Lusánt's work, no doubt . . ." He pulled his drab cloak off and handed it to Tepic. "Take this, boy." Standing outside in the graveyard, Voldigar could see that Tepic had grown taller and his face a little older. The cloak almost fit.

"He controls the weather now?" Medellai asked in a mocking tone.

"And the tides," Voldigar said quietly. "Let's not linger."

Voldigar concealed the sword in his own cloak and made for an alleyway through a tangle of dead and twisted hedges. With a final glance at the strange sky, they disappeared into overhanging shadows. There were many delays and hurried dashes on their winding way, but with a little help from

Gardoric, they went unseen until they passed nervously through a small gate that Voldigar knew well. They briefly kept pace with a throng of commoners making their way to the shantytowns pressed between Arregalt's wall and river. But with a subtle nod, Voldigar signaled to break off and reverse their course.

They were soon swallowed in a fold of scrubland and headed for his shallow ford. Voldigar glanced anxiously behind for footprints and was glad to see that snow had not yet clung to the ground. For some distance, anyone caring to look from atop the walls might see them, but there was hope that they were just four more dirty peasants, wandering on mundane business through an unexpected cold.

"When we're over the ford, take Tepic to Liadov's shrine," Voldigar said quietly. He walked close and slid the sword to Medellai. "Be quick, and be sure you're not followed."

Medellai nodded and took the weapon reverently in two hands before burying it in his cloak. "The first piece of the puzzle. I'll stay to the river, and the coast."

Voldigar continued. "I meant to examine the weapon myself, but there's no longer any time, and we can't risk it at my house. Impress upon her the urgency, Medellai. Find out what you can. Whatever she's to do, she has to decide *now*."

"Liadov acts in her own time, Brother."

Voldigar looked at the sky and shook his head. "Not even the seasons act in their own time anymore."

Gardoric went on ahead to scout the ford and soon returned to wave them carefully across. There they parted quickly. Medellai and Tepic turned sharply northward, and Voldigar found himself releasing a long sigh as he walked alone with Gardoric. They dipped through a familiar depression of thick-growing beech and maple—he'd be home soon. One more narrow escape, one more crisis averted. A stretch of brush, his aspen grove, and then his fieldstone house. He hoped Hobyn and Wulf had had the sense to bring in firewood for Gwenyth.

Underbrush gave way to a gentle rise in the land, and Voldigar hurried his pace into the aspen grove. He froze.

Before him through the trees, in his field, about his house, upon the road, and extending off into the distance were horsemen—hundreds and hundreds of horsemen—bearing the imperial livery of General Gamad.

———◈———

Gardoric stifled a cry and reached for his hatchet. Voldigar caught his wrist. "Wait!"

Gardoric twisted back and looked at him with wild eyes.

"Wait," Voldigar repeated. "Disappear."

"What?"

"There are too many, Gardoric. Disappear and watch." He held him intently in his gaze. "Someone must tell the others what happened. Disappear."

Gardoric took another look at the army before them, and with a helpless glance to Voldigar, he retreated to the shadows and vanished.

Voldigar squeezed the hilt of his Daneki blade and wished for not the first time that he had his maul instead. When plans had changed, he'd left it leaning in the corner of his home. He strode forward.

The soldiers caught sight of him, and several turned their horses. He ground his jaw and lowered his head. One step at a time. It took every fiber of resolve not to rush forward. As he emerged from the grove, he saw that it was not just hundreds, but perhaps two thousand men, mostly mounted, spreading into the distance. General Gamad himself was on a nearby rise of the road, astride a huge warhorse whose neck was as thick as its body. He gripped the reins tightly in his one good hand. Hobyn was on the bench beside the sevenbark, burying his face in his hands and rocking back and forth. The door stood open, and soldiers passed in and out.

One mounted man spurred forward to Voldigar and spoke in a severe tone "Lord Anteres—"

"Where is my wife?" Voldigar said over him.

"Hold yourself, old man—" the soldier began, but Voldigar did not hear another word. The rider moved as if to bar his way, but Voldigar shoved his horse stumbling to the side and sprang forward in four leaping strides. He was through the door in an instant and there sent another soldier sprawling on his back.

The crowded room erupted with the ringing of steel as no less than a dozen men cried out and wheeled on Voldigar.

"Peace! Peace!" shouted a familiar voice. It was Lusánt. He sat upon a chair by the hearth with his palms outstretched. Gwenyth was close by his side in her rocking chair, hands trembling and her face ashen white. "Peace!" he cried again. "Stay yourselves." Two men were grasping at Voldigar's arms. "Let him be, it's alright."

Lusánt slowly lowered his hands, first with his eyes wide and then with a glare while palpable tension hovered in the air. "Sun, Moon, and Star, people! We're in the presence of a woman with child."

"Get out of my house," Voldigar said through gritted teeth. He could see Wulf and Lyrusia now too, standing near the window of what made for his kitchen. Their faces were set like stone, save for fearful, darting eyes.

Lusánt's Xerimadi bodyguard moved forward as if to strike Voldigar. Lusánt caught his trailing arm first with his long, olive fingers. "No, no, no," he said with a strained smile. "The lord of the house is just surprised. Please, let's be civil." Lusánt adjusted his seat with a creak and gestured to the only other chair, empty near the center of the room. Hobyn had recently reconstructed both. Voldigar stood unmoving.

Lusánt dropped his gesture slowly and let out a small cough as he flicked his fingers. "We're just here to talk." He looked around the room. "Gods, man! How do you live like this?"

"What do you have to say to me?"

Lusánt eyed him sidelong and gave a disappointed frown. "Right to it then?" He straightened himself toward Voldigar and leaned forward in his chair. "Where is Tepic Banari?"

"I wouldn't tell you if I knew," Voldigar replied.

"I was afraid you'd say that." Lusánt leaned back and absently rocked the empty cradle that sat near the hearth. Pain flashed across Gwenyth's face, and she gripped the arms of her chair.

"Your wife is very ill, it would seem. She's family you know. I could send for Doctor Challeric. I would hate if her condition worsened."

"If you touch my wife, every man in this room will die," Voldigar said. His eyes remained fixed on the Emperor.

Lusánt released the cradle and tossed a nearby piece of firewood into the hearth instead. He sighed. "I thought you might say that as well. I think we're getting off on the wrong foot." He shook his head and looked at his dirty palm for a moment. "You have such an awful lot of firewood, Voldigar." He tossed another piece in. "Did you know Winter was coming so soon?"

The room was still, save for the crackling of fresh wood.

"So taciturn," Lusánt went on. "I'm sure your lovely friends told you that Tepic was missing from my household. For all their wisdom, they didn't seem to know where he was either. Isn't that strange?" Lusánt twisted in his chair and gestured all around him. "That's what all this is for. I'm in the field with my cavalry to rescue my retainer. Very romantic I think. We stopped by Maghaltani this morning."

Lusánt tilted his head and watched Voldigar intently. Voldigar swallowed hard but gave no other response. Lusánt steepled his fingers. "I found the village empty. Where are all your people?"

Voldigar glanced at Wulf a moment and back to Lusánt. "What do you mean?"

"What does 'empty' mean, Voldigar?"

Voldigar scowled. "The greater part of my order has gone on to defend Eastfort, since no one else will, Your Highness. But we did not leave the village empty."

Lusánt narrowed his eyes. "What a mystery then."

Voldigar's lip shook into an uncontrollable snarl. "What have you done?"

"What have I done? Nothing! I asked you a simple question. 'Where are your people?' Apparently, you don't know where *anyone* is." Lusánt held up his arm with an exaggerated shrug.

Voldigar balled his hands into fists but released them again.

"You seem agitated, old fellow. I thought the peasant's life was supposed to be . . . pastoral? Didn't I give you leave to live out your days in peace? You haven't been up to other things, have you?"

"You have two thousand cavalry in my field," Voldigar said.

"And in your woods, and on the road, and on the hills. All the places I think your dancing little feet have been carrying you, Elder of Aramon."

Tepic. Medellai. Voldigar blinked and lowered his eyes, but did not otherwise react.

"I heard a curious story the other day." Lusánt rose to his feet and started moving from spot to spot, knocking on the floor with his feet. *Tap tap.* "I heard that two guards were lured outside by someone and overpowered in the middle of the night by a single old man. It happened this summer." *Tap tap.* "Do you know anything about that?" He stopped long enough to watch Voldigar's face. *Tap tap.* "I've been studying you know. The Eighth Code. *'A Brother does not lie.'* Did I say it right?" He tapped the floor a final time. "Tepic isn't hiding here is he?"

"I don't have a cellar," Voldigar said.

"Right," Lusánt replied with pursed lips. "Those are expensive." He walked to the door. "Please, everyone, come with me. Up now. That's good."

Voldigar glanced briefly at Wulf again and shook his head, then did the same to Gwenyth. The soldiers were pouring through the front door, and Voldigar followed warily alone. Snow was coming down thicker now, and the barest layer stuck to the ground.

"By all accounts, you've had a very fine harvest," Lusánt said. "Look, three lovely granaries, as tall as I am. You could fit a person in these." Lusánt crossed the yard and tapped the first granary with his knuckles. Hobyn looked up from his hands.

"Hello?" Lusánt called loudly. "Tepic Banari? Are you in there?"

"Your Highness, they're full of grain," Hobyn called in his wavering voice. "No persons in there."

"Is that so?"

A soldier stood by with a maul resting head down in the dirt. It was a crude thing of black iron, half the size of Voldigar's weapon, heavy but mundane. Lusánt grabbed the tool and tested its weight in his hands. A look of horror crossed Hobyn's face and he tottered to his feet from the bench to shuffle as quickly as he could across the yard.

"No, no!" he cried. "Just open the top. I can show you."

"Couldn't get a very good view that way," Lusánt complained. He gave the maul one final twist and then struck it against the side of the first granary with a grunt.

"Stop!" Hobyn cried in a tortured gasp and stumbled forward.

"Stop!" Lusánt mocked as he swung again.

Voldigar winced with each strike. "Hobyn, no."

Lusánt swung again and again. Wood splintered and grain began to pour onto the wet ground, slowly at first, and then in a great flood of ocher seeds.

"Stop!" Hobyn cried again and grasped at the Emperor's shoulder. Voldigar jerked forward but it was too late. Lusánt spun in white-eyed fury and rammed the handle of the maul into Hobyn's chest. The old man folded with a pitiful whimper and crashed awkwardly to the hard earth in a splash of barley.

"No!" Voldigar cried and rushed toward the Emperor. Men were upon him in an instant, clutching his arms and pulling at his cloak.

Lusánt turned on him, menacing with the maul in hand. "We've been through this before, Voldigar! Don't play the fool again."

There was nothing he could do. "Please," Voldigar said with what calm he could muster. He did not resist the men as they dragged him backward. "It's all we have." He looked sideways to see Hobyn groaning and trying to right himself.

Lusánt shook his head in disgust and turned back to the granaries, smashing each one in turn, watching grain spill onto the rapidly piling snow.

In the chaos, Lyrusia had somehow come to kneel beside Hobyn and tend to the old man. In moments, the grain had all drained to the ground, and Lusánt turned back around to glare at Voldigar, his chest heaving. He smiled and wiped his hand across his mouth. "Well, I guess he's not here."

Voldigar opened his mouth to respond, but in that moment a flurry of activity erupted on his right. A crowd of soldiers were dragging a man into their midst. He was haggard and wounded, and black circles showed starkly on the dark skin around his eyes. It was Lanathor.

Chapter Thirty-Six

MEDDLING

"U nhand me!" Lanathor cried as he struggled against the soldiers' arms.

Lusánt snapped his head to him with an expression of genuine surprise. He dropped the maul. "Well, well . . . what a merry gathering this is. My savior Lanathor arrives." He gestured dismissively and the soldiers let him go. "Do the Brethren always gather so thickly at your humble farm, Voldigar?"

"What is this?" Lanathor said as he looked around in horror. "What have you done to the grain?"

Lusánt blinked. "I was looking for a fugitive. You haven't by chance seen Tepic Banari, have you?"

Lanathor flicked his gaze to Voldigar but quickly looked away. "No, Your Highness," he replied.

"Pity."

Dismayed, Lanathor turned his head from side to side, trying in vain to make sense of what he saw. The apothecary, Lyrusia, was moving Old Man Hobyn aside while another group of soldiers seemed to think they were restraining Voldigar. Wulf stood in the door with a glare.

He tried to shake the cobwebs from his thoughts. He'd ridden hard for hours only to be accosted at the picket lines of an entire brigade of cavalry, spilling out for acres around the meager home of his friend.

"Why are you here, Elder Lanathor?"

Lanathor squinted and refocused his mind. In all his many trials, he had never been so exhausted as he was now. He'd ingested three bulbs of Falam Root while they battled in the pass the night before, all he had. His ears still rung from the violence, and in the fading of the root, it was as if the world spun while he walked on the ocean floor.

"E-Eastfort has fallen," he managed to stammer. "Is that why . . . the army is here?"

A murmur went up among the soldiers, and Lusánt's face twisted. He coughed a short laugh, then rolled his eyes and looked into the sky. With a deep breath, he exhaled an exasperated yell. The snow muffled its echo.

"Gods above, Lanathor! Is that where you've been?" The Emperor was smiling.

Lanathor looked on incredulous. "What?"

Lusánt began to pace with his arms stretched wide. "Meddling, meddling, meddling. Why?"

Lanathor's face fell. "Emperor. Our border has . . . collapsed. Four hundred men gave their lives, many of my brethren among them, and more will succumb to their wounds. We've fallen back to Westfort. I don't know how long we can hold."

Lusánt stomped his feet and strode to Lanathor to cup the sides of his face. "Your men didn't have to die, Lanathor! *Why?* Why do you Brothers of Aramon never *trust* me? Why must you always be meddling?"

The earth swayed, and Lanathor struggled to maintain his balance. "We did what we must, Your Highness—and there's still time. You must ride at once. They've nearly broken through."

"Must I?" Lusánt shook his head and patted Lanathor's cheek. "You shouldn't have been there at all. Do you think I don't know there's a horde upon my doorstep? You told me yourself!"

Lanathor's mouth hung open. "Then . . . what will you do?"

"I told you already, but you didn't listen," Lusánt said. "You must trust me! If I have chosen to let the border forts fall, did I not choose it wisely? Do I not have my reasons? I will deal with this horde in the way of my choosing. Shall I always go about getting the approval of yesterday's men?"

Lanathor blinked. "There are two thousand souls in the pass Lusánt, mostly families. You would let them die?"

Lusánt drew his mouth into a line. "Let? Heroic sacrifice must be made in war," he said quietly. He patted his face again and then backed away. "Whatever you're about to say, Lanathor, don't. I'm still fond of you."

A man hurried to Lusánt's side and handed him a folded paper. Lusánt broke from Lanathor's gaze for a moment to read it, then nodded at the man. He held his finger out to catch a snowflake and raised his voice high. "What I see, is a merry band of conspirators meeting at this little farm." He stopped to lick the flake from his finger and then regarded the brethren coolly. "I do not approve. See that you do not *conspire*, Brotherhood of Aramon."

A horse was brought to his side, and Lusánt quickly mounted. General Gamad had also lumbered near and sat there upon his steed with a scowl.

Lusánt looked down at them from his saddle. "If you hear the whereabouts of Tepic Banari, I am to be told at once. Do not disappoint me, and do not meddle anymore. Consider this your *final* warning." Lusánt turned his horse about, and the column began to form and flow toward the road.

"You will not defend your border then?" Lanathor cried.

"I *shall* defend it, in my own way," Lusánt said, looking over his shoulder with a smile. "Turns out I may have a lead on Tepic's whereabouts—and other malcontents in my realm." Lusánt's lip curled into a sneer. "Goodbye, Brethren—sorry about the grain."

Lusánt snapped his reins, and the vast cavalry rolled into motion, heading toward the capital. After a thundering minute, Lanathor and the others stood alone, silent in a trampled field, watching the strength of Aramon ride west while their danger loomed to the east.

Chapter Thirty-Seven

WIELDING WISDOM

I T GREW COLDER AND colder while they walked, but the cloak Gardoric gave him was enough to blunt the chill. Tepic was not fond of cold, but he took pride in bearing it for hours on end. He remembered with a smile how in all seasons, the old stableground never closed. The clang of blunted steel rang while he danced through the snow at swordplay, waiting for the Festival of Midwinter. His skin always stung in the wintry air, but he'd been proud to go on manfully at his training.

Medellai led him swiftly on for an hour or two, north and east of the ford through a barren land of rocky soil and low, gnarled trees. Like Sword-Lector, the man seemed grave and wise, but he spoke little, looking lost in his thoughts. Tepic had never been here before, and it seemed few others had either. There were no farms or villages, and the air was so quiet he imagined he could faintly hear the ocean somewhere on ahead. The only other sound was the crunching of his feet where snow had just begun to stick.

"This is it," Medellai said.

Tepic nearly bumped into him before he looked up from his feet. Just ahead was one of the many gnarled trees, but this one far larger. It looked to him like some kind of willow, and snow gathered heavily on a thicket of the low-hanging branches that obscured its base. Beyond it, the terrain rose slightly and disappeared into the haze.

"Is that the sea?" Tepic asked and pointed ahead.

"Yes," Medellai replied, "and this is Sister Liadov's home." He paused. "Tepic, you must never show this to anyone. Do you understand?"

Tepic nodded. "She lives in a tree?"

Medellai smiled. "Follow me."

Pushing the branches aside, Medellai forced his way between them and uncovered a dark hollow in the earth. Tepic followed him down stone steps into the gloom where only spare light poked through and the branches swung back with a shower of snowflakes. Before them was a cold stone wall with many symbols in a grid across its face.

With a twinkle in his eye, Medellai pressed firmly on a few, and the stone wall slid aside. "Quickly now," he said.

They stepped into the dark and the door slid shut. It was pitch-black, and Medellai's voice called out from ahead. "Come along."

Tepic had spent enough time underground to know they were descending, and rapidly at that. He held his hand against the wall, and soon the tunnel leveled out, revealing a gentle gray-blue light far ahead. Medellai stopped at the opening and knuckled a wooden door that stood ajar. "Sister?" He stepped in with a gesture to Tepic.

The room was small and round and the stone here faintly brown, polished to a sheen. Most of the surfaces were covered by shelves, laden with a bewildering sea of books in the muted leathers of a thousand hues. Embossments of gold and silver graced the spines of many, and some were encased in ivory shells or clasped with clever latches. Here and there, cloudy lamps flickered in blue and white. The rest of the space was compactly furnished with dark wood, desks and chairs thickly stained countless times under the salt sea air. To their right, the wall opened in two graceful arches to a balcony that overlooked the ocean. In the left of these, a tall woman stood in a white gown, staring into the distance.

Liadov turned her head and smiled. "Welcome friends. I perceive this is an unusual gathering."

"Head and Heart," Medellai saluted. "We've found the first key."

Liadov dropped her gaze to Tepic, and he was struck silent by the radiant echo of Kyriana that stood before him. Her skin was pale and young and her hair of shining gold, but the same quality of deep age hid behind her wide blue eyes. "You are Tepic Banari then?"

Tepic forgot to answer, and her smile broadened as she gestured to a table close behind. Medellai produced the sword and, unwrapping it, laid it on the surface. Liadov's smile faded from her face as she stared intently at the blade. She was quiet a long time, breathing slowly while her eyes moved along it.

"This *is* a Prism of the Heavens," she said at length, "and the very one that I have once seen before." She turned to Tepic. "Draw the blade, young man, and place it back upon the table."

Liadov watched him with unblinking eyes as he licked his lips, removed the scabbard, and let the blade linger in his hands. He gently placed it on the table, careful not to make a sound.

"How came you by this thing?" Liadov asked.

Tepic shook his head. "It was on my mantle. I wasn't supposed to take it, but I did—once. I'm sorry."

Liadov laughed softly and smiled. Tepic stared at the floor. "Please, tell me more, young sir," she said.

Tepic swallowed and locked his eyes on the crystal hilt. "It was my grandfather's. But Lusánt—the Emperor, he wanted it. It seems like everyone wants it. Sword-Lector told me not to let him have it though." He looked up to make sure they understood. "Lusánt thinks the sword can do terrible magic. He wanted me to use it."

"And did you?" Liadov asked.

Tepic looked at the floor again and nodded. "I did, but just a little, and not like he wanted."

He was surprised to feel Liadov come to his side and lay a gentle hand on his shoulder. She said nothing more to him though and spoke to Medellai instead.

"Things are in motion, Elder—moving of their own accord."

Tepic watched Medellai's reaction. He didn't seem nervous, just serious. He nodded. "What have you foreseen?"

"Danger," Liadov replied. "Grave danger, and a dark grasp is closing around you, Brother Medellai, you and the rest of the Brotherhood. Yet I cannot turn your path, only watch as you are all consumed. Still, you will not turn aside?"

"You know that we cannot, Liadov."

Liadov shook her head sorrowfully and walked away from the table. "There's still time, Medellai. There's another path."

"Will you use the sword?" he asked.

Liadov turned and strode back to the table. She looked down again at Tepic. "May I, Lord Banari?"

Tepic startled at her question but nodded quickly several times. Liadov stretched forth her hand and slowly wrapped her fingers around the hilt. With a steady grip, she raised it flatly to the height of her eyes and held it glinting before her face. She stared into her reflection for a long while before she turned her eyes to Medellai. "Would that I could." She smiled, but Medellai's shoulders dropped.

"There is much that I have learned, more still unknown." She laid the sword back upon the table. "This Prism of the Heavens is only a danger to me, as they are to all those who are bonded with them."

"Can you destroy it then?" Medellai asked.

"I could," Liadov replied. "Much as you might destroy any other object, but as yet I cannot."

"Why not?" Tepic asked. He was surprised at the sound of his own voice.

"Because I would die, Tepic. And do not think I overvalue my own life—I would gladly give it to right a wrong. No, the Prisms are woven together. Were I to break this one, its power would only bleed into the others. One more your Emperor holds, and the other is . . . far away."

"Then you've found it?" Medellai asked urgently

"No, but in all my searching I know at least that it is not here. God has revealed to me that it will soon be found."

"But how?" Medellai asked.

"Why can't you use it?" Tepic interrupted.

Medellai frowned, but Liadov held her hand up gently and turned her eyes to Tepic. "These things, Lusánt's orb, your grandfather's sword, they are very old and very strange. In one way they are mundane objects, a blade and a glass ball, but in the right hands they are terrible indeed."

She turned her attention to Medellai again. "I know only what has been revealed to me, Elder. The Prisms of the Heavens are older than the Brotherhood, as old as Aramon itself. When our enemy still walked openly and the Builders were at war, Tymicha bade the Singers make them, one for each great house, Tavaana, Nabénes, and Sispérus. They were meant to bind the First Sorcerers, but as with all the corrupt things of men, sweet fruit was made bitter."

Tepic was listening to her story intently, but his mind wandered at the sound of a strange name, and he dared to interject again. "I know that name," he said.

Medellai blinked, and a flicker of annoyance crossed his face. Liadov stopped her tale and glanced at him. "What do you mean?"

"Nabénes. That's my mom's name," Tepic went on with a shrug. "Claras Nabénes, but she's Banari now." For the first time, Liadov's calm, wise face looked puzzled. Tepic felt his face go red, and he stuck his hands in his pockets. "Sorry," he muttered.

Liadov did not look away but stared at him intently. "What was your grandfather's name?"

"Arliman."

Liadov's eyes opened wide, and she followed with a broad smile. "How often do the wise neglect simple questions. So you are a son of Arliman?" She said it more as a statement than a question and glanced at Medellai again. "Only the heirs can use the Prisms."

Medellai's mouth hung open and he tilted his head. "Crazy Arliman had a daughter?"

Tepic wasn't sure what he'd done and resisted the urge to apologize again. Liadov took a step toward him and spoke in a quiet voice. "What did you mean when you said you used the sword? What exactly happened?"

"I-It glowed gold, and my arms, they f-felt . . . they felt . . ." Tepic stammered.

Liadov placed a hand on his shoulder again. "I understand, Tepic, and I'm sorry I did not hear you before." She narrowed her eyes, but he could no longer meet her gaze. "You must stay here for a while, we have much to discuss. You'll be safe. Do you understand?"

Tepic nodded.

"Good," Liadov said. "Brother Medellai, return to the others, swiftly. Tell them what you've heard. We cannot turn back now, for all that I might wish, there is only one path that remains."

Tepic licked his lips. "Ma'am, I know everyone thinks I'm young, and I am, but I'm thirteen and a half now. I can understand some things. Please, who are you, and what is this sword?"

"I am the sword Tepic, the sword is me—and you are its Wielder. I will tell you all, but it will take us time."

"Can Tepic use it then?" Medellai asked. "Can we teach him?"

"Time, Elder. We need time." She looked steadily into Medellai's eyes until he quickly dipped his head. "God be with you, Medellai," she continued. "You will not see my face again."

Chapter Thirty-Eight

Conspirators All

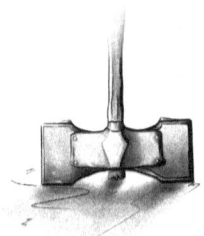

Voldigar did not know how long he'd stood there numb in his barley field while snow piled around his ankles. Hobyn had shooed Lyrusia away, and with tears streaming from his old eyes, he crawled on hands and knees, helplessly salvaging any grain he could. Lyrusia stopped trying to check him for injuries and instead, cupped seeds into her hands, pouring them into the broken shell of a granary.

"Elder?" a voice asked quietly.

Voldigar blinked and saw that Lanathor and Gardoric now stood before him.

"I saw everything," Gardoric said.

Lanathor breathed heavily, his face distant and resigned.

"Gwenyth," Voldigar muttered and turned back to his door.

Wulf had wandered off toward the road to Arregalt and stood there with his great two-headed axe in hand, staring at the great tower looming in the distance.

Gwenyth had taken his place in the doorframe and leaned weakly upon it, one hand over her belly. Her shoulders sagged, and her drawn skin was pale as alabaster. Her face twisted with rage and despair, eyes fixed upon the grain. She lurched and stumbled from the door, but Voldigar caught her as she fell.

"Gwen! Gwen, no . . ."

A long wail tumbled from her lips as she choked and sobbed and beat her arms against him, struggling toward the scattered barley.

Voldigar's chest felt like wax as tears of his own welled in his eyes. "No, Gwen . . . just come inside."

"No!" she screamed in return. "No . . ." She feebly swiped at the air twice more and then fell limp. Voldigar lifted her in his arms and hurried to the mat in the back of his house. Lyrusia was close behind.

He pulled blankets about her while Lyrusia placed her hands upon Gwenyth's cheeks and brow. Her breathing was shallow between quiet moans.

"M'lady," Lyrusia said softly, "don't fret, don't fret. *Please*, just rest."

"Brother," Lanathor said from the door.

Voldigar glanced at him and shook his head. He turned back to his wife and cupped her hands gently in his own.

"Brother," Lanathor said more firmly.

"Not now."

"Now is all we have," Lanathor croaked hoarsely. "Westfort is falling."

Lyrusia patted Voldigar's shoulder and took Gwenyth's hands from him. "She's . . . she just needs to rest."

Voldigar swallowed hard and took one more look at his wife. Her lips shuddered and the closed lids of her eyes trembled on an ashen face. Gardoric had gathered in the door as well.

"Not here," Voldigar said. "Don't talk here."

In a daze, he tore his eyes away and led the men outside across his field to the rear of Hobyn's shack. "Wulf," he called out. The shaggy man shook flakes from his mane and joined them there. Voldigar looked each man in his eyes in turn. "We never should have waited."

"I'm sorry about your harvest, Brother," Lanathor said softly.

"It's just grain!" Voldigar snapped. "Tell me what happened."

Lanathor swallowed. "Dantic called the retreat from Eastfort early this morning. Help never came."

"How many brethren were lost?"

"Nine, and more will succumb to their wounds. Vasherk is hard pressed."

Voldigar dropped his gaze to the snow for a moment. "And what followed?"

"Our enemy did not realize we'd abandoned the wall, for a little time at least, but they came on in a fury when we were only partway through the pass. Their numbers are countless, Voldigar. All of hell is poured out. Zedr brought the mountain down upon them, just in time."

"The initiate?"

"Yes. At a narrow point, he made a great ruin of stone and secured our escape. He wasn't ready for Telling of that magnitude. His body is crumbling now. Vasherk is with him, but I fear he will soon return to the earth he loved so well."

Wulf scowled. "My axe is hungry. How long do they have?"

Lanathor shook his head. "The rocks won't stop them forever. They are not mindless. The wall of Westfort is less broad, and Dantic can defend it with fewer men, but he is alone. I fear he may only last a day, maybe two—even with the Order. Taro I left in command."

"Then let us return and die with them!" Wulf said.

Voldigar shook his head. "What does that gain us? We can still strike at the head of the snake. It is a nearer path."

Their conversation was interrupted by a creaking sound. Though muffled by the snow, the rolling of wheels was unmistakable. They rounded Hobyn's hut and saw there a covered wagon, drawn by four fine Maghaltani horses. Lutz was on its seat and hopped down into the snow the moment it came to rest. "Head and Heart, Brothers." His face was grim. "I bring ill tidings. What dark news have you?"

<hr/>

Wulf answered first. "Arregalt. We go to strike the head."

Lutz secured the wagon and handed the care of the horses off to Hobyn who had limped over at his arrival. "It's regicide then, is it?" Lutz said.

Voldigar's eye twitched at the comment, though he otherwise held still. "The horde has broken through Eastfort, and Westfort holds by a thread—while the Emperor ignores it. I say we can strike the artifact he wields and end this nightmare."

Lutz raised his eyebrows. "Would that even work? How did Eastfort fall?"

"Tell us what happened to you first, Lutz," Lanathor interjected.

Lutz wiped his hands on his jerkin. "We had a visit from His Highness, very early this morning, him and a host of cavalry. Thank God we had warning, and long before. We considered fighting, but it would have been thirty brethren against two thousand, with almost two hundred women and children to protect besides." Lutz shook his head regretfully while the lenses spun and ticked around his eyes. "No, we hid in the Seaward Gulch hours before they arrived."

"You made the right choice," Lanathor said.

"What happened then?" Voldigar asked.

"I wish I could say we returned to Maghaltani in peace, Elder, but I can't. When I dared come back from the gulch, half the village was burned and the other half was torn to pieces."

The brethren gasped and Wulf growled. "Regicide appeals to me more and more."

Voldigar narrowed his eyes. "Our true enemy is in the east. Stay yourself. Where is everyone now?" he asked.

An eyebrow slid up from behind Lutz's eyepiece. "We gathered everything we could, and every horse and wagon. Emptied Maghaltani and made for Pirvale. We're taking shelter in those hills until the weather clears."

Voldigar looked up and sighed. "I fear it's only going to get worse."

"It may," Lutz said and patted the wagon. "This one is for Gwenyth. I know she's been sick, and it seems I judged rightly that you'd be visited too." Lutz scowled as he looked about the farm and Voldigar followed his gaze.

The twisted granaries gaped like three broken mouths, holding only a handsbreadth of seed in their bases. Snow had accumulated thickly on the ruined grain before their splintered wood. Hobyn shook his head pitifully as he walked the last of the four horses past them and then under the harvest shelter nearest to his hut. There he laid blankets on their broad backs and they huddled together to stave off the cold. The old man sagged to the ground between them to bury his face and weep.

Voldigar took a deep breath. "We're not plotting to kill our King, Brothers, only to do what we must—to take the orb and destroy it."

Lanathor shook his head. "It's folly, Voldigar, and you know it. Nothing in Aramon will be more closely guarded."

"He cannot stop us all," Voldigar said.

"All? Shall we take everyone from Pirvale and leave their families alone? Will I ride back to Westfort and empty it while the horde is beating down its gate?"

Voldigar set his jaw and thought to respond, but he knew Lanathor spoke true. All paths were madness and despair. Gardoric interjected. "Wulf had the right of it at first. Why don't we shore up Westfort, hold the horde off? Stand with our brethren! And if we give Liadov more time . . ." He held up his hands.

"What? What then?" Lanathor asked.

"She has the sword now," Gardoric protested. "Medellai took Tepic there with it this morning."

"That is some news," Lutz said. "What will she do with it?"

"We don't know," Voldigar said. "And that's the trouble. We have no certainty, and we have no time."

The men stood quietly for a few long moments. Voldigar wandered in his own thoughts and weariness. He had little else to say. He felt like a weather vane, spinning in the wind. The argument was the debate of dead men, choosing a plot in which to be buried. He found himself Chanting under his breath, letting his eyes close, and searching for some glimmer of hope.

Lutz broke the quiet. "You all look awful. Have you slept? Eaten?"

Voldigar blinked a few times and took a deep breath. He'd not slept since the night before last, nor had Gardoric, and Lanathor looked as though he'd been awake for a week straight.

"Rusted rods!" Lutz exclaimed. He waddled to the back of his wagon and scrambled up. The men followed, and there he rummaged through blankets and trunks, shoved a pair of saddles against the wall, and finally produced a box with several loaves of bread and fine summer fruits. "This! Fresh fruit in winter," Lutz said with a laugh. "Who'd have thought?"

The brethren thanked him for the provisions and gathered under a shelter that Lutz pulled from the wagon's side. There they ate in silence for a while until conversation struck up again. They argued and explained, made point and counterpoint, but in the end, Voldigar knew he'd simply have to decide.

"It's certain death to the west, and certain death to the east," Voldigar said at length. "But the most certain death of all is if we stay here arguing until we're buried in the snow." He took a deep breath and stole a long lingering glance at the Spire, its ominous height barely visible behind veils of falling snow. He let his gaze drop to his little home instead and sighed. "Let us make for Westfort, hold there as long as we may, and pray that Liadov uncovers the mystery of Tepic's sword."

The brethren all looked at him with raised brows. "I'm surprised at your choice," Lanathor said.

"As am I," Voldigar replied. "But you're right, and I would rather take my last breath facing our foe than facing our kin."

"And I'd rather not take a last breath at all," Medellai said loudly as he rounded the wagon and knocked snow from the canopy above their heads. He was red-faced and winded. "I have good news and bad."

━━━◆━━━

Voldigar turned to Medellai, too weary to be surprised. He opened his mouth to speak, but Medellai held his hand up while he breathed. "A moment. I heard everything." The brethren knew better than to ask him how.

He caught his breath and straightened to speak. "The bad news, Brethren, is that Liadov cannot use the sword."

Wulf groaned while Voldigar looked on in quiet consternation. Medellai held his hand up again. "The good news is that she believes the third Prism will soon be found, and that she also knows by whom and how the sword might be used."

Voldigar allowed a flicker of hope to cross his face, but Medellai shook his head and swallowed the last of his exhaustion. "It's not like you think. It's the boy, Tepic of course. But we cannot check the enemy that way, not yet at least. If we wait, all of Aramon will long be overrun."

"What do we do then?" Wulf cried in dismay. "Curse counsel, and curse indecision. Give me fire and give me foes!"

"Why don't we just let Westfort fall?" Medellai asked quietly.

Five blinking faces were Medellai's response. "What?" Lanathor asked.

"Hear me out. What lies before Westfort?"

"The Great Span," Wulf said.

"Yes, The Great Span—and a sheer chasm nearly half a mile deep and just as wide. It's the only way into Aramon by land. Evacuate Westfort, and bring it down."

The silence that followed was so vast it could hardly be described. Were it not broken by the sudden click and whir of Lutz's goggles, Voldigar thought he might hear the distant ocean as it crashed against the scree far below Liadov's shrine.

Lutz's gravelly voice had never sounded so thin. "Bring . . . down . . . the Span? You cannot bring down the Span!"

"You've said so yourself, Lutz. The center pillar of the Span bears all its great weight. Is there no one in our mighty order able to break it?" Medellai asked.

"It does, and I did!" Lutz protested. "But no, no there isn't! There are more enchantments on that pillar than on the entire Spire. A Singer of old could not bring it down, the first Artificer would go mad in solving that equation."

"Zedr might have done it," Lanathor said sadly. They fell silent again.

"I could do it," Voldigar said quietly.

The brethren looked at him incredulous, Lutz most of all.

"I could do it, I said," Voldigar repeated.

Medellai frowned. "The Wilding would be upon you before you'd bent a stone."

"Maybe. Maybe not."

Wulf began to nod his head. "It would give way before him."

"You'd be crushed in a thousand thousand tons of rock!" Lutz cried.

"Then I'll be crushed!"

Lutz frowned and the silence returned until he lifted his chin and spoke again. "Black Fire."

All eyes were now on him.

"Black Fire?" Voldigar asked.

"Yes, Black Fire," Lutz repeated with irritation. "I should have thought of it before. If there's one thing that doesn't give two coppers about enchantment, it's Black Fire—mokja explosives, and of the worse kind, mixed with miridas combustibles."

"You have this?"

"No, but I know someone who can make it . . . or I did. He's in Undercity now. The only sheep in the family blacker than present company, and the only one Bajk hates more than me. He got expelled making the stuff."

Realization flashed like a spark in Voldigar's mind. "Cozi?"

Lutz looked up with his jaw slack, and the telescoping over his eyes made his goggles shift down half an inch. He quickly pushed them back up. "How do you know that name?"

"I don't," Voldigar said, "but Tepic does. He befriended him in Undercity."

Lutz looked wildly from side to side. Voldigar could almost hear the gears of his mind working over the gears on his face.

"Lutz," Voldigar said, "this is the answer to our riddles. Cozi owes Tepic a favor, a huge favor. We just have to get to him."

Lutz nodded warily, but excitement was spreading on his face. He stopped short with a painful frown. "How can we get to Undercity?"

"Let us handle that," Gardoric replied.

"But the elements . . . The Miridas will not cooperate with us."

"Half a dozen of their vessels foundered in low tide, Lutz. We may not need their cooperation," Medellai said with a smile.

"Gather yourselves, Brethren," Voldigar said. "We have no time to lose."

———◆———

The plan was set and the brothers stood in a circle in the midst of the snowy barley field to make their final preparations. Their faces were stern, but the relief and excitement of a decision made shone in their eyes. Lutz's little meal was a help as well. Hobyn listened close by and Lyrusia had come out the front door to sit upon the bench. They still spoke in low tones, but Voldigar did not care whether the others heard or no. They were all conspirators now.

"Will we need the wagon?" Voldigar asked.

Lutz crossed his arms and shook his head. "No. We can carry everything we need. I know the component parts, but we have to convince Cozi to give me the catalyst—and the accelerant. If he's as indebted as you say, and we're lucky, maybe he'll even tell me how they're made."

"How do we know this Black Fire works?" Lanathor asked.

The lenses on Lutz's goggles narrowed. "It works, Elder. And you better keep away from me once I have everything in hand. The explosion looks slow at first, like frost on a window pane. But it spreads like molten iron, hotter than hellfire. Touch a drop of it and you'll lose your finger, and the arm behind it. Once it's begun . . ." he shook his head and the aperture of his goggles spread wide ". . . there's no stopping it. We have to time it perfectly. The Span will hold for a little and then come crashing down all at once. Black Fire eats stone like Wulf eats eggs."

Wulf grinned.

"Wulf," Voldigar said, "I want you to go to Pirvale. Tell everyone to head east and stay north of the Adionel. They go to the Anteres lands. There's an old well there."

"I thought you said it was all a swamp now," Medellai interjected.

Voldigar waved it off. "Mostly, yes, Don't let anyone near the well or the bogs, obviously. Stay west of that. Get every fighting man you can spare out of the wagon train, and go on ahead to Westfort with all speed, as many by horse as you can. Tell Taro our plan. When all is set, I'll send a messenger, and you evacuate with a rearguard. If we're lucky, we'll send a host of our enemy back to hell when the bridge falls."

"What then? What of Lusánt? We can't hide in your old lands forever." Gardoric said

"No, we cannot. There's a ford over the Adionel, just past where the river splits. We cross there as soon as the job is done, join everyone at the well, and head north to the Far Marshes."

Wulf's eyes widened. "The Far Marshes? No one goes there."

"Exactly," Voldigar said. "But that's where we'll go, and oppose Lusánt from there, disappear into the swamps. Gardoric, you know the old paths. It won't be easy, but we can bide our time while Liadov uncovers her mysteries and the horde rages impotent on the other side of the Chasm."

"There's a hidden pass beyond the marshes too, or so my people say," Gardoric added. "It's very high and slips into Danek, I doubt even the horde would come that way."

Voldigar nodded. "In need, we could use it."

"What about Gwenyth?" Wulf asked. Lyrusia was leaning forward on the bench now, listening intently.

Voldigar pointed at the wagon. "Take her, and Lyrusia and Hobyn, to Pirvale first. They can travel with the others." With that, he looked from face to face. It was settled.

The others moved to prepare the wagon while Medellai followed Voldigar to the house. Lyrusia stood up and shook her head.

"Sir, your wife cannot travel. She cannot be moved."

Voldigar stopped and blinked. "She has to, Lyrusia."

Lyrusia moved as if to bar his entry. "She needs rest, Elder. I don't think you understand. Her body's giving out."

Voldigar gently moved her aside. "You said she'd be alright."

"Yes, and I said she needed rest." Lyrusia took hold of his other arm as he pushed open the door.

Voldigar stopped and turned toward her. "We have no choice. This house is . . . condemned, Lyrusia. We're all leaving."

Lyrusia's face twisted in frustration and Medellai stepped forward. "How bad is it?"

"That's what I'm trying to tell you!" She wiped a tear from her eye. "She's dying, and her child too." Lyrusia turned her face aside and buried it in her hands. "You have to let her sleep. *Please*, don't move her."

Voldigar turned away and moved swiftly inside, Medellai was close behind. It was dim within and the light a shade of blue. He moved quietly across the floor and peeked beyond the curtain that was now drawn shut. Gwenyth lay there still, save for the shallow rise and fall of her chest. Her skin was gray.

Medellai came near at hand. His face grew pale and a deep frown showed through his beard. He stood as a man struck, quietly staring for a long while before he spoke in a cracking whisper. "Voldigar . . . you don't have to come this time."

Voldigar dared not speak but shot an angry glance at Medellai. He padded softly into the room. There he took Gwenyth's cold hand in his and watched her sleep, feeling her weak breaths barely touch the back of his fingers. He moved his mouth in silent words, first to her and then to God, while his face tightened and he fought back tears. "You'll be alright, Gwen," he whispered. "We'll all be alright."

Medellai stood in the door with his arms folded. Fire crept into his eyes, smoldering frustration on his lips, but he turned and walked outside again.

Voldigar didn't know how long he'd sat there by her side, in quiet memory of his summer bride, of the earth-dug home they shared beneath the tower of Maghaltani, of her slender arms wrapped around his shoulders, whispering good news into his ears.

Lyrusia entered the room. "She's barely holding on. Please, Voldigar."

Voldigar blinked and squeezed her hand again. "She'll hold on. Care for her, Lyrusia. Do all you can." Voldigar kissed Gwenyth's forehead. He let his lips and eyes linger a moment more, then rose and slipped from the room and through his front door.

Medellai was on him in an instant. "You're not going!" he cried.

Voldigar flinched. "We've been over this!" he snapped back.

"You came to guide us before, but Lutz knows the city better than you. No more excuses, Voldigar. No more!"

"Excuses?" Voldigar roared back, "This is my duty!"

"No it isn't!" Medellai caught Voldigar by the collar of his shirt and drove him toward the house. "It isn't," he repeated through gritted teeth. He blinked tears out of his eyes.

Voldigar grasped one of his wrists but caught his words in his mouth. Medellai went on. "You'll kill her, Vol! You'll kill her. Is that what you want?" He loosened his grip on Voldigar's shirt. The others were all watching now. Medellai pinned him sharply with his green eyes, with Gwenyth's eyes. "For once, Vol, just stay. We can do this without you!"

A firm response rose up in Voldigar's chest, practiced words he'd said a thousand times. His mouth moved, his teeth set, but the words never came. In one baffled moment, it was as if the strength drained from his limbs and poured onto the ground. A rigid beam inside his mind snapped and crumbled away. He let go of Medellai's wrist and let his eyes fall to the snowy earth.

"Send for Liadov," Medellai said more softly. "She'll come. She'll help Gwen."

"I can fetch her," Hobyn said.

Voldigar narrowed his eyes at the old man, but still he had no words.

"It's just walking," Hobyn continued, "and it isn't far."

"I'll go with you," Lyrusia added.

"No, my dear," Hobyn said as he rubbed his chest. "I'm not hurt, just my pride. Stay here with the mistress."

Medellai turned his face back to Voldigar and let go of his shirt. "Just wait for Liadov, Brother. And when Gwenie is ready to travel, you put her in that wagon, and you meet us at the well. That's all. We'll take care of the bridge."

Voldigar's shoulders sagged, and he felt as though another man were speaking through his tongue. He nodded. "Go then . . . and God go with you." He rested his hand upon the doorframe. ". . . We'll see you at the well."

A few more minutes preparation, and Voldigar was standing alone, staring dazed at a wagon and three inches of snow, some of it blowing to the side in a gentle wind. Bundled in whatever warm things they could find, Medellai, Gardoric, Lanathor, and Lutz traveled west. Hobyn to the north, and Wulf east. The Eldest watched them go in silence then turned through his door and stepped softly back to Gwenyth's bed.

Kneeling, he grasped her hands gently in his own again and dropped his head to the edge of the mat. "I'm staying this time, Gwen. I'm staying with you."

She squeezed his hand and breathed more deeply.

Chapter Thirty-Nine

The Heart of Winter

S NOW CAME THICKLY DOWN as the heart of Winter donned its hoary crown. Through archways that overlooked the sea, Tepic could hardly perceive the water beyond a thick curtain of plump white flakes. Medellai left some hours before, and for all her cryptic promises of having much to discuss, Liadov had not said ten words since. Instead, she sat hunched over a desk with a quill moving swiftly over a stack of small parchments. Periodic dips into her inkwell were the only sound besides the scratching of her pen and the crackling of a brick hearth.

Tepic dared not interrupt and was content for a while, first to try sleeping, and then to let his mind drift while he watched the snow. He thought of the Brethren and he thought of his sword, but bitter images of Kyriana crowded all the rest. "*There's nowhere you can go that I won't find you,*" she had said. Why did she want the sword in the first place? Or worse, why did she want Lusánt to have it? She seemed as kind as he was cruel, but was it all feigned? In the end, she had betrayed him—and poor Galomar too. He'd been a fool. He narrowed his eyes and imagined what he might have done in that jail cell had he just been more decisive, like the hero of an old tale, cutting down villains with his magic sword.

After a while, his thoughts were no longer good company, and he perused Liadov's books instead. He watched her back pensively as he pulled one from the shelf, but she didn't seem to notice. Laying the heavy tome on the center table, he quietly turned its deep blue cover. The language he did not recognize, and the next four were much the same. He finally found a promising title written in Aramoni, *Battles and Sieges in the Reign of Ramikus*, but soon discovered it was nothing more than a long roll of dry facts and drier figures. He sighed and drooped his head into his hands.

"You will put those back where you found them, yes?" Liadov asked.

Tepic looked up with a reddened face to see she had stopped writing and now observed him with a smirk over the back of her chair.

"Yes ma'am. Of course, ma'am."

She rose from her seat to help as he hurried to replace the books on their shelves. He found himself gawking at her strange wise face as she stood beside him. She smiled again. "Young men should read old books. It's good that you are curious. You wish to ask me a question?" she said.

Tepic didn't quite know how to broach the subject of his sword again and shifted his weight from foot to foot. "What were you doing?" he asked instead.

"Writing," she replied.

"What were you writing?"

"Prophecy."

"Oh." Tepic stopped and stared at his feet. "Really? I always thought—well, I thought there would be voices or glowing lights or something like that."

A musical laugh rolled from Liadov's lips, like the ringing of bells in a temple, so similar to Kyriana. "Not every wind must be a storm, my young friend."

Tepic nodded. "I suppose I didn't know."

"Well, that's the use of questions. Prophecy is the word of God." She fastened the clasp on a final book.

"Can you tell the future?"

"God's word is the future, and the past as well."

"Oh." Tepic found himself looking at the floor again. "Was God . . . talking to you while you wrote?"

"No. I was writing things he said to me before."

Tepic's eyes widened. "You wrote for such a long time. How can you remember so much?"

Liadov caught Tepic's eyes with her piercing blue gaze. "Would you forget God's words if he said something to you, Tepic?" Her face softened. "What was it you really wanted to ask me?"

Tepic glanced at the sword, still lying on the table. Liadov smiled again. "Walk with me," she said before he could say more.

She handed him a thick coat of furs, then led him to the balcony and through a small gate he'd not noticed before. It opened onto a narrow walkway, cleverly carved into the face of the cliffs. A low wall guarded its border, and it lazily wound its way high above the sea. Far below, the waters were striped with many shoals and reefs and jutting stones. It was strange to see snow fall so near the ocean and Tepic thought it a shame that with their feet they marred the pristine white that lay upon the path.

"It's easier to speak when you walk, don't you think?" Liadov asked. "Whatever is on your heart, young Banari, ask and I will answer. I require only that you speak honestly."

Tepic thought for a moment. "Is the sword evil?"

"No, but it's like any sword. It can be used for evil."

"I wouldn't use it for evil."

Liadov shook her head. "I believe you, but do you think Lusánt wanted to do evil with the orb?"

Tepic blinked. "I . . . Lusánt is wicked."

"Yes. Yes he is. Full of iniquity, corrupt, and headed for disaster—but there is a reason the orb was hidden, and the sword once was too." Liadov stopped walking and turned to Tepic. "The Prisms are both door and key, and there is corruption lurking in your heart too, and in mine. It desperately wishes to escape."

"Lusánt is a villain."

"All men are one decision away from being villains, Tepic. Do you think of him as your enemy?"

Tepic licked his lips and considered.

"Remember that we speak our hearts here," she went on.

Tepic nodded. "I do think he's an enemy."

"And so do I, despite my better judgment. But you must know something. Our enemy is not made of bones and blood and the flesh of men. It goes unseen and lives in a place far more real than the dim shadow we walk in now."

"I'm not sure I understand."

"Nor can we fully, but know this, Tepic. There is an evil behind Lusánt that is far more wicked than he. He is a foolish boy and a mortal vessel, but he is not so different from you or me. Do you know where evil enters our world?"

Tepic shook his head.

Liadov reached her finger out and poked him in the chest. "Right here, young man, and don't forget it. If you wish to master evil, start here."

Tepic looked back up the path to the tiny sanctuary she called her home. "Lector Voldigar said I should never use the sword. Is that true?"

Liadov followed his gaze. "Should? Tell me this, Tepic. How often do you think of it?"

Tepic looked at the ground. "A lot, I suppose."

"I suppose so too," Liadov said. "I'll tell you again: there is good reason for this sword to be hidden. Whatever your intentions, there are forces that would corrupt you. Will you give those forces the key and the door?"

Tepic swallowed. "No."

"That's a good decision. And yet, you must bear this weapon all the same. It is yours to carry, and I am sorry for it."

Liadov fell quiet, and they walked the rest of the way to where the pathway abruptly ended in a little hollow. She turned to lead him back and spoke again. "Corruption will seek after you, Tepic. It will speak to you, and when it does you must not listen. You must resist it. Do you understand?"

Tepic nodded. "I think so. Is that a prophecy?"

Liadov smiled. "It is, and one for every man."

Tepic opened his mouth to ask another question, but Liadov looked ahead with sudden alertness. "We have a guest. Come along now."

Once inside, Liadov hurried to the wooden door and swung it open. Tepic was surprised to see none other than Old Man Hobyn from Voldigar's farm shiver across the threshold. His lips were bluish and he trembled wretchedly as he stumbled into the room, rubbing furiously at his arms.

"Hobyn, what happened?" Liadov said as she led him near the hearth.

"S-s-so much colder, th-than it should be," Hobyn chattered. "C-couldn't remember the pattern on the door. Took me forever."

Liadov snatched a blanket from nearby which the man wrapped tightly about himself with a grateful nod. Hobyn blew into his hands and rubbed them together.

"The weather's really t-turned," he said. "Could be a storm coming, but no time to wait."

Liadov narrowed her eyes. "What's wrong?"

"It's the lady of the house, she's very sick, very sick indeed. The Emperor visited, and..." Hobyn trailed off and hung his head, shutting his eyes with a grimace. "... and he wrecked the whole harvest. Set us all to a terrible fit he did. A tremor came over her, and she can't bear such things right now, Liadov. She just can't. The Brethren are all ten ways about the land in a terrible anger and gathering at the old Anteres Well when all is said and done. Maghaltani is burned. But the young lord, he stayed with Gwenyth."

"Did he?

Hobyn nodded. "Aye, and we're all to travel to the well together, just as as soon as the mistress is able. But for now, he calls for aid. Needs you right quick. The apothecary girl is there, but she's very grim."

Liadov drew her lips into a line and signaled for Tepic to add wood to the fire while she ushered Hobyn to a chair and stuffed a pillow behind his back.

"You're hardly dressed for snow," she said.

"Shouldn't be snow. We're not a week past harvest."

"There's *shouldn't* and there's *is,* Hobyn. It's freezing cold, you reckless old man." She fetched another fur coat, like the one Tepic had worn, and dropped it over Hobyn who closed his eyes and scooted closer to the fire.

"What there is, is a message. Old Hobyn said he'd bring it to you, young lady—so that's what he did."

"At least wear boots next time."

"I don't own boots," he said as he leaned his head back and shook with another shiver that traveled from his toes to his nearly bald head.

"I'm going to the farm, Tepic," Liadov said. She stared strangely at him for a moment, but the look passed as quickly as it came. "Make sure Hobyn rests, and give him something warm to drink. There's a kettle by the hearth." Without another word, she wrapped herself in furs of her own and sped out the door.

———◦———

Tepic found the kettle easily enough and filled it from a little waterfall running off the cliff at arms-length over the balcony. It flowed in nothing more than a trickle now with tiny icicles hanging from the lip.

He hung the kettle on some hooks beat into the brick and looked around to see if Liadov had any tea. Scribes and priests always seemed to have tea. He found a little box with some nice-smelling leaves in it but wasn't sure if it was edible. He held it out.

"Is this tea, Hobyn?"

Hobyn did not reply. His head was lolled over the chair, and his chest rose and fell evenly. He was quietly snoring. Tepic frowned and put the lid back on the box, then pulled the kettle off before it got noisy.

He couldn't make sense of Hobyn's story and nearly woke him to ask, but the old man looked peaceful, and color was returning to his lips.

Lusánt had visited the farm? The Brethren were in terrible anger? His sister was there? None of it made any sense, and no one seemed to tell him anything. It was irritating.

Tepic found some dry bread and brought it to the table where he considered grabbing another book to read. There were a dozen other laden shelves, and surely something would be interesting. Instead, he just listened to the sound of his chewing while he scowled and watched the old man sleep.

His eyes fell to the sword lying by his hand, and he did his best to recount all of Liadov's words and warnings as they wandered through his thoughts. He was both its wielder and should never wield it. It wasn't evil, but it would always do evil. Lusánt was an enemy, but not the real enemy. "Paradoxes," Lector Lanathor called them. He hated paradoxes. Tepic wished he knew better what to ask and how to speak to Liadov. He wished he had a year to ask it. What was happening in Aramon?

"It doesn't matter," he told himself. *"What would I even do?"*

Tepic drummed his fingers on the table and looked up at Hobyn again. The snores were now more of a low rumble. It reminded him of his dad and how his snores could travel all the way up the stairs like the noise of a hibernating bear, waking him and Ru.

"Liadov didn't say I had to stay here," he told himself next. *"Maybe I could help. What if Ru's in trouble? And what about Sword-Lector? He helped me, I should help him."*

Tepic stared at his sword a long while more until he finally made up his mind. He found a scrap of paper and borrowed Liadov's quill.

Can't find tea. Water's hot. Went to your farm. - Tepic B.

Satisfied, he set the note by the kettle, then wrapped the last of Liadov's fur coats tightly around him. He covered that in Gardoric's cloak and pulled the hood close around his face. It took only a moment to swelter in the small room, but he knew he'd soon be glad of it. Last of all, he quietly lifted his sword from the table and snuck out the door.

In the dark tunnel, it took an awkwardly long time discerning how to slide the stone panel away, but soon he was pushing through willow branches and then blinking in the haze of an afternoon snowfall. An astonishing blanket of snow had accumulated on the ground since last he'd been outside. It fell so thickly here that he could see hardly fifty feet ahead, but Liadov's footprints still showed faintly, leading away to the south.

A gusting breeze blew the snow sideways. It stung his nose and stuck to his eyelashes. For a moment, he peered into the formless white and considered turning back, but how could he? Tepic pulled the hood as low as he could, hung the sword over his back, and padded through the snow—eyes fixed like a hawk on Liadov's tracks.

Chapter Forty

Black Fire

"**D**on't 'ave time for this!" Cozi bellowed. "Work to do—and more tin-heads every minute. How'd you even find me?" His reaction to Lutz had been immediate and explosive. If anything, worse than Lutz had warned.

Someone loudly pounded at the door and called for Cozi in a thick Undercity accent.

"Sod off!" Cozi yelled back. "Five minutes!" The mokja pressed his eye against the tharmskolp again and muttered something to himself.

Lanathor's fingers were numb, and a profound sense of weariness wrapped around his head and shoulders like a sodden cloak. He'd taken so much root the night before, all he had, and the fade would go on for hours yet. All the while, aching grogginess worked over his bones. Gardoric seemed no better. His skin gleamed with sweat in the pale lamplight, and his agitated fingers scraped against the driftwood countertop while he watched Lutz and Cozi go round and round.

"You owe Tepic Banari a favor, Cozi. I'm telling you, we're here on his behalf," Lutz said.

Cozi turned to a scrawny youth sitting on a barrel worrying at a dry biscuit. "These Dove's friends, Ferret?"

The boy looked up. "Two of 'em is." He pointed a pocket knife at Medellai and Gardoric.

"Fine. I'll chat wif' these buggers then." He glared at Lutz and then gave a sweet smile to Medellai. "How can I be of service, my gracious, masterful lord from above?"

"We need Black Fire, Cozi, and quickly," Medellai said.

Lutz struck his palm against his forehead and groaned.

After a frozen moment, Cozi raised one eyebrow, tilted his head back, and roared with laughter. It took him a solid ten seconds to recover.

"Black Fire? Black Fire! Presently, I'm engaged in evacuating a couple 'fousand of my friends, and you want Black Fire? I'll tell you how I repay Tepic's favor—by not 'frowing you twits 'eadlong over the edge. There. Repaid!" Cozi thrust the map back to his eye.

Lanathor hoisted himself from against the wall with a grunt. "We mean to use it against the Emperor, Cozi, Son of Brol."

Cozi blinked and looked at Lanathor like he'd just seen a three-headed mermaid. "Excuse me?"

"'Brol' is ye da's name?" Ferret interjected

"Shut it."

"You heard me right," Lanathor continued. "We saw the deployment on our way in. We found you at great risk to ourselves as well. We are your allies—at least by circumstance."

"My pimpled arse!" Cozi looked at Lutz. "Is this another cruel joke?"

"Brethren do not lie," Lanathor said.

Lutz only glared.

"So the bruvs of Aramon is gonna blow up Lord Sispy Rats wif' Black Fire?" Cozi laughed again, this time forced and with a wary eye. He didn't take his gaze off Lutz. "Getting me expelled wasn't enough, eh?"

"You got someone killed, Cozi!" Lutz protested.

"Science is dangerous!" Cozi shouted back.

"Please!" Lanathor swallowed. "We're not lying to you, and I did not say we're blowing the Emperor up. I said we need to use Black Fire against him. He's made an enemy of us too, and all of Aramon, not just Undercity"

"Ask 'em for coin," Ferret chirped from the barrel.

"Shut up," Cozi barked.

"We can pay you," Gardoric said and rubbed his eyes.

Lutz's goggles whirled. "The Emperor burned our village, Cozi. We're not going back. You . . . you can pick it clean, everything I own."

Cozi spit. "'Fink I'm going topside? Go blind as you, Lutz?" Cozi shook his head. "Sorry, bubs. I couldn't 'elp yous, even if I was a cracked fool. You need 'fings I don't 'ave."

Lanathor inhaled and pulled something from his pack. It was a stone about the size of his forearm. Dark and jagged, it caught a little of the light in its crystalline blackness. Most unusual of all, it pulsed slowly with its own violet glow. "We already have some of what we need."

Cozi's eyes expanded like saucers. "Tym'cha's crooked teef'!" He reached his hands toward the rock and Lanathor instinctively pulled it back. Cozi looked up at him. "How'd you get this?"

"There's a lot of chaos right now, and we are very resourceful."

Cozi licked his lips. "You're not lying . . ."

"We just need the accelerant, the catalyst, and—" Lutz began.

Cozi cut him off. "And a stone's worth of Tarpane Crystals."

"Ten stone," Lutz said.

It turned out that Cozi's eyes could get even wider. "Ten stone? What in Tymie's name are you blowing up? The moon?"

"Something like that," Lutz said.

"We intend a very large explosion and a very large distraction, Cozi," Medellai said. "I am confident we'll draw the Emperor's attention away from Undercity."

At this, Cozi's eyes narrowed and the room fell silent for several long moments. He began to pace and mutter, watching the floor as he scratched furiously at his chin.

"Just tell me how to make the parts, and we're gone," Lutz said.

Cozi looked up with disgust plastered on his gnarled face. "Ha! Don't press your luck, you hairless rat."

"Hairless . . . my luck?" Lutz gathered his hands into fists but Medellai stayed him with a glance.

Cozi's mouth twisted into a coil of twitching scowls. At length, he let out a deep sigh and dropped his shoulders. "Maybe I am a cracked fool . . ." He retreated behind the countertop and stopped to rhythmically wrap his knuckles while he eyed each brother in turn. "I don't want to know what you's doing, but . . . fine. I 'fink I like the sound of it."

With a grunt, Cozi disappeared into the back room. A moment later he returned with a small pouch. This he handed to Lutz. He vanished again and emerged with a sealed clay pot, carefully cradled in his hands.

"Which one of you 'as the steadiest 'ands?" Everyone looked to Gardoric. "Good. Don't go standing next to Lutz. Trust me."

Gardoric awkwardly took the jar and shuffled off to the side.

"Don't set this off anywhere near Undercity," Cozi said.

"We don't intend to," Lanathor replied.

"An' yous all better be as resourceful as you say, 'cause I don't have ten grain of Tarpane Crystals, let alone ten stone."

Lanathor's heart fell. Time was flowing away. Every minute hastened the collapse of Westfort. He closed his eyes and inhaled.

Lutz spoke up again. "I know someone who has a ton, but he won't be happy to see me either."

As it happened, Lutz categorically prohibited any attempt at speaking to Bajk.

"On account of Voldigar *liking* that pig," Lutz said, "he seems to think it's a funny sibling spat. It's not, and don't believe otherwise. Bajk would feed me to the rats if he could cut me small enough."

They were now huddled in the dark outside a small door. The rhythmic thumping of machines beyond the wall filled the air. "I was saving this little secret for a rainy day," Lutz said. "Well it's raining, so don't muck it up." He let a sliver of lamplight pass from face to face.

"Locked?" Medellai asked.

"Of course."

"Have your picks?"

"Of course! But there's nothing to pick," Lutz said. He shined the lamp on the door. Sure enough, it was nothing more than a flat board, not even a handle. "Only opens from the other side. Your turn, Lanathor. I'm not going in there." He walked a few paces back down the tunnel.

Lanathor narrowed his eyes. "What will the Tarbane Crystals look like?"

"Coarse, gray salt."

Lanathor sighed. "I mean what are they stored in?"

"Barrels, and they'll be labeled 'T.C.' He's an Artificer, not a chimney sweep. You need two, and make sure they're full."

Lanathor considered a moment. "How will I carry two?"

"I don't know, find a cart or something," Lutz said with irritation. He crossed his arms and turned back to the wall, muttering under his breath.

"Just let me in after," Medellai said. "We can each carry one."

Gardoric leaned forward. "No. I'll go. We don't want to be seen." His breathing was hard.

Medellai frowned at him briefly. "Save your strength, Gardoric. You've done enough already—we'll be careful."

Gardoric gave an appraising look at Lanathor. "He's no less weary than I."

"Maybe so, but Tellers don't suffer The Wilding."

"No," Lanathor added with a grimace. "If I push too hard, I just die."

Gardoric frowned but did not argue further. He settled back on his haunches to wait, carefully clutching the little jar.

Lanathor closed his eyes. The threads were still there, faint but within reason. He breathed deeply. "See you in a moment."

He wasn't sure if the spinning was better or worse in the pitch dark, but a split second later he was standing against a wall, trying to swallow bile before it filled his mouth. *Good, not spent yet.* He unlocked the door to let Medellai through, but Lutz stood there scowling instead.

"You'll probably just get lost," Lutz said and shouldered into the room while he closed off his lamp.

The momentary light revealed they were in some kind of closet, complete with mops and a drain in the middle of the floor.

Lanathor cracked the next door and peered through with one eye. No one was nearby that he could see, but many voices rang dimly through a cloud of steam and the metallic clank of huge machines. The room was crowded but tidily organized. Stacks of crates and boxes were piled in a tightly spaced labyrinth. Everything was wet and dripping and smelled of soot and hot oil. They emerged from the closet, gingerly stepping over slick stonework. Lanathor held his breath and peeked around the corner.

It was easier than expected to find their quarry. First, a limping mokja walked by carrying a jar with two handles, but Lutz heard him and pulled at Lanathor's robes. Lanathor ducked his head back around the edge and let him pass. But another look and there they were—a neat pile of barrels, the imprinted black 'T.C.' labels all pointing in the same direction. They were enclosed in a metal cage, but its gate hung open. The real problem was another mokja, sitting shirtless on a stool in the intersection directly in front of them. The strap of his goggles dug into the back of his wrinkly head, and he was working something in his hands they couldn't see.

Lanathor had not used it in years, but it was one of the simplest tricks he'd discovered as part of his unusual magic. "Oi, you slack-jawed rat. Get off your backside and help me with this!" He said the words in his best impression of a cross between Cozi and Lutz. The sound, however, emerged from a fair distance away, round the far corner of the crates.

The shirtless mokja looked up. "What? Slack-jawed rat? I'll slack-jaw you, you pig-faced filth!" He rose to his feet and stomped toward the voice.

Lutz raised an eyebrow along with the corner of his mouth, but gave a shake of his head in place of whatever it was he thought to say. They hurried into the cage and grabbed a barrel each, hefting to make sure they were full.

The bulk was considerably more than Lanathor had hoped. While Lutz seemed to bear the weight with ease, Lanathor balanced it awkwardly and wondered for a moment if he should roll it. Perhaps it would have been easier without numb hands.

Heavy as they were, there was no time to delay. Lutz set off back to the closet, and Lanathor waddled after him as fast as he could over the wet floor, praying not to fall.

Bajk stood directly in front of the closet door holding a mop. The Artificer was twirling his long white beard and chewing something—he turned just in time to see them round the corner. The chewing stopped, his mouth fell open, and his magnified eyes widened like two huge telescopes.

There was a long, pregnant moment of silence where all parties considered each other, wishing for all the world to go back to five seconds ago, but there was nothing for it. Bajk's face twisted in rage and alarm, and he cried out indignantly in his high, nasally gravel. "You beardless gutter filth nag pony hag loving scum—"

Lutz simply dashed ahead, overpowering the sputtering Bajk with his bulging belly and the weight of his barrel. Lanathor stumbled after, and Bajk crashed to the floor with a grunt. His shrill voice echoed through the engine room.

"Thieves! Thieves! Help! Help!"

They burst through the door while the sound of many voices gathered behind. Lutz swept his lamp into his hand and somehow managed his barrel in a single arm.

"Go! Go!" Lanathor shouted. "We're discovered!"

It took only a second for the other two to comprehend their sudden peril. They took off in a flash of swinging lamplight. It looked ridiculous, but Lanathor really did roll the barrel now.

"No! No!" Lutz yelled. "Pick that up. Follow me!"

He darted out in front, barrel and all, and his squat legs worked furiously, leading them through a tangle of chaotic twists and turns. The clamor of countless small legs and feet slapped the stone behind them, and a voice howled down the halls. "Lutz! You treacherous goat! I'll have your giblets! Curse the day you were born! You can't run forever!"

Losing the uninitiated in the Delvings was one thing, but it proved impossible to shake the mokja. Lutz glanced back several times with a look of growing despair until he finally pointed sharply to a turn.

The brothers careened around the corner into a dead-end.

"We have to disappear Gardoric. Now!" Lutz hissed.

Gardoric swallowed and blinked and moved in turn to touch each man with his eyes closed, coming last of all to Lanathor. He thought Gardoric might collapse and began to set his barrel down to help.

"No, no," Gardoric gasped. "You have to hold it, don't set anything down." He touched him, and then last of all, he himself rippled out of sight.

Lanathor did not move and dared not breathe. The barrel grew heavier in the stillness, and the edges of it were still slick from the engine room. He could feel it slipping from his grip and dug his fingers in until they ached. He could not see his own hands or any of his companions.

It only took a few seconds for a group of mokja to come into view, swinging bright lanterns and torches left and right. One stopped and peered directly into the dead-end hall, briefly shining his lamp against the far wall. Lanathor stared the fellow in the eyes, but there was nothing. The whole pack of mokja sped off again into the darkness.

Lanathor waited several more seconds to let his breath out and rest the barrel on the floor while one by one his friends reappeared. Gardoric slid his back down the wall until he was seated and then rested his head in his hands.

Medellai knelt in front of him with darting eyes and a frown. "No more, Gardoric. No more," he said firmly.

Gardoric nodded weakly. His eyes were glassy and his cheeks looked hollow and gray.

"We have to keep moving," Lutz whispered. "We can double back."

"Where will we go?" Lanathor asked.

"One more rainy day secret," Lutz said with a wild grin.

<hr/>

Lutz's final "rainy day secret" was a passage that extended a few miles beyond Arregalt, all the way to the reservoir beneath the Trakast Bridge that rested between Voldigar's farm and Maghaltani. It emerged there in a small cave, covered by a frozen waterfall. All brethren knew that the Delvings held secrets, but a passage that bypassed the very walls came as a great shock, doubly so that it had never been closed off.

"Last chance," Lutz said as they passed through the opening into dim light showing through the ice. "This won't open from the other side. Make sure you've got everything."

The brethren secured Cozi's compounds along with Bajk's barrels and stepped through. After one final lamplit scan, Lutz followed with a hop. The moment his weight left the floor behind, the heavy stone door rumbled closed, seamless and smoothly concealed in the natural rock around it.

Lanathor rubbed his temples and felt for his heartbeat while they caught their breath. "Will we be followed?"

Lutz frowned. "Yes, probably. Bajk knows about this too. He'll have to suspect it."

Lanathor's heart pounded—appropriate for the effort of lugging a seventy-pound barrel through miles of tunnel. He was recovering remarkably from three bulbs of Falam Root, but it also meant he'd be fully sober of its effects within an hour or two.

"We have to keep moving," Lanathor said.

The other brothers were resting, Medellai on the stone floor and Gardoric sagging on the barrel that Lutz had finally set down. They rose without complaint though, and Gardoric carefully knocked the ice away with his hatchet. It chipped a little at first until suddenly the whole sheet tore away and crumbled into the canyon. A gust of cold air took their breath away.

To their left, the huge dam barring the Adionel should have been visible. Below them, a deep river valley should have stared up. What met their eyes instead was a blinding torrent of snow, tearing through the air and whipping on a howling wind.

"Well . . ." Medellai said, "if they do follow us, they're madmen."

There was a brief debate on whether they should cross the dam itself or skirt the lake to use the bridge. It didn't last long, as the folly of trying to traverse the dam in the wind was readily apparent. They were more likely of course to be seen on the heavily trafficked Trakast Bridge, but whoever was upon it would have to be within twenty feet to have any hope at all—and only fools would dare the blizzard.

After a wet scramble from the valley and a weary trudge around the rapidly freezing reservoir, they were soon atop the bridge where they found they could at least slide the barrels along with little difficulty. Even Lutz preferred this method. Upon the road, the depth of snow did not delay them much, but outside the valley's protection, the blasting gale drove against the brethren. They huddled close together and gave up trying to speak in low voices.

"We won't make the Span in two days at this rate," Medellai said over the squall. "We need a sleigh, a cart—something! And horses."

"Where do we go though? Voldigar's house?" Lutz asked.

Medellai shook his head. "No. Not there. Leave the old man be. What about Maghaltani?"

Lanathor wondered if perhaps his store of Falam Root lay untouched in his tower. He was nearly convinced by that alone but abandoned the thought quickly. "No, we can't go there. They know it was us in the engine room. Maghaltani's the first place they'll search—blizzard or no."

"Pirvale then," Lutz said. They were all shouting at this point, and Lanathor looked nervously over his shoulder. "It's closer than Maghaltani anyway."

The sense of it was obvious, and the others joined Gardoric in his quiet posture, head down, trudging wearily across the bridge. Walking to Pirvale before the Span would add a few miles to their journey, but mounts and something to haul the cursed barrels were now necessities.

Rather than build two bridges, the Trakast Bridge had been expanded centuries before and split two ways. One southward toward the eastern road and the ten or so miles to the Span. The other broke off roughly northward where they would soon turn east to Pirvale. This direction they took and went on without incident for some time, staving off the hypnotic snowfall as best they could. At length, Medellai stopped and turned around.

"What is it?" Lanathor asked.

Medellai held up a finger. "Shhh."

The brothers stood breathless for a long while and looked back fruitlessly into the swirling snow.

"What do you hear?" Lanathor asked again when he could bear it no more.

"I think we're being followed."

"Are you certain?"

"No. It's all a tangle in the wind, Lan, but I thought I heard something." He squinted. "There's nothing now."

Lanathor stood still a moment and listened to the shrill howl. He peered hopelessly behind toward where the Trakast Bridge ought to be. Nothing.

"Let's just keep moving. Speed, that's all we can hope in now."

They redoubled their efforts, and Lanathor soon found himself breathing hard. The hairs in his nose froze with every inhale, only to thaw again.

He couldn't help but remember his long trek through Danek, towing Liadov behind. The memory brought a shiver to his spine, even colder than the storm that raged about them.

By habit, he reached for his pockets and the empty capsules within. He would long be past the root's effects by the time they reached the Span—nightfall if they were fortunate. He could still feel Liadov's fingers on his wrist, her eyes upon his own, but now was not the time for uncertainty. For how close it was to Arregalt, Pirvale was surprisingly provincial. Isolated in a blind valley, he doubted they would have a proper apothecary—but he could hope. He sighed and bent into the wind.

The road was hardly visible anymore, but long before it bent toward Voldigar's home, Medellai turned them aside to the east. The dirt track that led to Pirvale was not visible at all, but the brethren trusted Medellai could lead them with his eyes closed. On they went, and familiar trees began to show here and there until their course was mostly enclosed in a sparse wood of elm. Medellai stopped and glanced rearward again.

Lanathor came to his side. "What now?"

"I hear it again."

Lanathor looked into the empty, whipping snow while he blew heat into his hands. He strained his ears.

"It could be horses, Lan. We have to get off this track. I'd hoped we'd lose them off the north road, but . . ."

"How far behind?" Lanathor asked.

Medellai shook his head. "I don't know. There's a ravine ahead, not far. The wood is thick there—a quiet way into Pirvale."

They set off again, as fast as they could manage, lifting their feet high over the snow and following hard after Medellai. The wood thickened, and their breath grew heavy until this time, Lanathor abruptly called a halt. "Hold."

Through the elms, he spied a tumble of long shapes buried in the snow that must be fallen trees. Most importantly, one of them had a sapling growing from its side, itself almost completely covered in snow. The growth was a sure sign the log had lain there rotting for some time.

"I need a moment," Lanathor said as he pushed through the trees toward the grove of fallen logs.

"No time," Medellai called out. The others had stopped there on the track to watch him. "The ravine is just ahead."

Lanathor ignored him but hurried his steps toward the log with the little tree on its side. Off the road, the snow was surprisingly deep and he had to half swim through it to reach the fallen trunk. Clearing the snow away, he was reminded that only a few days ago it was summer. The signs of it were buried here under several inches of snow.

He had to move fast. It took only a few seconds to find his prize. It was pitifully small but glistened with the delicate, unmistakable flower of Falam Root. His knife was in his hand in a flash, working at the base of the tiny plant.

Just as it popped free, he spied a second stalk, further along the log. He waded to its side and set to work again. This one was larger, and its bulb was deep in the rotting wood. In his concentration, he did not notice Gardoric had come to his side.

"What are you doing?" Gardoric said urgently.

"Just a moment, I said," Lanathor replied. "It's very rare."

"We have to go."

"I'm hurrying. I'm almost done."

Gardoric sighed and tramped back to the path. He shouted something to the others, but it was lost in the wind.

The second bulb came free, and Lanathor struggled to push it into a capsule with his numb and trembling hands. It rolled out of his fingers. A voice carried over the wind again, and he opened his mouth to respond. He froze. There were many voices.

Lanathor flattened himself against the ground and peered through the trees. The little bulb of root lay crookedly in the snow. He could barely make out the shapes of his brothers, standing exposed in the middle of the road. Behind them, and now fanning out all around, were the hazy forms of horsemen, dozens of them, one the size of an oxcart.

". . . stand down . . ." he caught the phrase, clipped in the muffling wind. Horses were circling now and kicking more snow into the air.

"Disappear, Gardoric," Lanathor whispered under his breath. "Disappear!" The three figures on foot still stood below the horses. Lutz's shape was clear, but Medellai and Gardoric looked much the same in the churning white. One of them raised his hands.

Lanathor could make out nothing more of what was said, but there were shouts of alarm and the sounds of a brief struggle. Men were dismounting and crowding round the center of the road. A moment later, some of the horsemen broke off in his direction.

Thoughtlessly, he grasped the root from off the snow and thrust it into his mouth. He blinked, looking for the Song to form around him.

"The tracks lead this way." A voice could now be clearly heard.

For a moment, Lanathor thought to fight, but the folly of it took only a second to register. He looked about frantically and then grabbed the threads as they rippled into view. With a twist, he vanished, only to reappear some thirty feet away in deep shadow under the low-hanging branches of an ancient elm that stooped under the weight of sudden snow.

Six riders emerged from the haze of snowfall in imperial livery and heavy winter garb. General Gamad himself was behind them, and by his side, another man rode beneath a heavy cowl, lined in black fur and pulled low over his face. Their horses breathed heavily and lifted their feet high through the deep snow. One circled the spot Lanathor had been only seconds before.

"Careful," one of the soldiers said. "You'll lame your mare."

"Snow's trampled," another said.

Gamad looked warily from side to side as his horse stamped. "To hell with your horse. Careful of the Chanters."

A thin, quiet voice emerged from the rider in the cowl. It was too soft for Lanathor to hear all of it. "*. . . no concern . . .*"

Gamad pointed at the ground, and one of his men dismounted to dig through the snow.

"Someone was here all right, chopping at the wood."

The cowled figure spoke again. "*. . . foraging . . .*" was the only word Lanathor heard.

"Where do the tracks lead?" Gamad asked.

"Nowhere," another replied.

One of the men spit. "They was probably just here dropping trou."

"Snow's clean."

"Interrupted then. Waste of time."

Gamad looked back and forth several more times. He appeared for all the world like a great mountain bear nosing at the wind. His eyes passed directly over the elm where Lanathor lay flat, but his gaze did not linger. "Back to the road," Gamad said at last. "We have prisoners to process."

Lanathor had held his breath the entire time they spoke. It came out now in a stream of fog over the powder before his face. *Think Lanathor, think.* He could swear they'd heard the beating of his heart against the ground. It was like a drum in his own ears. He thought of a hundred spells and a hundred ways to put down dozens of horsemen in a snowstorm, but all his imaginings ended the same way—four dead Brothers bleeding out on the road to Pirvale.

The shapes in the distance receded back the way they'd come. Their voices grew more faint. Soon there was no one left on the road, but Lanathor still lay motionless.

Tears welled in his eyes. *"What have I done,"* he whispered to himself. *"Dear God, what have I done?"*

Chapter Forty-One

Falling Leaves

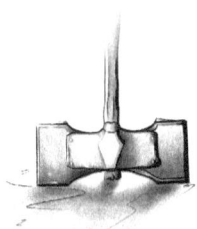

V OLDIGAR BALANCED SEVERAL MORE splits of quartered firewood in one arm, and with the other, he pressed the door shut against a howling wind. In reply, the warm red of his fireplace stood straight again, free of winter's blast. The storm beat and whistled against his home but came no further.

Save for the buffeting that dully pierced his walls, it was quiet within. Lyrusia dozed in Gwenyth's chair with a forgotten bundle of snow-wet herbs lying on her lap. Liadov sat upon the floor by Gwenyth's mat, holding her hand and stroking her cheek.

"How is she?" Voldigar asked quietly as he knelt beside them.

"Much better than she was," Liadov replied. "This one, I think, is strongest of us all." She smiled. "But I'm glad you sent for me."

Voldigar nodded. "As am I." He searched Gwenyth's face. There was a sheen of sweat across her brow, but color had returned, and her breathing was even.

"How soon can she travel?" Voldigar asked.

Liadov met his gaze. Questioning, at first she seemed, but the deep blue pools of her eyes grew distant, and her face fell in subtle pity.

Voldigar narrowed his eyes. "Liadov?"

Wordlessly, she placed Gwenyth's hand in his own and gently cupped his face. With a sad smile, she rose and left them, pulling the curtain shut behind.

Gwenyth stirred and Voldigar turned to her. Her eyes fluttered open, and he brushed an auburn strand from her face. She smiled weakly. "Is it Midwinter yet, my love?"

Voldigar smiled back. "No, Gwen, not yet." Liadov and Lyrusia had given her many cures and tinctures in her fitful waking. He did not know if she jested with him or if the medicines were playing on her mind. In either case, he would see to her comfort.

Gwenyth released a long sigh and closed her eyes again. "Where are we going?"

"To Pirvale, and then to my old well," Voldigar said quietly, "as soon as this storm blows over. Lutz brought you a very nice carriage."

A small frown emerged at the corners of her lips. "It won't do," she muttered. "Our little prince . . . must be born on the farm . . ."

Voldigar squeezed her hand. "That's a way off yet, Gwen. Maybe we'll be back by then."

"No . . ." She said the word in a long sigh. "Shouldn't he . . . be born with the first snow . . ." Her words trailed off into silence. She seemed to be sleeping once more, and Voldigar contented himself to gently run his hand through her hair while the light faded and heaviness grew over his sight. . . .

A deep, rolling rumble of the wind against their wall drew them both awake. Gwenyth turned her head to Voldigar and stared into his eyes. "Vol?" she asked. "Tell me everything will be good again."

"Everything, Gwen. Of course it will. Everything will be good."

Lyrusia padded softly into the room, rubbing sleep from her eyes and holding a steaming cup. She stood quietly until Voldigar finally nodded and rose to his feet. Lyrusia helped Gwenyth to sit upright as Voldigar returned to the hearth.

Liadov was moving her gaze slowly from one corner of the room to another and seemed to take no notice of him. A pale and subtle light of blue crept through the imperfections of his door and shutters. The faintest hint of sevenbark still lingered in the air. Voldigar squatted down to add more wood to the fire.

"You have a beautiful home, Voldigar," Liadov said. "For all the world that rages on outside . . . remember how it looks in here—right now."

Voldigar turned his head to reply, but at that moment, a muffled knock sounded on his door.

"Lanathor?" Voldigar asked as he held the door open. Lanathor indeed stood upon the threshold with his shoulders stooped and his chin against his chest. Snow was blowing across his dark head.

"I'm sorry, Brother," Lanathor said shakily.

"What? Come out of the cold."

He hurried Lanathor inside and shut the door.

"I'm sorry," Lanathor repeated. His eyes were closed, and his shoulders still hung low.

Voldigar glanced at Liadov and leaned in closer to Lanathor. "For what?"

"I've made a terrible mistake."

Voldigar grabbed his arm. "Come on, Lan. Snap out of it. What happened?"

Lanathor looked up and blinked. "I . . . we were caught, everyone's caught." He shook his head. "It's my fault. I've ruined everything."

"I don't care whose fault it is, Lanathor. Just tell me what happened!"

"The Black Fire," Lanathor said, "Gamad and his men have taken it. Gardoric, Medellai, Lutz—they're all gone."

A stone dropped in Voldigar's stomach. "Are they . . . alive?"

"I don't know, Eldest. They've been taken prisoner. We've lost everything."

Voldigar ran both hands along his head and took a deep breath. "The Span . . ." he whispered.

"It's over," Lanathor said. His face twisted in agony. "The horde is upon us and all will be swept away. I have done this."

Voldigar grasped Lanathor by his shoulders and shook him. "Stop it! It's not over. It's not. Pity yourself later!"

Lanathor closed his eyes again, and two tears streaked down his cheeks.

"Look at me, Brother," Voldigar said. They locked eyes. "Saddle two horses." He flashed his face to Liadov and took another wavering breath. "Bring everyone to the old well, Liadov—as soon as she can travel."

Lanathor's eyes widened and he shook his head. "No, Brother," he whispered. "It's beyond our reach now."

Voldigar followed Lanathor's gaze over his shoulder and saw that Gwenyth was on her feet. She was trembling in the frame of his bedroom door, bracing with one arm and holding her belly with the other.

Voldigar whipped his eyes back to Lanathor. "You're wrong. Saddle the horses I said!" He half shoved Lanathor through the front door and turned back to Gwenyth.

Lyrusia was at her side now, coaxing her with gentle words, but Gwenyth paid her no mind.

"What's happening, Voldigar?" she asked. Her mouth hung open. Her eyes were sharpened in growing terror.

"Gwen, lie back do—"

"Why is Lanathor here?"

Voldigar blinked and grit his teeth. "They caught the others. . . . I have to ride."

"No," Gwenyth said shakily. "No, no, no . . ." Lyrusia caught her under her arms as she leaned against the frame, but Gwenyth swiped her hands away. She gathered herself and crossed to Voldigar where she grasped the sides of his face with desperate strength. "No," she said again. "Your part is *done*."

"Gwen, I . . . I can't . . . I have to. There's no one else."

Gwenyth shook her head and dropped her hands to his shoulders. "That's not true. It can't be true."

"Gwen—"

"Choose me, Voldigar." She buried her head in his chest and sobbed. "Choose me . . ."

"Don't say that," he replied through his own shaking breath.

"Choose us!"

"Gwen. Please. There's no other way. I have chosen you. I *have* chosen us! Don't—"

Voldigar wrapped his arms more tightly around her as she sagged toward the floor. He embraced her there while her strangled weeping flowed onto his neck.

"It's not safe here anymore, Gwen. I'll return for you," he said, "when the storm clears . . . Liadov . . . she's taking you to the old well. It'll be alright."

Gwenyth was wracked by another sob and weakly pounded one fist against Voldigar's arm. Lyrusia hurried behind her and placed a hand on her back.

Voldigar felt strength sapping from his hands and from his heart. He had to move. He grasped her hands in his own and backed away, but she clung to him with inconsolable grip until her feet dragged along the floor.

A dam broke in Voldigar's chest, and he choked on a wrenching cry.

"You won't come back," she moaned. "You *won't*."

Slowly, like driving a dagger through his own heart, he peeled her small, pale hands from his shirt. Liadov and Lyrusia both were at her side now, holding her weight. Voldigar grasped the handle of his door but could not find the strength to move it. "I promise, Gwen. We'll meet at the well. We'll be safe. I promise."

Somehow the door had opened, and Voldigar felt the cold wind blasting against his back as several flakes blew past his eyes and vanished before the fire. He took one step backward. His eyes were fixed on Gwenyth. "I promise," he said again. Another step.

Gwenyth lurched forward and stumbled, but she was out of reach now. Another step. Liadov caught her but could only lower her gently to her knees as she sobbed. The howling lash of the storm tore sideways between them and obscured his vision. Backwards, another step.

He could see only Gwenyth now, a single starlight shining through a flowing sky of frost, her hands outstretched as she receded. The roar of the blizzard filled his ears until her sobs were voiceless murmurs. He felt nothing on his skin. The clamor of the wind descended into formless gray until he heard nothing either. Another step. Another step.

In a sudden moment, all the cyclone of winter froze like a crystal before his wet eyes, and he knew if he looked for another agonizing second, he would never take another step. He would rush forward and wrap her in his arms. They would lie down in the snow and perish as a dark wave swept over Aramon, but they would perish together.

He turned away.

Lanathor was there upon one of the huge Maghaltani steeds, another saddled by his side. His face was grim, and his dark eyes shone in wonder at his friend. He dared not look back either, and in a breathless plunge, Voldigar leapt upon the other horse. With the wind upon their backs, the two Elders charged over the snow, flinging powder into the air, and with cloaks billowing behind, the great pounding of their hooves drowned out the cry of the storm and the last falling of a thousand red aspen leaves.

Chapter Forty-Two

Beacons on the Span

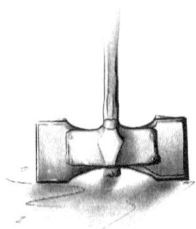

V OLDIGAR DID NOT REMEMBER the long miles consumed under the pounding hooves of their sure-footed steeds, only the cold spray of winter across his eyes as they blindly trusted their horses to feel the road beneath them. Evening had come by the time the arching expanse of The Great Span loomed in the dusklight. Its huge mass faded into the distance before the mountains, and tiny lights flickered on its turrets that receded into gloom.

The blustering wind had blown itself weary in the preceding hours, and the snow came down now in a gentle cascade. In the last sliver of sunlight behind them and the glowing torches before, there was a quiet calm, a sense of memory of winters past and high holy days. Voldigar slowed as they approached.

"We must act soon. If Westfort still holds, go on before me, and prepare its retreat. I will descend the Chasm to the base of the Span and watch there for your signal. When all are across, make certain your sign to me, and I will bring it down."

Lanathor nodded grimly and peered into the darkness beyond the Span. "And if Westfort does not hold?"

"Then we give battle worthy of the end of The Brotherhood of Aramon." Voldigar smiled, but Lanathor did not reflect his face.

"I will assemble a rearguard," Lanathor said, "that the others may escape. If fortune holds, we'll lure our foe onto the bridge before you bring it down. I will see it done." Lanathor looked at Voldigar with a far-off gaze.

Voldigar nodded and moved close enough to lay a hand on Lanathor's shoulder. "Do nothing rash, Brother, and do not despair. Whatever blame you give yourself, remember that risks are taken in war. Not every arrow strikes its mark. Set your mind on the task at hand."

Lanathor swallowed and cast his eyes to the snow. "I . . ." He stopped and fell silent before he looked at Voldigar again. "Are you certain you can do this, Voldigar?"

"No . . . but there is no other way, and I must try."

"How will you escape?"

Voldigar took a deep breath. "Does it matter?"

Tears welled in Lanathor's eyes again. He bared his teeth and drew his eyebrows together, but he could only rock in his saddle until he shook his head and turned away. Together, they moved to the edge of the Span in silence.

"Do not wait for us past dawn," Lanathor said, "and do not hesitate if the horde is on the bridge before us. Westfort perishes with them if it must. It is a small price to pay for all of Aramon."

The only footprints they found in the snow were long since buried and showed softly in firelight. The marks were those of men, likely the torchbearers. Voldigar thought of their long, despairing vigil as he dismounted and handed his reins to Lanathor. The watchmen had awaited help from their Emperor that never came, yet still they lit their beacons in hope of his arrival. Instead, they would receive only one weary rider in the night and an old man who worked his will against the stone.

"I'll wait as long as we dare, Lanathor. I need only a few hours to reach the bottom." Voldigar looked into the deep purple sky beyond the fold of the mountains where Westfort lay. An ominous plume of smoke rose against the horizon, but as yet, nothing stirred on the foothills below.

"Head and Heart, Eldest." Lanathor struck his hand against his chest. "Whatever happens down there, I'll bring you out."

Voldigar gave a small nod and swung his legs over the Chasm's edge. "Head and Heart, Lan."

Chapter Forty-Three

Buried in the Snow

Too many hours passed, and Tepic knew that he was hopelessly lost. The wind grew violent shortly after he left the shrine, and it did not take him long to abandon his purpose and turn back. The problem though, was that he did not know which way "back" was. By the time he'd corrected and recorrected his direction, all the world was a whirlwind of blinding white. Liadov's tracks were long since washed away. No longer did he speed over the wintry plain like a bird of prey. Now he staggered, bent in the wind, stumbling through snow that grew ever deeper around his legs.

His foot caught against something buried below, and he fell headlong into the powder. He found that though his face was pressed into the snow, it was strangely comfortable. He could still breathe through the length of cloak he'd pulled over his nose and mouth, and the fur of his coat was like a bed of down. He could not remember the last time he'd really slept. It had been so long, a lifetime ago on a pile of rags in the corner of the old tannery. It was getting dark. It was so soft here, and as he lay, the cold was forgotten.

He was sitting now at a long table with servants all around. It was so much like his old table in the house atop the Citadel, but why were his family so far away? The table stretched out like a dock over the sea, narrowing into the distance. Ru was there, and Mother, and Father. They were speaking, but he couldn't hear a word. His feet felt wet, and as he looked at the floor below, he saw now that it really was water, and it really was a dock.

The water splashed against his eyes, and he was face down in the sea, sinking like a stone. He wanted to swim, but his arms and legs were locked in place, splayed out beside him. The ocean floor was racing up to meet him, and there were faces there with gaping mouths. Caliras and Gamad. Lusánt and miridas crones—

He felt a tap upon his shoulder.

"Tepic," Liadov said. "Do you know where evil enters our world?"

Tepic startled awake and jerked his head up from the snow. He was alone. Flakes in his eyelashes blurred his vision, and his body shuddered with a profound sense of cold. He wished for all the world to lay back down, but he refused. The air had grown dim all around, and night must soon be falling. He had to move on, in whatever direction it was that he faced. Somewhere on ahead must be a river or the sea. He rose shaking to his feet.

As night hastened on, the storm mercifully ceased its roaring, and snow now fell gently about him in flakes as thick as his thumb. In the distance, a few shadowed shapes emerged. At length, he discerned that they were willow trees—and of a sort familiar to him. He passed a few and continued on until he saw to his right the great northern sea cliffs of Aramon. Soon he stood before a final gnarled tree, overhanging the river where it plunged into the sea.

Despite the snow upon the ground, he knew that it was here those months ago he'd faced the Orun, rising green from the waters, and Caliras with his gray-cloaked men. So many turns in so little time. It seemed like the world was ending, but he lingered on—one lost boy in the snow.

He rested his hand upon the cold trunk and stared out over the waters, looking for the very branch he'd grasped to save his life. He saw no such limb and wondered at its absence. There were only roots of the willow, curling meekly under the icy bank. Tepic whispered a prayer of thanks and sighed in relief. He knew now where he was. Voldigar's farm was only a few miles to the south.

Chapter Forty-Four

FOR THE ELDEST

THE BRETHREN STOOD IN a ring about Lanathor, faces ashen and eyes dark. Dantic was there too. His armor was tattered, his forehead bruised, and overlapping cuts on his face and arms added to the look of wide-eyed, weary madness that he wore. Only Vasherk seemed to hold any semblance of repose on his mild face. The old brother looked at Lanathor with earnest eyes, steeled to whatever command he next would bring.

Thus far, they'd held the narrow wall of Westfort desperately but successfully against wave upon wave of the enemy. Zedr's delay had given them time to assemble a new defense, but little more. The smoke Lanathor had seen was a raging fire that Urias or another Teller maintained rhythmically, a vile inferno of the corpses of their foes, burning at the far wall's base. The stench was unbearable, but the blaze kept the horde at bay while its red anger lit the night and ashes fell like rain. It was during one such respite that they now spoke.

"So the old man will really do it then . . ." Wulf said. His gruesome axe was still in hand, and he glanced often to the stone arch that led back to the battlements.

Lanathor nodded. "The Black Fire is beyond our reach, lost by my own folly—but our conspiracy is otherwise unchanged."

The others did not question what he meant but somberly nodded their heads as they imagined what the end might be.

"There are civilians here," Dantic said. "It will take time to order our retreat."

"Yes," Lanathor replied. "Though I fear the Emperor will soon deduce our design and ride here in all fury, we should have some hours yet before we must depart. When we do, we give a final volley from the eastern wall and then engage a rearguard—to delay the horde upon the Span while the wounded and infirm are brought on as quickly as they may."

Dantic nodded. "Your plan is sound, save for this madness of bringing down the Span."

"Voldigar will do it," Wulf said. "Few understand Chanters, and his power least of all. It's not the strength of his arm but the strength of his will. The Span will break before he does."

Dantic inhaled deeply, grimaced, and pulled at a strap in his armor. "I hope you're right. I will be in the rearguard, and two score of my swiftest men."

"As will I," Lanathor said. "But I lay no charge on anyone. Many of us will fall upon the Span."

"Where else would I go?" Wulf asked with a grin.

"And I'll not let Wulf have all the glory," Vasherk added. "Count me in."

Lanathor nodded and looked to Taro. "And you I suppose, will not be parted from Vasherk?"

Taro smiled and tapped the end of *Skullcrusher* on the ground.

"We will need some final deed, at the last," Urias said, "to put distance between us and our pursuers. I too will go. They fear my fire."

"When they are at the center then. Hold them there, and then we flee to signal Voldigar," Lanathor said.

The men fell quiet and looked from face to face.

"What about the Eldest then? What will happen to him?" Taro asked.

Lanathor sighed and looked away. "I don't know, Taro. But when we are clear of the bridge, we must do what we can to help. I won't leave him down there."

"Nor I," Vasherk said. "I won't let him die."

Lanathor saluted. "For the Eldest then."

"For the Eldest," they echoed.

Chapter Forty-Five

The Mocking Stone

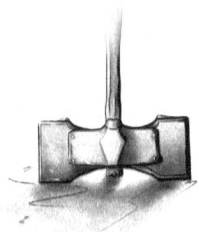

C LIMBING DOWN THE CHASM was an exercise in terror. Voldigar hoped it would prove easier than his wet ascent upon the sides of the Spire that rainy summer night an eternity ago, but it was not so. The Chasm opened below like the black maw of the underworld. It had no discernible bottom or opposite lip, lost in never-ending night. From its depths raged a howling wind, cold breath of a mountain's ghost who would brook no trespass.

The Chasm's walls were only a little more rough than those of the Spire, and while they were not slick with rain, the cold of the rock and the numbness of his fingers drove him to grip harder and harder as he descended. "*Good,*" he thought, "*the better to bar our enemy's way.*"

He believed the climb might take him an hour, but no less than a watch of the night had passed before he finally felt his feet touch upon level ground and the noise of the river Haroel was joined by its cold air upon his back. The darkness here was nearly absolute, but he could dimly see the shape of his hands. He held them upright and saw a darker paint upon his fingertips—blood, no doubt. He wondered if any flesh remained, and the pain that grew as feeling returned soon told him that it must be so.

The river was lower and not so loud as it had been in spring. Voldigar stood quietly, listening for any sound above. Distant voices echoed down the canyon, but there was no panic in their timbre. These must have been the first evacuees, civilians moving across—and not in fear. He sighed with relief and whispered thanks to God. Westfort still held. Ahead of him was the greater difficulty of reaching the center of the Span.

Voldigar walked in darkness for a stone's throw until he squatted near the bank of the black river and peered into the night, trying to make sense of the faint shapes he saw. Near at hand and before, many pillars descended into the waters in a long receding line. He'd passed several on dry land already, and despite his near blindness, he found it was within his power to leap from base to base out over the water and continue on his journey. He knew these bore little of the massive bridge's weight—his prize lay in the center of the river.

At length, he reached the final pillar in this foremost row, but from there, he could see nothing further in the darkness. Wherever the central support stood, it was beyond his sight, no matter how he squinted. He squatted down again and stayed there a long time while he glanced up at the sky. The snow had ceased its falling while he climbed, and he hoped perhaps soon the gloom would also clear. He was not long disappointed as first one star and then another twinkled into view behind swift-moving clouds.

In time, the moon itself rose distant but huge over the faraway edge of these high, hollow depths, a great, green, lidless eye. It was a glowering moon, a maliced moon, a new moon unseen before in all of Aramon's long years. But Voldigar did not fear its hatred, and instead, he stole its light to turn against his enemies. Its radiance did not belong to them. He peered into the darkness once more.

Faintly now, he could see it—the mighty central pillar which he sought. Like the others, it rested on a broad base that rose out of the rapidly flowing Haroel. It was enormous though, twice again as broad as his own house and made of thick stones, each higher than his head and stacked one upon the other. The lip of its foundation was hundreds of feet away. In need, the Virtue of his Chanting allowed him to leap distances that could scarcely be believed, but this length was far too great a feat. He would have to swim.

Voldigar laid his cloak and boots beside him and then drew his Daneki blade as well. He stared sadly at its steel awhile and wondered if it might be found again. It was the last memory he had of his mother, a thing given to him from her far country long before he knew its use. Sadly, it occurred to him, the priceless object would likely be crushed with him beneath a mountain of falling stone. Even so, he took a little hope and flung it with all his might back in the direction from which he'd come. Perhaps someone would find it. It glittered until it disappeared into the darkness, but there was neither splash nor clatter.

With a great breath, he coiled himself and sprung out against the current of the river. All the air was ripped from his chest as he plunged into bitter cold. Icy fingers tore at the sides of his aching head, but he knifed through the depths with forceful strokes. Soon he surfaced and made desperately for the pillar, struggling against the waters. He caught its edge that nearest broke the rippling flow and heaved himself to the platform above where he sat breathless against the mighty stone, sputtering and coughing with his eyes closed against the pain.

The shock of winter upon his soaking flesh drove tears into his eyes, and he wrenched the wet garments from his body to lay them dripping by his side. He shook himself free of what moisture he could and then lay panting and trembling on the stone, retreating into his thoughts and away from the biting cold.

Voldigar soon hoisted himself against the pillar again and rung his garments out as best he could. Reaching into the pockets of his trousers he grasped an old, empty pouch—Gwenyth's medicine bag. He gazed at it a long while, forgetting the sting upon his skin. How fared she now? He took comfort that the blizzard had ended, and wondered if Gwenyth traveled even as he huddled in the dark. He could almost see her, gently bumping down the road while Liadov drove Lutz's cart onward to the old well.

He wondered too if he would see her again, or if some sad weeks from now, Gwenyth would welcome their child into the world alone. And for a father, this little one would have only stories of an old man who perished one cold night in a tangle of rock. He rubbed the empty pouch with his thumb and bitterly considered how they would live, penniless, with what little wealth they had poured into the snow by a petulant boy.

What clumsy words had he said to her as he backed into the snow? Were they the things he should have spoken if they were to be his last? His face twisted fiercely as he remembered they were only promises, likely to be empty. No assurance of his love. No farewell of a devoted husband. Just the lie of '*I promise*' from a man doomed to die.

And for what then was his death? The great column of stone loomed quiet by his side, mocking him to try. Hundreds of souls were no doubt stirring now, thousands of feet above, trusting that he alone would somehow do the impossible. They pinned all their hopes on him. They would flee from the security of Westfort only to be overrun by a sweeping wave of darkness, biting at their heels as they ran fruitlessly into the hinterlands.

Voldigar could bear his thoughts no longer and let them float away on the icy river at his feet. His mouth began to move in the Chants he knew so well. He would let the songs tumble from his lips in precious words until he heard or saw a signal above. When his brethren called for him to play his part, he would be ready. He would tear the mocking stone away, or die in the attempt.

CHAPTER FORTY-SIX

MORNING'S MESSENGER

Dim light shone about the shuttered windows of Voldigar's low-roofed home, and a billow of woodsmoke poured from its chimney. Tepic's heart leapt to see it, and he stumbled forward in his weary joy.

Lyrusia opened the door warily when he knocked, but her suspicious face burst in a sudden gasp of gladness. "Tepic!" she cried and stood holding the door in wonder.

Tepic stiffly took the last step of his journey and sagged into the warm embrace of his sister.

"Tepic," she cried again. "What are you doing here? My goodness, you're cold to the touch! How long have you been outside?"

"A long time," Tepic muttered. He took the sword from off his back and leaned it against the hearth.

"You brought it here?"

"I couldn't leave it!"

Lyrusia pursed her lips and led him to Gwenyth's chair to sit him down before she hurried to cover him with a rough, heavy blanket that smelled of horses. "Liadov is in the other room with the lady of the house." Lyrusia grimaced. "The lady thinks she's in labor, but it's far too soon. She's very sick."

Tepic nodded, trying to make sense of what she said with his cold-addled mind. The heat of the fire on his numb ears was the most pleasant sensation he could recall. "Labor?" he asked.

"Her baby, you dolt. She thinks she's having her baby!"

"Oh," Tepic managed.

Just then, a mournful whimper sounded from the back of the house, and Liadov pulled aside the curtain just enough to show her face. "Tepic Banari," she said. "How little I'm surprised."

Tepic looked away to consider what he might say.

"Think nothing of it. I'll deal with you later. I hope you are here on good purpose." Liadov ducked behind the curtain again.

"Why *are* you here?" Lyrusia asked again.

"I thought I could help," Tepic said.

Lyrusia frowned. "Help? With what?"

"Everyone's in trouble!" Tepic said. "Everyone's in danger, and I was stuck with books and tea kettles."

Lyrusia sighed. "You look awful, little brother." She wiped her hand across his forehead and brushed his lengthening hair aside. "And you're supposed to be hiding."

Tepic thought to complain but realized then how terribly tired he was and how miserable he must truly appear. He let the words die in his mouth and closed his eyes while he pulled the blanket up around his neck.

"I have to help the lady," he dimly heard Lyrusia say. "I'll leave some food out for you . . ." Her words faded into the rhythm of his own breathing and the sound of her receding footsteps as he fell into a blissful, dreamless sleep.

———◆———

Tepic startled awake to an anguished wail. His body tensed, but he soon remembered where he was and saw Lyrusia stomping past him with a bucket swinging in her hands and one of her medicine satchels strapped to her side.

"What? What's happening?" Tepic asked.

Lyrusia stopped. Her look was grim. "If you want to help so much, Tepic, fetch us water and every blanket and linen you can find." She dropped the empty pail on the floor.

Tepic scrambled to his feet and regretfully cast his warm blanket aside. "Why?"

"The lady is giving birth."

Another painful cry rang out from the room beyond the curtain. He didn't know what to say. "That's . . . that's wonderful!"

Lyrusia's face twisted. She trembled and shook her head, then hurried back beyond the curtain.

Tepic's feet were bare, but a wash of energy came over him. He rushed out the door with his bucket in hand. The snow had stopped, and stars shone everywhere through scattered clouds. A thin band of light in the east promised morning soon. It would have been beautiful, he was sure, had there been any time to look, but his heart was full of urgency, and he sped to the well to tie his bucket to the line.

He was soon diving into the back of the wagon, grabbing every piece of cloth he could find, and then darting back to the house with his bundle and a sloshing bucket.

"No! Not in here," Lyrusia barked. "Set that by the fire. Let it warm a little! Put those blankets over here!"

Tepic did his best to obey and then watched his sister dash back into the room, only to emerge a moment later and rummage through Voldigar's cupboards.

"Why are you so upset?" Tepic asked.

Lyrusia spun to Tepic and took a deep breath. She spoke softly. "Because, Tepic. The baby will die. It's too soon."

A lump formed in Tepic's throat, and words formed on his lips. "Die? But . . . why?" He was interrupted by Liadov hurrying into the room as well. Her face was stern.

"The baby will not die, Lyrusia—not if we can help it. Pray God we can. Come with me."

Tepic turned to follow as well, but Lyrusia wagged her finger. "Stay out here." She yanked the curtain closed.

Tepic sat in silence, back in Gwenyth's chair, rocking, for he knew nothing else to do. The wails of the lady carried through the air, one anguished cry following another. It was awful. This went on for nearly an hour until the mournful sounds abruptly ceased and all the house filled with a dreadful silence. Tepic held his breath and blinked, but nothing followed.

The chair creaked and he let his breath out in a long sigh, glancing from side to side, but still, the quiet went on. He could hear a hurried shuffling now behind the curtain, but no hint of what had happened. He closed his eyes and began earnestly to pray. "Dear God, don't let Lady Gwenyth's baby die. Please." He let his head fall and tightly held his eyes shut. The fire cracked and his ears rang, but even the shuffling stopped.

Like a sudden pierce of sunshine through a storm-tossed day, the most wonderful sound followed. It was the tiny cry of an infant.

<hr />

The single cry was all it gave at first, and then Tepic heard more quiet murmurings. Not long after, Lyrusia emerged with a beaming smile. "Come here, Tepic."

Tepic rose from the chair with his eyes as wide as dinner plates. He didn't know why, but he tiptoed as softly as he could on his cold bare feet until he was staring down at Lady Gwenyth who sat upright on a mat upon the floor. Liadov was behind her with a weary face, and in Gwenyth's arms was the tiniest person he had ever seen, wrapped snuggly in a pale blue shirt he'd rummaged from the wagon. His hair was charcoal black, like the Sword-Lector's, but his eyes were green and clear, as green as the moon, and a mirror of his mother's. Gwenyth's gaze was fixed on him, tender and joyful, yet fierce and resolute.

"His name is Olwis," Gwenyth said quietly.

Liadov smiled. "Will your husband have no say?"

"He has done his naming. This one will be mine," she said with a smile.

Liadov laughed, and Tepic watched as sorrow melted from her fair face. "Then Olwis he shall be, the prince that Voldigar loved best."

Tepic was overcome with an emotion he could not describe. It carried through his chest and suffused through his face until it settled across his shoulders. Words came out that he did not expect. "Voldigar should hear this news—fast as we can give it." He licked his lips. "I can go to the well."

At first, all three women looked at him in surprise, then Lyrusia's eyes narrowed and her nostrils flared. She looked ready to pounce. Liadov laid a gentle hand on her arm and rose to her feet. "It is a noble thought, Tepic—but unwise."

"Why?"

"You are fortunate to have made it here unharmed."

"But . . . Voldigar has to know!"

Liadov sighed. "And he will, in time. As for us, when the lady has rested, we're returning to my shrine."

"But Hobyn said we're to meet them at the well!"

Liadov lowered her brow. "Tepic—"

"But—"

"Tepic," she said more firmly. "The lady needs her rest now."

His lip quivered, and his hands balled into fists, but he didn't know what else to say. He dropped his gaze to the floor and retreated to the hearth where he sank back into Gwenyth's chair. Liadov stood a moment longer in the door frame, watching him, until she raked the curtain closed. He was alone again with his crumpled boots drying by the fire.

Tepic folded his arms and closed his eyes. The image of his sword-lector's kind face staring through his high window on a stormy summer night filled his thoughts. It seemed so long ago now. What had he risked to come all that way? The old man had done so much for him . . .

What if he dies?

Tepic shifted uncomfortably to the side and stared at his boots again.

What if he dies and never even sees his tiny little son? What if he never even knows?

It was then something like a plan began to form in Tepic's mind. A terrible, foolish, awful plan. He grasped his boots and slid them onto his feet. He thought he knew where the Anteres lands were . . . the old well. Somewhere at the end of the Adionel . . .

Liadov pulled the curtain aside and walked two paces into the room. She stopped and stared at him warily. His heart leapt into his throat.

"Tepic?"

He froze like a rabbit.

"Your boots aren't dry yet. Take them off." Liadov crossed the rest of the room and plucked the sword into her hand. She stopped there by the hearth and pinned him with her eyes. He thought her angry at first, but a glimmer of sorrow whispered across her face, like the last mist of an autumn rain, caught in the wind of winter. It passed as quickly as it came. She turned and carried the sword back behind the curtain.

It may have been a minute before he breathed again. The sound of rustling commotion struck up once more from the other room, and Tepic found himself staring at his unlaced boots and empty hands. Without the sword, he thought himself a far less dashing messenger. He sighed and reached down to pull the boots from off his feet, but his hands stopped an inch away.

What if he never even knows . . .

Tepic's hands worked like lightning, lacing both boots and snatching up his fur coat again. He swept the loaf of bread Lyrusia left him off the table and tucked it under his arm. A moment more and he was tiptoeing through the front door, then sprinting through the barley field, and finally looking back only once to see the little farm shrinking behind in the dimness. *Free as a bird.*

"Tepic!" Lyrusia bellowed from somewhere behind.

Tepic's eyelids nearly shot off his face, and one foot caught on the other. He stumbled headlong into the snow and swallowed a mouthful of it. Choking the powder away, he looked back to see Lyrusia sprinting over the open fields with her skirts flailing wildly in the wind, her satchel bouncing against her side. He'd never seen her move so fast. In wide-eyed terror, he scrambled to his feet and ran again, pretending not to hear.

"Tepic, you mule-eared dolt! Stop!"

He didn't stop.

"Stop!"

He nearly tripped again and dared another look behind. She was gaining on him. They ran on until he leapt over something buried in the snow and found the drift twice as deep on the other side. He was nearly wading now, flailing his arms in panic.

"Tepic!" she roared as she vaulted after him and plunged into the snow. Another leap and she had his ankles. They went down in a heap of thrashing arms and legs. The loaf of bread he carried twirled and stuck in the snow like a javelin. He was on his back in a little hollow of snow, pinned helplessly under the ungodly strength of older sisters.

"What do you think you're doing!" she shouted in his face.

"I have to tell him!" Tepic sputtered, struggling to blow snow out of his eyes. She had both his wrists pinned now. "I have to!"

"No you don't, you half-wit! It's a dozen miles through the hinterlands. You'll freeze to death—Liadov! Liadov!" she yelled.

"Stop!" cried Tepic. "Stop it."

Lyrusia twisted her head around her shoulder. "She can't hear me anyway—but she'll come looking soon enough. And when she does, you'll be in *so* much trouble."

Tepic closed his eyes and groaned. "I just want to help him. I'm not a child anymore, Ru. You can't stop me." He fruitlessly jerked his arms from side to side.

"Watch me."

Tepic looked again and was surprised to see tears welling in his sister's eyes.

"Ru—"

"Everything's all wrong, Tep. You can't always go off to play the hero."

"I don't want to be a hero. I just want to help. What if he never knows, Ru? What if he never even hears?"

Lyrusia twisted her lip and they stared at each other in silence, breathing heavily in little puffs of steam.

"You can't sit on me all day."

"Can't I?"

"When you get up, I'll just run again."

"I'll catch you."

Tepic gave a fruitless push, but he was pinned fast. "What if you never knew about me?" he asked.

"What?"

"What if you never got to meet me, never even knew I was alive? You would have been all alone."

"That doesn't even make sense, Tepic."

He managed to pull a wrist free and hid it under his back before she could grab it again. Maybe she was tiring.

"If I let you up, will you promise not to run?"

"No," Tepic protested.

"Fine—Liadov!" she yelled again. Her shout echoed through the morning air, but there was no reply. There they stayed on the ground for several long minutes while the stars twinkled out of view in the early light.

"I have to be a man someday, Ru, and make my own decisions."

"Not today, you don't"

"I just want to be brave."

"You are brave, but you're a dummy too."

Tepic squirmed one leg free and dug his heel into the dirt beneath the snow.

"Why won't you listen to me, Tep?"

"Let me up and I will."

Lyrusia frowned.

"I promise then! I won't run," Tepic said.

Lyrusia narrowed her eyes but slowly released his other wrist. They were sitting in the little snow hollow now, facing one another in a wary truce. Tepic could see the farmhouse, tiny in the distance, but there was no sign of Liadov or anyone else. "What do you want to say then? I'm listening."

Lyrusia sent a puff of air out of her nose. "You're too reckless, little brother—and you scare me."

"Maybe I am, and maybe I do. But I help too! I escaped the Spire, I stopped Caliras, I lived a whole month on my own in Undercity."

Lyrusia blinked and narrowed her eyes again. She pushed her lips into a flat line.

Tepic sighed. "All I want to do this time is tell Voldigar some good news for once. No adventures. I don't even have the sword!"

Lyrusia too looked over her shoulder at the farmhouse.

"It's nearly daytime anyway, sis. And look, it's not even snowing anymore. Just a winter walk."

"What if they take you again? You don't even know the way."

Tepic frowned and pointed west into the darkness where the Spire was beginning to show against a faintly glowing sky. "Lusánt's that way . . ." He whipped his hand back to the east. ". . . and the old well is that way. Can't you just let me go?"

Lyrusia sighed and caught Tepic's eyes for a moment before she looked away at the ground between her feet. "It's north of the river, where the marshes start and you can't go any further. You didn't even bring any food."

Slowly, Tepic got his feet. He dared not move away, but was she cracking? At least she didn't lunge to grab him. "I'll be safe, Ru. Just a few hours walk. And look!" He drew the old loaf of bread from its snowy sheathe. "I did bring food!"

Lyrusia smirked and crossed her arms. She too stood and gave him a long hard look.

"What?" Tepic asked.

Lyrusia shook her head. "What even are you?"

Tepic laughed. "A mule-eared dolt."

Lyrusia rolled her eyes and abruptly pulled the satchel off her side to rummage through it.

"Isn't that your medicine bag?"

"It is," Lyrusia replied as she plucked a tiny vile into her hand. "I hardly have anything left, but I do have this."

"What is it?" Tepic asked.

"Jarnath leaf. It's awful stuff. No one ever bought it, but it's very rare." She held it out to Tepic.

Tepic opened the lid to take a smell and immediately recoiled. "It smells like liquor!"

"Careful," Lyrusia said. "It is liquor. The leaves are fermented and distilled. It will make your skin feel cold, but inside you'll be warm as dragonfire."

"You want me to drink it?"

"All of it."

"Now?" Tepic eyed the vial suspiciously.

Lyrusia nodded.

"So . . . you're letting me go?"

Lyrusia frowned. "I didn't say that."

"Why not come with me?"

She frowned again. "I'm staying to help Lady Gwenyth. And you should too. What do you think the Brethren are doing out there? Nowhere's safe."

Tepic looked at her sidelong for a beat but decided not to answer. With a shrug, he tipped the vial back and drank the little cordial down. He resisted the urge to cough and smiled bravely instead while his eyes watered.

Lyrusia pulled the collar of his coat tighter. She pursed her lips and then squinted and held her hand up flat to move it between their heads. "You really are taller than me now, aren't you?"

Tepic grinned. "I have been, for a while."

Lyrusia emptied the satchel of a few more small bottles and then held the bag against his chest. "Put your loaf in there . . . dummy."

Tepic dutifully obeyed and then stood awkwardly while the liquor worked its way into his toes. "Well?"

"Well what? Go off before I change my mind." Tepic's eyes widened and he opened his mouth to speak, but Lyrusia embraced him then, wiping a tear from her face. "Be careful, Tep, and bring my satchel back when you're done. I want to hear exactly what old Voldigar looks like when you tell him." She worked a weary smile onto her face.

"I will, sis. I promise." Tepic hesitated a moment longer, his hand on her shoulder. "Please, don't worry."

"I should club you and drag you back."

For a moment, he thought she might, but instead, she nodded and took a backwards step. Tepic bit his cheek and waited until he could finally will himself around, taking a few tepid steps into the light of a rising sun beyond the mountains. He stopped to look back.

"Ru—" he began, but Lyrusia had already turned to swiftly walk away. He faced the mountains again. Somewhere, far over the horizon, the sword-lector would soon be gathering with his men, awaiting the best news of his life—and Tepic would be the one to bring it.

CHAPTER FORTY-SEVEN

DEMONS TO SLAY

D AWN WAS COMING SOON, and Lanathor stood in Westfort's courtyard, staring up at the falling snow. In the last hour, it had resumed
its slow tumble while the final preparations were made to flee. The gentle
flakes appeared like winter's fireflies in the torchlight and floated past
his face. It should have been beautiful. It should have been serene, but
Lanathor felt nothing. The root of Westfort's apothecary was strong upon
his mind. All the better as he buried the thoughts of his great misdeed in
yesterday's storm.

Before him, a huge cloud of smoke billowed over the far wall—the latest
putrid burning of their endless foe. Already he could hear them scrabbling
against the earth, amassing again in a thick mob to surge forward with
crushing weight when the flame subsided.

Palizar, the other Fire Teller, and Urias's own initiate, had long since left
with the wounded or those otherwise unfit to fight. He'd given all he had
and would have given more, but Urias dragged his limp body from the wall
and forced him to go in an earlier wave of evacuees—along with Soris, who
could barely stand or speak and could no longer muster any magic at all.

Urias himself now sat upon a crooked chair, his head sagging toward the
ground before a great pile of wagons, furniture, linens, and anything else
flammable they could find. It was stretched from end to end across the
entire length of Westfort, awaiting his attention for when the command

would finally be given. His body was covered in soot, his long hair singed and wild, and he rocked unsteadily from side to side with unseeing eyes.

"You're certain you have something left in you?" Lanathor asked.

Urias blinked until he could focus a glare on Lanathor. "It's just fire, Elder, rivers of fire. The world never runs dry of it, and it never fails to yield." He steadied himself with a blistered hand on a nearby crate.

"It must be quite a tale you tell, to make yourself so angry for so long."

Urias hazarded a weary smile. "It's many tales. Everything makes me angry." He wiped his mouth with the back of his other hand, but it did not make it cleaner. "Though I confess, there is one I've thought of most of all tonight."

"Oh?" Lanathor asked.

Urias grinned again. "Better I not share it. More potent that way." He scowled once more.

Dantic emerged into the torchlight with a helm under his arm and a horn in his hand. His face was grim and dark. "Everything is ready."

Urias rose to his feet, and Lanathor nodded. Wulf was standing by, braced against a huge wagon laden with many barrels that waited near the only gap in the massive barricade of wood and debris. Forty men with pike and shield stood at the ready behind Dantic.

Lanathor took a breath. *I will not fail this time.* "Give the command."

Dantic raised the horn to his lips and sounded a tremendous blast. Many more sounded in return, and then a whistle of arrows split the night. As quickly as the volley had released, once and again, a stream of some hundreds of men came pouring back from the wall and down into the courtyard. Many limped and stumbled as they ran. Most were tattered and bloodied. All carried the flint-hard look of men too long bound in the grip of terror. It was all that remained, but they had held Aramon through its longest night. On they went, swiftly through the gap, and forth to fly through the western gate. As the last ran by, Wulf wedged his shoulder against the wagon and drove it into place.

"Stand back!" Urias said. Wulf hurried to obey and with him Taro and Vasherk, Lanathor and Dantic, and forty men with heavy arms. The taciturn initiate Eadom had joined them as well. This half dozen brethren and two score of Aramon's guard would be last to leave.

"The enemy will not tarry as they did at Eastfort!" Lanathor cried. Even now, he could hear them laying beams against the wall and beginning to climb. "When the barricade is lit, stop for nothing. We make our stand at the narrow entrance of the Span while the others flee to safety. Then, it is a running battle until Urias holds them at the center." He paused only a moment to look across their faces. "Now, Urias!"

The Teller's hands had worked silently while Lanathor spoke. Now, they erupted in a spout of flame that brightly swallowed the great wagon and washed a wave of shimmering heat across his face. The wagon burst with acrid sulfur and a flash of white fire. Waving his arms like the bellows before a furnace door, Urias lit the entire mass ablaze.

"Go!" Dantic cried over the roar of the inferno.

As one, the rearguard sprinted for the gate while searing heat licked at their heels.

The wind whistled in Lanathor's ears as he ran swiftly down the hill. The rearguard with him carried a few sputtering torches that streamed alongside in the darkness. Daring to look up from the treacherous ground beneath his feet, he saw small shapes of the much larger garrison fleeing on ahead. They would soon round the fold of the mountain pass and then be on to the final approach of the Span.

The helmets of Dantic's nearby men bobbed as they ran in the dim light, pulling into a column two abreast. Vasherk and Taro, Wulf and Eadom were among them, but where was Urias? Lanathor whirled his head about to see the exhausted Teller stumbling on behind.

"Come on, Urias!" Lanathor yelled as he worked his arm under the man's shoulder.

Urias tried to wave him off. "I'm fine, I can fight!"

"I know you can, but you have to run first!"

Wulf was now at Urias's other side, and together they hoisted him along. Lanathor stole another rearward glance, only to see the first creatures vomiting forth from Westfort—a vanguard of hell, leaping through a shadowed cloud of smoke that billowed from the gate. Many were aflame and their tortured fury echoed off the mountain while their hideous kin trampled on their backs. The barricade had hardly held them. The rest of the rearguard was pulling on ahead. The brethren were moving too slowly.

Wulf saw the same and silently concurred with Lanathor. He grit his teeth and swept Urias off his feet like a child. "Put me down!" Urias cried, but Wulf gave no reply and bolted off ahead. Lanathor charged on too, struggling to keep pace.

Soon they'd rejoined the column, and the lip of the Span was in sight. Its length disappeared far away into the gloom of spare predawn light and the few torches still burning upon its turrets. The snow became slush under their heavy feet. It was a wonder that no one fell, but Dantic had chosen his men well. The ground soon leveled, and the rearguard charged forward, heedless of any further formation. The horde was gaining fast, a river of death gushing down the slope.

Breathless, the men skidded to a halt where the stones of the Span met the road from Westfort. Dantic ordered his guards into a double line, facing back while the brethren took their place among them. Lanathor looked warily at Urias, but the man was already deep into his Telling, working his hands in subtle circles with his eyes tightly closed. Fire and blood seeped from fissures in his arms and steamed upon his fingers.

Turning back to the mountains, the enemy looked almost frail at first—nothing more than a disordered stream of misshapen forms, but soon a wall of their vile ilk formed and swelled across the hill, flooding into the valley. Their number was impossible and grew as brackish water, pouring forth from the ruin of a ruptured sea.

"Stand fast!" Dantic cried. "Stand fast for Aramon! Now comes the final test! Now comes the hour of our acclaim!" His blade shook in his hand above his head, but his face shone dauntless in the firelight. The rolling tide surged forward until all the ground was covered in an avalanche of shadow. The earth shuddered under their rumbling advance, and their glistening eyes flashed into an endless line of hateful lights, deep red and ghastly green. A wailing shriek arose from their midst to resound across the snowbound peaks.

There was a wide-eyed madness on the face of young Eadom as he trembled and rocked on his feet. Vasherk laid an even hand on his shoulder, and Lanathor could hear his quiet words. "Steady now, Eadom. God has brought you to this moment. His strength is in your arms."

The guardsmen set their pikes and locked their shields as the first wave swept into their choke point. There was a terrible crash, but the line held. Gibbering Bashevi leapt high, yet Taro beat them from the air with *Skull-crusher*. Wulf's great axe flashed in glimmering circles and tore through his foes like firewood in the gaps between the pikes.

Lanathor willed a wide upheaval of force through the air over the heads of the men that caught the weight of their foe just as Urias arced a geyser of liquid fire into the same. The enemy fell back, if only for an instant, and Lanathor glanced behind. The rest of the garrison had disappeared into the dim gray.

"Fall back!" he cried. "Fall back!"

As one, the rearguard of Westfort backed away, only to reset their feet and absorb another terrible charge. In this way, buttressed as they were by the strength of the Brothers of Aramon, the rearguard covered a quarter of the bridge unbroken and unbowed as the howling horde clambered over their fallen allies. It was then that men began to fall.

The right side of the line faltered, and into the breach rushed Taro and Vasherk, rapier and staff dancing together, fell and terrible as lightning while the sun began to rise. Eadom and Wulf took up the center at Dantic's side when it began to crumble. Eadom's sword was dashed from his hand, but now his face was set as steel. The initiate plucked a pike from off the ground and fought on with righteous fury. Step by step, they retreated to the center of the Span.

"Now, Dantic!" Lanathor cried. "Now, Urias!"

Dantic fell back a few more paces from the line and sweeping his horn from off his waist, he sounded several times.

"Down! Down! Down!" Lanathor cried as he descended deep into the trance of his power. The men were but shadowed shapes of leaves before his eyes while the world faded into the reality of spinning threads beneath it. He saw the rearguard surge against the foe a final time and then dip their heads low for the moment he had warned them.

Lanathor thrust his hands forward, and the force of a thunderclap burst from between them. Like a stone he was cast away, skidding upon his back, but a rippling distortion flared from edge to edge of the Span and rushed onward, tearing up the paving of the bridge before the feet of the men and smashing into the wicked mass beyond them. The foremost of the Oruni simply shattered into a powdery mist. Those behind were hewn limb from limb, and further on, their bodies whipped downward to dash against the ground. In a deafening instant, a hundred feet of the enemy were flattened to a writhing black mass upon the bridge.

Lanathor breathed heavily as he saw his companions rise to their feet and sprint toward where he lay. Now would be Urias's greatest fire and their final escape. He would expend all that remained to create a conflagration in the foremost ranks of their foe.

Nothing came.

Lanathor flashed his eyes to the side as he raised himself onto his hands and there saw Urias bowed upon his knees. His head drooped against his chest. Smoke rose from his hands and hair.

"Urias!" he called. "Now, Urias!" But there was no reply. The man swayed and slumped. His hands looked as though they would rise, but then sagged again. He fell forward to lay upon his face.

Wulf was there in a heartbeat and swept Urias up in a full sprint. The others were close behind, stampeding away from the small gap Lanathor had created for them. Urias's fire was supposed to follow—it had to follow. Without it, the creatures would be across far too soon.

Dantic furiously blew his horn and cried aloud as he ran. "Voldigar! Voldigar!" The others took up the cry as the horde regained its footing and surged after them. The wrathful clamor of their foe swept into the air like the trashing of a hurricane. Deaf but for their howl, Lanathor found himself in the rear, running last of all between Taro and Vasherk. Their pursuers were gaining.

"We're almost there!" Lanathor yelled. "Keep going!" His voice was lost to the whirlwind.

Wulf had gone on far ahead, and Lanathor saw him there, laying Urias gently in the snow. The huge man then wrenched a torch from off a turret and thrust it into a nearby cart, setting it ablaze. Over the edge of the Chasm he hurled it and took up the cry himself in his booming voice. "Voldigar! Voldigar!"

In a moment, all had crossed over and spun back to face the encroaching swarm of Oruni. They were coming on far too fast, perhaps only two hundred yards to go. The bridge stood as firm as the pillars of the earth, unshaken since the day it was wrought. Lanathor peered over the side into the dark, but dawn had not yet pierced the gloom of the canyon's depths below. What had become of their brother?

"Voldigar needs more time! I'm going back." Lanathor cried. "Follow me!"

He rushed onto the bridge, and the brethren hurried to his side. Wulf clutched him by the shoulder. His eyes were wide with fury.

"No!" Wulf bellowed. "Stay here and prepare another blast, let us handle this."

Lanathor moved forward again, but Wulf jerked him back. "No, curse you! You're the only Teller standing. Let us fight. You must battle at the last."

Dantic continued to blow his horn while his men ran on.

Lanathor had no time to think, but he knew Wulf was right. He saluted the man with a fierce fist against his chest and narrowed his eyes to seek the threads. Wulf bared his teeth and whirled with a roar.

Forward he charged with Vasherk, Taro, and Eadom at his side. Axe and pike, staff and sword, dagger and fist, flared before them like the brands of heaven come down into the hands of men. Dantic's guards saw now what had happened and surged back to rejoin the battle, but Lanathor shot up his hand. "No! No! It's too late!" The momentary distraction pulled the threads apart. His body shook as he tried to refocus his mind.

He saw Wulf cleave two odomo with his axe just as Taro turned his staff to the side and charged into a mass of gray-skinned bashevi. He disappeared beneath their clawing hands, and Vasherk darted forward with a cry. The old man's rapier flashed and dove, pierced and flayed, while all the while his left hand worked a furious dance, too fast to comprehend. Eadom's weapon moved in unison with his, eyes again wild in the only battle the young Chanter had ever known. They were soon buried in a swirling flood of vile flesh, and Lanathor could watch no longer. He had to close his eyes to complete his work. He had to close them against the horror that he saw.

A thick braid of the Song slid into his fingers. "Get down!" he cried. He knew it would be useless, but warn them he must, on whatever vain hope he still had to save his friends. Cheerful Taro, Wild Wulf, Charming Vasherk, and Young Eadom. He would save them if he could, and remember them if he could not. He opened his eyes just as the blast flew from his hands.

The bridge was swaying.

Only for an instant did Lanathor glimpse this strange sight, for once again he was thrown to the ground. A spray of dirt covered his face, but he slapped it away, sputtering on the taste of blood. Crawling to his hands and knees, he peered into the chaos. He could not mistake it now. The bridge buckled and rocked as though struck by an earthquake. Its turrets bobbed like the masts of ships while stones rippled to the side. A great grinding sound was echoing from the canyon. The horde fell back.

Mad creatures held their ears and tore at one another, vainly fleeing the way they'd come. Others fell, then scrambled to their feet to fly forward once again, but the Span was sinking beneath them. Before them all, and well ahead of the collapsing stone, three men ran, Wulf and Eadom and Taro last of all—carrying Vasherk in his arms.

— ◆ —

The exhausted brothers, wounded and despairing, collapsed together before Lanathor where he knelt upon a patch of summer grass. The snow was raked from the earth where he'd been thrown down. His hands and his mouth trembled as he raised his eyes to their weary faces.

Taro, he was struck by first of all. His wide, kind face was streaked with tears, and he looked down mournfully at Vasherk who lay across his knees. "Wake up old man, wake up," Taro said.

From the evacuees, Soris too had found his way back and now stood unsteadily over the brethren. His pale skin was drawn in folds under his deep, sad eyes.

Lanathor put his hand beneath Vasherk's head and spoke softly. "Vasherk?"

Vasherk's eyes fluttered open, and he stared first at the sky before he weakly turned his eyes to Lanathor. The man's body was crushed, and deep blue bruising showed swollen beneath his skin.

"Brother . . . Brother, heal yourself," Lanathor said.

Vasherk coughed and smiled dimly. "I can't, Brother. My arms are broken."

A strangled cry broke on Taro's lips, and he reached down to stroke Vasherk's face. He tried to speak but seemed unable. He looked away again.

Lanathor shook his head and stared numbly at the old man's wispy white hair. His arms hung limply at his sides. "You old fool," he whispered. "You old fool, I told you to die in peace."

"Did you?" Vasherk coughed again, and a line of red flowed from the corner of his mouth. He looked up into Lanathor's eyes. "We all have our demons to slay, Lanathor." The old man closed his eyes, and slowly a smile formed on his lips. He opened them again. "Elder . . . I am at peace." His gaze turned away, over Lanathor's shoulder and to the snowflakes that fell softly on his brow. There he looked into the winter sky and breathed his last, with rest upon his face.

Taro wailed and Wulf turned away to cry, his great shoulders heaving. Lanathor knew what he should feel, he knew that a great sorrow should go up from his chest for Brother Vasherk, the passing of an irreplaceable man from the earth, and the passing of his dear friend—but there was nothing. The Falam Root still wound about his mind, and Lanathor reviled it. What he felt or no, there was no time to grieve, for the stone of the Span had torn away and was falling to the side.

"Voldigar!" Lanathor cried as he gently laid Vasherk in the grass. "We have to help Voldigar!"

Chapter Forty-Eight

No Time for Doubts

IN SOME FAR HOUR of the night, the Chanting on Voldigar's lips fell away, and the man was taken by the sleep he'd so long held at bay. As he always did, he dreamed.

It was early autumn, as it should have been, and a swift sun rolled along the southern sky, scattering the shadows of his aspen grove like spokes upon a spinning wheel. Their ribbons sped across his feet and hands, and Rory was there at his side, resting as he scratched his ears. The shadows lengthened, and the sky dimmed from orange to red, purple to gray. Night began to fall.

Rory suddenly stood upon his feet and stared off into the dark. The hairs of his back bristled as he sniffed the air, and then Voldigar heard them too—hunting horns in the distance and the baying of many hounds.

"Rory, no!" Voldigar cried, but it was far too late. His dog darted into the woods in a spray of leaves. Voldigar rose and gave chase, but his legs were leaden as he ran. On he stumbled, crying as he went. "Rory! Rory!"

The dark pillars of the trees crowded about him, tighter and tighter as the sound of Rory's rapid footfalls receded, and the black of night closed in. Soon all was pitch, and Voldigar blindly felt his way forward.

"Rory!" he called again and again until his voice was hoarse, but the sound echoed away before him into nothing.

A pale light emerged, somewhere on ahead, and the trees thinned against Voldigar's sides until he swept away a final curtain of their branches and peered into a quiet, moonlit glade.

A man sat there upon a rock, huddled and stooped, his bare arms wrapped about his chest and his blonde hair stirring in a steady breeze. His eyes were cast to the ground and his fingers trembled.

Voldigar took a pair of cautious steps toward him. "Young man?"

"Why . . .?" the man muttered as he rocked back and forth. "Why . . . Voldigar?"

Voldigar stopped short and narrowed his eyes. The voice was so familiar, but its memory so fleeting. Like the noontide of a summer's day, forgotten save for its lingering shimmer.

"Who are you?" Voldigar croaked through his cracked lips.

"Why?" the man asked again, yet now his words were clear and present.

Voldigar's heart froze. He tried to speak, but his tongue clove to the roof of his mouth.

The man's arm shot forward like a serpent and grasped him by the wrist. His head tilted back, and only the whites of his eyes could be seen under his golden hair that now whipped wildly in a sudden gale. His mouth was wide with agony.

"Why did you leave me?" he cried in a deep, resonant voice. "Why did you leave me here?"

Voldigar violently recoiled, but he was stuck fast. The man clawed into his arm and reached for him with his other hand.

"Why?" he bellowed again. "The veil! The veil is so *hollow*. . . . The veil is so thin! *Why?*"

Voldigar jerked awake with a cry, clutching the little key that still hung about his neck. All was bitter cold and dim, and he was naked against the frigid stone where still he sat, gasping for air. The sound of hunting horns lingered in his ears, and frozen tears clung to the corners of his eyes. There he sagged against the stone, rigid and blanketed in frost, trembling while he sought for his wits.

He slowed his breathing and bit by bit, blinked away the terror of his vision, until at last he could finally peer into the sky. For long moments, he perceived nothing of what he saw but soon realized that the earliest pale light of morning was creeping into the world, thin and remote, a mere ribbon across the high fringe of the canyon.

Morning!

Voldigar lurched to his feet and held his breath to listen. The horns had followed from his dream. Still they blared down the Chasm's walls, and faintly he could hear the distant roar of many voices. He shook the last vestige of the night from his mind. Surely, this was the signal meant for him.

He turned to face the glowering stone that loomed there huge before him, vanishing into the gray above. A sudden chill of fear overtook the icy stiffness of his body as his thoughts came rushing back. A weight beyond all measure—a deed beyond all possibility. How could this stone yield to him? All this way he'd come, but had he been a fool? What hope had he? The effort would break him, like ice upon a branch. And what if he did tear it down? He would descend into the deepest tomb, unseen again in all the ages of the earth, unseen by wife and child who would only know him in a tale. Death's fingers wound upon his heart and whispered of the grave.

"No time for doubts, old man," Voldigar muttered to himself. He placed his hands against the stone and braced his feet upon the rock. One hand he slid above his head. The other he kept close beside his chest. He closed his eyes.

"My God. My Almighty. My True King. Grant me this; that if you have called me to this moment, and called my brethren too, bring down this stone and save us, save my wife and child, come what may."

Voldigar opened his eyes, and there, high above him, a ball of flame plummeted through the air. As a great beacon in the dim of morning, its fiery tail illuminated the snow which had begun again to gently fall. The flaming cart crashed into the riverbank and burst into a million sparks.

He pushed.

With all his might he pushed. With every fiber of his will, he pushed. With the name of every Brother on his lips and the memory of Gwenyth beating in his heart, he pushed. His hands drove into the stone, but the pillar only looked on and mocked. *"You cannot,"* he heard it say. *"But I must,"* his bones replied.

A shard of stone splintered away and gashed his hand. Blood poured out and over his wrist, but still, he pressed on. The agony was exquisite, the force of all his foes held up inside his grasp, but the love he had of home and of his brethren and of his people, he told himself, was heavier even still.

He felt and heard a snapping sound behind his elbow, but to him, it was nothing more than the whip upon an ox's back. Still he pushed and cried out to God with all his voice and will. On he drove until all the world shook before his hands.

In a sudden crack, the stone before him began to move, and then the rock above him shuddered and burst. A great shower of dust and debris sprayed outward and rained over his head. He pressed on, and the stone continued to move. He felt the mighty bearing of the Span list above him and settle into place again. On he strained until a great shelf of terrible mass loomed and bowed darkly over the crown of his head.

In one hushed moment, it was done. The mocking stone had given way before him and The Great Span of Aramon was conquered. His legs would have surely buckled and his pounding heart burst within his chest, but a single image of Gwenyth crying out for him in the storm flashed before his eyes. Voldigar gathered himself and leapt away just as the rock above came crashing down.

With strength renewed, he plunged into the icy water again and swam against the current with all his strength. His arms were a world of fire and pain, but he knew behind him all the endless bulk of the Span convulsed in a terrible dance of ruin.

A huge block crashed into the river, so close to his side that it raked along his thigh. The water displaced and sent him hurdling from the river and careening through the air. He splashed in again, a handsbreadth from one of the other pillars he'd leapt from in the night before. He wrenched himself onto its base and saw now that this pillar too was bulging to the side as the thunder and deafening crack of destruction boomed and echoed from the walls of the Chasm.

He leapt free, just as the column burst into a rain of mighty stone. He was fleeing now in earnest, leaping from base to base. The pillars collapsed behind him as fast as he could run and vault. No sooner did he land on one than it would shatter and he sprang into the air again, searching for the next with his feet.

His lungs burned with the coarse grit of obliterated stone swirling in the air. He was near blind with its smoke and terror as he finally leapt upon the shore. The bridge was toppling toward him, and he thought for a moment to pass beneath and so avoid its awful collapse. To his dismay, before him was nothing less than a rushing waterfall of rock, racing forward to crush him where he stood.

Away he fled along the riverbank as fast as he could fly. He did not look back nor to the way beneath his feet, but with what strength remained, sped and plunged ahead. He felt the ground shudder and buckle as massive stones fell like meteors upon the earth.

They grew closer now, perhaps sixty yards behind, now fifty, now forty. The huge footsteps of a titan, smashing down to pursue him. Thirty, twenty. Voldigar sprinted on as the dust overtook him in a cloud of blinding gray. Ten. Five. He knew his flight was in vain. Just behind now, he felt the jolt of an impossible force land only inches from his feet. He was launched, hurled through the wind as stones pierced his body in a thousand wounds. In the deafening clamor, he was sure he heard a sound, Gwenyth, singing in the barley. A great weight drove him down, and all the world blinked into nothing.

CHAPTER FORTY-NINE

ECHOES IN THE CANYON

THE VILE HANDS OF many foes reached up in a final desperate gesture as the Span crumbled beneath their feet. For an instant, the Oruni hung suspended on the air in madness, and then fell away like the offscouring of a filthy dish. Countless thousands of gibbering devils cried out in frantic terror as the Chasm swallowed them. The great stones of the bridge mingled with their plunge and crushed them even as they fell.

Lanathor saw little of this as he raced along the canyon's edge, searching with his eyes and ears for the Eldest, at the mercy of the peril far below. Taro was close behind, vainly calling out his name over the roaring collapse of the Span. Even Soris followed on his limping legs while Wulf gave chase to all.

Dimly, in the gray of morning, a small figure rushed past the ruin of the tumbled cart Wulf had thrown over the edge. It was Voldigar, speeding along the near bank of the river as rocks and bodies crashed down from high above.

"Voldigar!" cried Lanathor as well, but surely, his Brother could not hear over the din of destruction. The falling stones were drawing ever closer. Lanathor slowed his pace and set his mind again. Rarely did he work his craft at such a height or distance, and only then at peril to himself, but there was no time to consider. He reached out over the vast gap below.

In his weariness, the strain was agonizing, like pulling the root of a mighty tree through coal-black clay. The faintest glimmer of violet light shimmered along the edge of a massive block, and it was thrust aside, narrowly missing Voldigar. Taro's hands burst in white light, and Soris tried to spin his ice in turn. Meager as it was, they cast forth their powers too, grasping helplessly at many stones.

Lanathor came completely to a halt and trembled as his hands worked. Still, Voldigar went on, but he was hardly visible now, obscured by the crumbling mass that came down all around. The chaos was too great, and Lanathor cried out as an immense boulder, huge as a ship upon the sea, hurtled directly at his friend. He could only stand despairing as the inevitable came.

The great stone was violently cast aside in a burst of red fire. Urias stood there at their flank with his hand outstretched until he wavered and slumped against Wulf's side. "Too many," he groaned, "too many . . ." then lay still upon the snow. Wulf stood helpless with axe in hand, his face white and hollow. The canyon filled with a cloud of dust and the rain of mighty stones. Voldigar disappeared as the ruinous flood finally overtook him and crushed him in the Chasms's depths.

━━━◆━━━

The better part of the day was spent by the time Lanathor and Wulf had made their way to the canyon floor over many winding paths and descents upon their ropes. The others, they had sent on to the Anteres Well, dead and wounded borne on carts and biers. Dantic they advised to go with them, but he refused and for his part, would not play the rebel. All that survived of the garrison, he brought back to Arregalt, and Lanathor wished them well.

Lanathor worked a final rope from off his waist and looked about while Wulf wrinkled his nose and peered at the ruin before him. The water split in many rivulets and trickled over a tangled mass of broken stone and broken bodies. It was oddly quiet, and all was still where snow had begun to layer over every surface not broken by the streams. The stench was indescribable. The decay of the twisted creatures set on more quickly than that of mortal men, and their vile odor steamed around them in mountains of their piled corpses.

Wulf covered his face with his sleeve and spoke in a muffled tone. "His body could be anywhere. How do we find him in all this filth? Curse them!"

Lanathor returned a grimacing nod. "He was buried somewhere near. Perhaps . . . perhaps he's still alive."

Wulf took on a pained expression. "Alive?" He shook his shaggy head.

"Perhaps," Lanathor said again.

Wulf nodded and pulled rocks aside while he kicked over the bodies of the Oruni. "Perhaps," he echoed Lanathor loudly. He tossed a mangled tree. "Perhaps!" he cried again through gritted teeth and wiped his arm across his eyes.

Lanathor joined him in his manic dance, clawing through the rubble, until after long and fruitless effort, they fell breathless to the ground. There they lay in despairing weariness until Wulf sat up with a shout. "His knife! It's stuck there in the sand!" He scrambled along the riverbank.

Lanathor hurried after him, and Wulf plucked it from the ground to hold it to the light. "Strange fortune," he said as he admired the blade. "It's not broken." Lanathor looked from left to right, trying for all his worth to peer through the stones themselves. A boot, a belt, anything—

He spied a tiny wedge of cloth, buried further down the shore. Weary as he was, Lanathor stumbled toward it with newfound strength and raked through the sand.

"What is it?" Wulf asked.

"It's a pouch . . ." Lanathor said as he rose back to his feet and brushed the dirt away. ". . . Gwenyth's medicine bag." He stared at it in silence until he dropped his eyes to the ground with a sigh.

Wulf renewed his mad dredging, tossing huge rocks aside and flinging mud into the air. On his hands and knees, he burrowed where the little pouch had been until the hole was as deep as his arms and he could scrape no further. His shoulders shook, and he leaned backward with bloody fingertips, heaving great tears and roaring at the sky.

"Where are you!" he bellowed. "Where are you, old man?"

The root had begun to fade, and Lanathor felt hot tears streaming down his face. He laid a gentle hand on Wulf and listened to his cry echo along the Chasm.

From behind him, the sound of a tumbling rock caught his ear. He whirled about and Wulf leapt to his feet to brandish the blade before them. They saw nothing at first, but then the faintest movement showed on the flanks of a great mound. It was the tips of fingers, a man's fingers, the color of stone, and thrust through the debris and snow.

They rushed toward the pile and desperately cleared the rubble away, still digging with their hands.

"Hold on, old man!" Wulf cried. "Hold on!"

"I . . . heard you . . . talking . . ." a faint voice came out of the dust-caked face that emerged. They pulled the final pieces of stone away and gently coaxed Voldigar's limp body from the makeshift tomb.

"Is the Wilding on him?" Wulf asked frantically as they continued to brush away the grit.

"I don't know how to tell," Lanathor said as his eyes darted over Voldigar. A fierce joy rose in his heart as he saw the life rising and falling in the chest of his dear friend.

Wulf fished a waterskin from his side and poured a trickle of it into the old man's mouth. Voldigar licked his lips and swallowed, but said no more.

"I can't believe it," Wulf said as he brushed more grime and washed it from Voldigar's face. "I knew you could do it, old man," he said while tears gathered in his eyes again. "I knew you could."

The faintest smile flickered across Voldigar's face. "You . . . came for me. . ."

Wulf nodded and turned again to Lanathor then looked up at the high canyon wall. "How do we get him out of here?"

"North," Lanathor replied, "along the riverbank. The canyon's more shallow where it meets the Adionel. The others will meet us there."

"Gwenyth . . ." Voldigar murmured.

"Hold on, Eldest. We'll bring you to her," Wulf said and scooped him into his arms.

CHAPTER FIFTY

LESSONS OF A KING

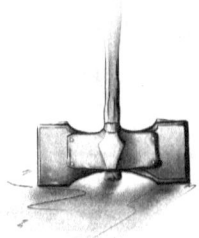

V OLDIGAR REMEMBERED LITTLE OF their journey. With what
meager strength he had, he clutched Gwenyth's medicine pouch
to his chest. His other arm hung limply while Wulf carried him as gently as he could. They covered long miles in the shadows of the canyon
until he lost consciousness again. When he awoke, others had joined
them. He heard them softly singing Arcus's Chant as they passed the
massive Rock of Tholc. That great hand of stone reached out there and
split the Haroel from the Adionel in vast, tumbling waterfalls. To him,
their Chant was as the voice of angels, bearing him on his way while
they hoisted him on a swaying lift, high over the falls and out of the
canyon at last. He wished to join them in their song, but he could not
find his voice nor even the power to open his mouth.

Soon they passed the fords west of the Rock and descended into the
marshy valley of his ancestral home. They left him there on the edge of the
bogs to sleep upon a cart under a shelter of rough burlap. When he awoke
again, the sun of late afternoon was low in the west, and on his other side,
he stared absently at a thick tangle of leafless weeping cherry trees. Faintly,

he could make out the distant shape of a half-sunk well that had stood on solid ground when he was a child.

Soris was by his side, recounting the names of fallen brethren in his somber tone. All around them, the now homeless residents of Maghaltani tended to fires and went about the business of camp with faces grim.

". . . Roldwin, Demeric, Maleth . . . and Vasherk." Soris stopped and closed his eyes with a sigh. "Twenty-six in all, Eldest. Twenty-four brothers and two of the sisters."

Voldigar sat in silence a long while until Soris shifted his weight in the snow and took a deep breath. "Would that we had Vasherk now, there are many wounded—you among them."

"Twenty-six," Voldigar repeated, "and three captured by Lusánt. That leaves us seventy-four that wear the red cloak." His voice was hoarse and thin.

Soris nodded. "And less than half of them fit for war."

"How many others?" Voldigar asked. "The families?"

"One hundred and seventy-one, Eldest. And mercifully, none of them are hurt. They came with all they could from Maghaltani."

Voldigar swallowed. "Has there been word from Liadov, or Gwenyth?"

Soris shook his head. "No, but they should be here soon. The storm has not returned."

Voldigar closed his eyes and nodded, but the voice of Taro as he stooped under the shelter pulled them open again.

"Awake, I see? Here." Taro handed him a bowl of something warm and fragrant.

With effort, Voldigar raised himself and swung his legs over the side of the cart. The blanket fell away, and he could see that someone mercifully had clothed him while he slept.

Taro's eyes widened. "Already strong as an ox again I see."

"My wounds are superficial," Voldigar replied.

"Superficial? You're one giant bruise," Taro complained with a smile, "and very fortunate. Honestly, Brother, I don't understand how the Wilding didn't strike you."

"How do you know it didn't?"

Taro shook his head and shrugged. "I know nothing you don't. Different for every Chanter, right? But you'd know. You'd have to know."

Voldigar cooled his soup a little and took an unsteady spoonful. There was something wrong with his arm, but he somehow managed not to drop the bowl. The soup was delicious. "Thank you, Taro. I'm sorry about Vasherk."

Taro's smile melted. "He's your friend too."

Voldigar nodded. "You were close."

"We were," Taro agreed, "and we are. We'll see him again, Elder. *Together in the Song*. Eat your soup."

Lanathor caught sight of their gathering and limped over to join them.

"What happened to you?" Voldigar asked.

"Nothing important," Lanathor said. "Not all of us climb like mountain goats." He smiled. "Glad you're awake."

Voldigar raised his brow with a nod and took another bite. "As am I. Retiring to my farm isn't working out quite the way I thought it would."

"Well, welcome back to your estate then, Lord Anteres," Lanathor said.

Voldigar chuckled painfully and held his side. "At least we made it."

"That we did. Most of us anyway." Lanathor's face darkened. "We'll have to move again soon, along the river and then deeper into the Far Marshes."

Voldigar nodded again. "Liadov should be here soon—with Gwenyth. We have to wait for them, and then all are accounted for." He looked his brothers in their eyes and lowered his brow. "Take heart, Brethren, and take hope. We'll not be followed in the Marshes. We did the right thing, and God . . . God sees all."

Lanathor folded his hands at his waist. "We built Maghaltani. We'll make the swamps bloom too."

"Would you look at that," Taro suddenly exclaimed. He pointed off to the west where a small shape cast his shadow over the snow.

<hr />

"Voldigar!" Tepic cried as he hurried his pace. "Voldigar!" Red of cheek, the boy came to a stop with a breathless smile that quickly faded to a frown. "Lector! What happened?"

Voldigar waved a hand. "I'm fine, Tepic. What on earth are you doing here? How did you find us?"

Tepic's face brightened. "Begging pardon, sir, but everyone talks in front of me. I heard where you were going. I have news!"

"News? Speak on."

Tepic shifted his weight and seemed unable to continue. He licked his lips and inhaled.

Voldigar's eyes narrowed and he leaned forward. "Well?"

"You're a father!" Tepic finally blurted out with his arms stretched wide.

Voldigar's face froze like he'd just been struck. He set his soup bowl down with a trembling hand, and his jaw hung open in dumbfounded silence.

"Voldigar?"

Voldigar blinked. "It's . . . it's too soon."

"No, no, the baby's fine! It's fine. Liadov, she . . . Voldigar?"

Voldigar looked at Tepic again as though he'd just seen him for the first time. A smile started to spread across his face, and Tepic nodded eagerly.

"He's got black hair—like you, Lector, and green eyes like his mum." In his excitement, a hint of Undercity touched Tepic's voice.

Voldigar's smile melted back into confusion. "Where are they? Why haven't they come?"

"They couldn't, not yet," Tepic hurried on. "The lady's very weak, but they're not coming here anyway, they're going to the shrine."

"What? Why the shrine?"

"She didn't say, but the sword is with her, and they have your mokja friend's wagon. They probably went already."

Voldigar opened his mouth to ask another question, but then shook his head and placed a hand on Tepic's shoulder. "Thank you for your message. I have to go to them." He put his foot on the ground to rise but Taro was suddenly at his side.

"Easy now, Brother, not yet. Send someone—I can go."

Voldigar stumbled and weakly tried to brush Taro's hand away. He steadied himself on the wagon to let the dizziness pass, then pulled himself upright again. Tepic was still grinning before him with his kind and earnest face. On the ridge beyond, a shadow stirred. Voldigar caught his breath.

"What is that?" he asked. The other men looked where he pointed, and all saw it at once. Where Tepic's tracks receded to the lip of the lightly wooded hill, a line of riders had come dimly into view. More were appearing every moment.

Voldigar's eyes flashed with anger. "The snow! Tepic, you fool, you've led them right to us!"

Tepic's eyes shot up in fear, and then his face twisted like he'd been stabbed. "What?"

"Gamad's men!" Voldigar said as loudly as his thin voice allowed. "They're here."

Tepic turned to look, but Voldigar spun him back. "Run, Tepic! Run now!"

The boy's eyes were full of anguish, and tears welled in them. Voldigar could see his words had wounded Tepic, but there was no time to mollify. He thrust the boy past him wordlessly, and Tepic ran madly to the east through the weeping cherries.

"Not the bog!" Voldigar shouted after him, but Tepic did not hear his wavering cry.

In moments, the riders had all gathered, and now they came thundering down the slope. Lusánt was at their head.

⸺ ◆ ⸺

A cry rose up in the camp as many backed away and others raced for their weapons or snatched flaming brands from the fire pits. All around, the mass of horsemen were closing in.

"Don't fight!" Voldigar cried out weakly and stumbled to his knees. "Don't fight!" Panic gripped his heart. Less than forty men were fit to battle, and thousands of cavalry had surrounded them, their families, and rows of wounded men. Taro lifted Voldigar from his knees and set him back to lean against his cart. His face was resolute.

Lanathor took up the cry in his baritone. "Stand down, Brothers of Aramon! Stand down!"

Lusánt kept his distance while others leapt down from their horses and brought a forest of bristling spears to bear. There was a ferocious look upon his young face, and he struggled to keep his impetuous horse under control.

"Where is Voldigar?" the Emperor cried out. "Find him, and find the boy!"

All about him, stern-faced brethren laid down their arms and held up their hands. They backed their families behind them. Several children had begun to cry. Voldigar staggered forward from under his shelter and held high his hand before he let it fall heavily to his side again. "I am here, Lusánt." He fell once more to his knees and tried to lift his hand again.

Lusánt saw him at once and reared his horse about with a scowl. "Him first! These adders bite!" Lusánt raised his eyes over the crowd and scanned wildly among them. "Bring me Tepic Banari!"

A tight cordon had now formed around the entire camp, save for the wet ground of the swamp. Voldigar glanced through the trees but could see no sign of Tepic. Silently, he prayed the boy had not stumbled to his doom in the treacherous waters.

A gap opened in the ring of soldiers, and through it walked a tall figure in a drooping cowl of black fur. By his side was none other than Bajk the Mokja in his brass goggles, and behind them, several soldiers pushed a cart, laden with a great mound of iron rings.

"Why are you here, Lusánt?" Voldigar asked.

Lusánt leapt down from his mount and whipped a long cavalry sword from off his waist. He stared at Voldigar but did not speak a word.

Bajk snatched one of the iron rings from the cart and walked forward, staring timidly at the ground. He hesitated. "I'm sorry, Voldigar," he muttered. He opened the ring at its center and snapped it around Voldigar's neck.

At once, a piercing pain shot through his head and down his spine. Voldigar gasped and clawed at the collar before he collapsed to the snow. A shrill whine on the edge of hearing filled his ears. He squeezed shut his eyes against the pain. More soldiers came forward and quickly bound his wrists while many rough hands hoisted him to his feet. There he would have fallen again, save for the arms that bore his sagging weight.

Through his squinting eyes, Voldigar could see that soldiers were now everywhere, clasping the strange collars about the necks of every man, woman, and child in the camp. The rings glowed faintly along their centers, and like him, many others cried out when the collars were made secure.

Voldigar struggled against the cords on his hands. Even in his injured state, they should have melted away like wax, but they may as well have been the jaws of a dragon. He could not free his wrists.

From the corner of his eye, he saw Wulf flailing against a mass of soldiers. They managed to place a collar on his neck too, but he snapped it off like cornwood and bellowed like an injured bear. Soldiers brandished clubs and beat at him but he snarled and swatted them aside.

"Don't fight, Wulf," Voldigar cried out breathlessly. "Don't fight!"

The cowled figure stepped forward, and a hollow voice came forth from his shadowed face. "I will deal with that one." He strode to Wulf, and ducking a wild blow, thrust his hand upward to catch him in the crook of his arm. Wulf yelped like a startled animal and went rigid before a sound like the tearing of a seam rang out. He fell stunned to the ground.

"Wulf!" Voldigar cried out again. "Wulf!"

Lusánt walked forward now and grasped Voldigar by the collar of his shirt. "Wulf is fine, old man. Stop your blubbering." He drove him backward until the soldiers released him. Voldigar stumbled and fell, seated now against the cart. Lusánt loomed over him a moment before he squatted down and stared him in his face.

"How does it feel, old man? To be weak and powerless? Unable to help the ones you love?"

Voldigar's head swam, and the whine of the collar rang relentless in his ears. He did not speak.

"What happened to my bridge, Eldest of Aramon?"

Voldigar groaned and looked away again. Lusánt slapped him hard across the face.

"I asked you a question."

The cowled figure had come to Lusánt's side now and spoke again. "This one is half-dead already." Faintly, Voldigar could see that steam was rising from inside his robes.

Lusánt regarded him sidelong for a moment before turning back to Voldigar. "Do you know who has done this thing? There is one road into Aramon, and now it is destroyed."

"The horde is stopped. There was no other way."

Lusánt narrowed his eyes. "Did I not command you; do not interfere? All the realm obeys me, Voldigar. But you, why are you the rebel? Oathsworn yet false, my protectors and my teachers, but faithless in the end . . ." Lusánt shook his head ruefully and sighed.

"They would have overrun all of Aramon, Lusánt."

"No! No, they would not! Do you still not understand, you old fool?" Lusánt thrust his sword into the earth and gestured wildly with his hands. "They would have come to the doorstep of my city and no further. While you refuse me, even the Oruni are mine to command. They would have bent to my will and to the symbol of my house—and then for the wretched, decadent people of this dying land, I would have been a god! I could have saved them from *themselves.* The greater the wound, the greater the deliverance. But now look what you've done." Lusánt grit his teeth. "Do not meddle with wisdom in the heart of a king! You! You who are sworn to obey!"

Voldigar's face twisted in horror. "What wicked madness is this?"

Lusánt slapped Voldigar again. His lips trembled.

"Hold your tongue, you coward! What do you know of wickedness? Lies and falsehood! Always you judge so small, Voldigar. You think of one, of solitary souls—but you see no further than a mirror, with a heart as weak as clay. I will teach you another lesson of a king."

"A king must judge the many, the masses, and that is my burden. Awakening—unity you could only dream of, a golden age of Aramon unseen since Tymicha rose like a morning star above the sea. But what do you bring, Voldigar? Destruction? I build, while you tear down. I command, while you quiver in doubt. You send Oruni to the abyss, but I make them my servants. My victory is total!"

The sun behind Lusánt had fallen almost to the horizon and blinded Voldigar where he sat. He searched within for any shred of strength but found only enough to steady his wavering voice. "What happened to you, son of Olwis? Who whispers in your ear? God have mercy on you . . . and on us all."

Lusánt rose again to his feet as two men approached and looked down darkly at Voldigar. "I am your Emperor. It is my mercy you should beg of now, Voldigar."

"My lord, we cannot find the boy," a soldier said.

Lusánt regarded the soldier with hollow contempt for a brief moment before his face contorted in rage. He turned back to Voldigar. "Where is he?"

"Who?" Voldigar asked.

Lusánt stepped forward and snatched the sword into his hand again. "Don't be coy with me, grandfather. I followed Tepic to your camp. Where are you hiding him?"

Voldigar turned his eyes to the cart against which he sat, resisting the urge to look again through the trees.

Lusánt slowly brought the tip of his cavalry sword to Voldigar's neck and pressed it there until a tiny drop of blood dripped over its cold metal. Voldigar raised his eyes to the Emperor and held him in his gaze. A gust of wind passed between them, but they were silent until Lusánt turned back to his men. "Don't let him get away. Scour the area. Call for dogs." He stared down the length of his sword again until he abruptly jerked it away, spun on his heel, and called for his horse.

"Voldigar," he said, as he held the pommel of his saddle, "you should pray that we catch Tepic Banari. Much of my mercy will depend on it."

The cowled man still stood by, and Voldigar thought he could see glittering eyes peering from under his furs. Lusánt turned to him. "Bring me the boy, and the sword he bears." The Emperor mounted his horse and waved his men on. "Back to Arregalt!" he cried. "We have a trial to prepare."

CHAPTER FIFTY-ONE

A LONELY VESSEL

TEPIC COULD ONLY LISTEN in horror and confusion to the struggle in the camp behind him. He dared not raise his head over the lip of the flooded well in which he now wedged himself. He gathered low beneath its stone, his chin touching the frigid water of the swamp. He could hear soldiers going back and forth in the camp and knew they were searching for him, even calling out his name in mocking tones. He was certain that at any moment they would hear the chattering of his teeth.

His skin felt as though it were frozen. The water, though not yet ice, was somehow even colder. Like a thousand tiny hands, it tore at him, reaching for his bones—but a warmth still smoldered in his body. The little cordial of foul liquor his sister had given him, that he'd hardly stopped from spewing on the ground, that had made him sweat profusely all his long travel in the day—now clung to his heart as he clung to his life in the frigid bog. Tepic held his breath and tried to send his thoughts far away.

Unbidden tears worked into his eyes as the catastrophe raced through his mind. The Brotherhood was taken, and he was to blame. A message he had meant for good had ruined all their careful plans. An hour before, he proudly bore his duty, but now he clenched his teeth in shame and regret, trying all the while not to make a sound. *I'm sorry, Voldigar. I'm so sorry.*

Night had long fallen, but the voices of soldiers still echoed out. He'd heard a mass of men moving away hours before, yet these still lingered. The lights of their torches flickered dimly on the rim of the well. As yet, he'd heard nothing enter the water, though many feet had gone by on its shore.

"Nothing," he heard a voice say. "They circled all the way to the rivers and back."

"Dogs will find him," another said.

"Pfft," the first man hissed. "P'raps he's dead, face down in the bog."

The cold finally touched Tepic's heart, and he held his breath, sinking lower in the water.

Harsh laughter rang out from the second voice. "Why don't you have a look then?"

"P'raps I will."

He heard the slosh of water as someone stepped into the shallows. Tepic sank until only his nose and ears were above the surface.

"Gods, it's cold!" the voice called out again. "It's all mud too!"

"Gods rest his soul," the other voice replied. "For his grave!"

He heard the man relieving himself into the water while the other took up his harsh snickering once more. Tepic did all he could to hold a whimper behind his lips. His heart was beating fast, pounding in his own ears. At length, the water sloshed again, and he heard the men wander away. He dared to breathe once more.

Eventually, all grew quiet. It took many long minutes of doubt before he finally willed himself to peek over the edge of the well. The night was still, and save for moonlight, it was utterly dark. No torches loomed, and no sound of booted feet wandered through the abandoned camp. He sighed with relief, slipped from the well, and started toward the shore. He'd not swam two feet before he caught a distant clamor upon the wind, barking and baying over the hills.

Tepic's heart nearly gave out within him, and he considered simply swimming to the shore and letting himself be taken. What hope did he have now? He looked to the well and thought to leap back in and hide until the morning, but that too would be hopeless. He'd hunted with his father. He knew the hounds would smell him, even over a hundred feet of shallow bog. Despite his despair, something within his soul told him he must go on, that he must not be captured. There was only one choice, come what may. Tepic turned and swam as hard as he could, deeper into the swamp, praying all the while and sputtering brackish water from his lips.

He could no longer sense his limbs, and though the Jarnath leaf still burned deep within, he wondered if he would ever feel his hands again. He wondered too what creatures might lurk below the surface. He had to put it out of his mind. All he did encounter were the strange remnants of a long abandoned manor. A fencepost here, the ragged frame of a building there, or a tiny tussock of shaggy ground, all poking like ghost stories through the surface of the water. Somewhere up ahead would be the river that had overflowed its banks so long ago to make this swamp.

On he went, slowly, and all the while the distant sound of the dogs grew louder, and a coiling mist rose over the surface of the dark water. He had almost given up hope when there ahead he saw the most beautiful thing in the world. It was a small patch of solid earth with a squat little tree and the current of the river just beyond. Most important of all, tied to the tree was the unmistakable shape of an old row boat.

Tepic pulled himself onto the land and found the cold even worse than in the bog. His eyes watered and his fingers stung, but hope was there before him. The boat had no oar, but the rope was loosely tied, and the hull of it looked as sound as he could tell in the dim light. He pushed it into the river and nearly lost it with his trembling grip. A moment more and he lay breathless in its belly. The current swept him away, a lonely vessel on a dark river, drifting into the hinterlands.

Chapter Fifty-Two

A Brother Does Not Lie

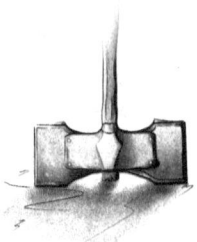

VOLDIGAR COULD HARDLY SEE. He swayed where he stood in the center of a cavernous hollow, engulfed in the belly of Lusánt's Golden Spire. It was all of ivory, and marble, and hammered gold. A gallery soared above him where cold men peered down from high-backed chairs between the light of many torches. His wrists and ankles were shackled in iron, his neck in the cruel collar that whined its shrill, high note. All about him, the room swelled with the press of his brethren and the muted fear of their families, identically restrained. Even wounded men upon their backs, lying on cots or on the hard floor beneath, were bound the same. Smaller children had been left in their cells, but here and there blinked the sullen eyes of boys who could not be more than ten. It seemed they were on an altar together, being sacrificed to the same capricious god.

"Let us begin," Lusánt called out from above.

From the edges of his blurred vision, Voldigar sought for Lutz and found him. Medellai and Gardoric too, stooped among the throng. Haggard and worn, at least they had survived their arrest. Three fewer names on Soris's rolls. For this, he whispered quiet thanks before he squinted up at the Emperor.

"Remove our shackles, Lusánt. We are no danger—"

"Silence!"

"At least the children—for pity's sake."

"I said silence!" Lusánt lifted himself halfway from his chair, and his words echoed off the marbled walls. An awkward moment passed before he lowered himself again and gestured to his left.

To that side, Voldigar saw another man, now standing in his own gallery, dressed in blue—Diocesan Ragat.

"Thus do we call to order lawful tribunal, under the gracious eye of His Majesty, the Emperor Lusánt Sispérus, Lord of Aramon and the Thirteen Provinces, presided over by Master Hyrodan, High Reverend of the Sun. The accused are gathered before you. Voldigar, House Anteres. Medellai, House Sispérus. Lanathor, Commoner and Lector. Lutz, former—"

Lusánt stood again and waved his hand. "Yes, yes, etcetera, etcetera. Gods, Ragat. Will you read every name?"

Ragat coughed, and his small round face reddened. He streamed a long sheet of paper through his hands and swallowed before he continued. "As this is a house of justice, the accused are offered first to present certified counsel."

The room fell silent while Lusánt shifted in his chair and frowned.

Ragat continued. "Seeing as the accused do not present counsel, they must represent themselves. Who shall prosecute for the Crown?"

"I will. Me," Lusánt said with a flick of his hand.

"Very well, " Ragat said as he sat.

From across the chamber, Master Hyrodan rose, all in white with an amused smile. "Charges," he announced. "The accused are charged with two counts of Treason with Malicious Conspiracy, one count of Trespassing, and one count of Harboring a Dangerous Malefactor. How do the accused plead?"

The room went quiet again, save for a low murmur in the galleries. Lusánt rose to his feet once more. "Bring forward the . . . titular head. Do you have nothing to say, Elder Voldigar? Sword-Lector, Hero of Aramon, and King of Maghaltani?"

"I am no king," Voldigar growled, "and we are guilty of nothing."

Lusánt clapped his hands. "Not Guilty then, very well. . . . And you must be a king, because it seems you do not recognize the rule of any other." Lusánt waved his hand dismissively. "No matter. You will have lawful tribunal. We would not dare to try the heroes of Aramon in any other way."

Hyrodan cleared his throat and spoke again. "Seeing as the accused deny all charges, I yield to the Prosecution."

Lusánt bent over the polished banister at his waist and looked across the faces of those below him with his mouth held open before he began. "The count of Trespassing, I dismiss."

"Stricken," Hyrodan boomed out.

"But the others I do not. These rebels before you first stole from my tower, then with wicked hands, they tore down the second greatest monument of Aramon that had stood for a thousand years. And through it all, to this very moment, they conceal a wanted criminal, the young man Tepic Banari, who has stolen an artifact and assaulted my general. For evidence, I ask only that you use your eyes. Stand, Gamad."

The old general sat eating from a bowl of shellfish and wiped his mouth with the tips of his thick fingers before he stood with a grunt. He held the dark wood of his false arm before him for all to see before he returned heavily to his seat.

"And if you wish to see the ruin of the Span," Lusánt went on, "you have only to ride there yourself and see its stone crumbled into the Haroel. Of the final matter, bring forth my witness."

In the rear of the hall, two doors opened and Bajk waddled in, shoving a barrel on a handcart through the press. He'd been cleaned up for the occasion, but his hands were still blackened by a permanent layer of soot.

Lutz glared as his brother entered the room, but his face twisted into a strange look of doubt when Bajk passed by. "Speak well of us, Bajk . . ." Voldigar heard him say. The rest of his words were lost while the two briefly met each other's eyes. Bajk's mouth twitched with some unspoken word before his attention was stolen away by Lusánt's voice.

"What do you have there, Artificer Bajk?"

Bajk turned his head away from his brother. "Tarbane Crystals, m'lord—one of two barrels these fellows tried to steal. Very dangerous."

He searched the crowd and pointed a grubby finger at Lanathor. "That's one of them."

Lusánt feigned shock and shook his head. "Awful."

Bajk stole a short look at Voldigar before he swiftly turned his eyes away. "What kind of trouble are these men in?"

"That's enough, Artificer Bajk," Lusánt said. He made a shooing motion with his hand, and the mokja was escorted from the hall as quickly as he'd come. Lutz's mouth hung open in a defeated frown, eyes fixed on the doors until they closed behind Bajk.

"That is all," Lusánt said as he sat back down and draped a hand over his chair. "The evidence is clear, and most importantly, rests on my own testimony. Let's not belabor things."

Hyrodan rose to his feet again. "The Defense may speak."

A door in the upper gallery burst open, and a murmur rose up in the crowd again. Dantic entered the hall. His face was flushed and angry, and he moved quickly to his seat.

Lusánt leaned forward. "Dantic! Must I remind you that you're only a Captain now? You were not invited to this tribunal."

"Your Highness, my seat does not rest on my rank but on my noble title. With your pardon, sir, this seat is permanent. I should have been notified."

Lusánt's face coiled in disgust, and he looked to Ragat while the galleries whispered again. Ragat shrugged apologetically and quickly turned his attention back to the long scroll he held.

Voldigar glanced at Dantic who looked down on him now with a hard face and a nod.

Hyrodan coughed again. "The Defense?"

"I will speak," Dantic said from the balcony above.

Ragat bolted to his feet and loudly protested. "Counsel has already been declared, Commander—Captain," he quickly added. Dantic gripped the railing in front of him but returned to his seat.

Voldigar was growing dizzy and leaned subtly against Lanathor. He blinked, and stared at the floor and at his arms. There were bruises from elbow to wrist, and most of his fingers were swollen. He could still taste blood in his mouth.

"Voldigar Anteres," Hyrodan said. "You may speak."

Voldigar raised his head with effort and searched the faces in the gallery. Most of them he recognized, lords and officers of varying degree. Some were neither, but there as guests to gape and gawk upon the spectacle. Against all hope and reason, he sought for Gwenyth's face among the crowd, but she was not there. The only friend he saw was Dantic. He knew his words meant nothing to the rest of them, and he'd grown weary of their mockery. All the same, they were his words to speak, and to the righteous souls who stood by his side, and to Dantic, he would give them at least a little truth.

"We have done . . . only as our duty required," Voldigar said, as firmly as he could. "Nothing more, and nothing less. Even to this hour, Lusánt Sispérus, we serve you, and we serve Aramon—though you see it not." Voldigar turned his eyes to his brethren round about, finding each in turn, gathering their strength into his voice. "Were a single man to remain or a solitary blade of grass, the Brotherhood would defend her still. Aramon is in our hearts. Look around you, Emperor. All the world has gone to madness and crumbles. Even the heavens shake. But we do not yield! Will you cloak yourself in lies and stand upon delusion? As for me, and those in my care, we still love the truth. Yes, we tore down your bridge. Yes, we stole into your city, and we have hidden Tepic Banari beyond your reach." Voldigar swallowed and steadied himself. "A Brother does not lie!" he cried. "Voldigar Anteres has spoken. God's honor!"

"Honor God!" the cries of the Brethren went up behind him, and every man crossed his arm over his chest. The sound reverberated through the hall.

Lusánt snatched up his scepter from beside him and beat it against the rail. "Silence!" he called once more. "Silence!" The head of the rod broke free and tumbled down to clang and roll across the floor where it settled at Voldigar's feet.

"You admit it then!" Lusánt cried. "Fools!"

Hyrodan rose to speak, but Lusánt cowed him with a glance and an outstretched hand. "The defense is over. We need no further testimony. Move to sentencing!"

Voldigar took a deep breath, looked from side to side, and then calmly into Lusánt's eyes above.

Lusánt sat again and held the scepter sideways before his face. There was silence for a space in the hall until he spoke again. "There can be only one decision. . . . I, Lusánt Sispérus, sentence you to die."

Murmuring arose again in the galleries above. The stifled weeping of many voices behind him mingled with the sound of his shackles as Voldigar shuffled forward. The fight was ended. "In my final words then, I ask your clemency, Emperor, not for me, but on those who stand beside. It was I who designed every deed. It was I who led these men and gave command. Do with me as you will, but spare the others."

"I told you how you might seek my mercy, Voldigar. It's too late for you to claim a crown. The time is past, and I must judge the many." Lusánt rose again. "Do any oppose?"

A few men shifted in their chairs, and a hush rested on all who watched. Dantic stood. "I oppose."

"Does any second?"

A pregnant silence extended through the hall for many long seconds. Then, to Voldigar's astonishment, General Gamad pushed himself from his chair. "I second."

No longer a murmur, the chamber erupted into chaos. Lusánt's eyes went wide, and lords bolted upright to shout and throw papers in the air. Ragat was on his feet, blustering in a furor and beating a gavel over and over again. "Order! Order!" he called.

Through it all, Gamad stood with a faint look of bemusement on his broad face. He worked his one good hand through his tangled beard while the room settled under Ragat's incessant pounding.

Gamad at length lifted his voice above the din. "We forget ourselves, men of Aramon. The Brotherhood are exempted from capital punishment, even for the highest of crimes. Tymicha's law is inviolable."

There was a woodenness in the man's voice, as though the words had been rehearsed a dozen times before. Voldigar looked to Taro, to see if he had somehow freed himself from his collar, but only confusion rested on his face.

"The motion is seconded . . . and sustained," Hyrodan said. He looked as though he'd swallowed a sour grape. "What do you propose, General Gamad?"

"Exile," the general said without hesitation. "Immediate and total."

Lusánt began to laugh, quietly to himself at first, but then hysterically with his head tossed back. "Gamad, Gamad. You old jester. Did you lose your mind as well as your arm? Recall, General, that the only road out of Aramon was lately lost." Lusánt went on snickering. "Shall I catapult them all into Kurath? I fear they might be injured."

Gamad did not laugh or even smile. "The tide returned this morning, Your Highness, and there are two ships of the Miridas. They are leaving on account of early winter, one of them as soon as tomorrow. They are large ships, very large, and one of them could easily take on all these prisoners."

Lusánt raised his eyebrow and let his chuckling cease. He tilted his head. "Tomorrow? Where would I send them?"

"Tharakhan." Gamad sat down with a smug look of self-satisfaction.

A slow smile spread across Lusánt's face. "The old slavers' lands?"

Gamad nodded and raised his finger. "But not as slaves, my lord—that would be illegal."

Lusánt nodded slowly. "So it would. Exile then . . ."

Dantic lurched to his feet. "Gods, man! There are women and children among them. This is execution all the same. They'll be slaughtered or starved to death! I oppose!"

Ragat began to beat his gavel again, and Lusánt whispered something to a group of soldiers that stood behind him. Voldigar looked to Lanathor and found only that his Brother's head was drooped toward the floor. His shoulders gently shook.

"Do any join the opposition?" Lusánt cried out. The room was deathly quiet, save for the muffled weeping of a boy that stood near at Voldigar's hand. "Then I amend my sentence as Gamad advised."

"Captain Dantic," Lusánt went on, "you speak true. They would not be safe there—at least . . . not safe alone. But they will not be alone." Lusánt stood again and held his hand out across the open space between the galleries. "I am sending Aramon's most decorated soldier to guide and protect them. Congratulations, Captain Dantic. You've been reassigned."

All the color drained from Dantic's face, and stunned, he gripped the arms of his chair. The door behind him opened, and soldiers filed into his gallery.

"On the ship then, tomorrow!" Lusánt announced. He spread his hands wide. "I tire of this mummery. The session is adjourned."

Voldigar lurched forward, and forgetting his shackles, nearly stumbled. "Let me see my wife!" he cried. "Before I go!"

Lusánt blinked as though he'd just seen Voldigar for the first time. He smiled. "You would have her stand trial too? I thought you'd be grateful she wasn't here this morning. As it happens, I couldn't find her at home." He shook his head sadly. "Tell me where Tepic is, old man. You have five seconds."

Lusánt crossed his arms and waited. He blinked again. "Pity. Well, I am not unjust. I drop all charges against Gwenyth Sispérus. I will restore her barley too, plus one fifth, and she shall have full access to my doctors."

Voldigar bared his teeth and stepped forward again. "You shame us!"

"You shamed yourself, old man." Lusánt turned away and called out as he left the gallery. "Return them to their cells!"

Chapter Fifty-Three

Even When it Crushes

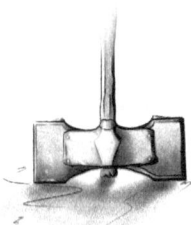

Voldigar sat on the cold floor of a dark cell with his chin against his chest and his back against the bars, breathing hoarsely while blood seeped from his nostrils. He was half asleep and half dreaming, winding round and round the same spinning image. He was in his barley field but it was bare, and he and Gwenyth were struggling against a stone together, fruitlessly trying to pry it from the earth. The dream faded with a distant, rhythmic sound.

The sound was that of footsteps, echoing louder as they came near. He cracked open his eyes to dimly see Lanathor across from him, likewise leaned against the yellowing stone with his eyes closed and mouth hung partly open. Voldigar wiped the blood from his lip with his two chained hands, and the footsteps stopped outside his cell. He turned and squinted into the lamplight.

"Voldigar," Gamad said. The lamp was hooked into his prosthetic hand, and in the dark behind him, the black-cowled figure stood with face obscured. "I've come to say goodbye, and thank you."

Voldigar tried to peer around Gamad's massive shoulders. "Who's your friend?"

Gamad glanced briefly behind him and shrugged "Him? An old ac-
quaintance, or a new one. Let's just say we've come to an understanding.
You can ask him whatever you like on the ship. You'll be there an awful
long time."

"Why did you object to execution?"

"Because, I'm a charitable man." Gamad smiled. "I can afford to be,
because I'm also a very rich man now."

Voldigar let his gaze fall to the corner of his cell. "You're selling us as
slaves?"

Gamad barked out a short laugh. "No. Not at all. I abide by the law.
You'll be free men in Tharakhan. I'm even sending your weapons along
to be given to you when you arrive—including your ridiculous maul."

Voldigar narrowed his eyes. "I don't understand."

"Oh, you will." Gamad smiled again then ran his tongue along his teeth.
"It was always a wonder to me how you could swing that maul. A shame
you can't anymore." Gamad reached his good hand through the bars and
flicked the collar on Voldigar's neck. "Like a lion without his mane."

Voldigar winced and shied away, but Gamad suddenly caught him under
his arm and dragged him to his feet, painfully against the bars.

"At the mercy of a one-armed man," Gamad hissed. "What a change of
fortune." He worked his hand down to clasp Voldigar's fingers in his own
and squeezed. "You're not much without your Chanter's tricks, are you?"

The pain was awful as Gamad twisted and wrenched. Voldigar ground
his teeth and groaned, but he refused to cry out. His thumb was bent
backward until he thought it would break while Gamad sneered on and
tightened his grip. The general abruptly released him, and Voldigar slid
back to the floor.

"Barley farmer, that's what you are. Not worth my effort."

Voldigar closed his hand reflexively and stared across at Lanathor who
was now stirring and struggling to sit upright.

"Let me see my wife, Gamad," Voldigar said without raising his eyes.

"I like your begging, Voldigar. I really do, and I'd even help you if I could.
I'm afraid no one knows where she is. Perhaps you'd show us?"

Voldigar took in a ragged breath but could think of no reply.

"Would you like to tell us where Tepic is?"

Voldigar drew his knees up to rest his arms on them and met eyes with Lanathor who was now fully awake.

Gamad wrapped his hand around a bar and leaned his head in close. "When I find that rat, I'll take both his arms. Have a nice trip, Voldigar Anteres."

The iron creaked as Gamad released it and returned the way he'd come. The cowled man lingered there, his hood turned to the rear of the cell. As before, Voldigar saw the same glimmer of eyes behind his shroud, but the man was otherwise obscured. His gaze was fixed on Lanathor, his head unmoving but for the smallest wavering of its cloth. Wordlessly, he turned and slipped away.

Lanathor stayed silent, watching the cowled man recede. When he was gone, the Elder lowered his head and began quietly to weep. Voldigar could not recall the last time he'd seen his reserved old friend cry openly in such a way. He could not fault him and knew only a thin dam covered his own heart. He took a deep breath and slid himself across the floor to sit near Brother Lanathor.

Voldigar rested there silently, huddled by the man as darkness closed about them and his eyes adjusted again to see their shadowy hands. Lanathor fell quiet, and Voldigar's thoughts turned to Tepic.

"I've done wickedly," Voldigar said at length. Lanathor lifted his head and Voldigar went on. "I stabbed that boy in the heart. He came to bear good tidings to me, innocently, and I gave him anger in return. I didn't have the chance to say I was sorry, Lan. I just yelled at him, and all he'll remember of his teacher are the hard words of a bitter old man." Voldigar felt his lips tremble as the grief worked through his chest.

"I'm sorry," Lanathor said. In the dim light, Voldigar could faintly see blackened streaks below Lanathor's eyes. "It was my fault, Vol."

"Don't say that anymore—"

"No," Lanathor said. Voldigar was startled by his sudden vehemence. "You don't understand. I've tried to tell you. It *was* my fault. It's *been* my fault—for a long time."

Voldigar blinked in confusion. "How could that be?"

Lanathor swallowed. "I'm not a Teller, Voldigar."

They sat in silence for a moment as Voldigar tried to comprehend what he'd just heard. "What?"

"You heard me. I'm not a Teller."

Voldigar sighed and let his shoulders drop. They'd been through so much. He couldn't tell if Lanathor was delirious or spoke in some form of riddle. "What does that mean, Lan?"

Lanathor turned toward him. "It means, I am not a Teller, Voldigar. I never was."

Voldigar shook his head. "What is this nonsense? Brother, reveal your riddle. We've served together for twenty years. You are the greatest Teller of our order. I've seen your magic a thousand times with my own eyes, you've taught others—"

"Stop, Vol. It was all a lie." Lanathor took a wavering breath. "My magic is different. I . . . I don't feel the Song, Voldigar. I can hear it, like you, like the Chanters, but I can *see* it too."

Voldigar blinked. "*See* it? But . . ."

"But I can only do it one way," Lanathor went on. "I consume the root, Falam Root." Lanathor looked away and shook his head. "So much Falam Root. Enough to stop the hearts of other men."

"All the Tellers use aromatics."

"No, Voldigar," he said vehemently again. "I've taken a hundred times a lethal dose. Not to attune to an emotion, not to feel the Song, but to feel *nothing*. There's a hole in my heart, Brother, and it's shaped like that poison. I don't even know who I am." His eyes welled with tears again, and Voldigar sat in stunned silence.

"I'm scared all the time," Lanathor went on. "A black terror in the pit of my stomach, and I only know one cure, Voldigar." He turned to him with tearful eyes. "I stopped upon the road, just to find more root, and that's why Medellai, and Gardoric, and Lutz were captured. That's why we lost the Black Fire. That's why—" Lanathor's whole body shook, and he choked upon his words. "It was my doing. My fault. And now it's led you here . . ."

Voldigar let the confession wash over him for a long and painful moment. The words were like a waking dream, but he knew that they were true. He sifted them in his mind, grasped at anger for a flickering second, and let them blow away.

"I know who you are," he said at last. "You're Lanathor. You're Lanathor, and I forgive you." Voldigar reached his two chained wrists clumsily over the other man's head and gathered him near in an embrace. "You're Lanathor, and you're my friend."

Lanathor sank his head against Voldigar and sobbed. "I didn't think you would forgive me."

Voldigar turned his eyes to the bare ceiling and whispered. "What have we in this world but each other now, Brother?

They sat in silence a long time until Voldigar spoke again. "This is not the end. I'll bring you back, we'll bring everyone back home. We'll return to Aramon—I swear it."

"What was it all for?" Lanathor asked.

"You do the right thing, Lan. Even when it hurts, even when it crushes. You do the right thing."

Chapter Fifty-Four

THE ALBATROSS

IT WAS THREE DAYS of bitter cold wandering before Tepic finally found the northern coast and followed it to the low-branched willow of Liadov's hidden shrine. His little boat had drifted deep into the hinterlands and would have gone on to the Far Marshes had he not abandoned it in a swirling shallow before it curved away.

He lived on the meager bread that survived in Lyrusia's wet satchel and begged warmth and dry clothing from an old farmer and his wife the morning after his escape. Oblivious to any trouble in Aramon, they were astonished when he gave his thanks and left as quickly as he'd come.

Today, he was wrapped in Liadov's furs again, warm and well-fed, though a deep emptiness lingered. She'd brought him to talk alone once more, walking together on her pathway above the sea. Hobyn and Lyrusia, Gwenyth and baby Olwis, rested peacefully inside while they spoke quietly under a gray sky.

Tepic felt as though he'd aged a year. He was certain he looked it too. From Liadov, he learned of the Brothers' exile and that his father had been sent away as well. Like wind-blown ash, his heart gave way within him. He was too late. He'd ruined all their plans. He walked half the way in numb silence before Liadov spoke again.

"They are beyond our reach now, Tepic. Be thankful that your mother and sister are well, and do not blame yourself."

Tepic watched his feet press into the snow and thrust his raw hands into his pockets. "How can't I?"

"Because it wasn't your doing."

Tepic shook his head. "I left a trail of footprints all the way from Lector's farm. They arrested everyone."

"And how was it that you left the farm?" Liadov asked.

The sound of breaking waves echoed up from far below. "I snuck away, when you weren't looking."

Liadov raised an eyebrow. "You think I didn't know?"

Tepic looked at her, incredulous. "You . . . knew?" He stared at his feet again. "But it isn't *your* fault!"

"Isn't it?"

"But I—"

"Tepic, I even took the sword away. Do you not think I suspected what you were doing?"

Tepic frowned. "I don't understand."

"If I let you leave, I am more to blame than you, young man."

"But it's *not* your fault, Lady Liadov."

"No, it isn't. Fault is hard to ascertain. Perhaps it's not as useful as you think."

Tepic glared and pondered as they walked on a few more paces. "Then it's Lusánt's fault."

Liadov smiled. "Closer, but you will not be satisfied with that answer either. Remember what I told you?"

"I hate him," Tepic said bitterly. "I'd cut him down and turn back the ship if I could."

Liadov stopped. "Be careful with your words, Tepic Banari. Vengeance is a base thing in the wicked hands of men. Justice is better. But that is the province of God alone, for men have unjust eyes."

"What's left to us then?" Tepic asked.

"To trust the word of God, to long and wait for his redemption, and to keep his ways and do your purpose, with whatever small power you possess."

"Then what's my purpose?"

Liadov took a long breath. "The right things are in motion, Tepic, and you'll soon know it. Do you think God was surprised by all that's happened?"

Tepic scratched his head. "I suppose not."

Liadov nodded. "Good. He wasn't. He will deal with Lusánt, with the instrument of his choosing.

Tepic frowned and returned to his thoughts as they walked on. "I never even got to tell Voldigar his son's name. He was so mad at me," Tepic said softly. He looked at the ground again. "I just want to tell him I'm sorry . . ."

Liadov stood still and rested her hand on Tepic's arm. "You still may." They had reached the end of the winding path. "Tepic, look at me."

Tepic found it hard to hold her gaze, for Liadov was now staring intently into his eyes.

"I have a word for you, and you must listen closely. You have a long path ahead, a journey you would not believe. But if you are swift to courage, then courage will give you trust. And if you will trust, then trust will show you love. And if you will love, then you will find your purpose. You will see what you were meant to see. Your heart will touch the waters above and your eyes the sea below. A black sun will quench the flames and you will find a guiding star. And if you will yield when you must yield, and stand as a rock when you must stand, then redemption is at hand. Go forth with blessing, Tepic Banari."

Tepic blinked and his mouth hung open. "Was that . . . a prophecy?

Liadov smiled. "They are words that you should not forget."

Tepic stood quietly and let his mind drift again. He licked his lips and found Liadov's eyes once more. "I want to help my dad, and the Brothers. Someone has to help them."

In the shadows behind where she stood, Liadov reached her hand, and when she drew it forth again, she held his grandfather's sword. She extended it to him.

"And you may help them yet. As I told you, you are this weapon's Wielder, and now you must take it far away."

Tepic's mouth moved, but he did not know what to say. The crystal hilt of the sword shone brilliantly in the morning light, and he received it reverently in his hands.

"Away? I don't understand," he said.

"You will in time. You must take this sword away, far away where the enemy will not find it. But you must also bring the Brothers home. Will you do this, Tepic?"

"Me?"

"You said you wanted to help them, did you not?" Liadov sternly held his gaze.

"But . . . why not you? Why not both of us?" Tepic asked.

She did not speak.

"I'm just a boy."

Liadov watched him steadily. "Each has his purpose, and mine is here. The Chasm will not hold back the horde forever, and many webs the Emperor has spun remain uncut. I will hold back the tide, Tepic—but you must bring back our allies. You are just a boy, too young, but we are all that remain."

"But what about Ru, and my mom, Hobyn, and Lady Gwenyth?"

"They will do their purpose too. Swift to courage, Tepic."

Tepic's head felt light and his vision blurred. He stared at the sword in his hands.

"Will you do this?" Liadov asked again.

Tepic looked out over the ocean where waves crashed across the distant shoals and rocks. Like a great albatross soaring high above, it was as if he watched himself, a tiny speck, insignificant below. He thought of home, and of the Undercity. He thought of the grave faces of the Brotherhood. He thought of the old stable ground, cold and empty, and a small flame lit within his heart. He took a breath and nodded. "I will do it, if I can. I'll find them. But will you help me? I don't know how to start."

"I will help you, in whatever way I can. There is one more ship leaving Aramon before our long winter. I can take you near, but then you must find the way."

"Ru won't understand," Tepic said.

Liadov nodded. "It's alright not to understand, but still we must act. Come inside, Tepic. We have much to prepare."

GLOSSARY

Many of the proper nouns and terms used in Return to Aramon: A New Moon are found below. The glossary may contain mild spoilers.

Adionel - The central watercourse of Aramon. It runs from the mountains north of the great pass all the way to the promontory under Arregalt where it drains into the sea.

Alazi - Survii's brother.

Aramon - A small but powerful and ancient state that rules over its neighbors. Its language and people are sometimes referred to as Aramoni.

Arbed - Captain of the Westfort Garrison. In service of General Gamad.

Arcus - A great teacher and healer of ancient Aramon. Tymicha's mentor. A famous Chant is named after him.

Arliman - A deceased treasure-hunter known for his eccentricity.

Arregalt - The capital city and seat of power in Aramon. A huge metropolis on a high promontory overlooking the sea.

Artificer - Architects, engineers, and inventors in service of the crown. For many years, only the Mokja have made up their ranks.

Azkushan - A land on the same continent as Aramon but far away. It is known for its tall men with ebony skin.

Baerdermyrch - Another name for the Thirteen Provinces. Sometimes used to refer only to Aramon's nearest neighbors: Danek, Tituria, and Kurath.

Bajk - Artificer of the Spire. Mokja. Brother of Lutz. Controls the engine room for the lift.

Blooded - A term used to described certain demons who've consumed adequate blood to take on a stable and powerful form. It also describes their victims.

Bashevi - Mythical blood-drinking demons from Titurian folklore that begin as nothing more than mouths. They are known as Varpan in the language of Tituria.

Bolran - A palace eunuch. Night scribe in the Spire.

Brelabbus - A greater demon. Fly Father.

Brol - A prolific mokja.

The Brotherhood of Aramon - An ancient order established at the founding of Aramon. They exercise various martial, judicial, and religious duties. They are known for adherence to their Code and to tradition, as well as vigilance against sorcery and the distinctive red cloaks they wear.

Builders - An ancient group of powerful kings who sought their own glory, creating massive monuments in an ever more dangerous and corrupting rivalry

Caliras - Lord Commander of the Stonepike Guard. Rumored consort of the widowed Empress.

Cassolke - A word of indeterminate origin. Possibly Mokjan. The unsharpened portion of a blade just beyond the guard. A "ricasso" in our world.

Challeric - The royal physician of House Sispérus.

Chanter - Counterpart to Tellers. Chanters can hear the harmonies of the Song and experience a special connection with the words of Scripture. Meditation on these words manifests particular powers in them. There are no known Chanters outside of The Brotherhood of Aramon.

Chasm, the - A huge canyon before the feet of the mountains at the edge of Aramon.

Citadel, the - The great fortress at the heart of Arregalt. The Spire is at its center.

Claras - Dantic Banari's wife. Tepic and Lyrusia's mother. The owner of a very curious sword.

Code, the - A set of oath-sworn rules adhered to by The Brotherhood of Aramon.

Cozi - A mokja fence and engineer in Undercity.

Dantic - House Banari. Commander of the City Guard in Arregalt and the garrison at Eastfort.

Danek - One of thirteen provinces of Aramon's empire. Objects and people from that land are often called "Daneki."

Delvings, the - The deeply tunneled and carved interior of the promontory on which Arregalt sits. It is labyrinthine.

Dizghizádè - The most prominent shrine of the Sun Cult. It is hidden in the mountains above Danek.

Eleanora - Queen and now Empress of Aramon and the recently conquered Thirteen Provinces. Lusánt's mother. Widow of Olwis.

Eadom - A young initiate of the Brotherhood. Pupil of Vasherk. Known for his formal personality.

Eastfort - The first of two forts guarding the pass into Aramon. It lies just below the summit of the pass and opens to the long stretch of road leading to the Thirteen Provinces.

Ekhebiri - A lost race of beings with some relation to the Miridas. Their homeland is a series of isles that float in the great circuit of the sky.

Falam Root - An aromatic root that grows on fallen trees. It has properties of cough suppression, anxiety reduction, and pain relief.

Far Marshes, the - A vast swampland beyond the hinterlands of Aramon. An ancient indigenous people live in scattered settlements there.

Ferret - A boy in Undercity missing his front teeth.

Fish - A boy in Undercity whose hair never grew back.

Fort Dromvedya - A fortification along the river Vedkorya in Danek's eastern valley.

Galomar - A young sergeant in Dantic's service. Assigned to guard Tepic's house.

Gamad - General of the Legions of Aramon, their famous, conquering field-armies.

Gardoric - A Chanter and Brother of Aramon. A man of the Far Marshes.

The Golden Spire of Tymicha - The royal palace and heart of Arregalt. It towers impossibly high and broad into the sky.

Gray Sun - The eight-pointed symbol of House Sispérus.

Great Dispute - A recent religious dispute in which the worship of Mirvánè (the moon) was outlawed due to the immoral practices of its priests.

The Great Span - An enormous bridge over a huge chasm at the edge of Aramon. It is the only way in or out of the country by land.

Gwenyth - House Sispérus. Voldigar's wife. Plagued by a long illness.

Halma - An old miridas woman.

Haroel - A great arm of the river Adionel that splits southward at the Rock of Tholc and into the Chasm beneath The Great Span.

Haslor - A sleepy porter guard in the royal apartments.

Hirigael - A long pole with a match on the end of it, especially useful for lighting gas lamps. In our world it might be called a wick, a linstock, or even a punk.

Hobyn - Old man. Voldigar's family friend. Lives and works on Voldigar's farm.

Hugan - The deceased highest officer and marshall of Olwis's military.

Hyfariel - A Sister of Aramon. Raises horses in Maghaltani. Known for her love of trees and living creatures.

Hyrodan - Master of the Cult of Tetrimázè (the sun).

Imperial Reformatory - A jail where young noblemen amend their ways.

Jarnath Leaf - A potent and foul herb that affects the regulation of blood flow and body temperature.

Lanathor - Once rescued by The Brotherhood of Aramon. Now an Elder of that order. A powerful Teller whose magic touches space and time.

Lector - A teacher, especially one who teaches nobility through exposition and lecture. Many Brothers and Sisters of Aramon are employed as lectors.

Liadov - A mysterious woman who was once a Sister of Aramon and like a daughter, dear to Voldigar. She lives among the sun worshipers in Dizghizádè.

Lusánt - House Sispérus. Son of Olwis and Eleanora. Heir to the throne of Aramon.

Lutz - A mokja Artificer. High ranking member of The Brotherhood of Aramon.

Lyrusia - House Banari. An apothecary. The young woman is Commander Dantic's daughter.

Kishket - A device used by the Brotherhood in their dangerous work.

Kurath - One of the Thirteen Provinces and part of the Baerdermyrch. A lowland of fertile fields.

Kyriana - Lusánt's advisor. A miridas girl.

Mack - A draft horse, belonging to Hobyn's nephew.

Maghaltani - The mountain village of The Brotherhood of Aramon and their families.

Manric - A Stonepike guard. Assigned to the Inner Vault.

Medellai - An Elder of The Brotherhood of Aramon. Gwenyth's brother. Voldigar's brother-in-law.

Mokja - A race of short and stout humanoid creatures, prone to mechanical expertise. Singular or plural, "mokja" is often used descriptively of their people and workmanship.

Miridas - A remarkable race of mariners known for their unusual gait, blue-green skin, and musical voices.

Mirvánè - The proper name of the moon. Used extensively in its worship.

Nabénes - An ancient House of Aramon that is mostly lost.

Odomo - A grotesque race of golemic creatures formed of broken things. They are known in Kurathian folklore.

Old Shrine - An abandoned holy site along the wild northern coast of Aramon.

Olwis - House Sispérus. "Olwis the Shield." The dead king of Aramon. Lusánt's father. Eleanora's husband. Once a dear friend and patron of Voldigar.

Orun - A demon from another plane that seeks to enter the material world.

Oxtail - A boy in Undercity with unusual hair.

Pacho - A resilient, edible plant that grows without light.

Palizar - Urias's initiate. A Fire Teller.

Patradavi - A name given by men to the Pole Star. Its true name is unknown.

Pavka Flower - The Daneki word for Falam Root.

Pig - A girl in Undercity with a remarkable nose.

Planting Day - An early day in spring, traditionally used for sowing seed in Aramon.

Podge - Slang. A watchman or other officer of the law.

Polic - A former leader and Eldest of The Brotherhood of Aramon.

Prism - A mysterious artifact of wondrous and dangerous power.

Qasimar - Beloved initiate of the Brotherhood. Once Voldigar's pupil.

Ragat - Diocesan of the Cult of Patradavi (the Pole Star).

Ramikus - An early King in the line of Tavaana.

Reader - The title of one who reads sacred texts, especially in an official capacity. So many of The Brotherhood of Aramon have served in this manner that the term became synonymous with their members.

Reverend - A title used loosely for any religious official.

Rock of Tholc - A massive granite rock near huge waterfalls that split the Adionel and Haroel rivers. Named for the First Sorcerer that ruled over the lands of ancient Aramon.

Rory - Voldigar's eight-year-old Titurian hound.

Rul - A Titurian soldier in Dantic's service.

Sanctum, the - A tavern in a quiet corner of Arregalt that was repurposed as a secret headquarters for The Brotherhood of Aramon during the reign of Olwis the Shield.

Scepter of Tymicha - The original symbol of Aramon's ruler, passed from one to the next. Also known as the Golden Scepter of Tymicha.

Sea Cliffs, the - Arregalt and its nearby coasts are notable for their high cliffs overlooking the sea—over a thousand feet in some places.

Seaward Gulch - A hidden ravine near Maghaltani.

Shift - A phenomenon of movement thought to be unique to Lanathor's magical expression.

Singer - Like Tellers and Chanters, Singers could harness the magic of the Song, but with vastly greater effect. It has been so long since any have been seen that more precise knowledge of their powers is lost.

Sispérus - The most noble House of Aramon. Rulers of the realm. Their sigil is an eight-pointed sun, gray on sable.

Soris - A powerful Teller and Brother of Aramon known for his mastery of ice and a quiet demeanor of fatalistic melancholy.

Spring Throne - The outdoor throne room behind the Spire.

Stonepike Guard - Caliras's personal security force. Charged with guarding the Spire.

Suramn - A storm-swept land north of Azkushan that borders the Baerdermyrch.

Survii - A Daneki farmer.

The Song of Creation - Also known simply as "the Song", it was made by God at the dawn of time. Its structure holds together all substance in the universe.

Spire, the - see The Golden Spire of Tymicha.

Tavaana - An ancient House of Aramon that is mostly lost.

Taro - A young Chanter and Brother of Aramon known for incredible powers of mind and spirit. A prodigy who reached his Fourth Virtue at a young age. Once an initiate of Voldigar.

Tarbane Crystals - A flammable substance used by Artificers.

Teller - To the common folk, a magician or wizard. Tellers are known to feel the Song and the echoes of its emotion. The only known Tellers in Aramon are all members of the Brotherhood.

Tepic - The adolescent son of Commander Dantic Banari. He is one of Voldigar's students.

Tetrimázè - The proper name of the sun. Used extensively in its worship.

Tharmskolp - A magnificent visual device made by mokja Artificers.

Tharakhan - An old slaver's outpost and wasteland on the other side of the world, at the far end of the Wending Sea.

Tif - Slang. A small coin.

Thirteen Provinces - The proper name of thirteen formerly independent kingdoms that were long dominated, but only recently conquered, by Aramon.

Tituria - Once independent. One of thirteen provinces ruled by Aramon. Known for its rolling hills and moors.

Tower of the Sea - An ornate tower on the very point of Arregalt's promontory behind the Spring Throne.

Tower of Maghaltani - The first structure of Maghaltani, around which the entire village was built.

Trakast Bridge - A bridge near the primary gate of Arregalt. It splits in three directions over a confluence of rivers.

Tymicha - The leader of the slave revolt that created Aramon in antiquity. She was their first queen and is deified among the people.

Tymicha's Arsenal - The weapons Tymicha commissioned after her Uprising.

Tymicha's Uprising - The stonecutting slaves of the Surgad, Roluma, and Fasheki peoples followed Tymicha in revolt against the Sorcerer Kings of the ancient world. Aramon was born from this rebellion.

Undercity - The Undercity is a network of tunnels and platforms built into and beneath the great promontory of Arregalt. A vast population lives there.

Urias - Brother of Aramon. Perhaps the most powerful Teller in the world. A master of fire known for his fierce countenance.

Vasherk - A aged Chanter of the Brotherhood of Aramon. Blessed with gifts of healing. He is not the "Eldest" by title, but he is the oldest living member of their order.

Vedkorya - A river in Danek running roughly west to east.

Veysara - A noblewoman of House Sispérus.

Vaults, the - The heart of the Delvings carved into the promontory below Arregalt. Separate from the rest, it holds the most secret treasures of the realm, especially within the Inner Vault.

Veskelti - A noble house of Aramon. A hart upon a field of green is their emblem.

Vessel - An object imbued with Virtue by a powerful Chanter.

Veyli - A ranking man in Fort Dromvedya.

Virtue - A euphemism for the manifestations of a Chanter's power. Also the specific principle of a Chanter's meditation leading to the abilities he possesses.

Vlacha - The capital city of Danek, in the far north of its valley.

Voldigar - House Anteres. Sword-Lector, Farmer, and retired leader of The Brotherhood of Aramon. He still holds the title of "Eldest," but has left the order to other "Elders."

Wending Sea - A great sea with a powerful eastward current that lies off the coast of Aramon. Beyond its protected bay, the sea's flow is so powerful that only the miridas can ply its waters in their magic ships.

Westfort - The pass out of Aramon is guarded by two forts. Westfort lies at the opening near the Great Span.

Whale - An appropriately named boy in Undercity.

Wilding, the - A malady that may strike Chanters.

Winter Throne - The indoor throne room at the heart of the Spire.

The Words of Ralm - One of the sacred texts of Aramon's old monotheistic religion. A favorite among Chanters.

Wulf - Brother of Aramon. A wild man renowned for his huge size and strength. He is neither Teller nor Chanter. Once Voldigar's initiate.

Wyrna - Half man, half animal. A twisted corruption of the demons. The legend of them is told in Danek.

Xerimadi - A northern race of men known for their hardy constitutions, dusky skin, and nomadic way of life.

Zedr - A mokja Initiate and Teller known for his love of stone and earth.

Zizechi - A Daneki word akin to 'foreigner.'

Acknowledgments

This book would not exist without the encouragement of so many who helped me along the way.

First and foremost, I acknowledge my King and Captain, Jesus. I spoke to Him every day and hope this story is worthy of His kingdom.

I am so thankful to my beloved wife of nearly thirty years, Elisha. She was my daily encourager, the first reader of every scene, and an incredibly thoughtful and kind listener with all the best questions.

My editor Anika Saphiloff is an extraordinary talent. Without her brilliant insight, this book would be a threadbare version of what it became. If you love any part of this book, thank her. If anything misses the mark, she warned me, but I was too stubborn to listen.

Johnny Voruz, my friend, without your encouragement I would have faltered on the first page. Thank you, sincerely.

Terran Gregory, my conspirator of days too numerous to count. There isn't room to acknowledge you properly, my friend. The flashes of inspiration fill a galaxy.

To all the great ones of Rufus Cubed, you are so very dear to me. Cole Miller, Ty Ovendale, and Emily Carlin.

There were so many more early readers, listeners, and commenters. I'm terrified of missing a name. You know who you are, but I give you my thanks. Deva. Jesse F. and Jesse R. Jesse and Justina. Isaac. Thomas. Ian, Kathy, and Brian. Eliott and Matt. Tim. Karen. Mike and Jennie, Ashley, Emilie, Justin. Kristy. Melody and Jim. Janeiro, Malia, and Bill. Hannah, Troy, Erika, Tyler, Jeff and Kirsten, Corinne, Zak, and Jenni!

If I forgot your name, it is to my eternal shame. Please forgive me, but know that you are loved and honored and join an august company of the great ones who do much for others from the quiet unknown.

Finally, I acknowledge my copilot Tinyo, The Professor, and all my glorious RPG buds, keeping it real since the primordial days of Fantasy. Stay great!

ABOUT THE AUTHOR

Ezra Ferguson lives in the Seattle, Washington area with his adorable wife of almost thirty years, countless animals, too many roleplaying books, and six fruit trees. He has two incredible adult children pursuing their dreams and tries to spend every morning in the Bible, in prayer, or at church. He loves weights, football, history, video games, and anything dwarven. God has been good to him every day of his life.